D0272019

Glouces

993326536 9

THE SILVER EAGLE

The Silver Eagle

BEN KANE

preface

Published by Preface 2009

10 9 8 7 6

Copyright © Ben Kane, 2009
Map © Jeffrey L. Ward 2008, 2009

Ben Kane has asserted his right to be identified as the author of this work under the
Copyright, Designs and Patents Act 1988

This book is sold subject to the condition that it shall not, by way of trade or otherwise, be
lent, resold, hired out, or otherwise circulated without the publisher's prior consent in any
form of binding or cover other than that in which it is published and without a similar
condition, including this condition, being imposed on the subsequent purchaser.

First published in Great Britain in 2009 by Preface Publishing
1 Queen Anne's Gate
London SW1H 9BT

An imprint of The Random House Group Limited

www.rbooks.co.uk
www.prefacepublishing.co.uk

Addreses for companies within The Random House Group Limited
can be found at www.randomhouse.co.uk

The Random House Group Limited Reg. No. 954009

A CIP catalogue record for this book is available from
the British Library

Hardback ISBN 978 1 84809 011 8
Trade Paperback ISBN 978 1 84809 012 5

The Random House Group Limited supports The Forest Stewardship Council (FSC),
the leading international forest certification organisation. All our titles that are printed
on Greenpeace approved FSC certified paper carry the FSC logo. Our paper procurement
policy can be found at www.rbooks.co.uk/environment

Typeset in Fournier MT by Palimpsest Book Production Limited,
Grangemouth, Stirlingshire

Printed and bound in Great Britain by Clays Ltd, St Ives plc

To my amazing wife Sair,
without whose love, support and tolerance
I would find things much harder.
This is for you.

BRITANNIA

Alesia

GAUL

Ravenna

Massilia

ITALIA

Rome

DACIA

Dyrrachium

Brundisium

Pharsalus

HISPANIA

ASIA
MINOR

GREECE

Mare Internum

AFRICA

Alexandria

N

EGYPT

R. Nilus

0 Miles   200   400
0 Kilometers   400

© 2008 Jeffrey L. Ward

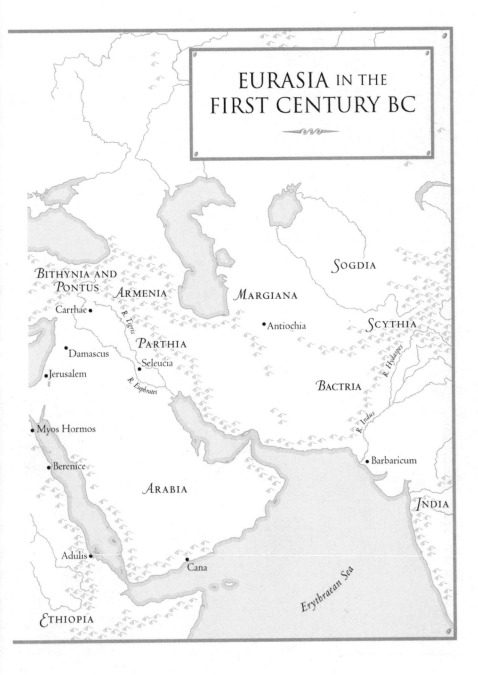

EURASIA IN THE FIRST CENTURY BC

BITHYNIA AND PONTUS

ARMENIA

Carrhae

Damascus

Jerusalem

PARTHIA

Seleucia

R. Tigris

R. Euphrates

MARGIANA

Antiochia

SOGDIA

SCYTHIA

BACTRIA

R. Hydaspes

R. Indus

Myos Hormos

Berenice

ARABIA

Barbaricum

INDIA

Adulis

Cana

Erythraean Sea

ETHIOPIA

Chapter I: The Mithraeum

Eastern Margiana, winter 53/52 BC

A good mile from the fort, the Parthians finally came to a halt. When the steady crunch of boots and sandals on frosty ground ceased, an overwhelming silence descended. Quiet coughs and the jingle of mail fell away, absorbed by the freezing air. Darkness had not quite fallen, allowing Romulus to take in their destination: a nondescript cliff face of weathered, grey-brown rocks which formed the end of a range of low hills. Peering into the gathering gloom, the powerfully built young soldier tried to see what had brought the warriors here. There were no buildings or structures in sight, and the winding path they had been following appeared to come to a dead end at the cliff's foot. Raising an eyebrow, he turned to Brennus, his friend and surrogate father. 'What in Jupiter's name are we doing here?'

'Tarquinius knows something,' grunted Brennus, hunching his great shoulders under his thick military cloak. 'As usual.'

'But he won't tell us!' Romulus cupped his hands and blew on them, trying to prevent his fingers and face from going completely numb. His aquiline nose already was.

'It'll come out eventually,' the pigtailed Gaul replied, chuckling.

Romulus' protest died away. His eagerness would not speed things up. Patience, he thought.

Against their skin, the two men wore cloth jerkins. Over these, standard issue mail shirts. While affording good protection against blades, the heavy iron rings constantly drained away their body heat. Woollen cloaks and scarves and the felt liners under their bronze bowl crested helmets helped a little, but their calf-length russet trousers and heavy studded *caligae*, or sandals, exposed too much flesh to allow any comfort.

'Go and ask him,' urged Brennus with a grin. 'Before our balls drop off.'

Romulus smiled.

They had both demanded an explanation from the Etruscan haruspex when he'd appeared in their fuggy barrack room a short time earlier. Typically, Tarquinius gave away little, but he had muttered something about a special request from Pacorus, their commander. And the chance of seeing if there was a way out of Margiana. Unwilling to let their friend go off alone, the pair also jumped at the chance of some information.

The last few months had provided a welcome break from the constant fighting of the previous two years. Gradually, however, their life in a Roman fort turned into a numbing routine. Physical training followed guard duty; the repair of equipment replaced parade drill. Occasional patrols provided little in the way of excitement. Even the tribes which raided Margiana did not campaign in winter weather. Tarquinius' offer therefore seemed heaven-sent.

Yet Romulus' purpose tonight was more than simple thrill-seeking. He was desperate for even the briefest mention of Rome. The city of his birth now lay on the other side of the world, with thousands of miles of harsh landscape and hostile peoples in between. Was there any chance he might return there one day? Like nearly all his comrades, Romulus dreamt of that possibility day and night. Here, at the ends of the earth, there was nothing else to hold on to, and this unexplained excursion might provide a sliver of hope.

'I'll wait,' he replied at length. 'After all, we volunteered to come.' He stamped resignedly from foot to foot. Suspended by a leather carrying strap, his elongated oval shield, or *scutum*, swung off his shoulder with the movement. 'And you've seen the mood Pacorus is in. He'd probably cut my balls off for just asking. They're better freezing.'

A laugh rumbled in Brennus' throat.

Short and swarthy, Pacorus was at the head of the party, dressed in a richly decorated jerkin, trousers and ankle boots, with a conical Parthian hat and a long bearskin cloak to keep him warm. Under the fur, a delicate gold belt circling his waist had two curved daggers and a jewel-hilted sword slung from it. A brave but ruthless man, Pacorus led the Forgotten Legion, the remnants of a huge Roman army defeated the previous summer by the

Parthian general Surena. Together with Tarquinius, the friends were now merely three of its rank-and-filers.

Once more, Romulus was a captive.

It was ironic, he thought, that his life should be spent exchanging one master for another. First it had been Gemellus, the brutal merchant who owned his entire family – Velvinna, his mother, Fabiola, his twin sister, and himself. Falling on hard times, Gemellus had sold Romulus at thirteen to Memor, the *lanista* of the Ludus Magnus, Rome's largest gladiator school. Although less casually cruel than Gemellus, Memor's sole business was training slaves and criminals to fight and die in the arena. Men's lives meant nothing to him. At that memory, Romulus spat. To survive in the *ludus*, he had been forced to end a man's life. More than once. *Kill or be killed*: Brennus' mantra rang in his ears.

Romulus checked that his short, double-edged *gladius* was loose in its scabbard, that the bone-handled dagger on the other side of his belt was ready for use. The actions were second nature to him now. A grin creased his face as he caught Brennus doing the same. Like all Roman soldiers, they also carried two iron-headed javelins, or *pila*. Their companions, a score of Pacorus' best warriors, stood in marked contrast to them. Clad in simpler versions of their senior's clothing, and with slit-sided woollen cloaks rather than a thick fur one, each man was armed with a long knife and a slim case which hung from his right hip. This was large enough to carry his recurved composite bow and a supply of arrows. Proficient with many weapons, the Parthians were first and foremost a nation of highly skilled archers. It was fortunate that he had met none of them in the arena, thought Romulus. All were able to loose half a dozen shafts in the time a man could run a hundred paces. And every one accurate enough to kill.

Fortunately, the *ludus* was also where he had met Brennus. Romulus threw him a grateful look. Without the Gaul's friendship, he would have soon succumbed to the savage life. Instead, over two years had passed with only a single life-threatening injury. Then, late one night, a street brawl had gone horribly wrong and the friends had had to flee Rome together. Joining the army as mercenaries, the general Crassus had become their new master. Politician, millionaire and member of Rome's ruling triumvirate, he was desperate for the military recognition possessed by his two colleagues, Julius Caesar and Pompey Magnus. Arrogant fool, thought

Romulus. If he'd been more like Caesar, we'd all be home by now. Instead of fame and glory, Crassus led thirty-five thousand men to a bloody, igno-minious defeat at Carrhae. The survivors – about one-third of the army – had been taken prisoner by the Parthians, whose brutality outstripped even that of Memor. Given the stark choices of having molten gold poured down their throats, being crucified or serving in a border force on Parthia's unsettled eastern frontier, Romulus and his comrades had naturally chosen the last.

Romulus sighed, no longer so sure that their choice had been correct. It seemed they would spend the rest of their lives fighting their captors' historical enemies: savage nomadic tribes from Sogdia, Bactria, and Scythia.

He was here to find out if that miserable fate could be avoided.

Tarquinius' dark eyes scanned the rock face.

Not a sign.

Differing in appearance to all the others, Tarquinius had long, blond locks held in place by a cloth band, which revealed a thin face, high cheek-bones and a single gold earring in his right ear. The Etruscan wore a hide breastplate covered with tiny interlinked bronze rings; a centurion's short leather-bordered skirt completed his attire. From his back hung a small, worn pack. Over his left shoulder, a double-headed battleaxe dangled from a strap. Unlike his companions, the haruspex had scorned a cloak. He wanted his senses to be on full alert.

'Well?' demanded Pacorus. 'Can you see the entrance?'

A slight frown creased Tarquinius' brow, but he did not reply. Long years of training under Olenus, his mentor, had taught him great patience. To others, it often looked like smugness.

The commander's eyes flickered off to the right.

Tarquinius deliberately glanced the other way. Mithras, he thought, Great One. Show me your temple.

Pacorus could no longer contain himself. 'It's not even thirty paces away,' he taunted.

Several of his warriors sniggered.

Casually, Tarquinius let his gaze slide over to where the commander had looked a moment before. He stared long and hard at the cliff, but could see nothing.

'You're a charlatan. I always knew it,' snarled Pacorus. 'It was a complete mistake to let you become a centurion.'

It was as if the Parthian had forgotten how he, Tarquinius, had provided the Forgotten Legion with its secret weapon, thought the haruspex bitterly. A ruby gifted to him years ago by Olenus had bought the silk which even now covered more than five thousand men's *scuta*, giving them the ability to withstand arrows from the previously all-powerful recurved bows. It had been his idea to have thousands of long spears forged, weapons which could keep any cavalry at bay. It was thanks to him that the massive Sogdian war band devastating towns in Margiana upon their arrival had been anni-hilated. In addition, his medical expertise had saved the lives of numerous injured soldiers. His promotion to centurion was a tacit acknowledgement of this, and of Tarquinius' esteemed status among the ranks. Yet still he dared not answer back.

Pacorus held all of their lives in the palm of his hand. Until now what had protected Tarquinius, and to an extent his friends, from torture or death was the commander's dread of his prophetic abilities. And, for the first time in the Etruscan's life, these had deserted him.

Fear – a new emotion – became Tarquinius' daily companion.

For months, he had existed on his wits, while seeing nothing of real signifi-cance. Tarquinius studied every cloud, every gust of wind and every bird and animal he saw. Nothing. Sacrifices of hens and lambs, normally an excel-lent method of divining, had repeatedly proved fruitless. Their purple livers, the richest source of information in all of haruspicy, yielded no clues to him. Tarquinius could not understand it. I have been a haruspex for nearly twenty years, he thought sourly. Never has there been such a drought of visions. The gods must truly be angry with me. Charon, the Etruscan demon of the underworld, came to mind, emerging from the earth to swallow them all. Blue-skinned and red-haired, he walked in Pacorus' shadow, his mouth full of slavering teeth ready to tear Tarquinius apart when the commander's patience reached its limit. Which would not take long. One did not need to be a haruspex to read Pacorus' body language, reflected Tarquinius wearily. He was like a length of wire stretched so taut it would break any moment.

'By all that is sacred,' Pacorus snapped, 'let me show you.' Grabbing a torch from a guard, he led the way. The whole party followed. Just twenty steps on, he stopped. 'Look,' he ordered, jabbing forward the flame.

Tarquinius' eyes opened wide. Directly in front lay a neat area of evenly cut paving stones. In the centre was a large, man-made opening in the ground. Heavy slabs of rock had been laid down to form a square hole. Their weathered surfaces were covered with inscriptions and etchings. Tarquinius stepped closer to see, recognising the shapes of a raven, a crouching bull and an ornate seven-rayed crown. Was that outline a Phrygian cap? It was similar to the blunt-peaked hats worn by haruspices since the dawn of time, he thought with a thrill of excitement. This tiny detail was intriguing, because it was a possible link to the uncertain origins of Tarquinius' people.

Before they had colonised central Italy many centuries previously, the Etruscans had journeyed from the east. Traces of their civilisation existed in Asia Minor, but legend had it that they came from much further away. As did Mithras. Few things excited Tarquinius, but this did. Years of his life had been spent searching for evidence of the Etruscans' past, with little success. Perhaps now, here in the east, the impenetrable mist of time was beginning to thin. Olenus had been correct – again. The old man had predicted he might find out more by journeying to Parthia and beyond.

'Normally, only believers may enter a Mithraeum,' Pacorus announced. 'The penalty for trespassing is death.'

His pleasure quickly dissipating, Tarquinius grimaced. Any information about Mithraicism came second to surviving.

'You are being allowed inside in order to foretell my future and that of the Forgotten Legion,' said Pacorus. 'If your words are unconvincing, you will die.'

Controlling his emotions, Tarquinius regarded him steadily. There was more.

'But before that,' muttered Pacorus, his gaze moving to Romulus and Brennus. 'Your friends will be killed, slowly and painfully. In front of you.'

Full of rage, Tarquinius' gaze bored into Pacorus. After a few moments, it was the Parthian who looked down. I still have some power, the haruspex thought, but the knowledge was like ash in his dry mouth. Pacorus had the whip hand here, not him. If the gods did not grant him some kind of meaningful vision in the Mithraeum, they would all be slain out of hand. Why had he insisted that his two friends came along tonight? It had been only the smallest of hunches to ask them. Tarquinius was unconcerned about himself, but guilt suffused his heart that big, brave Brennus and Romulus, the young man he had come to love as a son, would have to pay for his failures. Meeting soon after joining Crassus' army, a close friendship had sprung up between the three. Thanks to the accuracy of his divinations, the others had come to trust Tarquinius utterly. After Carrhae, when escape under the cover of darkness had been an option, they had followed his lead and stayed, blindly pinning their fates to his. Both still looked to him for guidance. It cannot end here or now, Tarquinius thought fiercely. It *must* not.

'So be it,' he cried, using his best prophetic tones. 'Mithras will give me a sign.'

Romulus' and Brennus' heads whipped around, and Tarquinius saw the hope flare in both their faces. Especially in that of Romulus.

Taking some solace from this, he waited.

Pacorus bared his teeth expectantly. 'Follow me,' he said, placing his foot on the first step.

Without the slightest pause, Tarquinius stepped after him.

Just one hulking warrior, Pacorus' personal bodyguard, took up the rear. In his right hand was a ready dagger.

The party of guards fanned out, planting their torches in specially placed gaps in the paving stones. An ash-filled ring fireplace was evidence that they, or others, had stood here before. Romulus was still amazed by the manner of Pacorus' and Tarquinius' disappearance. He had noticed the large, shaped slabs but not fully appreciated that they formed an entrance. Now, with the whole scene relatively well lit, Romulus saw the carved drawings on either side of the hole. Excited, he began to under-stand. This was a temple, to Mithras.

And Tarquinius seemed sure that something would be revealed inside.

Desperate to know more, he moved to follow the haruspex, but half a dozen Parthians blocked his way.

'Nobody else goes down there,' growled one. 'The Mithraeum is hallowed ground. Filth such as you are not welcome.'

'All men are equal in Mithras' eyes,' Romulus challenged, remembering what Tarquinius had told him. 'And I am a soldier.'

The Parthian looked nonplussed. 'The commander decides who may enter,' he barked eventually. 'And you two weren't mentioned.'

'So we just wait?' demanded Romulus, his temper rising.

'That's right,' replied the warrior, taking a step forward. Several of the others copied him, their hands falling to their quivers. 'We all stay here until Pacorus says so. Clear?'

They glared at each other. Although the Parthians and the legionaries had now fought together a number of times, there was little love lost between the captors and captives. As far as the Romans were concerned, there never would be. Romulus felt the same way. These men had helped slaughter his comrades at Carrhae.

He felt Brennus' arm on his. 'Leave it,' said the Gaul calmly. 'Now's not the time.'

Brennus' intervention was a simple gut reaction. Over the previous four years, Romulus had become like a son to him. Since they had been thrown together, the Gaul had found his own tortured existence much easier. Romulus provided him with a reason not to die. And now, thanks to Brennus' repetitive and unrelenting training, the seventeen-year-old was a skilful fighter. Tarquinius' efforts meant that Romulus was also well educated; he could even read and write. It was only occasionally, when he was severely provoked, that Romulus' temper got the better of him. *I was like that once*, Brennus thought.

Taking a deep breath, Romulus stalked off, leaving the Parthian smirking at his companions. He hated always having to back down. Especially when he had the chance of witnessing something so important. But, as usual, walking away was the prudent choice. 'Why did Tarquinius bother dragging us along?'

'Back-up.'

'Against whom? Those miserable dogs?' Incredulously, Romulus indicated the Parthians. 'There are twenty of them. With bows.'

'Bad odds, it's true,' shrugged the Gaul. 'He doesn't have anyone else to ask, though.'

'It's more than that,' Romulus shot back. 'Tarquinius must have a reason. We *need* to be here.'

Brennus turned his blond shaggy head this way and that, taking in the barren landscape. It was vanishing into the darkness of another bitter night.

'I don't know what,' he concluded. 'This is a godforsaken spot. Nothing out here but dirt and rocks.'

Romulus was about to agree when his attention was caught by two spots of light reflecting the radiance from the torches. He froze, squinting into the gloom. At the limit of his vision was a jackal, watching them. Motionless, only the creature's bright eyes revealed that it was not a statue. 'We're not alone,' he hissed delightedly. 'There! Look.'

Brennus smiled proudly at the sharp observation. An expert hunter himself, he had missed seeing the small predator. This was becoming more common. Romulus could now follow animals over bare rock, possessing an uncanny ability to notice the smallest detail. The twig out of place, the blade of grass bent double, the change in prints' depth when the quarry was wounded. Few men had such skill.

Brac had been one.

Old emotion welled up inside Brennus: grief that his young cousin would never have the chance to stand with him like this. Like Brennus' wife, baby son and his entire Allobroge tribe, Brac was dead, massacred by the Romans eight years before. At exactly the same age Romulus was now. Trying to ease the sharp claws of his ever-present grief, Brennus shook his massive shoulders and silently repeated the Allobroge druid Ultan's words. The secret prophecy that Tarquinius had somehow known.

A journey beyond where any Allobroge has gone. Or will ever go.

And on Margiana's eastern border, some four months' march east of Carrhae and more than three thousand miles from Gaul, Brennus had truly done that. It remained to be seen how, and when, his journey would end. His attention was drawn back to the jackal by Romulus' eagerly pointing arm. 'Belenus above,' Brennus breathed. 'It's acting like a dog. See?'

Strangely, the animal was sitting back on its haunches, like a hound might watch its master.

'That's the gods' work,' muttered Romulus, wondering what Tarquinius would make of it. 'Has to be.'

'You could be right,' Brennus agreed uneasily. 'Jackals are scavengers, though; they feed on whatever dead flesh is around.'

They exchanged a glance.

'Men will die here tonight.' Brennus shivered. 'I can feel it.'

'Maybe,' said Romulus pensively. 'But I think this is a good sign.'

'How?'

'I don't know.' Falling silent, Romulus tried to use the snippets that Tarquinius occasionally let fall. Concentrating on his breathing, he focused on the jackal and the air above it, searching for something more than his blue eyes could see. For an age, he did not move, his exhaled breaths clouding round him in a thick, grey layer.

Brennus let him be.

Intent on starting a fire, the Parthians were ignoring them.

At last Romulus turned away. The disappointment on his face was clear.

Brennus eyed the jackal, which hadn't moved. 'Couldn't see anything?'

Romulus shook his head sadly. 'It's here to watch over us, but I don't know why. Tarquinius would, though.'

'Don't worry,' said the Gaul, clapping him on the shoulder. 'There are four of us against twenty now.'

Romulus had to smile at that.

It was far colder where they were standing, but both felt more kinship with the jackal than with Pacorus' men. Instead of seeking heat by the fire, they huddled down together by a large boulder.

In the event, it was that decision which probably saved their lives.

Tarquinius felt his pulse quicken as they descended the crudely formed earthen steps, which were easy to see thanks to Pacorus' torch. The narrow staircase had been dug out of the soil, with timber joists to hold up the sides. Neither the commander nor his guard spoke, which suited Tarquinius. He used the time to pray to Tinia, mightiest of the Etruscan gods. And to Mithras, even though he never had before. Mysterious and unknown, Mithraicism had fascinated Tarquinius ever since he had heard of it, in Rome. The religion had only been carried there a decade previously by legionaries who had campaigned in Asia Minor. Highly secretive in nature, Mithras' followers were sworn to uphold the values of truth, honour and courage. Rites of great suffering had to be endured to move between the levels of devotion. That was all the haruspex knew.

Of course it was not surprising to see evidence of the warrior deity here, in Margiana. This area was where the cult was strongest, perhaps even where it had originated. The discovery might have been in better circumstances though. Tarquinius smiled sardonically. He and his friends were under threat of immediate death. So it was time to be bold. With luck, the god would not be angered by a request made by a non-initiate, entering a Mithraeum in this unorthodox manner. After all, *I am not just a haruspex*, he thought proudly. *I am a warrior too.*

Great Mithras, I come with a humble heart to worship you. I beg for a sign of your favour. Something to placate your servant, Pacorus. He hesitated for a moment, and then dared all. *I also need your guidance to find a path back to Rome.*

Tarquinius sent his prayer up with all the force he could muster.

The answering silence was deafening.

He tried not to feel disappointed – but failed.

Eighty-four stairs later, they reached the bottom.

A wash of stale air wafted up the tunnel. It was a mixture of men's sweat, incense and burnt wood. Tarquinius' nostrils twitched, and goose bumps formed on his arms. There was palpable power here. If the god was in a favourable mood, perhaps his divining skills *did* have a chance of being revived.

Half turning, Pacorus noticed his reaction and smiled. 'Mithras is mighty indeed,' he said. 'And I will know if you are lying.'

Tarquinius met his stare. 'You will not be displeased,' he said quietly.

Pacorus restrained himself from saying more. Originally, he had been awed by Tarquinius' ability to anticipate the future, and to pluck the solutions to overwhelming problems from thin air. Although he would not openly admit it, the Forgotten Legion's initial successes in driving out the marauding tribes had almost exclusively been thanks to the haruspex. But some months ago, Tarquinius' accurate predictions had dried up, to be replaced with vague, generalised comments. At first Pacorus had been unconcerned, but this had soon changed. He needed the prophecies because his position as commander of Parthia's eastern border was a double-edged sword. While a huge promotion from his previous rank, it came laden with expectation. Pacorus relied on divine help just to survive.

Attacks by war bands from neighbouring lands had been frequent for some time. The reason for this was simple. In anticipation of Crassus' invasion, all local garrisons had been emptied more than twelve months previously. King Orodes, the Parthian ruler, had diverted every available man to the west, leaving the frontier region with few defences. The nomadic tribes had quickly seized the opportunity to rape and pillage every settlement within easy reach of the border. Growing bold on the back of success, soon they were vying to carve up Margiana.

Pacorus' mission from Orodes was simple: to smash all opposition and restore the peace. Fast. This he had done. But his very success jeopardised his position: the king was wary of any officer who became too effective. Even General Surena, the leader who had achieved the stunning victory at Carrhae, had not been safe. Nervous of Surena's new-found popularity, Orodes had ordered his execution not long after the battle. The news kept officers such as Pacorus in constant uncertainty: eager to please, unsure how to proceed – and desperate for aid from sources such as Tarquinius.

Fear is my last psychological advantage over Pacorus, thought the haruspex. Even that had worn thin. Weariness filled him. If the god revealed nothing, he would have to come up with something believable, enough to convince the ruthless Parthian not to kill them all. But after months of stringing Pacorus along, Tarquinius doubted his imagination was capable of any more.

They walked in silence along a passageway constructed in the same way as the staircase. At length, it opened out into a long, narrow chamber.

Pacorus moved left and right, lighting oil lamps which sat in small alcoves.

As light flooded the room, Tarquinius took in the paintings on the walls, the low seats on each side and the heavy wooden posts supporting the low roof. Inevitably though, his eyes were drawn to the end of the Mithraeum, where a trio of altars was positioned below the dramatic, brightly painted image of a cloaked figure in a Phrygian cap crouched over a kneeling bull while plunging a knife deep into the beast's chest. Mithras. Stars glittered from his dark green cloak; a mysterious figure bearing a flaming torch stood witness on each side of him.

'The tauroctony,' whispered Pacorus, bending his head reverently. 'By killing the sacred bull, Mithras gave life to the world.'

Behind him, Tarquinius sensed the guard bowing. He did the same.

Slowly Pacorus led the way to the altars. Muttering a brief prayer, he bent from the waist. 'The god is present,' he said, stepping aside. 'Let us hope he reveals something to you.'

Tarquinius closed his eyes and gathered his strength. Unusually, his palms were sweaty. Never had there been an occasion where he needed help more. He had made momentous predictions before now, many of them, but not under the threat of immediate execution. And in here, there was no wind, no cloud, no flocks of birds to observe, not even an animal to sacrifice. I am alone, the haruspex thought. Instinctively, he knelt. *Great Mithras, help me!*

He looked up at the godly figure depicted above him. There was a knowing expression in its hooded eyes. What can you offer me? it seemed to say. Other than himself, Tarquinius had no answer. *I will be your faithful servant.*

He waited for a long time.

Nothing.

'Well?' demanded Pacorus harshly, his voice echoing in the confined space.

Desolation swamped Tarquinius. His mind was a complete blank.

Furious, Pacorus uttered a few words to his guard, who stepped in close.

This is it, Tarquinius thought angrily. Olenus was wrong in thinking I would journey back from Margiana. Instead, I am to die alone, in a Mithraeum. Romulus and Brennus will be slain too. My whole life has been wasted.

And then, from nowhere, an image seared his retinas.

Nearly a hundred armed men creeping in on a score of Parthian warriors sitting around a fire. Tarquinius' skin crawled. Talking among themselves, the Parthians were totally unaware.

'Danger,' he blurted, jumping up. 'There is great danger approaching.'

The guard paused, his knife still ready for use.

'From where?' demanded Pacorus. 'Sogdia? Bactria?'

'You don't understand,' cried the haruspex. 'Here! Now!'

Pacorus' eyebrows rose disbelievingly.

'We must warn the others,' urged Tarquinius. 'Return to the fort, before it's too late.'

'It's night-time, in midwinter,' scoffed Pacorus. 'Twenty of the finest men in Parthia are on watch outside. So are your friends. And nine thousand of my soldiers are only a mile away. What possible danger can there be?'

His guard leered.

'They are about to be attacked,' answered Tarquinius simply. 'Soon.'

'What? This is how you cover up your incompetence?' shouted Pacorus, his colour rising. 'You're a damn liar!'

Instead of denying the accusation, Tarquinius closed his eyes and brought back the image he had just seen. Somehow he did not allow panic to take hold. *I need more, great Mithras.*

'Finish it,' Pacorus ordered.

Tarquinius could sense the knife approaching, but he remained still. This was the ultimate test of his divining ability. There was nothing else he could do, no more he could ask of the god. Cool air brushed Tarquinius' neck as the guard's arm rose high. He thought of his innocent friends above. Forgive me.

Carrying down the tunnel, the unmistakable sound of a man shouting the alarm reached their ears.

Shock filled Pacorus' face, but he regained control fast. 'Treacherous dog. Told your friends to cry out after a certain time, eh?'

Tarquinius shook his head in silent denial.

There was a long pause before the air filled with blood-curdling yells. Far more noise than two men could make.

Pacorus blanched. He hesitated for a moment, then turned and ran from the chamber, his guard close on his heels.

Rising, Tarquinius was about to follow, when he felt a surge of power.

The god's revelation was not over.

But his friends were in mortal danger.

Guilt mixed with anger, and desire for knowledge. He knelt again. There was time.

A little time.

A long half-hour passed. The temperature, which had been hovering just below freezing all day, fell much further. Using a stockpile of timber left there for the purpose, the Parthian warriors fed the blazing fire until it was the height of a man. While a few stood guard on a perimeter roughly thirty paces out, the remainder hunched around it, talking between themselves. Few even glanced at Romulus and Brennus, the interlopers.

The two friends stamped up and down, doing their best to keep warm.

It was a futile battle. Still they felt no inclination to join the Parthians, whose attitude towards them was at best contemptuous. Brennus fell into a deep reverie about his future while Romulus studied the jackal, hoping to understand its reasons for staying. His efforts were in vain. Finally the animal stood up, shook itself in a leisurely manner and trotted off to the south. It was lost to sight instantly.

Later, Romulus would remember the timing with awe.

'Gods above,' muttered Brennus, his teeth chattering. 'I hope Tarquinius is done soon. Otherwise we're going to have to join those bastards by the fire.'

'He won't be long,' Romulus replied confidently. 'Pacorus has reached the end of his tether with him.'

Everyone in the Forgotten Legion knew that when their commander lost his temper, men were executed.

'The prick's been looking twitchy,' agreed Brennus, counting the Parthians for the umpteenth time. There are too many of them, he decided. 'Probably order us all killed next. Shame the jackal didn't stick around to help, eh?'

Romulus was about to reply when his gaze fell on the two furthest sentries. Wraithlike figures had appeared behind them, bearing long knives. He watched disbelievingly for a heartbeat before opening his mouth to shout a warning. But it was too late. The Parthians toppled backwards and out of sight, silent sprays of red jetting from their cut throats.

None of their companions noticed.

'To arms!' Romulus roared. 'We are under attack from the east!'

Alarmed, the other warriors scrambled to their feet, reaching for their weapons and staring out into the pitch darkness.

From it, fearsome yells rose into the freezing air.

Brennus was beside Romulus in an instant. 'Wait,' he cautioned. 'Don't move yet.'

'They're spotlit by the fire,' said Romulus, understanding.

'Fools,' muttered Brennus.

The first arrows descended as they watched. Fired from beyond the firelight, they fell in a dense, deadly rain. A perfectly laid ambush, it was bizarrely beautiful to watch. More than half the Parthians were killed outright by the volley, and several others were wounded. The remainder frantically grabbed their bows and loosed shaft after blind shaft in response.

Romulus raised his silk-covered *scutum* and was about to race forward, but Brennus' great paw stopped him again. 'Tarquinius . . .' he protested.

'Is safe underground for the moment.'

Romulus relaxed a fraction.

'They'll charge next,' the Gaul said as the terrifying shouts increased in volume. 'And when they do, let's give them a little surprise of our own.'

Brennus' guess was correct. What he had not foreseen was the number of attackers.

There was another shower of arrows and then the enemy came in at a run. Dozens of them. With bows like those of the Parthians slung over their shoulders, they waved swords, knives and vicious-looking short-headed axes. Dressed in felt hats, ornate scale mail and knee-high boots, the brown-skinned men could only be one nationality: Scythian. Romulus and Brennus had already encountered the fierce nomads in skirmishes on the border. Although their empire's heyday had passed, the Scythians still made unrelenting enemies. And their hooked arrow heads were coated in a deadly poison called *scythicon*. Anyone even scratched with it died in agonising pain.

Brennus cursed quietly, and Romulus' stomach clenched.

Tarquinius was still in the Mithraeum, and they could not just leave him to his fate. Yet if they tried to rescue the haruspex, certain death would come to all of them. There were at least fifty Scythians visible now, and more were appearing. Bitterness filled Romulus at the randomness of life. The idea of returning to Rome now seemed laughable.

'They can't have missed the noise,' Brennus whispered. 'Pacorus is no coward. He'll come charging out at any moment. And there's only one way to save their lives.'

'Go in, quick and silent,' said Romulus.

Pleased, Brennus nodded. 'Hit any Scythians by the temple's entrance. Grab Tarquinius and the others. Then make a run for it.'

Clinging to his words, Romulus led the way.

They ran hard and fast, their cold muscles aching with the effort. Thankfully, adrenalin soon kicked in, giving them extra speed. Javelins in hand, both cocked their right arms back, preparing to throw when the time was right. Engrossed with the surviving Parthians, the Scythians were not even looking outwards. They had encircled their foes, and were closing in.

With a century behind us, thought Romulus wistfully, we'd smash them into pieces. Now though, they had to trust that Tarquinius emerged at the right time and they could escape into the night. It was a slim hope.

Like two avenging ghosts, they closed in on the Mithraeum's unguarded entrance.

Still they were not seen.

Cries of fear filled the air as the last Parthians realised that their fate was sealed.

A few steps from the hole, Romulus was beginning to think that they might just do it. Then a lightly built Scythian straightened up from a prone Parthian, wiping his sword on the corpse's clothing. His mouth opened and closed as he saw them. Snapping out an order, the Scythian rushed forward. Nine men followed, some quickly sheathing their weapons and unslinging their bows.

'You look for Tarquinius,' yelled Romulus as they skidded to a stop by the opening. 'I'll hold them.'

Trusting his friend implicitly, Brennus dropped his *pila* by Romulus' feet. Ripping a torch from the ground, he clattered down the steps. 'Won't be long,' he yelled.

'I'll be dead if you are.' Grimly, Romulus closed one eye and took aim. With the ease of long practice, he threw his first *pilum* in a low, curving arc. It hit the lead Scythian twenty paces away, skewering right through his scale mail and running deep into his chest. He dropped like a pole-axed mule.

But his comrades scarcely paused.

Romulus' second javelin punched into a stocky Scythian's belly, taking him out of the equation. His third missed, but the fourth pierced the throat of a warrior with a long black beard. Giving him a little more respect now, three Scythians slowed down and strung shafts to their bows. The four others redoubled their speed.

Seven of the whoresons, Romulus thought, his heart pounding with a combination of madness and fear. Poison arrows too. Bad news. What should

I do? Suddenly, Cotta, his trainer in the *ludus*, came to mind. *If all else fails, take the battle to an unsuspecting enemy. The element of surprise is invaluable.* He could think of nothing else, and there was still no sign of Brennus or Tarquinius.

Yelling at the top of his voice, Romulus charged forward.

The Scythians smiled at his recklessness. Here was another fool to kill.

Reaching the first, Romulus used the one-two method of punching with his metal shield boss and following with a thrust of his *gladius*. It worked well. Spinning away from his falling enemy, he heard an arrow strike his *scutum*. Then another. Thankfully, the silk did its job and neither penetrated. A third whistled past his ear. Knowing he had a moment before more were loosed, Romulus peered over the iron rim. Two Scythians were almost on him. The last was a few steps behind, while the trio with bows were fitting their second shafts.

Romulus' mouth felt bone dry.

Then a familiar battle cry filled his ears.

The Scythians faltered; Romulus risked a glance over his shoulder. Springing from the entrance like a great bear, Brennus had launched himself half a dozen steps forward.

Next came Pacorus, screaming with rage. He was followed closely by the hulking guard, waving his knife over his head.

There was no sign of Tarquinius.

Romulus had no time to dwell on this. He spun back and barely managed to parry a powerful blow from a Scythian. He stabbed forward in response, but missed. Then the man's comrade nearly took off his sword arm with a huge downward cut. It missed by a whisker. Sparks went flying upward as the iron blade struck the flagstones, and Romulus moved fast. The second Scythian had overextended himself with the daring blow, and in the process, exposed his neck. Leaning forward, Romulus shoved his *gladius* into the unprotected spot between the man's felt hat and his mail. Slicing through skin and muscle, it entered the chest cavity, severing most of the major blood vessels. The Scythian was a corpse before Romulus even tried to withdraw his blade. Shocked, his comrade still had the presence of mind to lower his right shoulder and drive forward into Romulus' left side.

The air left his lungs with a rush, and Romulus fell awkwardly to the frozen ground. Somehow he held on to his *gladius*. Desperately he pulled on it, feeling the blade grating off his enemy's clavicle as it came out, far too slowly. It was hopeless.

His lips peeled back with satisfaction, the Scythian jumped to stand over Romulus. His right arm went up, preparing to deliver the death stroke.

Bizarrely, Romulus could think only of Tarquinius. Where was he? Had he seen anything?

The Scythian made a high, keening sound of pain. Surprised, Romulus looked up. There was a familiar-looking knife protruding from his enemy's left eye socket. He could have shouted for joy: it belonged to Brennus. Somehow the Gaul had saved his life.

With a hefty kick, Romulus sent the Scythian tumbling backwards. Craning his neck, he looked for the others. Brennus and Pacorus were within arm's reach, fighting side by side. Unfortunately, the guard was already down, two arrows protruding from his belly.

But they now had a tiny chance.

Carefully retrieving his *scutum*, Romulus sat up, protecting himself from enemy shafts.

One immediately slammed into it, but he was able to take in the situation.

The trio of archers were still on their feet.

And at least a score of Scythians were running to join the fray.

With arrows raining down around him, Romulus managed to retreat unhurt to Brennus' side.

'Give me your shield,' Pacorus ordered him at once.

Romulus stared at his commander. My life, or his? he considered. Death now, or later? 'Yes, sir,' he said slowly, without moving. 'Of course.'

'Now!' Pacorus screamed.

As one, the archers drew back and loosed again. Three arrows shot forward, seeking human flesh. They took Pacorus in the chest, arm and left leg.

He went down, bellowing in pain. 'Curse you,' he cried. 'I'm a dead man.'

More and more shafts hissed into the air.

'Where's Tarquinius?' shouted Romulus.

'Still in the Mithraeum. Looked like he was praying.' Brennus grimaced. 'Want to make a run for it?'

Romulus shook his head fiercely. 'No way.'

'Me neither.'

As one, they turned to face the Scythians.

Chapter II: Scaevola

Near Pompeii, winter 53/52 BC

'Mistress?'

Fabiola opened her eyes with a start. Standing behind her was a kind-faced, middle-aged woman in a simple smock and plain leather sandals. She smiled. Docilosa was Fabiola's one true friend and ally, someone she could trust with her life. 'I've asked you not to call me that.'

Docilosa's lips twitched. A former domestic slave, she had received her manumission at the same time as her new mistress. But the habits of a lifetime took a while to discard. 'Yes, Fabiola,' she said carefully.

'What is it?' asked Fabiola, climbing to her feet. Stunningly beautiful, slim and black-haired, she was dressed in a simple but expensive silk and linen robe. Ornate gold and silver jewellery winked from around her neck and arms. 'Docilosa?'

There was a pause.

'Word has come from the north,' said Docilosa. 'From Brutus.'

Joy struck, followed by dread. This was what Fabiola had been asking for: news of her lover. Twice a day, in an alcove off her villa's main court-yard, she prayed at this altar without fail. Now that Jupiter had answered her requests, would it be good news? Fabiola studied Docilosa's face for a clue.

Decimus Brutus was sequestered in Ravenna with Caesar, his general, who was plotting their return to Rome. Conveniently situated between the capital and the frontier with Transalpine Gaul, Ravenna was Caesar's favourite winter abode. There, surrounded by his armies, he could monitor the political situation. Above the River Rubicon, this was allowed. But for a general to cross without relinquishing his military command – thereby entering Italy proper under arms – was an act of high treason. So every winter, Caesar watched and waited. Unhappy, the Senate could do little about it, while Pompey, the only man with the military muscle to oppose Caesar, sat on the fence. The situation changed daily, but one thing felt certain. Trouble was looming.

Fabiola was therefore surprised by Docilosa's news.

'Rebellion has broken out in Transalpine Gaul,' she revealed. 'There's heavy fighting in many areas. Apparently the Roman settlers and merchants in the conquered cities are being massacred.'

Fighting panic at this new threat to Brutus, Fabiola exhaled slowly. *Remember what you have escaped*, she thought. *Things have been far worse than this.* At thirteen, Fabiola had been sold as a virgin into an expensive brothel by Gemellus, her cruel former owner. Adding to the horror, Romulus, her brother, had been sold into gladiator school at the same time. Her heart ached at the thought. Nearly four years of enforced prostitution in the Lupanar had followed. *I did not lose hope then.* Fabiola eyed the statue on the altar with reverence. *And Jupiter delivered me from the life I despised.* Rescue had come in the form of Brutus, one of Fabiola's keenest lovers, who bought her from Jovina, the madam of the brothel, for a great deal of money. *The impossible is always possible*, Fabiola reflected, feeling calmer. Brutus would be safe. 'I thought Caesar had conquered all of Gaul?' she asked.

'So they say,' muttered Docilosa.

'Yet it has seen nothing but unrest,' retorted Fabiola. Aided by Brutus, Rome's most daring general had been stamping out trouble since his bloody campaign had ostensibly ended. 'What is it now?'

'The chieftain Vercingetorix has demanded, and received, a levy from the tribes,' Docilosa replied. 'Tens of thousands of men are flocking to his banner.'

Fabiola frowned. This was not news she wanted to hear. With the majority of his forces stationed in winter quarters just inside Transalpine Gaul, Caesar could be in real trouble. The Gaulish people were fierce warriors who had vigorously resisted the Roman conquest, losing only because of Caesar's extraordinary abilities as a tactician and the legions' superior discipline. If the tribes were truly uniting, an uprising had catastrophic potential.

'The news gets worse,' Docilosa continued. 'Heavy snow has already fallen in the mountains on the border.'

Fabiola's lips tightened. Brutus' most recent message had talked about coming to visit soon. That would not now happen.

And if Caesar couldn't reach his troops in time to quell the rebellion before spring, the trouble would spread far and wide. Vercingetorix had picked his moment carefully, thought Fabiola angrily. If this revolt succeeded, all her well-laid plans would come to nothing. Doubtless thousands would lose their lives in the forthcoming fighting, but she had to ignore that heavy cost. Whatever her desires, those men would still die. A quick victory for Caesar would mean less bloodshed. Fabiola desperately wanted this because then Brutus, his devoted follower, would gain more glory. But it was not just that. Fabiola was ruthlessly focused. If Caesar succeeded, her star would rise too.

She felt a twinge of guilt that her first thought had not been for Brutus' safety. A keen career soldier, he was also extremely courageous. He might be injured, or even killed, in the forthcoming fighting. That would be hard to bear, she reflected, offering up an extra prayer. Although she had never let herself love anyone, Fabiola was genuinely fond of Brutus. He had always been gentle and kind, even when taking her virginity. She smiled. Choosing to lavish her charms on him had been a good decision.

Previously, there had been many such clients, all powerful nobles whose patronage could have guaranteed her progress into the upper echelons of Roman society. Keeping her eyes on that prize, Fabiola had somehow managed to disassociate herself from the degradation of her job. Just as they used Fabiola's body, men were to be taken for whatever she could gain: gold, information or, best of all, influence. From the start, Brutus had been different from most clients, which made sex with him easier. What had finally tipped the balance in his favour was his close relationship with Caesar, a politician who had aroused Fabiola's interest as she eavesdropped on conversations between nobles relaxing in the brothel's baths. The pillow talk that she cajoled from her satiated customers had also been full of promising pointers towards Caesar. Perhaps it was Jupiter who had guided her to become Brutus' mistress, thought Fabiola. While at a feast with Brutus, she had seen a statue of Caesar which reminded her strongly of Romulus. Suspicion had burned in Fabiola's mind since.

Docilosa's next words brought her back to reality. 'The Optimates threw a feast when the news of Vercingetorix' rebellion reached Rome. Pompey Magnus was guest of honour.'

'Gods above,' muttered Fabiola. 'Anything else?' Caesar had enemies everywhere, and particularly in the capital. The triumvirate which ruled the Republic had been reduced by one with the death of Crassus, and since then Pompey had seemed unsure what to do about Caesar's unsurpassed military successes. Which suited Caesar admirably. But now the Optimates, the group of politicians which opposed him, were openly courting Pompey, his sole rival. Caesar could still be the new ruler of Rome – but only if Vercingetorix' uprising did not succeed and if he retained enough support in the Senate. Suddenly Fabiola felt very vulnerable. In the Lupanar, she had been a big fish in a small pond. Outside, in the real world, she was a nobody. If Caesar failed, so did Brutus. And without his backing, what chance had she of succeeding in life? Unless, of course, she prostituted herself with someone else. Fabiola's stomach turned at that idea. Those years in the Lupanar had been enough to last a lifetime.

This called for dramatic measures.

'I must visit the temple on the Capitoline Hill,' Fabiola declared. 'To make an offering and pray that Caesar crushes the rebellion quickly.'

Docilosa hid her surprise. 'The voyage to Rome will take at least a week. More if the seas are rough.'

Fabiola's face was serene. 'In that case, we shall travel by road.'

Now the older woman was shocked. 'We'll end up raped and murdered! The countryside is full of bandits.'

'No more so than the streets of Rome,' Fabiola replied tartly. 'Besides, we can take the three bodyguards that Brutus left. They'll be enough protection.' Not as good as Benignus or Vettius, she thought, fondly remembering the Lupanar's huge doormen. Despite their devotion to Fabiola, they had been too valuable for Jovina to sell as well. Returning to the capital might allow her to investigate that possibility again. The tough pair would be very useful.

'What will Brutus say when he finds out?'

'He'll understand,' answered Fabiola brightly. 'I'm doing it for him.'

Docilosa sighed. She would not win this argument. And with few diversions other than the baths or covered market in Pompeii, life had become very mundane in the almost empty villa. Rome would provide some excitement – it always did. 'When do you wish to leave?'

'Tomorrow. Send word to the port so that the captain can ready *Ajax*. He'll know in the morning if the weather is good enough to sail.' Upon his arrival in the north, Brutus had immediately sent back his treasured liburnian to lie at his lover's disposal. Powered by one hundred slaves working a single bank of oars, the short, low-slung ship was the fastest type of vessel the Romans could build. *Ajax* had been lying idle at the dock in Pompeii and Fabiola had not foreseen needing its services until the following spring. Now, things had changed.

Docilosa bowed and withdrew, leaving her mistress to brood.

Visiting the temple would also afford Fabiola another opportunity to ask Jupiter who had raped their mother. Velvinna had only mentioned it in passing, but for obvious reasons, she had not forgotten. Discovering her father's identity was Fabiola's driving purpose in life. And once she knew, revenge would be hers.

At any price.

Taking charge of the rundown *latifundium* when Brutus left had greatly intimidated Fabiola. But it provided her with satisfaction too. Being mistress of the large estate surrounding the villa was tangible proof of her revenge on Gemellus, who had originally owned it. And so she had thrown herself into the job from the start. An initial tour of the house proved that, as in his residence in Rome, Gemellus' tastes were crude and garish. It had given her great pleasure to have every single opulent bedroom, banqueting hall and office redecorated. The merchant's many statues of Priapus had been smashed, their massive erect members reminding Fabiola too much of the suffering that she had witnessed Gemellus inflict on her mother. The thick layer of dust covering the mosaic floors was swept away; the fountains unclogged and cleared of dead leaves. Even the neglected plants in the courtyards had been replaced. Best of all, the walls of the heated bathing area had been repainted with bright images of the gods, mythological sea creatures and fish. One of Fabiola's most powerful memories of her first day in the Lupanar was seeing such pictures in its baths. She had determined to have the same luxuriant surroundings herself one day. Now it was a reality.

And yet it was hard not to feel guilty, she thought later that day. While she lacked for nothing, Romulus was probably dead. Tears pricked the corners of Fabiola's eyes. While in the brothel, she had left no stone unturned in her efforts to find him. Incredibly, after more than a year, she had discovered that her twin was still alive. In the savagery of the gladiatorial arena, Jupiter had protected him. The further revelation that Romulus had enrolled in Crassus' legions could not dampen Fabiola's spirits, but then disaster struck. A few months before, the devastating news of Carrhae had reached Rome. At one stroke, Fabiola lost virtually all hope. To survive one horror only to end up in a doomed army seemed cruel beyond belief. Eager to help, Brutus had done his best to find out more, but the news was all bad. The defeat was one of the worst ever suffered by the Republic, with huge numbers of men lost. Certainly Romulus was not among the remnants of the legion that had escaped with the legate Cassius Longinus. Plenty of cash had been spread amongst the veterans of the Eighth, to no avail. Fabiola sighed. Her twin's sun-bleached bones were probably still littering the sand where he had fallen. Either that or he was gone to the ends of the earth – to some god-forsaken place called Margiana, where the Parthians had sent their ten thousand prisoners.

And no one had ever returned from there.

Rare tears rolled down Fabiola's cheeks. While the slightest chance remained of seeing Romulus again, she would not despair totally, but now stubbornness was taking over from faith. Jupiter *Optimus Maximus*, hear me, she thought miserably. Let my brother still be alive – somehow. Determined not to lose control of her emotions, Fabiola dried her eyes and went in search of Corbulo, the aged *vilicus*, or steward, of her *latifundium*. As usual, she found him busy supervising the workers. Never having lived in the countryside, Fabiola knew little about it, or agriculture, so she spent most days in Corbulo's company. The news from Gaul would not change that. The *latifundium* was her responsibility now.

Fabiola knew from Corbulo that the days of citizen farmers working their own fields were disappearing fast, as cheap grain from Sicily and Egypt put them out of business. For more than a generation, farming had been confined to those rich enough to buy up land and work it with slaves. Fortunately for such people, the Republic's war-like tendencies had provided no end of unfortunate souls from all corners of the world to generate them wealth. Gemellus' former estate was no different.

Recently freed, Fabiola hated slavery. At first, being the owner of several hundred people – men, women and children – troubled her. Practically, though, she could do nothing. Freeing the Greeks, Libyans, Gauls and Numidians would achieve little other than bankrupting her new property. She resolved instead to consolidate her position as Brutus' lover, cultivate noble friends if possible and try to discover her father's identity. Perhaps in the future, with help from Romulus, she would be able to do more. Fabiola remembered how her twin brother had idolised Spartacus, the Thracian gladiator whose slave rebellion had shaken Rome to its core only a generation before.

That thought brought a smile to Fabiola's face as she reached the large yard behind the villa. Here, the slaves' miserable, damp living quarters were a stark comparison to the solidly built storage areas. Something would have to be done about their situation, she decided. There were also stables, a two-storey mill and numerous stone sheds. These last were built on brick stilts to allow continuous airflow underneath and to prevent rodent access. Some were filled to the ceiling with harvested grain and oats, while others contained the estate's rich variety of produce. Resin-sealed jars of olive oil stood in well-balanced stacks. There were tubs of *garum*, a popular and strongly favoured fish paste, sitting beside barrels of salted mullet and clay vessels full of olives. Ready to be used over the winter, apples, quinces and pears were packed neatly in rows on beds of straw. Muddy bulbs of garlic were arranged in small pyramids. Dried hams hung from the rafters beside bunches of carrots, chicory and herbs: sage, fennel, mint and thyme.

Wine, one of the premium products, was prepared and stored in special cellars in yet another building. Firstly fermented in *dolia*, huge pitch-lined jars that were partially buried in the ground, the juice from the crushed grapes was then sealed in and left to age. Only the best vintages were decanted to amphorae and moved to the main house, where they were laid in a special depository in the roof space over one of the main hearths.

Fabiola was fond of checking each of the stores herself, still amazed that the food belonged to her. As a child, hunger had ruled her life. Now, she had enough to eat for a lifetime. The irony was not lost on her and she made sure that her slaves' diet was adequate. Most landowners barely gave their slaves enough to live on, let alone survive beyond early middle age. She might not be setting them free, yet Fabiola was determined to be a humane mistress. The use of force might occasionally be necessary to ensure obedience, but not often.

The main labour for the year – sowing, tending and harvesting crops – was almost over. Today though, the yard was a hive of activity. Corbulo was stalking up and down, shouting orders. Fabiola saw men re-forging broken ploughs and repairing worn leather harness for the oxen. Alongside them, women and children emptied carts of the late ripening vegetables such as onions, beet and the famous Pompeian cabbage. Others worked in groups on the wool which had been shorn from the sheep during the summer. Now it was being combed out and washed, before being spun.

Corbulo bowed when he saw her. 'Mistress.'

Fabiola inclined her head gravely, careful to maintain an air of un-accustomed command.

His brown hair shot with grey, the round-faced, stooped figure would scarcely attract a second glance. His clothes were nondescript. Only his long-handled whip and the lucky silver amulet dangling from a thong round his neck showed he was no mere agricultural slave. Seized as a child on the North African coast, Corbulo had lived his life since on the *latifundium*.

Having a youthful woman as his owner seemed to trouble the old *vilicus* little. Brutus had made it perfectly clear that in his absence, Fabiola was the mistress of the household. Corbulo was delighted just to have someone to tell him what to do to stop the estate falling into rack and ruin, as it had been for years.

'What are you doing?'

'Supervising this lot, Mistress,' said Corbulo, indicating the nearby slaves. 'Always plenty of routine jobs to keep them busy.'

Fabiola was intrigued by daily life on the *latifundium*. She could not imagine her former master feeling the same way. 'Did Gemellus have any real interest in this place?'

'When he first bought it, yes,' Corbulo answered. 'Used to come down here every few months.'

Fabiola concealed her surprise.

'He brought in the new olive trees from Greece and had the fish pools constructed,' the *vilicus* revealed. 'Even picked which hillsides to grow the vines on.'

Fabiola disliked the thought of her former master having a creative side.

He had only ever shown brutality at the house in Rome where she and Romulus had grown up. 'What happened then?' she asked.

There was a shrug. 'His businesses started to do badly. It started with goods from Egypt. I can still remember hearing the news.' Corbulo's lined face grew anguished. 'Twelve ships sank on the way here from Egypt. Can you believe that, Mistress?'

Fabiola sighed expressively, showing her apparent empathy. In reality she was trying to understand how a man such as Corbulo could care if his master's fortunes took a turn for the worse. She had been delighted when Brutus revealed the circumstances that had led to Gemellus' sale of the *latifundium*. Yet it was inevitable for slaves to identify with their owners in some way, she supposed. Fabiola could recall how proud Romulus had been about safely bringing back a note from Crassus' to Gemellus' house, dodging the moneylenders' men who were always lounging opposite the front door. Yet her twin had hated Gemellus as much as she did. Even those with no freedom had some pride in their lives. So she should not judge Corbulo on that alone. Although he had worked for Gemellus for over twenty years, the *vilicus* had thus far proved loyal, reliable and hard-working.

Almost on cue, Corbulo barked at a male slave who was sharpening a scythe with slow, indifferent strokes. 'Put a proper edge on that, fool!' He tapped the whip hanging from his belt. 'Or you'll feel this across your back.'

Hastily the slave bent over the curved iron blade, running an oilstone back and forth along its entire length.

Fabiola smiled approvingly. While not a brutal man, Corbulo wasn't scared of using force either. It was a good sign that the threat was enough. 'I thought his fortune was huge,' she said, probing for more information.

'It was.' Corbulo sighed. 'But the gods turned their faces away. Soon, everything the master did turned to dust. He began to borrow money, with no means of repaying it.'

She could remember the heavies waiting outside Gemellus' *domus* day and night and the rumours in the kitchen where the slaves gathered to gossip. 'Brutus mentioned a venture with animals for the arena being the final straw.'

Corbulo nodded reluctantly. 'Yes, Mistress. It should have made

Gemellus a king's ransom. He had a third share in a *bestiarius'* expedition to capture wild beasts in southern Egypt.'

Fabiola felt a pang of nostalgia: her brother had often pretended to be a *bestiarius*. Grief quickly dissolved her happiness. Instead, Romulus had become a gladiator. Yet no emotion showed on her face. The Lupanar had endowed her with the ability to conceal her feelings from everyone, even Brutus.

Suddenly an old memory surfaced. Not long before they were sold, she and Romulus had overheard Gemellus and his bookkeeper having a conversation. It had concerned the capture of animals for the circus, a venture with the potential for huge profit. The twins had been shocked that the merchant could not afford the initial outlay. As poor household slaves, his wealth always seemed immeasurable. 'That should have cleared his debts,' she said calmly.

'Except the vessels sank,' Corbulo announced. 'Again.'

'All of them?'

'Every last one,' replied the *vilicus* grimly. 'A freak storm.'

Fabiola gasped. 'Bad luck indeed.'

'It was more than that. The soothsayers said Neptune himself was angry.' Corbulo swore violently, then his face coloured as he remembered whom he was speaking to. 'Sorry, Mistress,' he muttered.

Fabiola abruptly decided to show her authority in front of the slaves. It was something she had seen Brutus do on a regular basis, ensuring that he was feared as well as respected. 'Remember who I am!' she snapped.

Corbulo bowed his neck and waited to be punished. Perhaps his new young mistress was no different to Gemellus.

In fact Fabiola had heard far worse in the Lupanar, but Corbulo had no knowledge of that. She was still learning to give orders, so his response gave her confidence. 'Continue,' Fabiola said in a more gentle tone.

The *vilicus* bobbed his head in gratitude. 'Gemellus was never one for prophecies, but there was one he mentioned just before those ships were lost.'

Her lip curled. 'Haruspices tell nothing but lies.' Hoping for a sign of release from their awful existence, many girls in the brothel spent large amounts of their meagre savings on readings from soothsayers. Fabiola had seen precious few predictions borne out. Those that had come true had been of minor significance, strengthening her determination to rely on no one but herself. And on the god Jupiter, who had finally answered her prayer for freedom.

'Indeed, Mistress,' Corbulo agreed. 'Gemellus said the same himself. But this one was not made by one of the usual shysters hanging around the great temple. It came from a stranger with a *gladius*, who only agreed to do a reading on sufferance.' There was a deliberate pause. 'And virtually all of it came true.'

Her curiosity was aroused. Soothsayers did not carry weapons. 'Explain,' she ordered.

'He predicted that Crassus would leave Rome and never return.'

Fabiola's eyes widened. It had been common knowledge that the third member of the triumvirate wanted military success to win public approval. Crassus' choice of the governorship of Syria had been little more than an opportunity to invade Parthia. Yet few could have predicted that his trip abroad would be his last – except a genuine soothsayer. Someone who therefore might have knowledge of Romulus. 'What else did he say?' she hissed.

The *vilicus* swallowed. 'That a storm at sea would sink the ships, drowning the animals.'

'Is that all?'

Corbulo's eyes flickered from side to side. 'There was one other thing,' he admitted nervously. 'Gemellus only mentioned it once, the last time I saw him.'

Fabiola pounced like a hawk on its prey. 'What was it?'

'The haruspex told him that one day a man would knock on his door.'

She tensed. *Romulus?*

'He seemed haunted by the thought,' Corbulo finished.

'Not a gladiator?'

'No, Mistress.'

Her spirits plunged.

'A soldier.'

And rose again from the depths.

Confused by her interest, Corbulo glanced at her for approval.

The *vilicus* got a perfunctory smile instead. Fabiola would give away nothing.

Not a gladiator, she thought triumphantly. A soldier, which is what her brother had become after fleeing Rome. Gemellus knew how much Romulus hated him: the prospect of seeing him again one day would have been terrifying. Now the journey to the temple of Jupiter had two important purposes. If she could find this mysterious soothsayer, she might be able to discover if Romulus was alive. It was a wild hope, but Fabiola had learned never to give up.

Dogged faith, and the desire for revenge, was what had kept her alive.

A deep baying sound suddenly rose from beyond the courtyard walls. It was a noise that Fabiola had heard occasionally since arriving in Pompeii, but always at a distance. As it grew louder, she could see fear growing in her slaves' faces. 'What's that?'

'Dogs. And *fugitivarii*, Mistress.' Seeing her blank response, Corbulo explained. 'Bounty hunters. They'll be after a runaway.'

Fabiola's pulse increased, but she did not panic. I am free, she thought firmly. Nobody is pursuing me.

Searching for the sound's source, they walked a little way out into the large, open fields which surrounded the villa. Stone walls, bare trees and low hedges separated each from its neighbour. This was flat, fertile land, most of it fallow at this time of year. Two weeks earlier, the soil had been tilled, leaving it to breathe before it was planted with seeds in the spring. Only the winter wheat remained, small green shoots poking a hand span from the earth.

Normally, Fabiola liked to stand and take it all in. At this time of year the landscape was stark, but she loved the noisy jackdaws flying to their nesting spots, the crisp air, the absence of people. Rome's streets were always thronged; inside the busy Lupanar had been little different. The *latifundium* had come to mean seclusion from the brutal realities of the world.

Until this.

Corbulo spotted the movement first. 'There!' He pointed.

Between the gaps in a hedge some two hundred paces away, Fabiola spotted a running figure. Corbulo had been correct. It was a young man, wearing little more than rags. A slave. Clearly exhausted, with his lower body covered in a thick layer of mud, his face was a picture of desperation.

'He probably tried to give them the slip by hiding in the river,' announced the *vilicus*.

Fabiola had taken pleasant walks along the waterway that separated her property from the estate belonging to her nearest neighbour. It would never seem the same again.

Corbulo grimaced. 'It never works. The *fugitivarii* always check under the banks with long poles. If that doesn't work, the dogs will catch their scent.'

Fabiola could not take her eyes off the fugitive, who was casting terrified glances over his shoulder as he ran. 'Why is he being hunted?' she asked dully, knowing the answer.

'Because he ran away,' Corbulo replied. 'And a slave is his master's property.'

Fabiola was intimately acquainted with this cruel reality. It was the same reason that had allowed Gemellus to repeatedly rape her mother. To sell her and Romulus. To execute Juba, the giant Nubian who had trained her brother to use a sword. Owners had the ultimate power over their slaves: that of life and death. Starkly reinforcing this, in the Roman legal system, the pride of the Republic, there was no retribution for the torture or killing of a slave.

A pack of large dogs burst from the cover of the nearest grove, their noses alternately sniffing the ground and the air for their quarry's scent.

Fabiola heard the young man wail with terror. It was an awful sound.

She and Corbulo watched in silence.

A group of heavily armed men emerged from the trees, urging the hounds on with shouts and whistles. Cheers went up as they caught sight of the slave, whose energy looked almost spent.

'Where's he from?'

The *vilicus* shrugged. 'Who knows? The fool could have been running for days,' he said. 'He's young and strong. I've known the chase take more than a week.' Corbulo looked almost sympathetic. 'But those bastards never give up. And a man can't run for ever on an empty belly.'

Fabiola sighed. Nobody would give food or help to a fugitive. Why would they? Rome was a state based on foundations of war and slavery. Its citizens had no reason to aid those who had fled captivity. Brutal punishments, terrible living conditions and a poor diet concerned them not at all.

Of course, not every slave was treated this badly, but they were still the beating pulse of the Republic, the labour which built its magnificent buildings, toiled in its workshops and grew its foodstuffs. Rome needed its slaves. There was little that other slaves could do either, Fabiola thought bitterly. The punishment for helping an escapee was death. And who wanted to die by crucifixion?

The drama was about to reach its climax. Having staggered to within fifty paces of them, the young man fell to his knees in the damp earth. He raised his arms in silent supplication and Fabiola had to close her eyes. Coming between a runaway and the men legally sent to catch him would not be a good idea. Without risking a lawsuit from the slave's owner, there was nothing she could do anyway.

Then the pack reached him.

Screams filled the air as the trained dogs began to savage the fugitive like a child's doll. Fabiola watched in horror. She thanked the gods a few moments later when the lead huntsman whipped them off. Gradually the rest of the *fugitivarii* arrived, more than a dozen tough-looking types clad in dull colours and armed with bows, spears and swords. From under their wool cloaks, the dull glimmer of mail could be made out. They gathered around, laughing at the deep bite wounds on the slave's arms and legs. This was part of their sport.

Fabiola held herself back. What could she do?

Engrossed with their capture, the *fugitivarii* seemed oblivious to their audience. Their brindle dogs had flopped down close by, red tongues hanging from wide, powerful jaws. Similar animals roamed around Fabiola's villa at night, used as protection against bandits and criminals. These heavily muscled creatures looked even more vicious.

Encircled now, the slave had rolled into a foetal position. He was moaning softly and only crying out when struck by his captors. Then something changed. The nearest thug finally noticed Fabiola and Corbulo. Seeing her rich clothing and jewellery, he did not speak, but muttered a few words to the stocky man in charge. Rather than respond, though, the figure delivered a huge kick to the slave's chest.

A muffled scream reached them.

Fabiola stared in horror. The blow had been enough to break ribs. 'Leave him alone,' she shouted. 'He's badly injured!'

Beside her, Corbulo coughed uneasily.

An opening appeared in the circle, hard, unforgiving faces turning towards the stunning woman and her *vilicus*. As they took in her beauty, leers distorted their features and lewd suggestions were made, albeit in whispers. The rich were still people to be respected.

Fabiola ignored the comments; Corbulo glared.

Bizarrely, the slave was then allowed to get to his feet. One of the *fugitivarii* drew his sword and poked him with its tip. Away from them, and towards Fabiola. Confused, the young slave did not move. Another sharp prod followed, prompting a sob. But he took the hint, and stumbled towards the villa. Laughs of derision met his efforts, and a number of the thugs threw clods of earth at him. His pace increased.

'What are they doing?' asked Fabiola in dread.

'They're playing with him. And us. Time to go inside, Mistress,' Corbulo muttered, his face a pale shade of grey. 'Before things get out of hand.'

Fabiola's feet were rooted to the spot.

The slave came closer. As well as the dog bites that covered his body, his torso and arms were a red ruin. Through an old, flittered tunic, oozing wounds were visible, crisscrossing his skin front and back in an ugly lattice-work. The marks of a whip, they were evidence of a brutal master. Was this why he had fled? The fugitive was young, Fabiola guessed, no more than fifteen. A boy. Sweat and tears had streaked the dirt on his face, which was pinched and hungry. And full of terror.

'Mistress!' Corbulo's voice was insistent. 'It's not safe.'

Fabiola could not take her eyes off the runaway, who did not dare to look at her.

In a trance, he shuffled past them, towards the courtyard. Like a mouse injured by a cat, he would not go far.

At last the *fugitivarii* began to move, and Fabiola's stomach twisted. She glanced around, but none of her bodyguards were in sight. Until now, there had rarely been a need for their presence and they spent much of their time around the fire in the kitchen, telling dirty jokes. Even the slaves who were in the yard had not appeared.

Corbulo's fear had grown so great that he actually took hold of her sleeve.

An urgent desire to help gripped Fabiola, and she turned to face the approaching men. Although fearful too, she was not about to scurry back inside her property to avoid these lowlifes.

Silently, malevolently, they drew closer.

'Who's in charge here?' Fabiola cried, holding her hands together to stop them trembling.

'That'd be me, lady. Scaevola, chief *fugitivarius*,' drawled the leader with an insolent half-bow. A squat, powerful figure with short brown hair and deep-set eyes, he wore a legionary's chain mail shirt that covered him from neck to mid-thigh. A *gladius* in an ornate sheath and a dagger hung from his belt. Thick silver wrist bands adorned his wrists, announcing his status. Hunting escaped slaves was clearly profitable work. 'Can I be of assistance?'

The offer came across as it was meant. Rude. Full of innuendo. It was met with sniggers of delight from the others.

Acutely aware of how powerless she was, Fabiola drew herself up to her full height. 'Explain what you are doing on my land.'

'Your land?' His eyes narrowed. 'Where's Gemellus then? You his latest piece of ass?'

This time his men laughed out loud.

Fabiola gave him an icy stare. 'That fat degenerate no longer owns this estate. I am the mistress now, and you will answer me!'

Scaevola looked surprised. 'I hadn't heard,' he admitted. 'We've been in the north for months. The pickings are good up there. Plenty of tribal scum fleeing Gaul.'

'What a pity you returned.'

'We just follow the work,' replied the *fugitivarius*. 'Been chasing this specimen for three days, isn't that right, boys? But no one escapes old Scaevola and his crew!'

'Does it amuse you to torture the slaves you catch?' asked Fabiola acidly.

Scaevola smiled, revealing sharp teeth. 'Keeps the lads here happy,' he answered. 'And me.'

His men chortled.

Fabiola gave him a withering look.

'The dirt bag would have more reason to scream if it wasn't so damn cold,' Scaevola confided amiably. 'I need a good fire to heat my iron! But that can be done later, back at the camp.'

Now Fabiola was filled with rage. She knew exactly what Scaevola was talking about. One of the commonest punishments was to brand escapees on the forehead with the letter 'F', for *fugitivus*. It was a savage warning to other slaves. And if another attempt was made, crucifixion was likely. It explained why most slaves accepted their lot. Not me, Fabiola thought fiercely. Not Romulus.

'Be gone!' She pointed back the way they had come. 'Now!'

'Who's going to make me, lady?' Scaevola sneered, jerking his head at Corbulo. 'This old fool?'

At once his men laid hands on their weapons.

The *vilicus* went pale. 'Mistress!' he hissed. 'We must return to the villa!'

Fabiola took a deep breath, calming herself. Her decision to confront Scaevola had been made, and other than a humiliating climb-down, she had little choice other than to continue. 'I am the lover of Decimus Brutus,' she announced in a loud, clear voice. 'Do you know who that is, you sewer rat?'

Scaevola's face became a cold, calculating mask.

'One of Julius Caesar's most important men,' she continued proudly, rubbing it in. 'A senior army officer.' Fabiola glared at the *fugitivarii*, daring any to meet her stony gaze. None would, except Scaevola. 'If anything happens to me, he would go to Hades to find the scum responsible.'

For a moment, Fabiola's words seemed to have worked. She turned to go.

'The whore of one of Caesar's lapdogs, eh?' Scaevola drawled.

Fabiola's cheeks burned, but she had no chance to respond.

'There are people in Rome who pay good money to see Caesar's supporters . . .' Scaevola smiled, making his words more chilling, '. . . removed from the equation.'

His men's interest picked up instantly.

Fabiola's heart lurched. There had been rumours in Pompeii recently about the brutal murders of a number of Caesar's less wealthy allies. Men who, previously, had had no need for many bodyguards. And she had just three.

'Expecting Brutus soon?'

Fabiola had no answer. The first fingers of panic clutched her belly.

'Not to worry.' Scaevola leered at her. 'You'll do. Boys?'

As one, the *fugitivarii* moved forward.

Horrified, Fabiola looked at Corbulo. To his credit, the *vilicus* was not backing away. Gripping his whip in his right fist, he moved to stand protectively in front of her.

Scaevola began to laugh, a deep, unpleasant sound. 'Kill the stupid old bastard,' he ordered. 'But I want the bitch alive and unharmed. She's mine.'

Jupiter, Greatest and Best, thought Fabiola desperately. Once more, I need your help.

Instead, the sound of swords being drawn from their sheaths filled the air.

Squaring his shoulders, Corbulo moved a step forward.

Fabiola's heart filled with pride at his brave, useless action. Then she looked at the thugs and her gorge rose. They were both about to die. No doubt she would be raped first. And she did not even have a weapon to defend herself with.

Just a few steps from Corbulo, the *fugitivarii* stopped and Scaevola's face went purple with rage.

Confused, Fabiola and Corbulo looked at each other. They sensed movement behind them.

Turning her head, Fabiola saw practically every male slave she owned coming towards them at a run. Gripping scythes, hammers, axes, and even planks of wood, there were at least forty of them. Alarmed by the escapee entering the yard, they had spontaneously come to defend their mistress. And yet not one knew how to fight like the *fugitivarii*. A lump formed in Fabiola's throat at the risks these unfortunates would take for her.

Reaching her, the slaves fanned out in a long line.

The thugs looked unhappy. Armed or not, they were vastly outnumbered. And after Spartacus' rebellion twenty years before, everyone knew that slaves could fight.

Fabiola turned to face Scaevola. 'Get off my *latifundium*,' she ordered. 'Now.'

'I'm not leaving without the fugitive,' Scaevola growled. 'Fetch him.'

His head bowed, Corbulo obediently moved a step towards the yard. 'Stop!'

The *vilicus* jerked upright at Fabiola's shouted command.

'You're not having the poor creature,' she said, allowing her fury to take complete hold. 'He stays here.'

Corbulo's face was a picture of shock.

Scaevola's eyebrows shot up. 'What did you say?' he demanded.

'You heard,' snapped Fabiola.

'The son of a whore belongs to a merchant called Sextus Roscius, not you!' the *fugitivarius* roared. 'This is totally illegal.'

'So is physically assaulting a citizen. But that did not trouble you,' responded Fabiola sharply. 'Ask Roscius how much he wants for the boy. I'll have the money sent the very next day.'

Obviously not used to being thwarted or to losing face, Scaevola's fists bunched with rage.

They glared at each other for a heart-stopping moment.

'This is not over,' the *fugitivarius* muttered from between clenched teeth. 'No one, especially a jumped-up little bitch like you, crosses Scaevola without payback. You hear me?'

Fabiola lifted her chin. She did not answer.

'I hope you and your lover have strong locks on your doors,' he warned. From nowhere, a knife appeared in his right hand. 'And plenty of guards. You'll need both.'

His companions laughed unpleasantly, and Fabiola forced herself not to shiver.

Fortified by his mistress's courage, Corbulo made a gesture. The slaves moved forward, their weapons raised.

Scaevola eyed them all with scorn. 'We'll be back,' he said. Gathering his men, he led them back across the muddy field. The dogs trotted at their heels.

The *vilicus* let out a long, slow breath.

Fabiola stood stiff-backed, watching until the *fugitivarii* were out of sight. Inside, she was panicking. *What have I done? I should have let him take the boy.* But part of her was glad. Whether her decision had been wise, only time would tell.

'Mistress?'

She turned to regard the *vilicus*.

'Scaevola is a very dangerous man.' Corbulo paused. 'And he's on Pompey's payroll.'

Fabiola flashed him a grateful smile, and the old *vilicus* fell wholly under her spell.

'The mangy dog meant what he said too,' he explained. 'His enemies just disappear. These men . . .' He indicated the slaves around them. 'Next time, they won't be enough.'

'I know,' replied Fabiola, wishing that Brutus were by her side.

She had made a real enemy. Journeying to Rome had become an urgent priority.

Chapter III: Vahram

Eastern Margiana, winter 53/52 BC

Screaming wild battle cries, the Scythians charged headlong at the two friends.

Using the dead Parthian guard's bow, Brennus had already taken down four, including the archers who had injured Pacorus.

They were still outnumbered by more than nine to one. It's hopeless, Romulus thought dully. There are far too many. He steeled himself, preparing for the inevitable.

Trying to use as many shafts as possible, Brennus loosed another arrow. Then, with a curse, he threw down his bow and drew his *gladius*.

They moved shoulder to shoulder.

Surprising Romulus utterly, first one and then another bright ball of fire came flying over his head, illuminating the scene wonderfully. The first landed and smashed apart in a great burst of flame, right in front of the Scythians, who looked suitably terrified. The second struck one of the enemy on the arm, setting light to his felt clothing. The blaze spread upwards with terrible speed, burning his neck and face. The man shrieked in agony. A number of his comrades tried to help, but their efforts were hampered by a further pair of burning missiles. The Scythians' charge came to an abrupt halt.

'They're oil lamps,' cried Romulus, suddenly understanding.

'It's Tarquinius,' replied Brennus, fitting another shaft to his bowstring.

Delighted, Romulus turned to find the haruspex only a few steps away. 'What took you so long?'

'I had a vision of Rome,' Tarquinius revealed. 'If we can get out of here, there is hope.'

Romulus' heart soared, and Brennus laughed out loud.

41

'What did you see?' Romulus asked.

Tarquinius ignored the question. 'Pick up Pacorus,' he said. 'Quickly.'

'Why?' Romulus demanded in a low voice. 'The bastard's going to die anyway. Let's run for it.'

'No,' Tarquinius answered, hurling two more oil lamps. 'The journey south would kill us in this weather. We must stay in the fort.'

Screams of terror rose from the enemy warriors as the lamps landed.

'Those are the last ones.'

They had to move. Cursing under his breath, Romulus took hold of Pacorus' feet. Brennus did likewise with his arms. Lifting him as gently as they could, they slung him over Brennus' shoulder. Pacorus lolled like a child's toy, the blood from his wounds soaking into the Gaul's cloak. By far the strongest of the three, only Brennus would be able to run for any distance with such a load.

'Which way?' shouted Romulus, peering around. The cliff face was to their back, so they could only go north, south or east.

Tarquinius pointed.

North. Their trust in the haruspex still strong, neither Romulus nor Brennus argued. They trotted into the darkness, leaving utter confusion in their wake.

Fortunately, the weather aided their escape. Dense flurries of snow began to fall, severely reducing the visibility and covering their trail. There was no pursuit, and Romulus presumed that the Scythians knew how close their camp was. Although he did too, his keen sense of direction soon went awry; he was very glad that Tarquinius seemed to know exactly which way to go. The temperature was dropping even further as the snow began to collect on the ground. If they strayed even a small distance off course, there was little chance of ever reaching the Roman fort. It and the clusters of mud-brick huts nearby were the only dwellings for many miles. Parthia's population was not large, with less than a tenth of it living on its far eastern borders. Few chose to dwell here other than the garrisons of soldiers, and captives who had no choice.

They marched in silence, stopping occasionally to listen out for the Scythians. At last a familiar rectangular shape appeared out of the gloom. It was the fort.

A tiny sigh of relief escaped Romulus' lips. He was colder than he could ever remember being. But once they were inside and warmed through again, Tarquinius might reveal what he had seen. The desire to know more was the only thing that had kept him going.

Brennus grinned. Even he was looking forward to a break.

On either side of the massive front gates sat a wooden guard tower. They were matched by similar ones on the corners and smaller observation posts in between. The walls had been constructed from closely packed earth, a useful by-product from the construction of the three deep ditches which surrounded the fort. Filled with spiked iron caltrops, the *fossae* were also within range of missiles thrown or fired from the timber walkway that ran along the inside of the ramparts. The only passage through them was the beaten-down dirt track to the entrance in the middle of each side.

They tramped down it, expecting to be challenged at any moment.

Surprisingly the huge fort was not a fighting structure: legionaries did not hide behind the protection of walls by choice. The impressive defences were to be used only in the case of unexpected attack. If an enemy presented itself, the officers would marshal the men together on the *intervallum,* the flat area that ran around the inside of the walls, before marching out to do battle. On open ground, the legionary was the master of all other infantry. And with Tarquinius' tactics and training, thought Romulus proudly, they could withstand the charge of any force, mounted or on foot.

Man for man, the Forgotten Legion could defeat any enemy.

'Stop.' Moving to Brennus' side, Tarquinius checked Pacorus' pulse.

'Is he still alive?' asked the Gaul.

'Barely,' answered Tarquinius, frowning. 'We must hurry.'

Reality struck as Romulus took in Pacorus' ashen features. Enough time had passed for the *scythicon* to do its deadly work. The commander would surely die soon and, as the sole survivors, they would be held responsible. No senior Parthian officer worth his salt would fail to punish the men who had allowed this to happen. They had escaped the Scythians to face certain execution.

Yet Tarquinius had wanted to save Pacorus. And Mithras had revealed a road back to Rome.

As a drowning man clings to a log, Romulus held on to those thoughts.

They were now less than thirty paces from the gate and within range of the sentries' *pila*. Still no challenge had been issued to check their progress, which was most irregular. No one was allowed to approach the fort without identifying themselves.

'The lazy dogs will be huddling around the fire,' Romulus muttered. Sentinels were only supposed to stay in the warm guardroom at the base of each tower for short periods; just enough to thaw out numb fingers and toes. In practice, they did it as long as the junior officer in charge allowed.

'Time to wake them up then.' Raising his axe, Tarquinius stepped forward and repeatedly hammered the butt on the gate's thick timbers. It made a deep thumping noise.

They waited in silence.

The Etruscan had raised his weapon to demand entrance again when suddenly the distinctive sound of hobnailed sandals clattering off wood reached them from above. As expected, the sentry had not been at his post in the tower. A few moments later, a pale face appeared over the ramparts.

'Who goes there?' Fear filled the man's voice as he peered down at the small group. Visitors to the fort were rare, let alone in the middle of the night. 'Identify yourselves!'

'Open up, you fool!' shouted Romulus impatiently. 'Pacorus has been injured.'

There was a disbelieving pause.

'You piece of shit!' cried Tarquinius. 'Move!'

The sentry's shock was palpable. 'Yes, sir! At once!' He turned and fled down the staircase to the rooms below, roaring at his comrades.

Moments later the heavy locking bar was being lifted. One of the doors creaked open, revealing several legionaries and an anxious *optio*. The delay in responding would surely result in some kind of punishment.

But Tarquinius pushed past without a word. Romulus and Brennus followed. Confusion filled the sentries' faces as they took in the prone shape on the Gaul's shoulder.

'Shut the gate!' Tarquinius bellowed.

'Where are Pacorus' warriors, sir?' asked the *optio*.

'Dead,' snapped Tarquinius. 'We were ambushed by Scythians at the Mithraeum.'

Shocked gasps met this comment.

Tarquinius was in no mood to reveal more. 'Advise the duty centurion and then get back to your posts. Keep your eyes peeled.'

The *optio* and his men hastened to obey. Tarquinius was also a centurion and could have punished them as severely as Pacorus. They would have to find out what had happened later.

Tarquinius hurried down the fort's main street, the Via Praetoria. Romulus and Brennus followed. On both sides lay parallel rows of long, low wooden barracks, each housing a century of eighty soldiers. Their interiors were identical: large rooms for the centurion, smaller ones for the junior officers and more cramped quarters for the men. Ten *contubernia*, each of eight soldiers, shared just enough space to fit bunk beds, their equipment and food. Like gladiators, legionaries lived, slept, trained and fought with each other.

'Romulus!'

Hearing the low shout, he half turned. In the shadows between two of the barrack buildings, Romulus picked out the features of Felix, one of his original unit. 'What are you doing up?' he demanded.

'Couldn't sleep,' Felix replied with a grin. He was already dressed and armed. 'I was worried about you. What's going on?'

'Nothing. Go back to bed,' replied Romulus curtly. The less anyone else had to do with this, the better.

Instead, Felix darted to Brennus' side, gasping when he saw the arrows jutting from Pacorus' flesh. 'Gods above,' he breathed. 'What happened?'

Romulus filled him in while they marched. Felix nodded, grimacing as he heard the details. Though smaller than Romulus and weaker than Brennus, the little Gaul was a fine soldier. Truly stubborn too. When their mercenary cohort had been cut off during the battle at Carrhae, Felix had stayed by their side. Completely surrounded by Parthian archers, just a score of men chose to remain with the three friends and Bassius, their centurion. Felix was one of them. He's his own master, thought Romulus, glad to have him along.

No one else halted the small party. It was still dark, and most men were asleep. Besides, only a more senior officer would dare question Tarquinius, and none of those were to be seen. At this time of night, they were also in bed. Soon they reached the *principia*, the headquarters. This was at the intersection of the Via Praetoria with the Via Principia, the road that ran from the east wall to the west, dividing the camp into four equal parts. Here also were Pacorus' luxurious house and more modest ones for the senior centurions, the Parthian officers who each commanded a cohort. There was a *valetudinarium*, a hospital, as well as workshops for carpenters, cobblers, potters and a multitude of other professions.

Tradesmen and engineers as well as soldiers, the Romans were almost self-sufficient. It was one of many things that made them so formidable, thought Romulus. Yet Crassus had managed to expose the Republican army's sole weakness. It retained almost no cavalry, while Parthia's forces consisted of little else. Tarquinius had spotted this long before Carrhae, followed soon after by Romulus. But ordinary soldiers had no say in tactics, he reflected angrily. Crassus had marched arrogantly into disaster, unwilling or unable to see what might happen to his men.

Which explained why the Forgotten Legion had new masters. Cruel ones.

Romulus sighed. Apart from Darius, his own cohort commander, the majority of the Parthian senior officers were utterly ruthless. What would happen when they saw Pacorus, only the gods knew. But it would not be good.

From the *principia*, it was not far to the high walls of Pacorus' house. Copying a Roman villa, it was built in the shape of a hollow square. Just inside the front gates were the *atrium*, the entrance hall, and the *tablinum*, the reception area. These led on to the central courtyard, which was bordered by a covered walkway giving access to a banqueting hall, bedrooms, bathrooms and offices. Having seen Seleucia, Romulus knew that his captors were not a nation of architects and engineers like the Romans. Apart from the city's great entrance arch and Orodes' magnificent palace, the houses there were small and simply built of mud bricks. He could still remember his commander's amazed reaction when he had first entered the finished structure. Pacorus had been like a child with a new toy. Now, however, he barely stirred as they reached the gates, which were guarded by a dozen Parthians armed with bows and spears. Legionaries were never trusted with this duty.

'Halt!' cried the swarthy officer in charge. He peered suspiciously at the body hanging over Brennus' shoulder. 'Who have you got there?'

Tarquinius' gaze did not waver. 'Pacorus,' he said quietly.

'Is he unwell?'

The haruspex nodded. 'Badly wounded.'

The Parthian darted forward, gasping as he took in Pacorus' grey features. 'What evil is this?' he cried, barking an order. At once his men fanned out, surrounding the party with levelled spears.

Romulus and his friends were careful not to react. Relations with their captors were strained at the best of times, let alone when they were carrying a critically injured Pacorus.

Drawing a dagger, the officer stepped close to Tarquinius. He laid the blade flat against his neck. 'Tell me what happened,' he hissed, his teeth bared. 'Fast.'

There was no immediate reply and the Parthian's eyes bulged with anger. He moved the razor-sharp metal slightly and cut Tarquinius' skin, drawing a thin line of blood.

His men gasped at his courage. Most Parthians were terrified of the haruspex.

Keeping silent underlines my power, thought Tarquinius. And this is not my time to die.

Felix stiffened but Romulus jerked his head to stop any reaction. Their friend knew what he was doing. To his relief, the little Gaul relaxed. 'We were ambushed by Scythians, sir,' said Romulus loudly. 'Check his wounds for yourself.'

No one spoke as the officer paced back to Brennus. Close up, no one could miss the distinctive Scythian arrows. But he was not yet satisfied. 'Where are the rest of the men?' he demanded.

'All dead, sir.'

His eyes widened. 'Why are none of you hurt?'

Romulus kept his composure. 'They fired volleys of arrows from nowhere, sir. We had shields. We were lucky.'

The Parthian's gaze darted to Brennus and Felix, but the Gauls were nodding in unison. The officer stared last at Tarquinius, whose dark eyes revealed little. He turned back to Romulus.

'The commander and Tarquinius survived because they were in the

Mithraeum,' Romulus went on. 'Brennus and I fought our way to the entrance to try and rescue them.'

The officer waited in stony silence.

'Pacorus was hit as we were about to escape,' said Romulus, guiltily remembering his delay in handing over his *scutum*. If Pacorus lived, he would remember that. But that particular bridge would have to be crossed if it appeared. At least he wasn't the one with three poison arrows in his flesh. 'And Brennus carried him back anyway.'

'Why?' The Parthian sneered. '*Scythicon* kills everyone. What do you care if the commander dies?'

Unsure what to say, Romulus tensed.

'He is our leader,' protested Tarquinius. 'Without him, the Forgotten Legion is nothing.'

Disbelief flared in the other's eyes. 'Expect me to swallow that?' he growled. There was little reason for any of the Romans to care about the health of their captors. Especially Pacorus. Every man present knew it.

'I can help Pacorus. Delay me any longer,' Tarquinius announced, 'and you risk being the cause of his death.'

Outwitted, the officer stepped back. Having witnessed the extent of his superior's injuries, he did not want to be accused later of slowing Pacorus' treatment. However odd the situation might seem, there was only one man in the fort capable of saving their commander.

Tarquinius.

'Let them pass!' the Parthian ordered.

His men raised their weapons and one quickly opened the heavy gate, allowing Tarquinius and the others inside. The *atrium* was simply built, with a baked brick floor rather than the ornate mosaic it would have had in Rome. Unsurprisingly, nobody was to be seen. An austere man for all his cruelty, Pacorus needed few servants.

'Bring my leather bag from the *valetudinarium*,' the haruspex cried, leading the way through the *tablinum* and into the courtyard. 'Fast!'

Shouted commands followed them as the officer sent men running to obey.

Word was also being rushed to the senior centurions, thought Romulus sourly. If they weren't already on their way. He swallowed, offering a fervent prayer to Mithras, a deity he knew little of. And although worshipped by the Parthians, the god had apparently shown Tarquinius a way out of here. There had to be a solution to their increasingly desperate situation. But Romulus could not see it. Help us, Mithras, he prayed. Guide us.

In Pacorus' large bedroom, they found a fire already burning. Its flames lit up thick wall carpets and embroidered cushions scattered on the floor. Apart from some iron-bound storage chests, a bed covered in animal skins was the only piece of furniture. Startled by their sudden arrival, two servants, local peasants, jumped up guiltily from the floor in front of the brick fireplace. Warming themselves in their master's quarters would be rewarded with a severe flogging at the least. Their mouths opened with shock and a little relief when they saw Pacorus lying over Brennus' shoulder. There would be no punishment today.

'Make light,' snapped Tarquinius. 'Bring clean blankets and sheets. And plenty of boiling water.'

The fearful men did not dare answer. One scurried off while the other lit a taper and touched it to each of the bronze oil lamps positioned around the walls. The illumination revealed a wooden shrine in one corner. It was covered with the stubs of candles: like anyone else, Pacorus needed the gods sometimes. Sitting on it was a small statue of a cloaked man in a blunt-peaked Phrygian hat, twisting the head of a kneeling bull upwards towards the knife gripped in his free hand. The god was unfamiliar to Romulus, yet he somehow knew who it was. 'Mithras?' he breathed.

Tarquinius nodded.

Romulus bent his head in respect, praying hard.

Aided by Felix, Brennus moved towards the bed.

Tarquinius eyed the figurine curiously. Before entering the Mithraeum, he had only seen an image of Mithras once, in Rome. It had belonged to a one-armed veteran who helped him to search for the killer of Olenus, his mentor. Secundus, had that been the cripple's name? A good man, the haruspex remembered, but secretive about his religion. Ever since, Tarquinius had longed to know more about Mithraicism. Now, in one night, he had been inside a temple and had a vision from the god himself. And if Pacorus lived, yet more might be revealed. Through him, Tarquinius might also discover information about the Etruscans' origins. A stream of orange-yellow sparks rose as a log noisily cracked in two. Tarquinius' eyes narrowed and he studied the tiny points of fire as they turned in graceful spirals and twists before disappearing up the chimney. It was a good sign.

Romulus saw the haruspex watching the blaze and took hope.

Great Mithras, Tarquinius prayed reverently. *Although this wounded man is my enemy, he is your disciple. Grant me the ability to save him. Without your help, he will surely die.*

Felix and Brennus laid the unconscious Parthian on to his bed.

The remaining servant gaped as Tarquinius drew his dagger.

His response provoked a chuckle. 'As if I'd kill him now.' The haruspex leaned over and began slicing open Pacorus' blood-soaked clothing, leaving the wooden shafts in place. A few moments later, the Parthian was as naked as the day he was born. His normally brown skin had gone a grey, unhealthy-looking colour, and it was hard to see the shallow movements of his chest.

Romulus closed his eyes at their commander's horrifying injuries. Around each, the flesh had already turned bright red – the first sign that the *scyth-icon* was having an effect. But the worst area was his chest wound. It was a miracle that Pacorus had not been killed outright by the arrow, which had punched between two ribs to lie very close to the heart.

'That means death,' said Brennus quietly.

Tarquinius lifted his eyebrows, silently contemplating his task.

Felix sucked in a long, slow breath. 'Why did you bother carrying him back?'

'He has to survive,' answered Tarquinius. 'If he doesn't, we're all dead men.'

His trust in the haruspex absolute, Brennus waited. This was the man who had known – incredibly – what his druid had predicted, before his whole tribe had been massacred.

But the little Gaul looked worried.

Romulus knew how he felt. Yet Tarquinius was right. The extremely cold weather meant that any long journeys were far too dangerous without proper supplies. They had had little choice but to return here. Now their fates rested with the nearly dead man lying before them. Or rather, in Tarquinius' ability to save him. Looking at Pacorus' injuries, it seemed an impossible peak to climb. Automatically, Romulus' gaze flickered to the statue on the altar. *Mithras, we need your help!*

It was then that a group of excited, upset servants arrived, led by the peasant who had fled on their arrival. Bearing blankets, linen sheets and steaming bronze bowls of water, they laid down their loads near the bed. At once they were urged from the room by Romulus. Only the two original men remained, to hold up more lamps by the bed, in turn providing the haruspex with light. Moments later a guard arrived, carrying Tarquinius' medicine bag. He blanched at Pacorus' appearance. Muttering a prayer, he backed away hastily and took up a position by the door.

Delving into the pack, Tarquinius produced a set of iron surgical instruments, a selection of which he dropped into the scalding liquid. The remainder were placed neatly alongside in case they were needed. There were scalpels, forceps and hooks. Strange-looking probes and spatulas lay beside different types of saws. A roll of brown, fibrous stitching material appeared, made from the outer lining of sheep's gut. Trimmed off, dried and then stretched into tough thread, it could be used to hold together most tissues using round-bodied or triangular cutting needles. Romulus had seen the haruspex use many of the metal tools before, operating on the injuries of soldiers with great success. Although skilful in their own right, the legion's few surviving surgeons had been amazed.

Beneath Tarquinius' healing hands, men who would normally have died had not. Torn arteries were tied off, preventing death through blood loss. Tendons were carefully repaired, restoring function to useless limbs and toes. After the scalp had been lifted, even a man's skull could be sawn open to allow the removal of a blood clot on the brain's surface. According to Tarquinius, the keys to success were an expert knowledge of anatomy, and absolute cleanliness. Such surgery fascinated Romulus and he moved closer to watch. This challenge would surely test his friend's abilities to the limit. Compared to the relatively clean wounds inflicted by the razor-sharp blades of spears and *gladii*, those made by the arrows were ragged and contaminated with *scythicon*.

Pacorus was already halfway to Hades.

Fully aware of the mountainous task facing him, Tarquinius looked at the figure on the altar and bent his head, once. *Mithras, help me once more!*

The significance of the gesture was not lost on Romulus.

Felix' face changed as Tarquinius prepared to begin. 'Time to get warm,' the little Gaul muttered, sitting down by the fire with a sigh. Few men chose to witness such gory work.

Romulus and Brennus did not move.

'Hold his arms,' said Tarquinius briskly. 'He might wake up. This really stings.' Pulling the cork stopper from a small flask with his teeth, he poured some strong-smelling liquid on to a piece of clean cloth.

'*Acetum*?' asked Romulus.

Tarquinius inclined his head. 'Vinegar is excellent at preventing blood poisoning.'

They watched him gently clean the wounds; Pacorus did not even stir.

The haruspex tackled Pacorus' arm first. Slicing either side of the wooden shaft, he used a metal probe to free the barbed arrow head. Any bleeding was stopped with special clamps and then tied off with gut. Following this, the muscles were closed in layers. Pacorus' leg was treated similarly. It was the chest wound that took the most effort, however. Gripping special retractors, Tarquinius pried apart two ribs to allow with-drawal of the arrow. Closing this wound was an urgent process, he explained. If too much air leaked into Pacorus' chest cavity he would die. As Romulus watched, his understanding grew. Keen to learn more, he ques-tioned Tarquinius closely about his techniques.

'You should have seen enough by now,' the haruspex pronounced with a sigh. 'The next test will be for you to operate on an injured soldier.'

Romulus flinched at the prospect. To dress a wound in the midst of combat was one thing, but this was another.

'There'll be plenty of casualties in the future,' said Tarquinius shrewdly. 'I can never treat them all.'

Romulus nodded in acknowledgement. It was brutal but true. As Romulus had witnessed himself, the haruspex treated only those whom he had a chance of saving. Very seriously wounded legionaries were often left to die. If they were lucky, they received a draught of mandrake or the painkilling *papaverum* to help them on their way, but most died screaming in agony. Any attempt to save their lives by him, however inexperienced, would be better than the lingering hell they currently endured. Determination filled Romulus to soak up all the medical information he could.

At last the prolonged surgery finished. Muttering under his breath, Tarquinius produced a tiny bag, allowing a faint dusting of powder from it to fall over the Parthian's wounds. The falling particles smelt strong and musty.

'I haven't seen you use that before,' commented Romulus curiously.

'Some call it *mantar*,' the haruspex answered, tying up the pouch. 'Few even know of it; I've only come across it once, in Egypt.' He weighed the bag carefully in his hand. It looked as light as a feather. 'This cost me three talents.'

'How much was there?' asked Romulus.

Tarquinius looked amused. 'When I bought it? About three small spoonfuls.'

They all stared at him with amazement. That amount of gold would let a man live comfortably for the rest of his life.

Tarquinius was in a talkative mood. 'It's excellent at killing infection.' The pouch disappeared inside his tunic again.

'Even that caused by *scythicon*?' Romulus could not conceal the strain in his voice.

'We will see,' answered Tarquinius, eyeing the figure of Mithras. 'I've saved a man's life with it before.'

'Where does it come from?'

The haruspex grinned. 'It's made by grinding up a particular type of blue-green fungus.'

Brennus was incredulous. 'Like the stuff that grows on bread?'

'Perhaps. Or on some varieties of over-ripe fruit. I have never been able to tell,' sighed Tarquinius. 'Many moulds are poisonous, so it's difficult to experiment with them.'

Romulus was intrigued by the incredible concept that something growing on rotting matter might prevent the inevitable, fatal illness that followed belly wounds or animal bites.

Resentment bubbled up in Brennus. 'It'd be better saved for our comrades.'

'Indeed.' Tarquinius' dark eyes regarded him steadily. 'However our lives depend on Pacorus recovering.'

The Gaul sighed. He was not worried about himself, but Romulus' survival was vital to him. And Tarquinius held the key to that, he was sure of it. Which meant that Pacorus had to pull through as well.

During the whole experience, the Parthian had not even opened his eyes. Only his faint breathing showed that he was still alive.

Sitting back, Tarquinius considered his handiwork. He went very quiet.

Romulus looked at him questioningly. It was the same way the haruspex behaved when he was studying the winds or cloud formations in the sky.

'He has a small chance,' pronounced Tarquinius at length. 'His aura has strengthened a little.' *Thank you, great Mithras.*

Romulus breathed a small sigh of relief. They might survive yet.

'Sit him up so I can place the bandages.'

As the servants obeyed, the Etruscan ripped several sheets into suitable sizes. He was about to begin wrapping Pacorus' midriff when the door suddenly slammed open. As the sentry snapped to attention, eight brown-skinned men barged into the room, their dark eyes angry and concerned. Dressed in fine cloth tunics and richly embroidered tightly fitting trousers, they wore sheathed swords and daggers on belts inlaid with gold wire. Most had neatly trimmed short beards and black, coiffed hair. 'What's going on?' shouted one.

Everyone except Tarquinius tensed. Romulus, Brennus and Felix jerked upright, staring straight ahead as if on parade. These were some of the Parthian senior centurions, the highest-ranking officers in the Forgotten Legion. Men who would be responsible for the legion if Pacorus died.

Still held in a sitting position by the servants, Pacorus' head lolled forward on to his chest.

The newcomers gasped.

'Sir?' asked another, bending down and trying to attract Pacorus' attention.

There was no response.

Rage filled the man's features. 'Is he dead?'

Romulus' pulse quickened and his eyes darted to Pacorus. He was immensely relieved to see that the Parthian was still breathing.

'No,' said Tarquinius. 'But he is near death.'

'What have you done?' barked Vahram, the *primus pilus*, or senior centurion, of the First Cohort. He was their own direct superior. A barrel-chested, powerful man in early middle age, he was also the legion's second-in-command. 'Explain yourself!'

Struggling not to panic, Romulus prepared to draw his *gladius*. Brennus and Felix did likewise. It was impossible to miss the threat in Vahram's words. These were no mere guards to intimidate and, like Pacorus, the senior centurions held the power of life and death over them all.

His nostrils flaring, Vahram gripped his weapon.

Tarquinius lifted his hands calmly, palms facing Vahram. 'I can clarify everything,' he said.

'Do so,' replied the *primus pilus*. 'Quickly.'

Romulus' fingers slowly released his *gladius* hilt. He stepped back, as did Brennus and Felix. It felt as if they were all teetering on the edge of a deep chasm.

In stony silence, the Parthians convened around the bed. Vahram scanned the others' faces suspiciously as he listened to the haruspex' account of what had happened. Of course no mention was made of returning to Rome.

When Tarquinius finished, no one spoke for some moments. It was hard to tell if the Parthians believed his story. Romulus felt very uneasy. But the die had been cast. All they could do was wait. And pray.

'Very well,' said Vahram at last. 'Things could have happened as you say.'

A slow breath escaped Romulus' lips.

'Just one more thing, haruspex.' Vahram's hand fell lightly to his sword. 'Did you know this would happen?'

The world stopped and Romulus' heart lurched in his chest.

Again everyone's eyes were fixed on Tarquinius.

Vahram waited.

Incredibly, the haruspex laughed. 'I cannot see everything,' he said.

'Answer the damn question,' growled Vahram.

'There was great danger, yes.' Tarquinius shrugged. 'There always is in Margiana.'

The tough *primus pilus* was not satisfied. 'Speak clearly, you son of a whore!' he shouted, drawing his sword.

'I thought that something might happen,' admitted the haruspex. 'But I had no idea what.'

Romulus remembered the watching jackal and how he and Brennus had stayed away from the fire to study it. A decision which had saved their lives. Was that not proof of a god's favour? He looked at Mithras crouching over the bull and trembled with awe.

'That's all?' demanded Vahram.

'Yes, sir.'

Romulus watched the *primus pilus'* face carefully. Like that of Tarquinius, it was hard to judge. He did not know why, but suspicion filled him.

'Very well.' Vahram relaxed, letting his blade drop to his side. 'How long will it be before Pacorus recovers?'

'He may never do so,' replied the haruspex levelly. '*Scythicon* is the most powerful poison known to man.'

The senior centurions looked anxious and a vein pulsed in Vahram's neck.

Pacorus moaned, breaking the silence.

'Examine him again!' barked one of the younger officers.

Tarquinius bent over the bed, checking Pacorus' pulse and the colour of his gums. 'If he lives, it will take months,' he pronounced at last.

'How many?' asked Ishkan, a middle-aged man with jet-black hair.

'Two, maybe three.'

'You will not leave this building until he is well,' the *primus pilus* ordered. 'For any reason.'

There was a growl of agreement from the others.

'My century, sir?' Tarquinius enquired.

'Fuck them!' screamed Ishkan.

'Your *optio* can take charge,' the *primus pilus* said curtly.

Tarquinius bowed his head in acknowledgement.

Brennus and Felix relaxed. A reprieve had been granted, but Romulus was not happy. Later he would realise, bitterly, that the feeling had been intuition.

'We'll leave you to it.' Vahram turned to go, and then swiftly spun on his heel. Snarling silently, he rushed at Felix with his sword raised. The little Gaul had no time to reach for his own weapon. Nor did his friends.

Vahram ran his blade deep into Felix' chest. The lethally sharp iron slipped between the little Gaul's ribs to pierce muscle, lungs and heart, emerging red-tipped from his back.

Felix' eyes widened with horror and his mouth opened. No sound came out.

The senior centurions' faces were the picture of shock.

Tarquinius also looked stunned. He had forgotten the heavy price that gods often required. They gave nothing away free. Normally, he would have sacrificed an animal when seeking important information. Tonight, Mithras had revealed much without any obvious payment. Anguish filled the haruspex. How could he have been so stupid? Elated at seeing a vision, and at the mere possibility of returning to Rome, he had failed to consider what might follow. Was Felix' life worth that much?

And then Tarquinius' vision filled with the image of Romulus, standing on the deck of a ship, sailing into Ostia, Rome's port. After the drought of the previous few months, it felt like a rainstorm. Felix had not died in vain, he thought.

But Romulus knew none of this. Grief flooded through him. Felix was completely innocent; he had not even been at the Mithraeum. In reflex, Romulus drew his weapon and took a step towards the *primus pilus*. Brennus was right behind, his face fixed in a rictus of rage. They were two against eight, but at that exact moment, neither cared.

Vahram extended a hand and pushed Felix backwards, letting him fall lifeless to the floor. A gush of blood accompanied the blade's withdrawal from his thoracic cavity. It formed around the little Gaul's body in a great red pool.

Weeping fat, angry tears, Romulus swept forward, ready to kill. It was six steps to Vahram. Two heartbeats.

Tarquinius observed in silence. Romulus would decide his own fate. So would Brennus. It was not for him to intervene. Romulus' journey back to Rome was not his only possible path. Perhaps, like many gods, Mithras was fickle. Maybe they would all die here tonight.

But Vahram did not even lift his bloodied sword to defend himself.

Disturbed by the squat *primus pilus*' calm, Romulus managed to pull himself back. As he had learned at the Mithraeum, gut reactions were not always the best. Killing Vahram now would burn all their bridges. It was also a sure way to die. But there was another option: walking out of here. If he did that, then Felix could be avenged – later. Somehow Romulus was sure of this. Quickly he held out an arm to halt Brennus' attack as well. Remarkably, the Gaul did not protest.

This is not a battle that no one else could win, Brennus thought, remembering the haruspex prophecy. I will know when it is.

Tarquinius exhaled with relief. *Thank you, Mithras!*

'You show intelligence,' Vahram snarled. 'Twenty archers are waiting outside.'

Romulus scowled. All of them had been outwitted – even Tarquinius.

'If one of us calls out, they have orders to kill you all.'

Romulus lowered his weapon, followed slowly by Brennus. He glanced
at the statue of Mithras and made a silent vow to himself. Gods willing,
my day will come, the young soldier thought savagely. For Felix, just as
it will with Gemellus.

'Get back to barracks,' Vahram snapped. 'And consider yourselves lucky
not to be crucified.'

Romulus' fists clenched, but he did not protest.

Great Belenus, Brennus prayed. Take Felix straight to paradise. I will
see him there.

Vahram was not finished. He pointed a stubby finger at Tarquinius. 'If
Pacorus dies, so will you.' His eyes glinted. 'And both of your friends
here.'

Tarquinius' face paled. The *primus pilus* was repeating, albeit unknowingly, Pacorus' threat. It was the vivid vision of Romulus entering Ostia
which gave him strength. He himself might not return to Rome, but his
pupil could. Quite how that would happen, Tarquinius was not sure. All
he could do was believe in Mithras.

Romulus' heart sank. Judging by the haruspex' response, the chances
of Pacorus surviving were slim to none. Like mist dispersed by the rising
sun, the promised path to Rome vanished again. What hope had they
really?

Brennus quietly led him away from Felix' body, but Romulus turned
in the doorway and looked back.

Have faith in Mithras, mouthed the haruspex, inclining his head towards
the small statue on the altar. He will guide you.

Mithras, thought Romulus numbly. Only a god could help him now.

Chapter IV: Fabiola and Secundus

Rome, winter 53/52 BC

Fabiola's pulse quickened as she raced up the last few steps to the top of the Capitoline Hill, nearing the enormous complex. She had not worshipped here for months and had missed it keenly. Sheer excitement had made her run ahead of Docilosa and the bodyguards, but this was now replaced by anxiety at what she might find. It might be nothing at all.

An appreciative wolf whistle from a passer-by dragged her thoughts down to earth.

Fabiola's common sense kicked in, and she slowed down. It was not wise for a woman to venture out alone in any part of Rome. Particularly not for her. Scaevola's threat had been no idle one – only a day after the incident with the fugitive, two of her slaves had been randomly killed in the fields. There were no witnesses, but the *fugitivarii* had to be the main suspects. The threat accelerated Fabiola's departure. She had hurriedly managed to recruit a dozen gladiators from the local *ludus*, leaving six to defend the *latifundium* with Corbulo. Joining her original three bodyguards, the rest had come with her to Rome. But that did not mean that the danger was gone. And like a foolish child playing hide-and-seek, she had just left her protection behind.

Already Fabiola could feel the stares of several unsavoury types who were loitering nearby. None looked like Scaevola, but a flutter of fear rose from her stomach all the same. Now was not the time to let something foolish happen. Retracing her steps, Fabiola steadied her nerves. Perhaps too it had been foolish to pin her hopes on finding the mysterious sooth-sayer. Yet the revelation about Gemellus' last divination had to be more than coincidence. On the voyage north, her mind had raced constantly with the possibilities of the stranger at Gemellus' door being Romulus.

Soon Fabiola had been joined by her followers. Her face perspiring from the climb, Docilosa was also red with indignation at her mistress's rash behaviour. Nothing she said ever made any difference to Fabiola's actions, so she scolded the guards mercilessly for falling behind. The nine muscle-bound men looked sheepish and shuffled their feet in the dirt. Even the new recruits had learned not to argue with her. Amused, Fabiola hurried towards her destination, confident that Docilosa was watching her back.

Dominating the open area before her was an immense marble statue of a naked Jupiter, his bearded face painted the traditional victor's red. On triumphal days, a wooden scaffold had to be erected to daub his entire body with the blood of a freshly slaughtered bull. Today, apart from its crimson visage, the beautifully carved figure was a muted, more natural white colour. Its position, on the very edge of the top of the Capitoline Hill, had been very deliberately chosen. The main part of the city lay sprawled below, directly beneath Jupiter's imperious gaze. In open spaces like the Forum Romanum and the Forum Boarium, citizens could look up and be reassured by his presence: Jupiter *Optimus Maximus*, the all-seeing state-god of the Republic.

No less impressive was the huge gold-roofed temple that stood behind, its triangular portico of decorated terracotta supported by three rows of six painted columns, all the height of ten men. This was the airy anteroom to the triad of imposing *cellae*, or sacred rooms. Each one was dedicated to a single deity: Jupiter, Minerva and Juno. Of course Jupiter's was in the centre.

Extending for some distance to the rear was an extensive complex of smaller shrines, teaching schools and priests' quarters. Thousands of citizens came daily to worship in this, the most important religious centre in Rome. Fabiola revered it greatly and was sure that she could feel a distinct aura of power within the *cellae*. The long, narrow plastered rooms had originally been built by the Etruscans, the founders of the city. A people who had been crushed by the Romans.

Her nose twitched. The air was thick with the smells of incense and myrrh, and manure from the sacrificial animals on sale. The cries of hawkers and traders mixed with the incantations of haruspices performing divinations. Tethered lambs bleated plaintively, resigned hens packed into wicker cages stared beadily into the distance. Scantily clad prostitutes cast practised, seductive eyes at any man who glanced their way. Acrobats jumped and tumbled while snake charmers played flutes, tempting their charges out of clay vessels sitting in front of them. From small stalls, food vendors were offering bread, wine and hot sausages. Slaves wearing nothing but loincloths slouched beside their litters, sweat from the steep climb still coating their bodies. There would be time for a brief rest while their owners prayed. Children shrieked with laughter, getting under men's feet as they chased each other through the throng.

Although more peaceful than the narrow streets below, an uneasy air hung over the area. It was the same throughout Rome. Upon their arrival, Fabiola had been struck by the palpable menace. There were few people about, fewer stalls with their goods spilling out on to the road, more shops securely boarded up. Even the beggars were not as plentiful. But the most obvious sign of trouble had been the large gangs of dangerous-looking men on many corners. They had to be the reason that no one was abroad. Instead of the usual clubs and knives, nearly all were wearing swords. Fabiola had also seen spears, bows and shields; many men were even wearing leather armour or chain mail. A good number had bandaged arms or legs, evidence of recent fighting. The city had always been full of criminals and thieves, but Fabiola had never seen them congregate in such numbers, in daylight. Armed like soldiers.

Compared to a rural town like Pompeii, the capital always felt a touch more dangerous. Today it was markedly different. This felt as if a war was about to break out. Her newly enlarged collection of nine bodyguards began to seem woefully inadequate, and Fabiola had lifted the hood of her cloak, determined not to attract attention. As they hurried past, she noticed that the various quarters seemed to be under the control of two distinct groups. She suspected they were those of Clodius and Milo, a renegade politician and a former tribune. Fortunately relations between the sides seemed poor, with colourful insults filling the air across the streets that demarcated the borders of their territory. A few fast-moving passers-by were of little immediate interest to either faction.

Clearly the situation had deteriorated badly since her departure just four months before, when Brutus had been worried enough to take her away from Rome. It had begun with a political vacuum that formed after the scandals that had seen elections postponed and numerous politicians indicted for corruption. Clodius Pulcher, the disreputable noble turned plebeian, had been quick to take advantage. Gathering his street gangs together, he started to take control of the city. Unimpressed, his old rival Milo had responded in kind, recruiting gladiators to give himself the military advantage. Skirmishes were soon taking place, intimidating the nobles and terrifying the city's ordinary residents. Fearful rumours had even reached as far as Pompeii. They centred on one word.

Anarchy.

Fabiola had paid little attention to the gossip. Safe on the *latifundium*, it had seemed unreal. Here in Rome, it was impossible to deny the truth. Brutus had been completely correct. With Crassus dead and Caesar far away in Gaul, there were few prominent figures to take a stand against the growing social unrest. Cato, the politician and outstanding orator, might have been one, but he had no troops to back him up. Cicero, another powerful senator, had long been rendered powerless by intimidation. When he had spoken out against the gangs' brutality, Clodius had been quick to put Cicero in his place, erecting notices across the Palatine that listed his crimes against the Republic. The citizens loved such public shaming, and Clodius' status grew even higher. Politicians would not be able to bring this situation under control. Rome needed an iron fist – someone not scared of using martial force.

It needed Caesar or Pompey.

But Caesar was stuck in Gaul. Meanwhile, Pompey was cleverly biding his time, letting the situation spiral out of control until asked to help by the Senate. The Republic's most famous general craved constant popularity and saving the city from the bloodthirsty gangs would give him unprecedented kudos. So the rumours on the street went.

To remain safe, Fabiola realised that she would need more protection than the hulks lumbering in her wake. Two men instantly came to mind. Benignus and Vettius, the Lupanar's doormen, would be an ideal nucleus for her force. They were tough, skilled street fighters and, thanks to her previous hard work, fiercely loyal to her already. Jovina, the brothel's owner, had refused to sell the pair before, but she would find a way to win the old crone over. Perhaps something would be revealed at the temple.

Disappointingly, the soothsayers clustered outside the shrine seemed to be the usual group of liars and charlatans. Fabiola could pick them out from a hundred paces away. Dressed in ragged robes, often deliberately unkempt and with blunt-peaked leather hats jammed on their greasy heads, the men relied on just a few clever ruses. Long silences, meaningful stares into the entrails of the animals they sacrificed and shrewd judgement of their clients' wishes worked like a dream. Over the years she had watched countless people being taken in, promised everything they asked for and relieved of their meagre savings in moments. Desperate for a sign of divine approval, few seemed to realise what had happened. In the current economic climate, jobs were rare, food expensive and opportunities to better oneself few and far between. While Caesar grew immensely wealthy from the proceeds of his campaigns and Pompey could never spend all that he had plundered, the existence of the average citizen was sufficiently miserable to ensure ripe pickings for the soothsayers.

Fabiola did not trust such men. She had learned to rely only on herself, and on Jupiter, the father of Rome. To find out that there was a genuine haruspex, someone who could predict the future, had been news indeed. Hoping against hope that she might find the armed stranger whom Corbulo had mentioned, Fabiola moved through the group, asking questions, smiling and dropping coins into palms.

Her search was fruitless. None of those she asked had any knowledge of the man she sought. Keen for business from an obviously wealthy lady, most denied ever having seen him. Tiring of their offered divinations, Fabiola moved to the temple steps, where she sat miserably for some time, watching the ebb and flow of the crowd. Her guards stood nearby, chewing on meat and bread Docilosa had bought. To keep them happy, she had purchased each a small cup of watered-down wine as well. Docilosa made a good mistress, thought Fabiola. She shouted when necessary and rewarded regularly.

'Not going inside to make an offering, lady?'

Startled at being addressed, Fabiola looked down to see a one-armed man regarding her from the bottom step. It was a place well situated to ask devotees for a coin as they passed inside the temple. Middle-aged, stocky and with close-cropped hair, he wore a ragged military tunic. A solitary bronze *phalera* on his chest was a proud reminder of the cripple's service in the legions. From a strap over his right shoulder hung a knife in a worn leather sheath. Everyone in Rome needed to be able to defend themselves. His gaze was direct and admiring, but not threatening. 'Perhaps,' Fabiola replied. 'I was hoping to find a real soothsayer first. There are none in Pompeii.'

The veteran barked with laughter. 'You'll not find any round here either!'

Noticing the interaction, one of Fabiola's men moved forward, reaching for his sword. Tersely, she waved him off. There was no danger in passing the time of day. 'Obviously,' she sighed. It had been a vain hope to think that someone whom Gemellus had briefly encountered several years before would still be here. 'Probably no such thing.'

'Best to rely on no one, lady,' advised the cripple with a wink. 'Even the gods are fickle. They've certainly deserted the Republic in recent days.'

'You speak the truth, friend,' moaned a fat man in a grubby tunic, sweating as he climbed the steps. 'We honest citizens are being robbed on a daily basis. Something has to be done!'

Hearing his words, other passers-by muttered in angry agreement. Well-dressed or in rags, they all seemed of the same mind. Fabiola took note. The situation in Rome *was* as serious as it seemed. These people looked genuinely worried. Troubled, she turned back to the veteran.

'As for me, I didn't miss one of Mars' feast days for ten years. Still lost this!' He waggled his stump at her.

Fabiola clicked her tongue. 'How did it happen?'

'Fighting Mithridates in Armenia,' came the proud reply. Abruptly his face turned sad. 'And now I beg for enough to eat each day.'

Immediately she reached for her purse.

'Save your money, lady,' the man muttered. 'It must be hard enough earned.'

Fabiola frowned. The comment had been made as if he knew her history. 'Explain yourself,' she snapped.

His face went puce with embarrassment and there was silence for a moment as Fabiola glared at him.

'Not many customers tip, do they?' he ventured eventually.

Fabiola went cold. It was inevitable that she would be recognised by some in Rome, but she had not expected it this soon. And low-ranking veterans were uncommon clients in the brothel. They could not usually afford the high prices. So how did he know her? 'What do you mean?' she demanded harshly.

The cripple looked down. 'I used to sit opposite the Lupanar, before the area got too dangerous. Watched you come out many times with that huge doorman. Benignus, is that his name?'

'I see.' She could not deny it.

'It was impossible to miss your beauty, lady.'

'I'm a free woman now,' Fabiola said in a low voice. 'A citizen.'

'The gods favour you then,' he said approvingly. 'Few escape Jovina's claws.'

'You know her?'

He grinned. 'Of course. She got to recognise me, too. Yet the old bitch never dropped a single *as* into my lap.'

It was Fabiola's turn to colour. 'Neither did I.'

'That's all right, lady. People don't notice me nowadays.' The corners of his mouth turned down. 'Lost my sword arm for nothing.'

Sympathy filled her at his plight. The legions stood for everything that she despised, protecting a state which was founded on slavery and warfare. Although this man had served many years in their ranks, he had also paid a heavy price. Fabiola found it impossible to hate him. She felt the opposite. With luck, Romulus might have had similar comrades. 'It wasn't for nothing,' she said firmly. 'Take this.'

Gold glittered in her outstretched hand and his eyes opened wide with shock. The offered *aureus* was worth more than a legionary earned in a month. 'Lady, I . . .' he muttered.

Fabiola placed the coin in the veteran's palm and closed his fingers over it. There was no resistance. She found it sad how extreme poverty could even grind down the pride of a brave soldier.

'Thank you,' he whispered, no longer able to meet her gaze.

Satisfied, Fabiola had turned to go when intuition made her pause. 'What's your name?' she asked softly.

'Secundus, lady,' he replied. 'Gaius Secundus.'

'You probably know my name,' she said, probing.

Secundus grinned in response. 'Fabiola.'

She inclined her head graciously, and another man came into her thrall. 'May we meet again.'

Secundus watched reverently as Fabiola climbed the steps towards the *cellae*. She was the most beautiful woman he had ever seen. And she had given him enough money to live well for weeks. The gods were smiling today.

'Perhaps Jupiter will answer my prayers,' she offered over one shoulder.

'I hope so, lady,' Secundus called out. 'Or Mithras,' he added in a whisper.

The poorly lit *cella* was jammed with people wishing to ask a favour of the preeminent deity in Rome. After each new arrival had made an offering, shaven-headed acolytes directed them where to kneel. Priests filled the air with low chanting. Small oil lamps dangled from brackets, their guttering flames creating a forbidding atmosphere. High on the back wall hung an image of Jupiter, a great circular piece of sculpted, painted stone with a diameter twice the length of a man. The god had a beaked nose and full, sardonic lips. His unsmiling face stared impassively at the worshippers, heavy-lidded eyes half closed. Below the carving ran a long, flat altar, covered with gifts. Hens and lambs lay side by side, blood still dripping from the fresh cuts in their necks. Tiny, crudely made statues of Jupiter huddled together in twos and threes. There were copper coins, silver *denarii*, signet rings, necklaces and loaves of bread. Little replica clay vessels contrasted with the occasional piece of ornate glass. Rich or poor, plebeian or patrician, all gave something. All had a request of the god.

Fabiola moved quietly to the altar. Finding a place to stack a small pile of *aurei*, she knelt down nearby. But it was hard to concentrate on her prayers. Distracted by the loud muttering from the eager citizens around her, she closed her eyes and tried to imagine her lover. Gradually the noise diminished as her concentration improved. Brutus was of average build, but his clean-shaven, tanned face was pleasant and his smile natural. Fabiola had not seen him for months and was constantly surprised by how much she missed him. Especially recently. Holding his picture bright in her mind, she begged Jupiter for a sign. Anything that could help Brutus, and Caesar, to overcome the Gaulish rebellion. And protect them both from Scaevola's menaces.

Her hopes were in vain. Fabiola saw and heard nothing but the other people in the tightly packed room.

Despite her best efforts, thoughts of Romulus began to replace those of Brutus. Perhaps it was because she had met Secundus? Fabiola found the images impossible to ignore. It had been nearly four years since she had seen her brother. Romulus would have grown into a man. He would be strong, as Secundus must have been, before he lost his arm. It was pleasing to think of her twin standing straight and tall in his chain mail, wearing a horsehair-crested helmet. Then her imagination faltered. How could Romulus be alive? Crassus' defeat had been total, shaking the Republic to its core. Fabiola scowled, unwilling still to give up hope. In turn, that meant conceding that Romulus was a prisoner of the Parthians, sent to the ends of the earth. To Margiana, a place without hope. In mental agony, Fabiola remembered her own personal journey to Hades. She had not fought physical battles or risked her life in the legions. Instead she had been forced into prostitution.

And she had endured. Somehow Romulus would too. Fabiola was sure of it.

She got to her feet and made her way to the door. Docilosa and her guards were waiting outside, but disappointingly there was no sign of Secundus. His place on the bottom step had been taken by a leper covered in filthy, weeping bandages. Although Fabiola hadn't realised it at the time, the veteran had given her hope. There had been no sign of the mysterious soothsayer, and she had not been given proof of her twin's survival, or of Caesar's future. But her journey to Rome had not been without reward. Now it was time to return to Brutus' residence in the city, a large, comfortable *domus* on the Palatine Hill. There she could gather her thoughts and find ways of helping Brutus, and dealing with Scaevola. Perhaps there would even be time to begin the search for Romulus? Caught up in its own troubles, the Republic would not be sending an army to retaliate against Parthia in the foreseeable future. Yet merchants journeyed to the east regularly, attracted by the valuable goods they could resell in Rome. For the right price, one might be persuaded to ask questions on his travels.

The idea was enough to make Fabiola forget her worries for a short time.

Several days went by, and Fabiola was able to learn more about the dire situation in the capital. Enough shops were situated near Brutus' house for her to venture out relatively safely and gather information. There was no sign of Scaevola, and Fabiola began to think he was still in the south, near Pompeii. She relaxed into the role of a country lady, ignorant of recent goings-on. After she had spent a decent sum buying food and other necessities, the grateful shopkeepers were happy to relate all the latest rumours. As Fabiola had suspected, the streets had been taken over by gangs loyal to Clodius and Milo.

Once the closest of allies, Pompey and the brutal Milo had parted company on bad terms some years before. Now Milo was allied to Cato, one of the few politicians to oppose the shrunken triumvirate's stranglehold on power. Crassus might be dead, but Caesar and Pompey still controlled the Republic, which was not to the liking of many. Desperate to prevent Pompey becoming consul as the new year began, Cato had put forward Milo as a candidate instead. This was too much for Clodius, and minor disturbances now occurred on a daily basis. Occasional larger pitched battles had claimed the lives of dozens of thugs. Caught in the middle, a number of unlucky residents had also died. The Senate was paralysed, unsure what to do. Most people, one trader told Fabiola, just wanted order restored. And the person to do it was Pompey.

With his legions.

'Soldiers on the streets of Rome?' Fabiola cried. The very idea was anathema. To prevent any attempts at overthrowing the Republic, its laws banned all military personnel from entering the capital. 'Sulla was the last man to do that.'

'I remember it well,' said a skinny old man who was buying lamp oil. He shivered. 'Blood ran in the streets for days. No one was safe.'

The shopkeeper shook his head heavily. 'I know. But have we any choice?' He gestured at his empty shelves. 'If there is nothing to buy, people will starve. What then?'

Fabiola could not argue with his words. If only Brutus and Caesar were able to intervene, she thought. But there was no chance of that. News had come that meant neither man would be back for many months. Braving snow that was higher than a man, Caesar had ridden through the mountains and successfully rejoined his legions in Gaul. Battle had already been joined against the tribes; Caesar had suffered initial setbacks before a stunning victory had forced Vercingetorix and his army to retreat to the north. Yet the intelligent Gaulish chieftain was unbeaten. Thousands of warriors were still flocking to his banner, so Caesar had no option but to stay put. The situation in Gaul was critical, and Fabiola's worries about Brutus grew by the day.

Loud shouts from the street drew her attention back to the present. Fabiola made to leave the shop, but her bodyguards blocked the doorway. Although Docilosa was in bed with an upset stomach, they had been brow-beaten enough times. 'Let me check it out, Mistress,' said Tullius, the most senior. A short Sicilian with crooked teeth and a bad limp, he was deadly with a *gladius*.

She frowned but obeyed. Danger lurked everywhere now.

'Clodius Pulcher is dead!' Sandals slapped loudly off the ground as the running person drew nearer. 'Murdered on the Via Appia!'

Placing his thumb between the forefinger and index finger of his right hand, the shopkeeper made the sign against evil. The old man muttered a prayer.

Cries of dismay rose from the passers-by who had dared to be out. Windows clattered open as the residents of the flats above street level heard the news. Their voices added to the swelling noise.

'I want to see what's going on,' demanded Fabiola.

Drawing his dagger, Tullius peered outside. One look was enough. With a grunt of satisfaction he darted forward, deliberately knocking over the messenger. Quickly the Sicilian dragged him into the shop, one arm wrapped around his throat, the other holding his knife tightly under the youth's ribcage.

Fabiola took in the youngster at a glance. Short, underfed, dressed in rags, he was typical of Rome's poorest dwellers. No doubt he had been hoping to get a reward from someone for bringing back such dramatic news.

The captive's gaze darted wildly from side to side as he took in the shocked shopkeeper, the old man, Fabiola and her other guards. 'Who're you?' he gasped. 'Not seen you round here before.'

'Shut it, arsehole.' Tullius poked him with his dagger. 'Tell the lady what you were screaming about just now.'

The youth was happy to obey. 'Clodius and a group of his men were attacked by Milo's gladiators. Near an inn just south of the city,' he said excitedly. 'Must have been outnumbered two to one.'

'When?'

'No more than an hour ago.'

'Did you witness this?' Fabiola demanded.

He nodded. 'It was an ambush, lady. The gladiators threw javelins first and then swarmed in from all sides.'

'Gladiators?' Fabiola interrupted, her mind, as ever, darting to Romulus.

'Yes, lady. Memor's men.'

She managed not to react. 'Memor?' she asked casually.

He seemed surprised. 'You know, the *lanista* of the Ludus Magnus.'

Fabiola shrugged as if it was unimportant but inside she was reeling. For a short period before Brutus had freed her from the Lupanar, Memor had been one of her clients. She had hated every moment of his visits, but the cruel, dispassionate *lanista* had been a possible source of information about Romulus. By repeatedly driving him wild with lust, she had managed to discover that her brother had indeed been sold into Memor's school. And then escaped with a champion fighter. A Gaul. But that was history. She had to keep focused. More important events were unfolding, and Memor seemed to be taking a prominent hand in the ongoing unrest. Why? Anger surged within Fabiola. 'Was he there?'

'I didn't see him, lady.'

'Or Milo?'

'He was there at the start, encouraging his men,' said the youth. 'Then he left.'

'Milo's a clever bastard,' pronounced the shopkeeper. 'He'll have gone somewhere very public, with lots of witnesses to prove it.'

The same goes for Memor, thought Fabiola. 'What happened next?'

'Clodius got hit in the shoulder by a *pilum* and fell down. Some of his men carried him inside the tavern for shelter. The rest tried to hold off the attackers, but there were too many. The door was kicked in and Clodius got dragged outside, screaming and crying for mercy.'

Fabiola shuddered at the dramatic and gory image. 'And you're certain he's dead?'

'He didn't have a chance, lady. They were like a pack of wild dogs.' The youngster swallowed. 'There was blood everywhere. Clodius' men are carrying his body back to the city,' continued the prisoner. 'His wife doesn't even know yet.'

'When she finds out, the gates of Hades will open,' said the shopkeeper grimly. 'Fulvia won't take this lying down.'

Fabiola's interest was piqued. 'You know her?'

'Not exactly. But she's a typical noblewoman,' he replied. 'Likes to get her opinion across, if you know what I mean.'

Fabiola raised an eyebrow.

The old man tittered.

Realising what he had said, the proprietor flushed. 'Not meaning to insult noble ladies, of course.'

Fabiola graced him with a smile to show that she had taken no offence. 'Release the boy,' she ordered Tullius.

Reluctantly the Sicilian obeyed.

Unsure what would happen to him, the youth shuffled his feet.

Fabiola tossed him a *denarius* and his eyes lit up at the unexpected reward.

'Thank you, lady!' He bobbed his head and ran off, eager to spread the news.

'We'd best return to the *domus*, Mistress,' said Tullius, looking concerned. 'This means trouble.'

Fabiola did not protest. The open-fronted shop was no place to linger at a time like this. Saying goodbye to the shopkeeper, they hurried on to the street. It was only a hundred paces to Brutus' house and the protection of its thick walls and iron-studded gates. In the event, that short distance was too far.

Round the nearest corner swarmed a horde of thugs armed with clubs, swords and spears. Being herded in their midst were many frightened-looking men, women and children: ordinary citizens. Talking in loud, angry voices, the group's leaders did not immediately see Fabiola and her guards.

'Quick!' hissed Tullius, gesturing frantically. 'Back into the shop!'

Fabiola turned, but slipped on a sliver of wet wood lying in the mud. The resulting splash was enough to catch the attention of the fast-moving rabble. Within a heartbeat, it had reached them. Before the Sicilian had time to do more than help Fabiola up, they were surrounded. Fortunately, the heavies seemed relatively good-natured. Shouts of laughter rang out at her misfortune and rough, unshaven faces pressed in close, leering.

'Come with us!' cried a bearded man who appeared to be one of the mob's leaders. His tone offered no option of refusal.

Tullius looked helplessly at his mistress. If he or his men touched their weapons, they would be killed out of hand.

Fabiola knew it too. Her heart pounding, she smoothed down her dress. 'Where?'

The answer was instant. 'To the Forum!'

She peered at the people who were being forced to accompany the gang members: their faces were twisted with fear. Law and order was completely breaking down, and there was no one to stand up for normal people like them. 'Why?' Fabiola asked stoutly.

'To witness what those bastards did to Clodius!' shouted the bearded thug. 'His body will be displayed for all to see.'

A furious roar met his words and Fabiola's heart sank. News of the murder had already reached the city. The young man had not been the first to return.

'Respect must be paid to the dead.' The gang leader raised his sword in the air. 'Before we rid this city of that bastard Milo. And everyone who follows him!'

This time the mob's response was an inarticulate roar. Primeval. Terrifying.

Fabiola could almost feel the Republic's foundations shake beneath the rabble's anger. Her own heart was thumping with fear, but it was pointless trying to resist.

The crowd moved off at speed, taking Fabiola and her men with it.

Chapter V: Discovery

Margiana, winter 53/52 BC

An entire cohort was sent out to the Mithraeum at dawn, but found only corpses. The surviving Scythians had disappeared on horseback, and their original purpose was presumed to be an attempt to assassinate Pacorus. Long-range patrols were mounted throughout the area, but found no evidence of enemy forces. Gradually the tension in the fort eased, although Vahram, now acting commander, insisted that the sentries were doubled day and night.

Nothing more was seen of the Scythians.

Weeks passed without any news of Tarquinius. There was no word of Pacorus either; complete secrecy reigned over the commander's house and only Parthians were allowed within. The senior centurions were deeply angry at what had happened and spoke only to those they trusted: in other words, to none of the Roman prisoners. Of course, Romulus and Brennus had told their roommates about the attack; the news spread like wildfire. Rumours filled the camp on a daily basis. Only one thing was clear. Because there had been no reprisals, Pacorus was still alive. Tarquinius' care was having at least some effect, but nobody knew more.

To ensure that they did not flee, Romulus and Brennus were closely watched at all times. No other overt threat was made, but their situation remained desperate. Vahram's threat was no idle one, and most Parthians made sure to remind the pair of it at every opportunity. They were constantly taunted with the manner of Felix' death as well. This sting to their pride was particularly hard to ignore: after all, their friend's murder had not been avenged, and it might never be. With a clenched jaw, Brennus dealt with the menaces silently. Romulus kept them at bay by praying daily to Mithras. He thought of home too, and of what exactly Tarquinius might have seen. Knowing it involved returning to Rome helped immensely.

All kinds of fantasies went through his head, from discovering his mother and Fabiola to torturing Gemellus. Taking on Vahram in a duel and killing him slowly was another favourite. Romulus also had time to relive the brawl that had caused him to flee the capital. During it, he had apparently killed a nobleman with a crack to the head from his sword hilt. At the time, panicked and desperate to avoid crucifixion, Romulus had not given it much consideration. Now, the veteran of innumerable battles, he knew that unless he was no judge of his own strength, the blow had probably not been enough to kill. When he asked Brennus, the big Gaul confirmed that he had only punched the angry noble a couple of times. It was a troubling realisation, because it meant that he, Romulus, was innocent. Which meant that he had had no reason to flee in the first place. So who had killed Rufus Caelius? It was impossible to know the truth of it, yet Romulus became consumed by thoughts of what might have been if the nobleman had not been slain. Although he talked it over repeatedly with Brennus, the Gaul was less concerned about what had happened. His destiny all along had been to take a great journey, and Brennus was convinced that was why he was in Margiana. Romulus did not have that comfort.

All he had was Tarquinius' advice to trust in Mithras, about whom he knew very little.

Unsurprisingly, none of the Parthians would talk to him about their god. Watched constantly, he had no chance of trying to visit the Mithraeum either. Then Romulus managed to procure a small statue from a wizened old man who came into the fort on a regular basis to sell knickknacks. All the ancient told him was that Mithras wore a Phrygian cap, and that the life of the bull he was sacrificing gave birth to humankind, the animals and birds of the earth, and its crops and foods. Romulus pressed him hard for more information, and discovered that there were seven stages of devotion. After this, the seller totally clammed up. 'You look brave and honest,' were his last words. 'If you are, Mithras will reveal more.'

At this, the window of hope in Romulus' heart opened a fraction.

He placed the carved figure on the special shrine which had been erected by the barracks entrance. Although it was dedicated to Aesculapius, the god of medicine, Romans were happy to worship more than one deity at the same time. Romulus spent every spare moment he had on his knees before the image of Mithras, praying for some good news about Tarquinius, and that he might discover how to return to Rome. Nothing was forthcoming, but he did not lose faith. Since childhood, life had dealt him one hard knock after another. Witnessing Gemellus rape his mother nightly. Being sold into the savagery of the *ludus*. The duel against Lentulus, a far more experienced fighter. A deadly mass combat in the arena. Escaping Rome after the brawl. Army life and the horrors of Carrhae. Captivity in Parthia and then the long march to Margiana. But each time death threatened, the gods had lifted him from harm's way. Consequently, Romulus was prepared to devote all his attention to Mithras. What else could he do?

During his time at the shrine, Romulus was touched by the devotion shown by his comrades. In normal circumstances, the Romans would have been pleased if Pacorus died, but now prayers for his recovery were offered up by the dozen. Almost all the men in the century stopped by the altar each day. Word of the threat to Tarquinius' life spread fast and there were visits from countless other soldiers as well. Soon the simple stone top was dotted with *sestertii*, *denarii* and even lucky amulets: offerings that men would not part with lightly. Everything that had been minted or made in Italy was now priceless. It proved to Romulus and Brennus how important Tarquinius was to the Forgotten Legion's sense of wellbeing.

One cold afternoon, Romulus was performing his devotions as usual. Deep in prayer and with his eyes closed, he became aware of loud muttering behind him. Presuming it was other soldiers asking for divine help, he ignored the noise. But when they started sniggering, he looked around. Five legionaries were standing just outside the door, peering in at him. Romulus recognised them; they were from a *contubernium* in his century. All had served in the legions for many years. Tellingly, he had seen none make any offerings at the altar.

'Praying for the soothsayer?' asked Caius, a tall, thin man with few teeth and bad breath. 'Our *centurion*.'

Romulus did not like Caius' tone. 'Yes,' he snapped. 'Why aren't you?'

'Been gone a while, hasn't he?' sneered Optatus, leaning against the doorpost. A strongly built figure almost as large as Brennus, he had a permanently unfriendly manner.

Romulus felt a tickle of unease. All five had been out on the training ground. They were in chain mail and were fully armed, whereas he was clad in just his tunic, with only a dagger for protection. 'I suppose so,' he said slowly, gazing from one to the other.

'Treacherous bastard,' said Novius, the smallest of the five. Despite his stature, he was an expert swordsman. Romulus had seen him in action before. 'Be conniving with Pacorus, won't he?'

'Coming up with more ways to have us slaughtered,' added Caius. 'Like he did at Carrhae.'

Romulus could scarcely believe his ears, but the others' heads were nodding angrily. 'What did you say?' he spat.

'You heard.' Caius' lips lifted, revealing red, inflamed gums. 'Crassus didn't lose the battle. He was a good general.'

'So how did it happen?' Romulus retorted hotly.

'That treacherous Nabataean didn't help, but it was more likely your Etruscan friend, meddling with evil spirits.' Novius rubbed at the phallus amulet hanging from his neck. 'He's always bringing bad luck on us.'

His companions muttered in agreement.

Absolutely astonished that men could think like this, Romulus realised it was best not to respond. The discontented legionaries were looking for a scapegoat. With his long blond hair, single gold earring and odd manner, Tarquinius was an obvious target. Arguing would make things worse. Turning his back on them, he leaned forward, bowing to the small stone figure of Aesculapius on the altar.

There was a sharp intake of breath from Optatus. 'Where did you get that?'

Romulus looked down and his heart banged in his chest. The sleeve of his tunic had ridden up his right arm, revealing the thick scar where his slave brand had been. After slicing the damning mark off, Brennus had cobbled the wound together with crude stitches. There had been a few questions about it when they had joined the army, but Romulus had managed to laugh them off, saying he had received the cut in a skirmish with outlaws. None in the Gaulish mercenary cohort had cared where he came from anyway. Already upset by the accusations against Tarquinius, he was disconcerted by the question. 'I can't remember,' he faltered.

'What?' Optatus laughed incredulously. 'Happened in your sleep, did it?'

Although his comrades sniggered, their expressions changed. Now they looked like a pack of hounds that have cornered a wild boar. Romulus cursed to himself. Who would ever forget how or when he was injured in a fight?

Novius stuck his left leg forward and jabbed a finger at the shiny marks on either side of his muscular calf. Their length and breadth meant that they had probably been made by a spear. 'I've no idea who did this,' he crowed. 'Didn't even feel the blade go in.'

Loud laughter met his remark. All had scars from their time in the army.

'It was a long time ago,' said Romulus defensively, knowing his answer sounded weak.

Caius' response was immediate. 'You're only a damn boy. You've not campaigned in a dozen wars or been in the legions half your life.'

'Like us,' snarled Optatus. 'And we remember every sword cut like it was yesterday.'

Romulus flushed, unable to mention his two years as a *secutor*. The agony of Lentulus' knife plunging into his right thigh was as vivid now as the moment it happened. But he could not mention it. Gladiators were nearly all slaves, criminals or prisoners of war; they were the lowest of the low.

'They say that for the right price, there are men who'll cut off a brand and stitch you up,' said Caius spitefully. 'Get rid of the evidence.'

Novius frowned.

Optatus swelled with outrage. 'Been to one of those, have you?'

'Of course not,' blustered Romulus. 'Slaves aren't allowed in the army.'

'On pain of death,' added Novius with a leer.

Caius stepped over the threshold. 'Where is it you're from again?'

'Transalpine Gaul.' Romulus didn't like the way this was going. He got to his feet, wondering where Brennus was. 'What's it to you?'

'Served there for three years,' said Novius, his eyes mere slits. 'Didn't we, lads?'

Optatus grinned at the memory.

Romulus felt nauseous. It was Brennus who came from that part of Gaul; he himself was a city dweller through and through. The lie had just been a way to get them into the army. At the time, Bassius, their old centurion, was happy enough to get two men who could obviously fight. He had not asked too many questions. To Bassius, bravery was all that had mattered. Then, as mercenaries in Crassus' army, they had not mixed with Roman legionaries until after their capture. And on the long march east, few had asked questions of other prisoners. Survival had been more important. Until now. 'So did half the army,' Romulus said truculently. 'Did you catch the pox there too?'

Novius did not respond to the jibe. 'Where exactly did you live?' The malevolent little legionary had everyone's attention.

'In a village, high up in the mountains,' replied Romulus vaguely. 'It was quite remote.'

But there was no end to his interrogation. Now Novius and Optatus moved inside, while the last two blocked the doorway. There was nowhere to go, other than further into the barracks, where it was even more confined. The young soldier swallowed, resisting the urge to draw his dagger. In this tight space, he had little chance against three men with swords. His only hope was to brazen it out.

'What was the nearest town?'

Frantically Romulus racked his brains, trying to recall if Brennus had ever mentioned such a place. Nowhere came to mind. A prayer to Mithras, followed by another to Jupiter, made no difference. His mouth opened and closed.

Novius' sword slid from the scabbard as he stepped closer. 'Can't remember that either?' he said softly.

'We come from near Lugdunum,' growled Brennus from the entrance to the corridor.

Romulus had never been so relieved.

'Allobroge territory, eh?' sneered Novius.

'Yes.' Brennus stepped into the room, forcing Caius to move backwards. 'It was.'

Optatus grinned. 'I remember that campaign well. Your villages burned easily.'

'Some of the women we raped were passably good-looking,' added Novius, forcing two fingers in and out of a ring made of his right forefinger and thumb.

The others laughed cruelly and Romulus burned with anger and shame for his friend.

The Gaul's face went purple with rage but he did not react.

Novius was not to be put off. 'Why is your accent different to his then?'
He jerked a dismissive thumb at Brennus.

Brennus did not give Romulus time to answer. 'Because his father was
a Roman soldier, like you shitbags,' he snapped. 'Explains his name too.
Happy?'

Ammias, Primitivus and Optatus glowered but did not reply. They were
bullies rather than ringleaders.

'And the mark?' persisted Novius.

'It's from a *gladius*,' answered the Gaul with a show of reluctance. 'The
lad could barely lift a sword, but he tried to fight back when you fuckers
were attacking our settlement. Naturally he didn't want to tell you.'

It was Novius' turn to look confused. Quickly he did the maths, calculating if Romulus' age as a boy tallied with the Allobroges' rebellion nine
years before.

It did.

'We fled south. Worked here and there,' Brennus went on. 'Ended up
in Crassus' army. With all our tribe gone, it didn't matter where in Hades
we went.'

It was commonplace for the warriors of defeated tribes to seek employ
in the service of Rome. Iberians, Gauls, Greeks and Libyans were among
the host of nationalities in its armies. Even Carthaginians joined up these
days.

The little legionary was visibly disappointed.

Romulus used the silence to shuffle closer to Brennus. Side by side, they
were an imposing pair: the huge Gaul with bulging muscles and his young
protégé, slightly smaller but just as solidly built. Although Romulus had
no more than a dagger, they would account for themselves very well if it
came to a fight. The pair glared at the five veterans.

Novius lowered his sword. 'Only citizens are supposed to serve in the
legions,' he said resentfully. 'Not tribal vermin like you two.'

'That's right,' agreed Caius.

The fact that they had served in a mercenary cohort under Crassus
was not mentioned. That Romulus was apparently half-Italian. Or the
fact that the Forgotten Legion was not a Roman army unit, but a Parthian
one.

'That's a different matter,' Brennus replied smoothly. 'Here we're all brothers-in-arms. It's us against the Parthians, miserable scumbags that they are.'

His words seemed to have the right effect on the veterans; they turned to go, Novius taking up the rear.

Grinning at the Gaul, Romulus began to relax. It was the wrong thing to do.

The little legionary turned at the door. Brennus gave him an evil look, but Novius stood his ground. 'Odd,' he said in a strange voice. 'Very odd.'

With a sinking feeling, Romulus saw that Novius was staring at Brennus' left calf, which had a prominent purple oval of scar tissue.

'What is it?' called Caius from outside the barracks.

'Instead of branding them on the shoulder, Governor Pomptinus made us mark the captives' calves on that campaign.'

'I remember,' came the response. 'So what?'

Although he had never asked, Romulus had always wondered why Brennus' mark was different to other slaves.

'It was to show they were his property,' crowed Novius.

'Tell me something I don't know.' Caius sounded bored.

'This brute has a scar just where his brand should be,' announced Novius delightedly, lifting his sword again. 'He's a damn slave too!'

Before he could do more, Brennus lunged forward and shoved the little legionary in the chest. Novius flew out of the door, landing flat on his back. His four friends scattered, their faces alarmed.

'Piss off, you son of a whore,' the Gaul said from between clenched teeth. 'Or I'll kill you.'

'Scum!' Novius wheezed, his face twisted with rage. 'You're both escaped slaves.'

Romulus and Brennus did not reply.

'Felix probably was too,' the little legionary added as the others reached for their swords.

'There's only one punishment for that,' snarled Caius.

'Crucifixion,' finished Optatus.

Primitivus and Ammias, their companions, raised their *gladii* in unison at that prospect. Five faces filled with hatred ringed the doorway.

Romulus' stomach constricted into a knot. He had seen the brutal method of execution carried out many times. It was a slow, agonising death.

'Just try it,' Brennus bellowed. His temper was fully up, and he stood in the door like a raging bull. Only one man could attack him at a time. 'Who's first?'

None of the veterans moved. They were no fools.

Romulus pelted back to their room, scooping up his *scutum* and sword. There was no chance to don his chain mail, but armed like this, he felt more of a match for their new enemies. When he got to the entrance, Brennus had come back inside.

'Bastards,' he growled. 'They're gone. For now.'

'They'll tell everyone,' said Romulus, struggling not to panic. The Parthian officers didn't care about their history, but it would not be popular among the others in their century. Or, for that matter, the whole legion.

'I know.'

'What can we do?'

'Not much.' The Gaul sighed heavily. 'Stay alert. Watch each other's backs.'

This felt all too familiar. Neither spoke for a moment as they considered their options.

There were none. Escape was out of the question: it was deepest winter. Where would they go anyway? And Tarquinius, the one man who might be able to help, was still incarcerated with Pacorus. They were alone.

Glumly, Romulus studied the burnished iron of his *gladius*. He was going to be sleeping with it from now on.

It took Novius little more than an hour to tell every man in their century what had happened. He didn't stop there. The little legionary seemed possessed as he moved between the low-roofed barrack buildings, spreading his gossip. Caius, Optatus and the others were just as busy. Informing over nine thousand men took time, but gossip travelled fast and by nightfall, Romulus felt sure that their secret was well and truly public news.

The hardest thing to take was the reaction of his comrades in the barracks. Eighty of them ate and slept cheek by jowl, sharing their equipment, food and lice. Although the unit had been formed after Carrhae, there was a real sense of camaraderie. Felix had been part of it too. Far from Rome, they only had each other.

That no longer applied to Romulus and Brennus.

Or Tarquinius.

Men tarred them all with the same brush and the altar to Aesculapius and Mithras was dismantled the same day, its offerings taken back. Who would pray for a man with slaves as friends? Yet when the legionaries had nothing to pray for, they had nothing to hope for either – so they needed something to fill the void. Unfortunately, that turned out to be distrust of the two friends.

Suddenly Romulus and Brennus were responsible for all the men's misfortune.

Crucifixion was not that likely. To earn that punishment, Romulus or Brennus would have to fall foul of a Parthian officer. But there were countless other ways a man could be killed. Petty arguments were commonplace and with every man in the Forgotten Legion a trained soldier, they could be ended quite easily. Poisoning food, the norm in Rome, was not as popular as the use of weapons. Because men dropped their guard when in the latrines or bathhouse, being jumped in those locations was common. The narrow gaps between the rows of barracks were also dangerous places. More than once Romulus had come across bodies covered in stab wounds just a few steps from their quarters.

But the most immediate danger was where they slept. Eight men had to share a small, cramped space and when one quarter of those were being ostracised, it made life very difficult. On hearing the news, a pair of legionaries had instantly moved to another *contubernium* that was two short. Their disgusted faces upset Romulus hugely. That left Gordianus, a balding veteran, and three soldiers on one side of the room, the friends on the other. Gordianus, the obvious leader now, had not said much in response to Novius' revelation.

This kept his companions quiet, for which Romulus was grateful. He could take silent resentment. While it was doubtful that any of their own *contubernium* would try to kill them, they could not be trusted. Like a viper sliding through the grass, Novius was forever appearing unexpectedly, muttering in men's ears and poisoning their minds. The little legionary had taken to hanging around in the barracks corridor, idly picking his nails with his dagger. When he wasn't there, Caius or Optatus were. While none made any overt signs of violence, it was most disconcerting. If Romulus and Brennus responded by killing any of their enemies, they would be severely punished. And there were too many of them to risk a night attack. Cutting five men's throats quietly was an impossible task.

So Romulus and Brennus cooked together every day and stood outside the latrines with a ready sword while the other went inside. They went on sentry duty simultaneously, and only one slept at a time. It was exhausting and demoralising.

'This is worse than the *ludus*,' muttered Brennus on the second night. 'Remember?'

Romulus nodded bitterly.

'There we could at least bolt the door on my cell.'

'And Figulus and Gallus had few friends,' Romulus added.

'Not thousands!' The Gaul gave a short, sarcastic laugh.

And so it went on. Romulus' prayers to Mithras grew ever more frantic, but their situation did not change. The days stretched into a week, and the pair grew haggard and irritable. There was one occasion when Novius and his friends attempted to jump them in the alleyway outside the barracks, but Romulus' quick knife throw stopped the attack in its tracks. Caius' left thigh was now heavily bandaged, and the veterans' relentless hounding slackened somewhat. But the respite would merely be temporary. They would not be able to keep up their guard for ever.

Both were therefore relieved when, one frosty morning, Vahram ordered two centuries – theirs and another – out on patrol. For a few days, there had been no news from one of the legion's outposts that were positioned east of the main camp. The seven fortlets, each with a garrison of a half-century and a handful of Parthian warriors with horses, had been built in strategic positions overlooking various approach routes into Margiana from the north and east. High mountains protected the south and south-east. There was usually little news from the small forts, but twice a week riders were sent back regardless. Whatever their faults, Pacorus and Vahram kept themselves well informed of everything going on in the area. The need for this had been bloodily reinforced by the attack at the Mithraeum.

Romulus' and Brennus' feelings were not echoed by their comrades as they prepared for the patrol. Loud curses filled the warm, close air as yokes were dug out of the tiny storerooms behind the sleeping space for each *contubernium*. Their destination was only twenty miles away, but Roman soldiers always travelled prepared. Besides, Vahram had ordered rations for four days. The yokes, long, forked pieces of wood, carried everything from a cooking pot and spare equipment to sleeping blankets. Along with his armour and heavy *scutum*, they brought the weight carried by each man to over sixty pounds.

'This is bloody pointless,' Gordianus grumbled, lifting another legionary's mail shirt over his head so he could put it on. 'A fool's errand.'

'We'll meet the messenger halfway there,' said the man he was helping. 'And watch the prick piss himself with laughter as he watches us walk back.'

There were vociferous mutters of agreement. Who wanted to leave the safety and warmth of the fort for no reason? It was probably all down to a couple of lame horses.

'I don't know,' said a familiar voice. 'A lot of things can happen on patrol.'

Romulus looked up to find Novius standing in the doorway. Behind him were their other main tormentors, Caius and Optatus.

Automatically the young soldier's hand reached for his *gladius*; Brennus did likewise.

'Relax.' Novius' smile was evil. 'There'll be plenty of time for that later.'

Romulus had had enough. Lifting his sword, he stood up and moved towards the little legionary. 'I'll gut you now,' he swore.

Novius laughed and was gone, followed by his comrades.

'Gods above,' said Romulus wearily. 'I can't take this much longer.'

Brennus' red-rimmed eyes told him the same story.

At first, little was said by anyone the next morning. It was cold and miserable, and marching while carrying full kit was not easy. While the men were well able for the task, it was necessary to get into a good rhythm. Inevitably, Gordianus began to sing. Smiles broke out as the tune was recognised, a familiar ditty involving a sex-starved legionary and every whore in a large brothel. There were endless verses and a bawdy chorus to roar at the end of each. The soldiers were happy to join in: it passed the time, which often dragged on such patrols.

Normally Romulus enjoyed singing the refrain, with its countless sexual positions and innuendos. Today, though, he was gloomily imagining what might happen during the patrol. If they encountered any trouble, Novius could use the opportunity to strike. In the midst of a pitched battle, it was all too easy to stab a man in the back without anyone noticing.

Brennus' nudge darkened his mood even further. They had reached a crossroads five miles from the fort; the Gaul was pointing at a crucifix that stood on a small mound to one side. Pacorus had ordered it positioned so that all who passed would see it. Like those outside the front gates, the cross had just two purposes: to slowly kill condemned men, and to give graphic warning of the punishments at Parthia's disposal.

The crucifixes were rarely empty. Falling asleep on duty, disobeying an order or angering Pacorus: all were common reasons for legionaries to die on the simple wooden structures. Even Parthian warriors who incurred his wrath were sometimes executed in this manner.

Gordianus' voice died away, his song unfinished.

Romulus closed his eyes, trying not to imagine himself and Brennus ending their lives in such a way. With Pacorus' life hanging in the balance, it was still a distinct possibility – if Novius and his lot didn't do the job first.

Despite the early hour, there were carrion birds clustered all around the crucifix: on the ground, on the horizontal crossbar, even on the lifeless shoulders of their prey. Bare-headed vultures pecked irritably at each other while ravens darted in opportunistically to take what they could. Overhead, the huge wingspans of eagles could be seen, gliding serenely in anticipation of a good meal.

By now, everyone's gaze was on the frozen corpse that sagged forward, its head hanging. Thick ropes were tied around the dead man's arms and long iron nails pierced his feet. Everyone knew him: it was a young legionary from Ishkan's cohort who had been caught stealing bread from the ovens two days before. Dragged on to the *intervallum* before the whole legion, he had first been beaten with flails until his tunic was shredded and his back a red, bleeding ruin. Then, naked except for a loincloth, the wretch was forced to carry his cross from the fort to the lonely crossroads. Ten men from every cohort had accompanied him as witnesses. By the time they had reached the desolate spot, his torn, bare feet were blue with cold. This was not enough to dull the pain of the sharp nails being driven through them.

Romulus vividly remembered the man's thin, cracked screams.

Around him, the other legionaries' faces were full of dull resentment – except those of Novius and his friends, who were laughing behind cupped hands.

Darius, their stout senior centurion, sensed the bad feeling and urged his men to march faster. They needed little encouragement. As the soldiers came alongside, the nearest vultures lifted their bloated bodies into the air with lazy wing beats. Others further away just waddled out of reach. In the depths of winter, food was hard to come by, and the birds were reluctant to leave this ready feast. There would be no let-up until a skeleton hung from the cross.

Romulus could not tear his gaze away from the frozen body. The only part to remain inviolate was its groin, covered by the loincloth. Empty eye sockets stared into nothingness; peck marks covered its cheeks, chest and arms. Its mouth was open in a last, silent rictus of pain and terror. Half-torn-off strips of flesh hung uneaten from its thighs, where the largest muscles were. Even its feet had been chewed, probably by a resourceful jackal standing on its hind legs. Had the man been alive when the vultures first landed? Felt the sensation of breaking bone as powerful jaws closed on his frozen toes?

It was revolting, but compelling.

Romulus blinked.

Beneath the horror, there was more.

Over the previous weeks, there had been time to study the air currents and the cloud formations over the fort. Romulus had become meticulous, noting every bird and animal, observing the pattern of snowfall and the way ice formed on the river that flowed past the fort. Having watched Tarquinius, he knew that literally everything could be important, could provide some information. It frustrated him immensely that little seemed to make sense. But by following the haruspex' instructions, predicting the weather had at last became simple enough. Of course this was of interest but Romulus wanted to know far more than when the next storm would strike. Annoyingly, though, he had seen nothing about Tarquinius, Pacorus or Novius and the other veterans. Nothing useful.

Now perhaps, there was an opportunity.

Romulus focused again on the corpse.

A single, shocking image of Rome flashed before his eyes. Suddenly he felt a real link to Italy, as if the savagery of the crucifixion had been a form of sacrifice. Was this what happened when the haruspex killed hens or goats? Real awareness surged through Romulus for the first time.

He saw the familiar sights of the Forum Romanum: the Senate House, the *basilicae*, the distinctive temples and statues of the gods. Normal activities here included trading, money lending and the announcement of court judgements. Not today. Romulus frowned, scarcely believing what he was seeing. Horrifyingly, in the heart of the city, there was rioting. In front of the Senate itself, men were cutting and slashing each other to pieces. Among them, innocent civilians were being killed in their dozens. Bloody, mutilated bodies lay piled everywhere. Bizarrely, some of the combatants even looked like gladiators. Stunned, Romulus could not take it in. How could the capital of the greatest state in the world descend into such chaos? Was his mind playing tricks? Was he going mad? His need to go home had never been stronger, or seemed more unlikely.

A great arm clapped him on the back, bringing Romulus back to his senses.

'We can't help the poor fool now,' said Brennus, sadly regarding the frozen corpse. 'Forget about him.'

Romulus' mouth opened with surprise, then he realised. The Gaul had no idea what he had seen. He was about to tell Brennus when something made him look over his shoulder.

Novius was waiting for his chance and immediately half raised both arms, mimicking the crucified man.

Miserably, Romulus turned away, the little legionary's mocking laughter ringing in his ears. The world was going crazy.

Chapter VI: Chaos Descends

Rome, winter 53/52 BC

F abiola struggled not to lose her footing as the crowd pressed forward; only Tullius' firm grip on her arm kept her upright. The other body-guards had also been swallowed up by the rapidly moving mass of people. Occasionally Fabiola caught sight of their confused faces, but for the most part she concentrated on what the gang members were saying. It seemed the ambush at the inn had taken them all by surprise. Traitors in their midst were suspected and dire threats being made against any who might have been involved. The thugs would not rest until Clodius' death had been thoroughly avenged.

Fabiola could sense more than a desire for retribution in the angry words filling the air. The men brandishing weapons around her were all plebeians. Poor, uneducated, malnourished. They lived in overcrowded, rat-infested flats and were destined to live short, miserable lives with almost no chance of betterment. In many ways their lives were little different to those of slaves. Yet they were Roman citizens. Mob rule offered them something more. Power. Respect from those who normally looked down on them. Money from the people they robbed. They risked death, certainly, but it was worth it to gain these things that would otherwise never be theirs. It was therefore no surprise that both Clodius and Milo had enormous follow-ings. But Fabiola could see that the rabble's methods were short-sighted. If anarchy reigned, there would be no *congiaria*, the free distributions of grain and money that kept the poorest families alive. They would simply starve.

The crowd's pulsing anger did not appeal either. Fabiola only had to look at the blameless and terrified captives to know that such uncontrolled violence affected the innocent as well as the guilty. Whatever the monstrosities perpetuated by the Republic, it was still an institution which provided a framework for a more peaceful society than that which had gone before. Innocent people were not killed out of hand by the state for the contents of their purses. Yet that would become the norm once more if mobs like this assumed control.

It did not take long to reach the Forum Romanum. Bordered by numerous temples and shrines, it was home to the Senate building and the *basilicae*, massive covered markets that were normally jammed with tradesmen, lawyers, scribes and soothsayers. It was the busiest place in the city, a location dear to the heart of every citizen. Public meetings were commonly held here, as were trials and some elections. Events which happened in the Forum tended to be remembered, which was precisely why it had been chosen for Clodius' wake.

Today, the *basilicae* were quiet and virtually empty. The usual wall of sound comprised of merchants' voices, lawyers arguing and food vendors competing with each other was absent. In its place were the hollow shouts of the bravest shopkeepers, those who had actually dared to open up their stalls. For weeks there had been few honest folk about. Most traders, lawmakers and salesmen stayed safely at home. Even the wily haruspices were not to be seen. With constant violence the only business on offer, there had been little reason to risk their lives. The nobles and well-to-do were also absent, secure in their thick-walled houses.

They would not be safe there for long, thought Fabiola, eyeing the angry, chattering men around her.

Although the rich were not present, the open space of the Forum was crowded with plebeians drawn, despite the threat of conflict today. Word of Clodius' death had spread through the crowded suburbs faster than the plague. Terrified of the future offered by the rival gangs, Rome's citizens still wanted to watch it unfold. Seismic events like this were rare. Not since Sulla, 'the butcher', marched on the capital more than thirty years before had there been such a threat to democracy. For all its faults, the Republic generally ran quite smoothly. But now it felt like a rudderless ship caught in rough seas.

The best vantage points – the steps to the *basilicae* and all the shrines – were jammed. Children sat on their fathers' shoulders, craning their necks to see. Even the statues were covered in spectators. In contrast, the central area was clear. Bloodshed was inevitable and anyone caught in the middle would risk being killed.

Claiming the moral high ground, Milo stood in front of the Senate, dressed in an immaculate white toga. A handsome, clean-shaven figure, he was surrounded by scores of his men, many of whom were gladiators. The dramatic implication was impossible to miss. Here stood the defender of Rome, waiting to repel those who sought to tear it down. Attempting to give divine approval to his cause, a group of priests had been prominently deployed on the Senate steps. Chanting, burning incense and raising their hands to the heavens, the white-robed men would give credibility to any cause. The ploy was working and many in the crowd began to shout Milo's name. His gladiators responded by beating their weapons off their shields, creating an almighty din.

Brutus had taught Fabiola the different classes of fighter at the arena. Eager to know more about the life into which Romulus had been cast, she had memorised every detail. Now she picked out *murmillones* in their characteristic bronze fish-crested helmets, their right shoulders covered in mail. Beside Samnites with plumed helmets and elongated, oval shields was a group of *secutores*. Fabric and leather *manicae* protected their right shoulders while a single greave covered each man's left leg. Even the *retiarii*, fishermen armed only with a trident and net, were present. The massed ranks of trained killers made a fearsome sight.

Facing them from the other side of the Forum was a larger, more disorganised crowd of Clodius' followers. Although less well armed, Fabiola calculated that they significantly outnumbered Milo's force.

Seeing his cronies, the leader of the newly arrived mob roughly pushed into the throng of waiting citizens. His men were quick to copy him, using the flats and even the edges of their swords on any who got in the way. Screams rang out, blood flowed on to the cobbles and a path instantly appeared for the thugs to join their comrades. A great cheer rose into the air as they joined ranks. Now their number was at least three times that of their enemies.

A strange calm fell. Both sides had assembled for battle, but the reason had not yet arrived. Clodius' body.

During the journey, Fabiola's guards had managed to wriggle and squeeze their way to her side. It was a small consolation, but she felt acutely vulnerable without a weapon. Whispering in Tullius' ear, Fabiola took the dagger he passed to her and slid it up one sleeve of her dress. Only the gods knew what would happen before nightfall. Rome might fall, but she wanted to survive. If the need arose, she was perfectly prepared to fight as well. Fabiola offered up a swift prayer to Jupiter. Protect us all, she thought. Let no harm come to me or mine.

It was not long before the sound of women's screams reached them. Carrying from some distance away, the cries rose and fell in clear ululations of grief. Sighs of anticipation swept through the crowd and heads craned to see the source of the piercing howls. Clodius' corpse was approaching. The strain grew too much for one of Milo's men, who threw his javelin. It flew up in a shallow arc towards the plebeians but fell short and skittered harmlessly across the cobblestones. Jeers and insults filled the air in response. The atmosphere grew even more tense, but, amazingly, none of Clodius' thugs responded. Their throbbing anger was being held in check until they had seen his body with their own eyes. Like everyone else, their eyes were fixed on the spot where the Via Appia entered the Forum. Fabiola glanced at Tullius, who, despite the critical situation, gave her a reassuring smile. Knowing that he was putting on a brave face for her, she warmed to the tough Sicilian. A good man: she needed more like him.

The keening slowly grew in volume until it was possible to make out a group of women clad in grey mourning dresses approaching the open space and the massed, eager audience. In their midst was a slim, blood-soaked figure staggering under the weight of a bulky, cloth-wrapped bundle.

Clever, thought Fabiola. Fulvia had done well to assemble her friends in such a short time. There were few better ways to whip up public hysteria than with such a chorus of wailing. And it was a master stroke for Clodius' widow to enter the Forum carrying his corpse.

Gradually the screams became intelligible.

'Look what they have done to my Clodius!'

'Murdered,' responded the women dramatically. 'Killed on the street like a dog!'

'Left naked as the day he was born,' intoned Fulvia.

Shouts of anger went up from many of the watching citizens.

'Scared of a fair fight?' A number of Fulvia's companions spat in the direction of Milo and his men. 'Cowards!'

A swelling cry of rage met this accusation. Many of Clodius' supporters began drumming sword hilts off their shields. Shifting restlessly, others stamped their feet on the cobbles. On the other side of the Forum, the gladiators did the same. Soon it was hard to make out a word through the crescendo of noise.

As the two sides continued challenging each other, the hot taste of acid filled the back of Fabiola's throat. This was what Romulus might have experienced just before Carrhae. Before he died. The pangs of a familiar sorrow were followed by an eerie feeling of acceptance. Maybe he is dead, Fabiola thought. Perhaps Jupiter has brought me here to die today: to join Romulus and Mother. She was briefly surprised that the concept satisfied her. Her family had meant everything to her, but they were long gone. Apart from Brutus and Docilosa, she was alone in the world. Yet neither were blood relatives, and revenge as a purpose in life could only sustain her so far. *Very well. Jupiter Optimus Maximus, do what you will.*

The faces of the terrified citizens around her still tore at Fabiola's conscience. They were not like her, who had little left to live for. Innocent of any crime, most of them probably had families. Yet they were about to die too. And things would get worse if order was not restored. Fabiola felt helpless and insignificant. What can I do? There was only one thing to ask for. *Jupiter, protect your people and your city.*

'Let's get those fuckers!' shouted a large man in the front rank.

Everyone cheered. Baying with fury, the mob lurched forward.

'Wait!' barked the bearded leader. 'We haven't seen Clodius' body yet.'

It was the right thing to say. The crowd swayed back into position.

At last Fulvia reached the centre of the Forum. An attractive woman in her thirties, she had painted her face with ashes and soot. Tears streamed down her blackened cheeks, mixing with smears of blood. But she remained in full control of her faculties. Ordering her friends to spread out, she reverently lowered her burden to the ground. She pulled back the red-soaked sheet, revealing her husband's mutilated corpse to the watching citizens. Gasps of outrage greeted her action. Fabiola could not help but wince at the number of Clodius' wounds. The young messenger had not been exaggerating. The renegade noble had been run through multiple times, each thrust enough to kill. Covered in cuts and slashes, his features were almost unrecognisable. One leg had been almost severed from his body and a bent javelin head still protruded from his left shoulder. Clodius Pulcher had not died well.

Sniggers and laughs rose from Milo's men as they studied their work.

Fulvia stood up, her grey dress saturated with blood. This was her moment.

Fabiola waited.

All of Rome waited.

Raising her arms dramatically, Fulvia beat her breast with her fists. Spittle flew from her lips as she began to speak. 'I call on Orcus, god of the underworld!' She levelled a quivering finger at Milo. 'To mark out this man.'

Milo visibly quailed. Superstition ruled the hearts and minds of most, and there were few people who would not be intimidated by such a public cursing. But he was a brave man. Squaring his shoulders, the noble prepared himself for Fulvia's next words.

'Carry him off to Hades,' she intoned. 'There let Cerberus rip him slowly to shreds. And feed on him for all eternity.'

Milo managed not to react this time, but he had no reply. His gladiators fell silent; not even his tame priests dared answer.

Throughout the crowd, men made the sign against evil.

Fulvia let her words sink in for the space of ten heartbeats. Then, carrying Clodius' body to the steps of the temple of Juno, she fell to her knees and threw herself on top of it. Her companions hurried to join the grieving widow. Great sobs began to rack Fulvia as she finally allowed the grief to take hold.

Fabiola had to admire the theatrics. The last and most dramatic part had been reserved until Fulvia had reached safety. She could guess what would happen next.

There were more wails as the group of women clustered around Fulvia, touching the dead noble's wounds and raising bloody fingertips for all to see.

It was the final straw for Clodius' men. Revenge had to be taken. An incoherent bellow of hatred left their throats and they swarmed forward towards their enemies. Fabiola, her guards and the screaming captives were carried along with them. There would be no clear lines of battle, just a chaotic mêlée of thugs and civilians.

The terrified priests shouted for calm. Too late, they realised that what had been unleashed was uncontrollable. This vast, inchoate fury threatened Rome itself, and they had encouraged it.

'Mistress!' cried Tullius. 'We must escape.'

Fabiola nodded grimly. 'Use your weapons only if there is no other way,' she ordered her men. She did not want any innocent blood on her conscience.

They had barely acknowledged her when the two sides met with a resounding crash. Trained fighters, Milo's gladiators had an instant advantage over the plebeian rabble. Forming a solid wall of shields, they easily withstood the initial screaming charge. *Gladii* stabbed forward viciously; tridents and spears shoved into unprotected faces and necks; javelins hummed through the air; blood spilled on to the cobbles. Fabiola watched in fascinated horror. This was far worse than anything she had seen in the arena. In the first few moments, dozens fell to the ground injured or killed. Inevitably though, weight of numbers began to tell. Enraged, filled with grief, Clodius' thugs threw themselves at their enemies like men possessed. A Samnite was the first to go down, shield bodily ripped from his grasp by two burly plebeians. Even as he skewered one through the throat, the gladiator was transfixed by a spear. Blood bubbling from his lips, he collapsed, leaving a gap in the defensive line. Those who were nearby immediately concentrated their attack on this spot. Next a *murmillo* was killed, then a *retiarius*. The mob advanced, forcing Milo's followers backwards and on to the steps of the Senate. The gladiators were not highly disciplined Roman legionaries, used to withstanding overwhelming odds. More holes appeared and were instantly expanded, further separating their ranks. The fighters' heads began to turn, seeking a way out. They had been promised good wages for street brawls, not death in a full-scale battle.

The fight was far from over, but Fabiola sensed that the tide had turned. Fortunately they were still some distance from the bloodshed. The thugs who had marched them to the Forum had disappeared into the mêlée. It was time to escape, if they could. She jerked her head at Tullius, who was more than happy to obey. He barked an order at the others. Forming a protective diamond shape around Fabiola, the nine bodyguards drew their swords, turned as one and began to beat a path out of the crowd. Thankfully, large numbers were also trying to flee. With their captors' attention diverted, all the prisoners had a chance to gain their freedom, brutally pushing, shoving and ignoring the weak, who were simply trampled underfoot. When Fabiola bent to help an old woman who had fallen to her knees, Tullius roughly pulled her away. 'Leave her!'

Shocked at being handled, Fabiola realised the Sicilian was truly worried about her safety. She looked back in anguish, but the lined, terrified face had already been swallowed by the heaving mass. Another innocent victim. But there was no time to grieve or to dwell on the gods' purpose today. Intent on their own survival as well as that of their mistress, Fabiola's guards battered on.

'Make for that!' Tullius shouted, pointing at the temple of Castor, the nearest building. Ducking their heads down, the bodyguards soon gained momentum.

Fabiola held her breath as they crept through the maelstrom. Occasionally Tullius or the others had to use the hilt of their swords across someone's head, but most gang members nearby were more interested in attacking the gladiators than stopping a few people moving away from the battle.

Finally reaching the carved stone steps, they worked around their base and into a narrow side street. Fabiola took one more glance at the Forum. The two sides were still fighting hammer and tongs, neither prepared to give or ask for quarter. Milo's gladiators had been broken up and were now in small groups, struggling for their lives against far superior numbers of plebeians. Any success cost the thugs dearly though: every *murmillo* or *secutor* who died was taking three or four men with him. The dead sprawled everywhere now, crushed underfoot, heaped on top of each other, prostrate in the entrances to temples. It was a massacre.

Rome was finally toppling into anarchy, and there was no one to prevent it.

'Hurry!' Tullius' sole concern was to get his mistress to safety.

It was foolish to linger, but Fabiola could not take her eyes off the scene. She watched as six plebeians emerged from the confusion some distance away, bearing Clodius' body. Led by Fulvia and the bearded leader whom they had encountered earlier, the group moved purposefully towards the

Senate entrance. Behind came a pair of men carrying flaming torches. Fabiola gasped. Clodius' funeral pyre was to be lit inside the Republic's most important structure: the Senate itself.

Tullius bobbed up and down unhappily, but Fabiola would not budge. And her guess was correct. Moments later, tendrils of smoke began billowing from inside the sacred chamber. No event in the city's history had ever been more dramatic. Five hundred years of democracy were about to go up in flames.

Even Tullius paused when he realised what they were witnessing. Politics affected slaves little, but certain things in the Republic were permanent – or seemed so. The building that housed the seat of government was one of them. To see the Senate being burned was extraordinarily shocking. If it could be destroyed, then so could any other structure in Rome.

The Sicilian came to his senses at last. 'We cannot stay, Mistress.' His tone was firm.

Fabiola sighed in acceptance and meekly followed Tullius away. Jupiter had spared their lives thus far, but they should not tempt fate. It was time to leave, before things got even worse. Only military force could bring back peace now. The senators would have no choice but to ask Pompey, the new consul, to intervene, which would swing the balance of power firmly away from Caesar. Brutus' position would also be weakened by this unrest. So, therefore, would hers. And what would happen in Gaul? If Vercingetorix' rebellion succeeded, Caesar's attempt to become the Republic's leader would fail completely. A defeated general could never retain the fickle public's approval. Fabiola steeled her resolve. Jupiter had shown her his favour by letting her escape the chaos. Only a short time earlier, she had been ready to die – well, no longer. No matter what happened, this would not be the end of her rise to power.

Fabiola did not even see the arrow strike. It was the gasp of pain which attracted her attention. She looked up to see Tullius toppling forward, looking faintly surprised. A feathered wooden shaft protruded from the middle of his chest, its iron point buried deep in his lungs. Mortally wounded, the Sicilian landed face down in the ankle-deep mud.

A heartbeat later, another guard followed him. Then a third.

Ducking down, Fabiola spat a bitter curse. How could I have been so stupid? she thought. Jupiter does not bother with the likes of me.

The way ahead had been blocked with piles of refuse, lengths of wood and broken pottery. Eager to get away from the Forum, Tullius had not seen it. Fabiola had not been paying attention either. On another day, she might have thought the waist-high rubbish just indicated a particularly poor street, a place where the inhabitants cared for neither health nor hygiene. Not today.

This was an ambush.

A fourth missile hissed through the air, taking the guard nearest to her through the neck.

They could not go forwards. Or back. Certain death awaited in the Forum. Eyes swivelling, Fabiola looked for the archer.

One of her five remaining followers pointed. Then he screamed, clutching at the arrow jutting from his left eye. Falling to his knees, he tugged frantically at the shaft, and Fabiola heard metal scrape off bone as the barbs pulled free of the socket. His face drenched in blood and aqueous fluid, the brave guard staggered upright, sobbing with pain. Now half-blind, he would be of little use in the impending fight.

From a side alley, ten ruffians emerged. Dressed in ragged, dull brown tunics, they were carrying an assortment of weapons: spears, clubs, knives, rusty swords. There was one bowman, an evil-looking type who smiled as he notched another arrow to his string. His companions were similarly unsavoury in appearance.

'Look what we've got here, boys,' said a spearman with a leer.

'A noble lady!' answered another. 'Always wanted to try one of those.'

The archer licked his lips. 'Let's see what's under that fine robe.'

The men moved in, their faces filling with lust. This would not just be robbery. Fabiola saw rape and death in their dark eyes. But instead of fear, anger boiled up inside her. These were the lowest of the low: the scum who waited to prey on the weak and unarmed fleeing the battle.

'Mistress?' asked her guards in unison. Without Tullius, they were unsure what to do.

She swallowed hard. None had shields, leaving them defenceless against missiles. If they did not act fast, they would all fall to the bowman. There was only one way to overcome their ambushers, who were most probably cowards. Producing the dagger Tullius had given her, Fabiola bared her teeth. 'Run straight at them,' she hissed. 'It's that, or we go to Hades.'

If this was the end that Jupiter had chosen for her, she would at least die well.

Seeing her determination, the guards' courage rose. Four raised their swords, and the one-eyed man unsheathed a knife. With his reduced ability to judge depth of field, a short weapon would be easier to fight with. In a heartbeat, the five were lined up beside her. Slaves or not, it was better to die fighting than to just be slain out of hand.

A scream of rage and defiance left Fabiola's mouth. Raising her blade, she charged forward. Everything was falling apart. The gods had answered her: she was surely alone in the world. If death took her now, it would be a release.

Her men roared in response and followed close behind.

The battle was brief, and brutal.

Acting on a hunch that she would not be killed at once, Fabiola ran straight at the archer, who was drawing a bead on someone over her left shoulder. She felt a rush of air as his arrow shot past her cheek and a strangled cry from behind her as it landed. Then she was on him. There would only be one chance: her blow had to disable or kill, instantly. Before the thug even drew breath, Fabiola had slammed her dagger deep into the point where his neck met his body. It was where she had seen Corbulo stick pigs as they were being slaughtered. A high-pitched scream left his lips and he dropped his bow. She didn't hesitate. Pulling her blade free, Fabiola stabbed him twice more, in the chest. His wounds gushing, the archer fell backwards and out of sight. He would be dead within moments.

Fabiola looked at the hand holding her weapon, her right. It was completely red, sticky with blood. It was sickening. It was hard to know which was worse: this, or having to couple with old, fat senators.

'Bitch!'

Instinctively she ducked, avoiding a wildly swinging sword. Facing her was an unshaven, skinny man wielding a rusty *gladius*. Although Fabiola had not been trained to use weapons, she had watched Juba teaching Romulus enough times. She had also seen the Lupanar's two doormen sparring with each other. This fool has no idea how to fight, she thought, feeling a surge of hope. But she had never been trained to do so either.

He lunged forward again but she easily dodged away.

'More used to stabbing people in the back, eh?' Fabiola sneered, wondering what to do next. To get within knife range, she would have to go dangerously close to his sword. The thug sensed her indecision at once.

'I'm going to enjoy fucking you when this is over,' he panted, trying to snatch her dagger.

She had him now. Fabiola slipped down the top of her dress, revealing her full breasts. Survival mattered far more than her modesty.

Eyes goggling, he dropped his guard.

'Like what you see?' she asked softly, cupping one invitingly.

The plebeian could not answer. The only women he could afford were the worn-out whores who lived around the tombs on the Via Appia: toothless, diseased, half drunk most of the time. In comparison, Fabiola was like a vision of a goddess. He licked his lips and moved a pace forward.

Her smile changed to a she-wolf's snarl as he drew near enough. In her mind, this could have been Gemellus, or a hundred others who had used her body. With a backwards slash, Fabiola cut the man's throat wide open, taking the blade so deep it grated off the cartilage of his larynx. As he toppled over, choking on his own blood, she grabbed his *gladius*. Two weapons will be better than one, she thought.

When Fabiola had pulled up her dress and looked around, nearly all her men were down, but they had killed twice the number of their attackers. Strangely, the guard whose eye had been taken out was still fighting. Her heart filled with pride at his loyalty and courage. Screaming from a mixture of pain and battle rage, he had disabled two thugs, spilling one's intestines all over the ground and burying his dagger in the thigh of another.

That left Fabiola and the injured slave against two of the lowlifes, who now looked decidedly less confident. The odds had improved and her spirits lifted a fraction. Jupiter is still watching over us. Do not turn away now, she pleaded. But Fabiola's hope vanished again as four more men emerged from the alleyway. Drawn by the sound of fighting, they cried out angrily when they saw their comrades lying dead and injured. Dismay was quickly replaced by lust at the realisation that they only faced two enemies, one of whom was a beautiful young woman.

'Mistress?'

Fabiola turned to face her wounded guard. Runnels of clotted blood covered his left cheek. They had even run into his open mouth, staining his teeth red. But his remaining eye burned fiercely from the clean, right side of his face. The effect was terrifying and must have given him an advantage over the thugs. 'What is it?'

'When I'm dead . . .' He paused, looking genuinely distressed. 'I don't want to be dumped on the Esquiline Hill, Mistress.'

Fabiola's heart went out to him. The slave wasn't afraid of dying with her. Instead, like many of his kind, he feared the indignity of being thrown into the city's open pits along with excess waste and the bodies of animals and criminals. Like her brother, he had pride as well as courage. Sadly, she didn't even know the man's name. 'If I survive, and you do not,' Fabiola declared, 'then I swear before all the gods that you will have your own grave, with a memorial over it.'

She could not promise any more. The odds were still stacked against them.

He stared at her from his good eye and nodded once.

This was how the bonds of comradeship were formed, Fabiola realised. Someone who would stand by another in the midst of battle, especially when they did not have to, was worthy of friendship. And trust. Whether they were a slave or not was irrelevant.

'Your name?' she asked.

'Sextus, Mistress.'

'Good.' Pleased that she would not die with a stranger, Fabiola studied the newcomers. They seemed vaguely familiar, but fortunately none was armed with a bow. There would be an opportunity to injure or kill at least a few before they died. Perhaps one would drop his guard as the fool with the *gladius* had, she thought hopefully. But she doubted the ruse would work again. By the way they held their weapons, the tough-looking men were used to fighting. Sighing, Fabiola moved shoulder to shoulder with Sextus. He smelt of blood and sweat. 'Let's charge them,' she whispered. 'If we break past, head into the alleyway. It will lead somewhere.'

'Be easier to defend as well, Mistress,' Sextus replied. 'Two men can barely stand alongside each other in there.'

She was delighted by his insight. In such a narrow space, their attackers would not be able to overwhelm them with superior numbers. 'Jupiter has preserved us both this far,' she said, taking heart. 'Now we need Fortuna's help as well.'

'The gods have never smiled on me, Mistress. I'm a slave.' Sextus' eye was world-weary. 'But I'll die rather than let these scum harm you.' He hawked and spat a gobbet of bloody phlegm in the thugs' direction.

There was no more time to talk. Angered by Sextus' action and full of confidence again, their enemies moved forward purposefully. After all, they now outnumbered their victims by three to one; any fear of injury or death was overcome by their strong desire to rape Fabiola. How hard could it be for half a dozen fighters to overcome a blood-spattered young noble-woman and a badly wounded slave?

Fabiola's new-found confidence began to desert her. Better armed and disciplined, the new arrivals were clearly more determined than their original attackers. Fear began to take root in her heart. Raising her *gladius*, she shuffled forward, trying to remember the practice moves she had once seen Romulus make. Sextus kept close beside her, probing forward with the spear he had picked up.

One of the thugs laughed; it was an unpleasant, threatening sound.

And Fabiola remembered where she had seen him before.

These were *fugitivarii*.

Almost on cue, a burly figure with brown hair and deep-set eyes strolled from the alley. Dressed in a legionary's mail shirt, he had thick silver bands circling his wrists. Behind him were another six of his men, all heavily armed.

The tip of Sextus' spear wavered at the sight; Fabiola's hand rose to her mouth in shock.

Scaevola bowed mockingly.

Her pulse became a trip hammer. This ambush had been planned.

Chapter VII: Ambush

Margiana, winter 53/52 BC

It was the silence which first drew Romulus' attention. The fortlet that they had marched all day to reach was at the bottom of a gentle slope in a wide defile, meaning that sound carried up to anyone approaching from the west. Normal noises should have been audible: during daylight, every Roman camp was a hubbub of activity. There were smiths hammering out dents in sword blades, men shouting during weapons drill or trumpets sounding the change of guard. Yet he could hear nothing.

Not a sound.

A frisson of fear caressed Romulus' spine. Since seeing the corpse on the cross, he had thought only of Fabiola and his mother. If Rome was descending into the total anarchy he had seen, what did that bode for his loved ones? Their fragile image in his mind, which he used to stay sane, had begun to disintegrate. This in turn brought him back to reality with a jolt.

Footsore and looking forward to a warm meal, his comrades appeared unaware. Even Novius' taunts had stopped. Clearly unconcerned, Darius and a junior officer were conferring about something. The column tramped onwards, passing a small inscribed stone tablet sticking out of the ground. There had been similar markers all along their route from the main fort. This last was positioned about half a mile from their destination and as the men saw it, their pace picked up.

Romulus' jaw clenched. Why had no one else noticed? 'I don't like it,' he hissed to Brennus.

The Gaul looked startled. Immediately his eyes narrowed and he scanned their surroundings. Although nothing was visible, he did not relax. 'What is it?' he murmured.

'It's too damn quiet.'

Brennus cocked his head and listened. Apart from the noise of iron hobnails crunching off the frozen ground, he too could hear nothing. Suspicion flared in his blue eyes. 'If you're going to say something, do it fast.' He pointed at Darius.

Very soon, the Parthian officer would come into full view of the outpost.

Uneasy, Romulus turned his head to the rear. Blinding light from the setting sun lit up the track, making it almost impossible to see. Yet there was no mistaking the figure on horseback that was watching the patrol from the high point of the defile. It was Scythian.

Romulus blinked. When he looked again, the rider was gone.

Seeing him, Novius drew a finger across his throat.

He studiously ignored the gesture.

'Are you going to speak to Darius?' asked Brennus, who had seen nothing.

'It's too late. They're behind us as well,' Romulus whispered. Quickly he filled the Gaul in.

Stifling a curse, Brennus glanced back, then forward. He felt a brief surge of pride at Romulus' keen eye. If he was right, they could do little. The Gaul assessed the situation. Their current position was impossible to defend. With slopes on either side, they would be at the mercy of any missiles fired at them. But it was not safe to turn around either. 'Got no choice, have we?' he growled. 'The best place to fight will be the flat ground in front of the fortlet.'

Pleased, Romulus nodded. That had been his thought too. 'I'd better tell Darius,' he said.

The *optio* was surprised when Romulus broke ranks to mutter in his ear, but gave permission for him to advise their commander.

With his yoke waving overhead, Romulus trotted forward until he caught up with the senior centurion. Darius' horse was ten steps from the edge of the ridge which overlooked their destination.

'Sir!'

Reining in, the stout Parthian smiled at the sight of Romulus. This was one of the best soldiers in his cohort. 'What is it?' he asked in Latin.

'An ambush, sir,' replied Romulus. 'There are Scythians behind us.'

Turning in the saddle, Darius studied the bare landscape. 'Are you sure?'

Romulus explained what he had seen and the Parthian's face darkened.

'Let's get down there fast,' he said. 'We'll have over two hundred men then. That'll see off the bastards.'

'If they're not dead already,' Romulus announced, deliberately speaking in Parthian. Everyone needed to be aware of the risks they faced.

Darius' guards looked alarmed.

'Explain yourself,' Darius hissed.

Romulus opened his mouth to do so when instinctively the senior centurion's horse stopped. It had reached a flat piece of rock, a place where a soldier might stop to glance back at his camp before beginning a journey, or where a weary patrol arriving after a long march could pause to savour their achievement. Behind them, the legionaries halted gratefully, grounding their yokes and shields while the opportunity presented itself.

Together they gazed down at the fortlet, which was now only a short march away. The same playing-card shape of all Roman forts, the small outpost had just one gate, at the front. A tall wooden watchtower was positioned in the centre, with an uninterrupted field of vision around the camp. There were defensive *fossae* and wooden battlements twice the height of a man; inside the low roof of a barracks could be seen.

Romulus stared. The ramparts were clear of sentries.

That meant one thing. Roman soldiers never deserted their posts.

The garrison was dead.

An experienced soldier, Darius also took in the situation at a glance. He looked questioningly at Romulus. 'How did you know?'

'I couldn't hear anything, sir,' he explained.

It made perfect sense. Darius scowled, but there was no time to be lost blaming himself for not noticing what one of his ordinary soldiers had. 'Vahram must know about this,' he muttered, barking an order at his guards. At once two turned their horses and rode off, separating as they did. In an attempt to outflank the enemy, one went directly south and the other north. The remaining warrior moved closer to the senior centurion, notching an arrow to his bow.

'Damn it,' growled Darius. 'We'll just go down there as if nothing's wrong. But I want everyone ready for combat. Advise the *optiones* and *tesserarii*, then resume your position.'

Romulus snapped off a salute and hurried to obey. Already warned by his *optio*, the other junior officers began to move down the ranks, quietly ordering the men to prepare themselves. Surprise, dismay, and last of all anger, filled the legionaries' faces. Novius looked most put out, as did his companions.

'Well?' asked the Gaul.

'We march on in,' replied Romulus. 'Check out the camp.'

Gripping their weapons tightly, the patrol marched along the track, down the incline towards the fortlet. All eyes were upon it, but for different reasons than just a few moments before. Now everyone could see that there was no smoke from cooking fires, no movement on the walkways. It resembled a graveyard.

Closer in, Romulus saw that one of the front doors was leaning slightly ajar. This was final proof that things were amiss. Far from the rest of the legion, all outposts were under strict orders to keep their gates shut at all times. Yet there were no signs of violence, no damage to the exterior structure. No arrows or spears stuck in the timbers, no evidence of fire. Whatever had happened here had not been thanks to a direct assault.

Darius had seen too. Immediately he ordered the *optiones* to have the men make a protective screen in front of the entrance. Piling their yokes in a heap, the legionaries fanned outwards in a semicircle, four ranks deep. It was done efficiently, without fuss, and soon a solid wall of shields had formed. Above the silk-covered *scuta* were bronze bowl crested helmets and steady, grim faces. Apart from the soldiers' lower legs, there was little for an enemy to attack. And, thanks to Tarquinius' tutoring, the front ranks always dropped to their knees when the threat of missiles was present. They were ready.

To investigate, Darius hand-picked a squad of six men, including Romulus and Brennus. For reasons best known to himself, he also chose Novius and Optatus. The veterans leered at the friends as they leaned their *pila* against the timber wall. Javelins would be no good at close quarters. Instead they all drew their *gladii*. Pulling his own blade free, the stout Parthian led them inside the camp. He was totally unaware of the tension between the men behind him. There was a brief delay; no one wanted to have his enemies at his back. Then Romulus darted through the gate with Brennus, leaving the others too far away to try anything. Mouthing silent curses, Novius and Optatus followed.

The dirt beneath their feet was hard-packed from the passage of men in and out of the fortlet, so their hobnailed *caligae* made no sound. A deathly silence greeted them. The atmosphere within was eerie. Unnerving. Part of the garrison might be on patrol, but there should have been at least some soldiers visible.

Not one was.

Where are they? thought Romulus. Was it possible that they had abandoned the fortlet?

Apart from the observation tower, a single barracks building and a small latrine block, the only structures were an earth oven under the west wall and a number of altars to the gods positioned here and there. Large, tell-tale dark stains marked the ground, bloody proof that all was not well. There were uneasy murmurs from the others at the sight.

Hairs prickled on the back of Romulus' neck. There was death here, its presence suddenly overpowering. He looked up, expecting to see clouds of birds of prey hanging high overhead. There weren't many though, and those present were probably just eyeing the refuse heaps that existed outside the camp. Why were there not more?

Brennus could sense it too. Nostrils flaring, he reached up to touch the hilt of his longsword, which was hanging from his back. In open combat, it was still his favoured weapon.

'What's that?' hissed Darius. They were now very near the barracks.

They froze, ears pricked.

A low sound reached them. There was no mistaking the moan of an injured man. A survivor.

Using the tip of his sword, the Parthian flipped open the flimsy door. It made a hollow sound as it banged off the wall. Inside, the floor was slick with blood. Drag marks led towards the small rooms shared by the *contubernia* of eight men. With only a half-century in this fort, there would be five such, and a larger chamber for the *optio* in command. Wrinkling his face with distaste, Darius jerked his head at Romulus, Novius and another soldier. 'You three go left,' he ordered. 'We'll go right.' Taking Optatus and the fifth legionary, he entered.

Brennus was left outside.

Romulus gripped the bone handle of his sword tightly. Jupiter, Greatest and Best, he thought, protect me. The narrow corridor echoed to the sound of their *caligae* as Romulus led the way, with the others one step behind.

All held their shields high, their *gladii* ready. He was acutely aware of Novius at his unprotected back.

'Don't worry, slave,' hissed the veteran. 'I want to see your face as you die.'

Romulus spun round, glaring. He longed to end the vendetta right then.

'Found anything?' bellowed Darius in an odd voice.

The question broke the spell.

'Not yet, sir,' Romulus answered, turning back. His voice died in his throat as he reached the first chamber.

There was no need to worry about being attacked. Each room was exactly the same. Their limbs at awkward angles, mangled corpses lay heaped untidily on top of each other. All the legionaries had been stripped naked, their mail shirts and faded russet tunics discarded on the floor along-side. Clotted blood lay in great pools around the still bodies and mounds of clothing.

Even Novius looked disgusted. 'Who does this to an enemy?'

'Scythians,' Romulus said calmly. Tarquinius had told him about their barbaric customs.

'Fucking savages.'

Every body was mutilated in the same manner: beheaded as well as partially skinned. Patches of skin were missing from chests, backs and legs, and there was no sign of the soldiers' heads. Romulus knew why. According to Tarquinius, the Scythians measured a warrior's courage by the number of heads he carried back from battle. They also used the tops of enemy skulls as drinking vessels, covering them in leather and even gilding them inside, while skins were used as drying cloths and scalps as decorative hand-kerchiefs on their horses' bridles. Revulsion filled Romulus at this level of savagery. Breathing through his mouth, he realised that he could smell very little. Even though these men had clearly been dead for more than a day, the bitter cold had prevented much decay.

'Why did they carry them inside?' asked Novius.

Romulus looked at him with scorn. The answer was obvious.

Realisation hit the veteran. 'So there would be no cloud of vultures overhead.'

He nodded.

Suddenly there was more at stake than their feud.

As one, they turned and ran in search of Darius. They had marched into a trap. Now it was surely about to be sprung.

The trio found their commander on his knees in the *optio*'s quarters. He glanced up as they entered, his face twisted with fury. The junior officer lying cradled in his arms had not been treated in quite the same way as the others. Remarkably, he was still alive. A strong man in his thirties, the *optio* had been scalped and entirely flayed. Barely conscious, uncontrollable shivers shook his bloody, ruined frame. He did not have long.

'Sir,' Romulus began.

'They posed as a trading party. Got inside the gates and then produced hidden weapons,' snarled Darius. 'Dirty Scythian dogs.'

That made sense, thought Romulus. But there was no time to waste. 'Sir. They hid the men in here so that the vultures would not warn us off.'

'Of course,' gasped the Parthian. 'And we just walked in, like complete fools.'

'Best get outside, sir,' said Novius, his muscles twitching with impatience.

Darius nodded briskly. 'And this poor creature?'

'Give him a warrior's death,' said Novius.

Rather than let the mortally wounded die in pain, Roman soldiers always performed a final act of mercy.

'I'll do it, sir.' Romulus' voice echoed loudly in the confined space. Novius and Optatus began to protest. Slaves could not perform this duty.

But a warning look from Darius quelled their objections. 'This man volunteered first,' he said, thinking they also wanted the honour. 'Outside.'

The malevolent legionaries had no choice but to obey. Saluting resentfully, they left, followed by the other two soldiers.

'Do it quickly.' Laying the maimed *optio* down with care, Darius passed his hand over his forehead in a blessing and strode from the room.

Lifting his *gladius*, Romulus stepped closer. It was right that this death should be his. Darius was not Roman, while Novius and Optatus were evil men who should end no one's life. The last two had not volunteered, so it was up to him to give the *optio* a dignified passage to the other side.

The man's eyelids opened and their gaze met. Both knew what was about to happen.

Admiration filled Romulus. He could see no fear in the *optio*'s face, just calm acceptance.

'Sir,' he said. 'Elysium awaits.' Brave men went to the warrior's paradise.

There was a single nod.

Gently Romulus helped the other to sit up. There was an involuntary gasp, rapidly concealed. Even a small movement must be agonising, he thought. Pity filled him.

'My name is Aesius. *Optio* in the Second Century, First Cohort, Twentieth Legion,' managed the injured officer. He looked round enquiringly. 'And your name?'

'Romulus, sir.'

Aesius' twisted face relaxed. 'A man should know who sends him to heaven.'

From outside came the clash of arms and Darius' voice, bellowing orders. The Scythians had attacked.

'Your comrades need you,' said Aesius.

Romulus knelt and took hold of Aesius' bloody forearm in the warrior's greeting. The weak *optio* could barely return the grip, but Romulus saw that the gesture meant a lot. 'Go well,' he whispered.

He moved behind Aesius, who lowered his chin on to his chest. This exposed the nape of his neck. Holding the hilt of his *gladius* with both hands, Romulus lifted it high in the air, its sharp tip pointing down. Without pausing, he stabbed into Aesius' spinal cord, cutting it in two. Death was instantaneous, and the *optio*'s disfigured body slumped silently to the floor.

He was at peace.

His heart heavy, Romulus studied the prone form at his feet. But anger gradually replaced the sorrow. Forty good men had been maimed for no good reason. And outside, more were dying. Bloody sword in hand, he turned and ran from the building. The others had already disappeared, so Romulus sprinted towards the gate. The clash of arms mingled with men's screams, the noise of horses' hooves and shouted orders from Darius. Battle had been joined. Wishing that Tarquinius were there too, Romulus emerged from the fortlet to a scene of complete mayhem.

In partial testudo formation, the two centuries were holding firm.

Beyond them galloped large groups of Scythian warriors, loosing arrows at the legionaries as they rode to and fro. It reminded Romulus of Carrhae.

But the bearded, tattooed horsemen were dressed differently to the Parthians, with marmot fur or wool cloaks, dark woollen trousers and knee-high felt boots. Few of the dark-skinned horse archers wore armour, yet they were armed to the teeth, carrying short-headed axes, swords and knives as well as their bows. Their mounts were a magnificent deep red colour, and their blue saddles were richly decorated with gold thread. These were wealthier men than the riders who had devastated Crassus' army.

Romulus glanced at his comrades. Thankfully, the silk coverings on their shields were safely stopping the Scythian arrows. Already their surfaces were peppered with them. But there were a few casualties. Four men had received wounds to their lower legs. Another must have been looking up when the first volley was released. Lying to the unprotected rear with the others, he twitched spasmodically. One hand still clutched the wooden shaft protruding from his throat.

One dead, four injured, thought Romulus grimly. And the fight had barely begun.

Loud screams drew his attention once more. Almost as one, the four legionaries had begun thrashing about, their faces contorted in pain. Their reaction was extreme, confusing Romulus. They all had routine flesh wounds. Then he remembered. *Scythicon.*

Tarquinius had told him how the poison was made. Adders were captured and killed, and left to decompose. Next, sealed vessels of human blood were allowed to putrefy in animal dung. The final mixture of rotting snake, blood and faeces formed a toxic liquid that killed within hours of wounding a man. It meant that every Scythian arrow provided a guarantee of death. How could Pacorus be any different?

But that was the least of his worries right now. A finger of fear tugged at Romulus' heart. He did not want to die screaming in agony. And the same emotion was evident in the faces of the legionaries in the rear ranks. The cries of the wounded were doing little for morale.

There were at least a hundred figures on horseback pinning them against the fortlet's wall. Pleasingly, about two score more lay sprawled in the dirt, taken down by the first shower of Roman javelins. Wary of using their last missiles, Darius had not yet ordered another volley. His last bodyguard was using his bow to deadly effect, however. Taking his time, the Parthian was loosing well-aimed arrows, invariably killing a Scythian with each shot. But his efforts would soon come to a halt. The case-like quiver on his left hip only held twenty to thirty shafts.

'Into line, soldier!' shouted one of the *optiones* at Romulus.

Spotting Brennus' huge frame at the front, he shoved his way through to join him. Even on his knees, the Gaul towered over the others. Lowering his *scutum* to meet the others in the shield wall, Romulus knelt down on the cold ground beside his friend. The men in the second rank held their *scuta* angled overhead to protect those in front while those behind covered their own heads. The testudo was an extremely effective defensive formation. Romulus' misery lifted a fraction. They could hold their own against these attackers.

'Stand fast! Protect yourselves from their arrows,' shouted Darius, his perspiring face determined. 'Let the bastards use them all up. We'll stay inside the fort, and in the morning we can march out of here.'

At this, there was a loud cheer. Not everyone would fall to the poisoned shafts.

Romulus turned to Brennus. 'Can't be that simple,' he muttered. 'Can it?'

'I doubt it,' replied the Gaul with a scowl.

'There aren't enough warriors to wipe us out.'

But there were no more visible, and clearly Darius thought that the riders pounding back and forth in front of them were their only attackers.

The nomads must have heard of the silk protection on their shields, thought Romulus. Word had spread fast through the border region about the Forgotten Legion's secret weapon, meaning that most tribes were wary of attacking unless in great force. No leader could think that a hundred horse archers would be able to stop two centuries marching out to freedom. Slow them down, yes. Annihilate them, no. And if Darius' messengers safely delivered their message, reinforcements would arrive by the next afternoon. What was going on?

Romulus peered over the iron rim of his shield, his eyes flicking from left to right. There was a small group of Scythians at the enemy's rear, directing operations, but no sign of any more warriors. *Mithras, help me!* He took a deep, uncertain breath as his gaze was drawn upwards, over the milling horsemen. Clear blue sky. On the horizon, a few clouds. A faint breeze coming from the north. Attracted by the fighting, vultures were already beginning to circle high above. Romulus considered what he saw for a long time. Dread filled his heart, but eventually he was sure.

'We need to fight our way out,' he muttered. 'Now.'

The big Gaul was surprised. 'Why? It's nearly nightfall. Better to do what Darius says.'

Romulus put his lips to Brennus' ear. 'The omens are bad.'

Brennus looked confused. This was normally Tarquinius' territory. 'You're sure?' he asked.

'Yes. I asked Mithras for help and he gave it,' whispered Romulus vehemently. 'These are the scouts for a much larger force that will arrive at dawn tomorrow.'

'They're just keeping us here?'

'Precisely,' finished Romulus.

Used to Tarquinius' accurate predictions, Brennus let out a heavy sigh. He scanned Romulus' features again, searching for proof.

'I don't understand either,' hissed Romulus. 'But I saw a vision of Rome earlier too.'

The Gaul spat a curse. 'Very well. Speak to Darius. Tell him what you saw.'

By now, the Scythians had stopped wasting arrows by firing at the silk-covered shields. Instead they were letting them fly in curving arcs that came down to the rear of the testudo. Pushing his way out, Romulus was greeted by the sight of the injured soldiers transfixed to the ground. The unfortunate men who had been treating them had also been hit. Now they would die too. Still uninjured, Darius was standing nearby, with his guard holding a discarded *scutum* over both their heads. Both their horses had been struck by arrows and were charging wildly around the inside of the fortlet. Not for long, thought Romulus grimly. The *scythicon* would already be pumping through their veins.

He darted over. 'A word if I may, sir?'

'What is it?' demanded Darius irritably. He looked harassed and angry.

'We must retreat, sir,' he blurted. 'At once.'

The bodyguard snorted with derision.

Darius was more tolerant. 'Just as it's about to get dark?' Then the senior centurion saw that Romulus was deadly serious. His actions bordered on insubordination, but Darius valued his men, especially this one.

Unlike the other Parthian officers, he did not instantly punish all wrong-doers. 'Do you know what temperature it drops to out here?' he cried. 'We'd all freeze.'

'Perhaps, sir.' Romulus swallowed, but his stare did not waver. 'But waiting until the morning will be even worse.'

Darius glanced back at the strong walls of the fortlet. It was a good position to defend for one night. With their grisly contents, no one would sleep in the blood-soaked barracks, but huddled by blazing fires under the shelter of the ramparts, his men would survive well enough until dawn. 'Why?'

Romulus saw him look. 'More Scythians are on their way, sir. A lot more.'

Darius stared at him, perplexed. Yet this legionary had seen the rider behind the patrol. And he was Tarquinius' protégé. 'How do you know?'

'I have seen it in the sky.'

The guard hissed with disapproval.

Darius' dark eyes bored into Romulus. 'What exactly did you see?'

'A large host on the march. Soldiers carrying torches to light the way,' revealed Romulus. 'Squadrons of horse archers and companies of infantry. Armoured cavalry.'

Darius frowned. It was uncommon for armies to travel by night. Most men were too superstitious to do so: it was the time when demons and evil spirits were abroad.

Romulus pointed at the enemy riders, who had pulled back for a rest. 'They're just delaying us, sir. Until the others arrive.'

Now the stout Parthian scowled. He was one of the few senior centurions who had bothered to learn any Latin and could understand Tarquinius; he had a great deal of respect for the haruspex, even though he was a foreigner. But it seemed ridiculous that the young man standing before him could possess the same mystical ability. Romulus was a soldier, not a soothsayer. 'Don't think I'm not grateful to you for spotting the Scythian, lad,' Darius growled. 'Your action saved many lives.'

Flushing, Romulus ducked his head.

'But you actually saw that warrior earlier,' the Parthian went on. 'Whereas these others are a figment of your imagination.'

He began to protest.

Darius' face hardened. 'Scythians do not move during the hours of darkness. Or make large-scale attacks in wintertime.'

'What about the attack at the Mithraeum?' Romulus countered. 'Sir.'

Darius' eyes bulged with anger at the other's confidence.

'Mithras showed me the Scythians,' said Romulus, risking everything. 'I prayed to him and he answered.'

'How dare you?' the Parthian snarled. 'Only initiates may worship Mithras, you insolent dog.'

His guard laid a hand to his sword.

Romulus hung his head. He had failed. Despite his friendly manner, their senior centurion was just another Parthian.

'Consider yourself lucky not to be whipped. Or worse,' Darius snapped. 'Resume your position.'

The guard smirked.

Hiding his anger, Romulus stalked back to his place in the front rank. The fool, he thought. Darius was blinded by his refusal to admit that his god might favour a non-Parthian. Yet Romulus felt sure that was where his vision had come from.

'Keep your damn mouth shut too,' Darius called out. 'Not a word to anyone.'

Under his shield nearby, Novius sniggered unpleasantly. To Romulus' disappointment, none of the veterans had been hit. Even if they survived the Scythian attack, he still had them to contend with.

Brennus' reaction surprised Romulus. Instead of being furious, as he was, his friend simply shrugged.

'The Scythian reinforcements will outnumber us more than ten to one,' Romulus said.

'We can't avoid our fate,' replied Brennus solemnly. *A day when your friends need you. A time to stand and fight. No one could win such a battle. Except Brennus.* Would tomorrow be that day?

Romulus suspected he knew the reason behind Brennus' calm. Ever since Tarquinius had revealed the druid's prediction to the Gaul, he had secretly worried about losing his friend here, in Margiana. Mithras had shown Tarquinius that there was a road back to Rome. But was it for all three of them? His stomach knotted, Romulus considered the sky once more. What he had seen had changed utterly. The cloud patterns, wind speed and birds visible now made no sense at all. Perhaps he and Brennus would die here, while Tarquinius survived? Romulus' head spun until it hurt. He heartily wished that the haruspex were with them, to provide guidance. But he wasn't. For all they knew, he could be dead. An idea surfaced. 'We could make a run for it tonight,' he muttered. 'Just the two of us.'

'Back to the fort?' asked Brennus. 'We'd be executed for desertion.'

Romulus dared not vocalise it. He had been thinking of heading south, towards the coast. Shame filled him that he could have even thought of leaving Tarquinius behind. Like Brennus, the haruspex had taught him so much.

'Trust in the gods,' said Brennus, clapping him on the shoulder. 'They know best.'

But Mithras might be playing with me, thought Romulus. Punishing a non-initiate for daring to worship him. What better way to do that than show a man his doom? Romulus' guts twisted with worry again as he remembered the Scythian host in his vision.

'And don't get hit by an arrow.'

He grimaced at the Gaul's bleak humour.

Brennus was not finished. 'Look around you,' he commanded.

Romulus obeyed, taking in the set faces of the legionaries all around them. There was fear there, but also a steely determination. No names or insults were being called now. Unlike Novius and his cronies, these were men who would stand and fight with him and Brennus, to the end if necessary. Even if they no longer thought it themselves, they were his brothers-in-arms.

That counted for a lot.

Romulus clenched his jaw.

In response, he got an almighty nudge. 'That's the spirit.'

He gave Brennus a grateful smile.

The pair settled down to watch the Scythians, many of whom had now dismounted. Occasionally an eager warrior would gallop in close to the Roman lines and release a few arrows, but the rest seemed content to keep the status quo. Using brushwood, some had even started fires. Darkness was beginning to fall and the air was chilling rapidly. It would not be long before the temperature dropped far below freezing. Knowing this, Darius withdrew his men inside the fortlet and closed the gate. Once sentries were in place on the ramparts and fires had been started, there was not much else to be done. Dawn would decide their fate.

Few men slept well. Knowing what lay in the nearby barracks didn't help. Neither did the piercing cold, which was just kept at bay by the fires and their woollen blankets. Nightmares, numb fingers and toes were inevitable, as were aching, painful muscles. But they were warm enough to stay alive. That was all the legionaries needed.

Romulus lay awake for hours, while beside him the Gaul snored loudly. Brennus had offered to keep watch, but the young soldier was so wound up that he had refused. Eventually weariness began to get the better of him though, and his lids slowly closed. He plunged straight into a nightmare that played out his vision of Rome again in horrifying detail. Mobs of armed plebeians and gladiators ran hither and thither, attacking anyone in sight. Bodies lay scattered in crimson piles. Swords rose and fell; men clutched at gaping wounds. Screams competed with the clash of metal on metal and the air was filled with smoke. Flames licked up the sides of the Senate building itself. Finally Romulus saw Fabiola. Surrounded by a few body-guards, his twin was caught up in the midst of it. Her face was terrified.

His body covered in a cold sweat, Romulus' eyes jerked open. The images had been terrifyingly vivid. Was Mithras playing another cruel trick on him? Was it just a dream? Or was it real?

He stiffened. There was movement nearby.

It was not Brennus: he still lay alongside, deeply asleep.

Careful not to lose his night vision by looking at the embers of the fire, Romulus turned his head. The small movement saved his life. With a great leap, Optatus landed on top of him, stabbing at his face with an arrow. Romulus grabbed the burly veteran's arms – a reflex action – and they rolled over, struggling for control of the shaft.

Starlight revealed a dark liquid coating the arrow's hooked point and terror constricted Romulus' throat. It was a Scythian arrow. And Optatus was far stronger than he.

Chapter VIII: Despair

Rome, winter 53/52 BC

With leering faces, the *fugitivarii* shuffled closer.

Sextus dodged forward, trying to gut one of them with his spear. His attempt failed; instead he just missed losing an arm to a cut from a shrewdly wielded sword. Such daring moves were too risky, so he and Fabiola moved back to back. It made little difference. At once their enemies began to encircle them.

Fabiola's heart sank. The narrow street was deserted. Even if there had been someone about, who would intervene against such determined lowlife? Rome had no official force to keep the peace. The natural result of this was surely the rioting in the Forum Romanum. Fabiola cursed. What had she been thinking, to leave the safety of the house earlier? After his previous humiliation at her hands, Scaevola would be less than merciful. And there was nowhere to flee.

Not that Fabiola would run. That was what cowards did.

A sudden rush by the thugs and it was all over. Fabiola managed to bury her blade in the thigh of one, and Sextus to pierce the throat of another, but the remainder swarmed in, knocking the pair to the ground in a flurry of blows. As Fabiola struggled to rise, a sword hilt connected with her head. She collapsed, semi-conscious. Sextus was less lucky, suffering a heavy beating before being trussed up like a hen for the pot. But he was not killed. Scaevola had seen how good the injured slave was with a weapon. Selling him to a gladiator school would be most profitable.

The *fugitivarii* clustered eagerly around Fabiola, lustful eyes drinking in her beauty.

'Get her up,' Scaevola ordered.

His order was obeyed instantly. With a strong arm under each of hers, Fabiola found herself hanging between two of the biggest men. Head lolling to one side, her long black hair fell over her face.

The chief *fugitivarius* grabbed a handful of Fabiola's tresses. With a brutal tug upwards, he revealed her stunning features.

Fabiola moaned in pain and opened her eyes.

'Lady,' said Scaevola with a cruel smile. 'We meet again. And your lover's still not here to protect you.'

She looked at him with utter scorn.

'He wasn't at the *latifundium* either,' said the *fugitivarius* regretfully. 'We came looking for you both the day after you'd left for Rome. Didn't we, lads?'

His men growled in acknowledgement.

Seeing her eyes widen, Scaevola smiled cruelly. 'Warned you, didn't I? Nobody crosses me without getting paid back.'

Fabiola struggled to keep her voice even. 'What did you do?'

'Attacked just before dawn. It's the best time,' he revealed with delight. 'Killed your pet gladiators. Torched the buildings and took all your slaves to sell on. Best of the lot, though, we recaptured the fugitive I'd been chasing. Naturally, he had to be punished.' There was a pause. 'They say that gelded men make good servants for women.'

Fabiola could not take in the devastating horror of it all. 'Corbulo?' she pleaded.

Scaevola was saving the worst for last. 'The old bastard was stubborn,' he said admiringly. 'Most fools talk quickly with their feet in a fire. Not him. Wasn't until we broke his arms and legs that he started talking.'

'No!' Fabiola screamed, trying to break free. 'Corbulo had done nothing.'

'He knew where you were,' responded the *fugitivarius*. 'That was enough.'

'You'll all rot in Hades for this,' Fabiola spat, tears running down her cheeks. 'And Brutus will send you there.'

Scaevola made a face. 'I can't see him anywhere. Can anyone else?'

Chuckling, his men shook their heads.

'Shame. We'll have to hunt down the whoreson later. The only good supporter of Caesar is a dead one.'

Fabiola was dumbstruck. *What have I done to deserve this, great Jupiter?*

'So it's just us, I'm afraid,' Scaevola said teasingly. Letting go of her hair, he took hold of the neck of her dress with both hands and tore it to the waist.

The view this allowed drew gasps from his followers.

Used to men seeing her naked, Fabiola ignored them. But her inner rage knew no bounds.

On the ground beside them, Sextus writhed uselessly.

Looking into her eyes, Scaevola caressed her full breasts. 'Like that?' he whispered.

The young woman did not give him the dignity of a reply. But real terror was now growing inside her.

His hand dropped, stroking her flat belly. It was all Fabiola could do not to pull away, but she knew that would only increase the chief *fugitivarius*' enjoyment. Next her torn dress was pulled off completely and dropped into the bloody mud. Fabiola's underclothes followed. The two thugs holding her shifted from foot to foot, peering at her beautiful body.

Scaevola's own eyes widened at the sight. 'Like Venus herself,' he breathed. A meaty hand reached down and cupped her groin. 'But this one you can fuck.'

Despite herself, Fabiola tensed. His touch brought back memories of Gemellus, the merchant who had owned her entire family, and of other unsavoury clients in the brothel.

The *fugitivarius* grinned and pushed a finger inside her.

It was too much for Fabiola. Surprising those restraining her, she managed to free her right arm. Raking Scaevola's cheek with her long fingernails, she left four deep gouges in his flesh. More shocked than badly hurt, he reeled backwards, spitting curses. She had no further chance to injure him; the thugs quickly manhandled her back under control. Against their strength, Fabiola could do little. It was best to conserve her energy for another opportunity. Her struggles subsided and stopped.

With blood running unchecked down on to his neck, Scaevola moved to stand before her once more. 'Quite the vixen, eh?' he said, panting. 'I like my women like that.'

This time, she spat at him.

He responded with a solid punch to Fabiola's solar plexus which drove all the air from her lungs. Stars burst across her vision and her knees folded, unable to take her weight. She had never known pain like it.

'Let her fall,' she heard the *fugitivarius* say. 'I'll take the bitch right here.'

Obediently the men released Fabiola's arms, and she toppled down on top of her torn dress. Standing back, they left their chief to it. It clearly wasn't the first time that this had happened.

Lifting his chain mail and tunic with a grin, Scaevola freed his erection from his *licium*, his undergarment. He moved closer, greedily eyeing the neat triangle of hair at the top of her thighs. Sexual violence was part of his job, and Fabiola was more beautiful than any slave he'd ever raped. He was going to enjoy this.

Dazedly, Fabiola looked up. Nausea washed over her and she struggled hard not to vomit. This would be worse than any of the sex she had endured as a prostitute. Those men had at least paid to be with her and, in an expensive brothel, the vast majority had never offered any violence. The threat of Vettius and Benignus was enough protection for Jovina's women. At that moment, Fabiola would have given all the money she possessed to see the pair of huge doormen appear.

Instead, she was totally alone.

Fresh tears pricked her eyes, but Fabiola quelled them ruthlessly. Self-pity would make what was about to happen far worse. The most important thing to do now was survive. Simply survive. She shuddered in anticipation.

Scaevola dropped to his knees and shoved her legs apart. Taking his time, the *fugitivarius* caressed the inside of her thighs, laughing at the goose bumps of fear this caused. Half stunned and incapable of resisting further, Fabiola's revulsion was still apparent.

His men gathered round, keen to see everything.

Scaevola could control himself no longer. With an animal grunt, he moved closer. The tip of his erection nudged forward, searching.

Fabiola turned her head away so she did not have to look at his face. This was what her mother had endured for years. If she could do it, so could her daughter.

At that exact moment, the thought did not make things any easier.

Shame filled Fabiola. After he had finished, Scaevola would let his men rape her as well, before one of them cut her throat. Then her body would be left like so much meat, among the others who had died. Trying to save the young slave who had run on to her *latifundium* had been reckless, yet somehow it still felt right. Not responding would have denied all that Fabiola was, all that she had come from. Sooner or later Scaevola would have attacked her property anyway, searching for Brutus.

The *fugitivarius* grabbed Fabiola's chin in a grip of iron and twisted her face towards his. Dark, murderous eyes bored into her. His foul breath made her gag. 'Look at me while I fuck you,' he muttered, leaning in to lick her breasts. 'Dirty whore.'

Finally, a sob escaped Fabiola. This was far worse than she could have imagined. She managed to wrench her face away again.

Between the legs of the men standing above her, there was a sudden blur of movement from the alleyway. No one else noticed. Totally engrossed by the rape, none of the thugs were looking anywhere but at her. Amazingly, Fabiola saw armed figures spilling silently on to the street. All were dressed similarly in faded, patched military tunics and battered chain mail. The occasional *phalera* decorated a chest. Bronze bowl helmets with upright horsehair plumes covered every man's head. Carrying *gladii* and elongated, oval *scuta*, they advanced in a solid wall. These could only be ex-legionaries: men who really knew how to fight. And they did not look as if they were here on friendly business.

Fabiola's mouth opened in astonishment.

Mistaking her reaction for one of fear, Scaevola laughed and prepared to enter her.

Far too late, his men realised that something was wrong.

Loud thumps rang out as heavy shield bosses slammed into the nearest ones' backs, knocking them off balance. These were followed by ruthless sword blows that pierced bellies and opened chests to the air. Many of the thugs were killed in the initial attack and chaos reigned as the remainder struggled to understand what had happened. Without speaking, the veterans pressed forward, herding the *fugitivarii* together, like sheep to the slaughter, merciless in the face of their enemies' confusion. This was something they had done countless times before.

Shouts of terror rang out as the surviving ruffians realised there would be no escape.

The chief *fugitivarius* cursed and pulled back from Fabiola's groin.

His erection totally vanished, he fumbled frantically to put himself back in his underclothes. If he didn't get up off the ground, he'd be dead very soon. Stumbling to his feet, Scaevola joined the fight.

Fabiola watched as one of the veterans tackled a heavily built thug who was armed with a short sword and dagger. Ducking down, he drove his gilded shield boss upwards at his opponent's face, forcing the man to lift his chin away in reflex and expose his throat. The classic move was followed by a swift *gladius* thrust. Blood ran down the straight iron blade in great streams. The *fugitivarius* was dead before the blade even pulled free, letting him fall to the ground.

Fabiola used the opportunity to pull on the remnants of her dress, partially covering her nudity. She picked up a discarded sword, ready to fight before anyone else laid a hand on her.

'Mistress! Cut me free.'

She turned in surprise. Sextus was lying a few paces away, still tied up. Fabiola crept over, quickly slicing through his bonds.

Nodding his thanks, the injured slave grabbed the nearest weapon, which was an axe with a notched blade.

They huddled together, waiting for the battle to end.

It did not take long. Surprised and outnumbered, the surviving thugs did not put up much resistance. Although used to fighting together, they usually only faced terrified, half-starved slaves: easy to intimidate and even easier to overcome. Several threw down their weapons and pleaded for mercy. It got them nothing more than a swifter death. Veteran of a score of skirmishes, Scaevola realised that the game was up. Spinning on his heel, he shoved one of his own men out of the way with an impatient cry. He bounded backwards, towards the Forum. Despite the rioting, he had more chance of escaping with his life there than here with his followers.

His eyes met Fabiola's.

Time stopped.

Full of bitter rage, the squat *fugitivarius* mouthed a curse at her. She did the same. Stung by her defiance, he lunged forward, *gladius* in hand. And was met by Sextus, swinging his axe.

Scaevola skidded to a halt. 'Curse you to Hades,' he spat before sprinting off up the street.

Overcome by terror and nervous exhaustion, Fabiola sank down into the mud. Sextus moved to stand protectively over her, his one eye bright with battle rage. As the last thugs fell, the veterans closed in on them and Sextus turned this way and that, waving his axe at any who came within range.

Fabiola closed her eyes. Their rescuers might prove to be nothing more than another group of would-be rapists. But they did not move any closer. Heavy *scuta* clattered on to the ground when they were done. Without speaking, the men took a brief rest, chests heaving, sword arms reddened. Killing was tiring work.

When nothing happened, Fabiola got to her feet, the rags of her dress clutched around her. Unshaven faces regarded her admiringly. Silently. And not one man moved. She did not know how to react. Neither did Sextus.

Finally one of the veterans surrounding them gave a shrill whistle. To Fabiola's utter surprise, Secundus emerged from the alleyway. A parting appeared in the circle, allowing him to approach. 'Lady,' he said, inclining his head.

Fabiola tried to be bold. 'You have my thanks,' she said, rewarding him with a beaming smile.

'What happened?'

'We were escaping the rioting,' Fabiola explained. 'And they ambushed us. They were going to . . . He nearly . . .' The words dried in her throat.

'You're safe now,' muttered Secundus, patting her arm.

She nodded jerkily, her emotions still in turmoil. Although Secundus seemed sympathetic, not every veteran's face was friendly.

Secundus regarded the nearest corpse with contempt. 'To think that we fought for fuckers like this, eh?'

It was a valid point. Since time immemorial, Roman soldiers had fought and died for their countrymen's sake. Meanwhile, other men robbed, raped and killed citizens on the streets of Rome.

'This ambush was planned,' Fabiola revealed. She filled Secundus in, blaming the attack by Scaevola and his crew on the fact that she and Brutus were supporters of Caesar. She made no mention of the young fugitive who had been the reason they met. Few would understand why anyone would want to intervene on behalf of a slave.

'Well, the scumbag's gone now,' said Secundus reassuringly when she had finished. 'He won't be back in a hurry. Most of his men are dead.'

Feeling calmer, Fabiola gazed down the alleyway. Like the Forum, it was now littered with bodies. A few thugs were still alive, but not for long. Secundus' men moved expertly among them, slitting throats and checking for money pouches. It was not pleasant to witness, but they deserved no better, she thought.

Wary of the violence in the Forum, Secundus began calling the veterans back. 'This is no place to linger, lady,' he said, ushering her towards the alleyway. Like a faithful hound, Sextus followed.

'Do you often intervene like this?' she asked.

He shrugged. 'From time to time.'

Fabiola was surprised. 'But why?'

Secundus laughed. 'It's hard to give up army life after ten years or more, lady. About fifty or sixty of us keep in touch; we like to keep the area fairly peaceable. Can't stop what's going on in the Forum, but this, we can. It's easy for us, being trained soldiers and all. And it pleases Mithras.'

Fabiola was confused by the reference. 'Your god?'

He regarded her steadily. 'Indeed, lady. The soldiers' god.'

She and Sextus owed their lives not just to Jupiter, but to an unknown deity. Fabiola was intrigued. 'I would like to offer my thanks,' she said.

'At the Mithraeum, lady?' he asked. 'Unfortunately not.'

Unused to being refused, Fabiola bridled. 'Why?'

'You're a woman. Only men may enter our temple.'

'I see.'

Secundus coughed awkwardly. 'It's not safe round here, though.' The noise of fighting could still be heard from the Forum. 'It would be permissible for you to wait in the anterooms. Tomorrow, when it is safer, we can escort you back to your *domus*.'

'My slave comes too.' She indicated Sextus.

'Of course,' he said sympathetically. 'Our medical orderly can treat his wound.'

Some of the veterans looked less than happy at Secundus' offer of shelter and treatment.

'Why are you helping me?' Fabiola asked.

There was another shy grin. 'You gave me an *aureus*, remember?'

The best money I ever spent, thought Fabiola. 'Strange that our paths should cross again so soon,' she said.

'The gods work in such ways, lady,' Secundus replied.

'They do,' she agreed passionately.

Leaving the dead sprawled uncaring in the mud, Secundus led them off through a series of narrow yet empty thoroughfares. His companions split up, some walking protectively in front, some behind. Despite their reservations about Fabiola and her slave, all kept their swords drawn and eyes peeled for more trouble. But there was no one else about. All of Clodius' and Milo's men had descended on the Forum and the noise of the rioting alone was enough to make any ordinary citizens remaining indoors stay where they were. Doors were shut and shop windows barred. Street fountains splashed noisily, unattended. There were no plebeian women collecting water in clay vessels or washing their clothes. The public toilets were empty of gossiping neighbours and urchins selling vinegar-soaked sponges on sticks. Rickety wooden stalls that would typically be displaying bread, pottery, ironmongery and simple foodstuffs stood forlorn and bare. Even the begging lepers and the familiar scavenging mongrels were nowhere to be seen. An occasional scared face peered from half-open shuttered windows above, but these slammed shut if any of the party looked up. It was an eerie feeling to move through the city unimpeded by traffic or throngs of people. Rome was normally a hive of human activity from dawn till dusk.

Not today.

After they had been climbing for a little while, the sounds of violence gradually began to diminish.

'This is the Palatine,' Fabiola exclaimed in surprise.

Secundus threw her a crooked smile. 'Expected us to be based on the Aventine or Caelian Hills, did you?'

Fabiola flushed at his accurate guess. Most of the Palatine's residents were wealthy, unlike the ragged, unshaven figures surrounding her.

'Soldiers are the true spirit of Rome,' he said proudly. There was a growl of agreement from the others. 'We belong here, at its ancient heart.'

Fabiola bent her head in respect. After all, legionaries were the men who fought and died for the Republic. Although she had little love for it, she could respect these veterans' bravery and the sacrifices they had made in its name. One only had to see the stump of Secundus' sword arm and the multitude of old scars on all the ex-soldiers to realise that. Flesh had been hacked off, blood lost and comrades slain, while the rich who dwelled around here had given little, if anything, for their state.

Working his way along a high, plain wall, Secundus came to a halt before a small door, its surface reinforced with protective iron studs. A simply forged knocker and a metal plate around the keyhole made it look the same as the back entrance to any other decent-sized house in the city. If they could afford it, Romans preferred to live in a well-built *domus*, a private, hollow square with an open air courtyard in the middle and rooms around the sides. The exterior of these dwellings was usually entirely ordinary, designed to avoid attention. Inside, they could be luxurious, like that of Brutus, or garish in the extreme, as Gemullus' had been.

Checking there was no one in sight, Secundus rapped on the timbers with his knuckles.

Instantly a challenge issued from the other side.

Secundus leaned in close and muttered a few words.

His answer was sufficient. There was a short delay as bolts were thrown back and then the door swung inwards on silent, oiled hinges. Framed in the portal was a powerfully built figure in a russet-brown military tunic, carrying a drawn *gladius*. With close-cropped hair and a scar running from his right ear to his chin, this had to be another ex-soldier.

Recognising Secundus, he sheathed his sword and thumped his clenched right fist off his chest in salute.

Returning the gesture, Secundus led the way into the *atrium*.

Fabiola and Sextus were close behind, followed by the rest of the group. The guard's eyes narrowed at the sight of the two strangers, one a woman, the other grievously wounded, but he said nothing. As the last man entered, the portal shut with a quiet click, blocking out the daylight. With the doors to the *tablinum* closed, the only illumination in the wide hallway running from left to right was from oil lamps in regularly placed wall brackets. Flickering yellow flames lit up a number of brightly painted statues, the most prominent of which was a cloaked deity crouched over a reclining bull. Shadows cast by his Phrygian cap prevented the god's face from being seen, but the dagger in his right hand showed clear intent. Like all animals in shrines, the massive ox was about to be sacrificed.

'Mithras,' announced Secundus reverently. 'The Father.'

As one, his men bowed their heads.

Feeling more than a little fear, Fabiola shivered. Although they had only entered the first chamber in the building, there was more power palpable here than in the *cellae* at the great temple on the Capitoline Hill. If she was lucky, and Mithras willing, some information about Romulus might be revealed. Unlike the falsehoods uttered by the soothsayers and the uncertainties found inside temples, a sign given in a place like this might carry divine authority. Fabiola snapped back to the present. Do not lose focus, she thought. There would be time to pray later. Bowing respectfully to the sculpture, she indicated Sextus' gaping, ruined eye. 'He needs treatment,' she said.

Her slave had not uttered a single word of complaint thus far, but his teeth were gritted in pain. The adrenalin rush of combat had subsided and now waves of pain were radiating outwards, filling his skull with thousands of stabbing needles.

Secundus pointed to their left. 'The *valetudinarium* is down here.'

'Who owns the house?' Fabiola asked. This was a far cry from the type of accommodation most citizens could afford.

'Better than an army barracks, eh?' laughed Secundus. 'It belonged to a legate, lady. One of us.'

She frowned. 'Belonged?'

'Poor bastard was thrown from his horse two years ago,' he answered. 'Left no family either.'

'And you seized his property?' It was not unheard of for this to happen. In the current uncertain political climate, those who acted with confidence often got away with totally illegal acts. It was how Clodius and Milo had conducted their business for years.

He regarded her sternly. 'We're veterans, not thieves, lady.'

'Of course,' Fabiola muttered. 'I'm sorry.'

'The *domus* belongs to Mithras now,' he said simply.

'So you live here?'

'We have that privilege,' Secundus answered. 'This is the most hallowed ground in Rome. It has to be protected.'

Leaving his men and the statue of Mithras behind, Secundus took them along the corridor and around what would be the corner of the central courtyard. Beneath their feet was a simple but well-laid mosaic, its pattern the typical Roman concentric circles, waves and swirls. Few of the many rooms they passed seemed to be occupied, their open doors often revealing bare walls and floors, devoid of furniture.

Secundus finally came to a halt before a chamber which smelt strongly of vinegar, the main cleaning agent used by Roman surgeons. 'Janus!' he cried.

Ushering Sextus in, Fabiola entered the *valetudinarium*, the soldiers' hospital. As she would learn later, it was laid out just as it would have been inside a tent in a marching camp. A low desk near the doorway formed the reception area. On a wall behind were wooden shelves covered with rolls of calfskin, pots, beakers and metal instruments. Open chests on the floor were full of rolled blankets and dressings. Neat lines of low cots lined the back of the large room. All were unoccupied. Near them stood a battered table surrounded by a number of oil lamps on crudely fashioned iron stands. Thick ropes hung from each of its legs and while clean, its surface was covered in dark, circular stains. They looked rather like old blood.

Standing up from his leather stool in the corner, a thin-faced man wearing a worn military tunic decorated with two *phalerae* bowed his head courteously at Fabiola. Like all the soldiers, he wore a belt and a sheathed dagger. The studs of his *caligae* clashed gently off the floor as he approached.

Respect filled Fabiola. Every single one of Secundus' men might initially look like a vagrant, but they all carried themselves with a quiet dignity. 'What's that?' she asked, nodding at the table.

'The operating theatre,' replied the brown-haired medical orderly.

Fabiola's stomach clenched at the thought of being tied down and cut open.

Janus ushered Sextus towards it. 'An arrow?' His voice was low, authoritative.

'Yes,' muttered the slave, bending his head to allow a proper examination. 'I pulled it out myself.'

Janus clicked his tongue disapprovingly, his fingers already probing the area for further damage.

Secundus saw Fabiola's surprise. 'The barbs scrape off flesh as they come out. Makes a ragged and very distinctive wound,' he explained. 'Knives or swords come out more cleanly.'

She winced. *Romulus!*

'In the legions we see them all, lady,' Secundus murmured. 'War is a savage business.'

Her composure cracked even more.

Secundus grew concerned. 'What is it?'

For some reason, Fabiola felt unable to conceal the truth. The gods had brought Secundus into her life twice in just a few days; as a veteran, he would understand. 'My brother was at Carrhae,' she explained.

He shot her a surprised glance. 'How did that come to pass? Did he belong to Crassus?'

Of course, he knew her past: that she had been a slave. Fabiola peered anxiously at Janus and Sextus, but they were out of earshot. The orderly had made her slave lie down on the table and was cleaning the blood from his face with a wet cloth. 'No. He escaped from the Ludus Magnus and joined the army.'

'A slave in the legions?' barked Secundus. 'That's forbidden, on pain of death.'

Romulus had not been discovered and executed for that reason, thought Fabiola. As crafty as she, her twin would have found a way. 'He was with a Gaul,' she went on. 'A champion gladiator.'

'I see,' the veteran answered thoughtfully. 'Might have joined a mercenary cohort then. They're not as picky.'

'Romulus was a brave man,' Fabiola snapped, bridling at his words. 'As good as any damn legionary.'

'My words were hasty,' he admitted, colouring. 'If he is like you, he must have had the heart of a lion.'

Unwilling to let it go, Fabiola pointed at Sextus. 'Look! He's a slave. Yet he fought for me when badly wounded. So did the others, before they were killed.'

Secundus lifted his hands in a placating gesture. 'I am not what you think.' He looked her in the eyes. 'Slaves are permitted to worship Mithras. With us, as equals.'

It was Fabiola's turn to feel embarrassed. Secundus was not then like the majority of citizens, who regarded slaves as little better than animals. Even manumission did not completely remove the stain: by now, she was well used to the patronising stares given her by many nobles who knew her past. Fabiola sincerely hoped that any children the gods might grant her would not suffer the same discrimination. 'What do you mean?'

'Our religion's main tenets are truth, honour and courage. Those are qualities anyone can possess, whether they are a consul or a low-born slave. Mithras sees all men in the same light, as brothers.'

It was an alien and incredible concept; one Fabiola had never heard of. Naturally, it appealed to her immensely. In Rome, slaves were permitted to worship the gods, but the idea of recognising them as equals to their masters was unthinkable. Their position in society remained the same: the very bottom. The only people who could perhaps have changed that, the well-fed priests and acolytes in the city's temples, were no more than mouthpieces of the state: they never expressed such revolutionary thoughts. That might upset the status quo, which allowed an elite class of tens of thousands, as well as the ordinary citizens, to rule over hundreds of times that number of slaves. To hear that a god – a warrior god – could see past the stigma of slavery was truly amazing.

Fabiola's gaze lifted to that of Secundus. 'What about women?' she asked. 'Can we join?'

'No,' he answered. 'It is not permitted.'

'Why not?'

Secundus' jaw hardened at her audacity. 'We are soldiers. Women are not.'

'I fought today,' she said hotly.

'It's not the same, lady,' he snapped. 'Do not presume too much on our hospitality.'

Chapter IX: Omens

Margiana, winter 53/52 BC

Illness had aged Pacorus considerably. The normal healthy colour of his brown skin had still not returned. In its place was a pale waxy sheen, which accentuated his sunken cheeks and the new grey streaks in his hair. The Parthian had lost a huge amount of weight, and clothes which had fitted him well now hung loosely on his bony frame. But, remarkably, he was alive. It was a minor miracle. Despite the high fevers that had racked his body and the foul, yellow poisonous liquids which had repeatedly erupted from his wounds, Pacorus had not succumbed. *Scythicon* did not kill every man, it seemed. But it was not just his tough nature: all of the haruspex' skill and another dose of the precious *mantar* had gone into his recovery.

And the help of Mithras, thought Tarquinius, eyeing the little statue on the altar in the corner. He had spent many hours on his knees before it, making sure when possible that the commander saw him. Half-delirious still, Pacorus had been susceptible to his muttered words and consequently overcome by devotion to his god. With little prompting, he rambled about some of the secret rituals practised by the Parthians in their Mithraeum. The haruspex listened eagerly, picking up valuable pieces of information. He knew now that the statue depicted Mithras in the cave of his birth, slaying the primeval bull. By performing the tauroctony, the god released its life force for the benefit of mankind. Like all killings, the sacred rite did not come without a price, which explained why Mithras was looking away from the bull's head as he plunged his knife into its throat.

Tarquinius had discovered that among the stages of initiation were those of raven, soldier, lion, sun-runner and the most senior, the father. Pacorus had hinted that interpretation of the stars was critically important, as was self-knowledge and improvement. Mithras was symbolised in the sky by the Perseus constellation and the bull by that of Taurus. Frustrating Tarquinius, the Parthian had said little else. Even severe illness was not enough to make him reveal any meaningful Mithraic secrets.

Tarquinius knew that there might be few chances to learn more. Although the commander had come back from the brink, he was by no means fully recovered. And rather than subsiding, Vahram's threats had sharply increased. He could see what was being done for Pacorus, and because of it the squat *primus pilus* had formed a personal grievance against Tarquinius. There could be only one reason for this, the haruspex decided. Vahram wanted Pacorus to die, thereby relinquishing command of the Forgotten Legion to him.

This was a possibility that filled Tarquinius with dread. Vahram was bull-headed and far less susceptible to his influence than many men. Yet, like most, he was swayed by superstition. Wary of Tarquinius and the reaction of his warriors, he did not yet feel secure enough to murder Pacorus out of hand. Vahram wanted a guarantee that his plans would not backfire. Every day, he badgered the haruspex for information. Busying himself with the preparation of medication and the changing of Pacorus' dressings, Tarquinius skilfully avoided giving Vahram anything other than a polite fob-off. Their commander's now frequent lucid moments also helped to prevent interrogations.

The *primus pilus'* anger grew steadily but he confined himself to taunts about Romulus and Brennus. Knowing that the two men were very dear to Tarquinius, Vahram used doubts about their safety as a way of intimidating the normally imperturbable haruspex. Verbal abuse rained down on his head and Tarquinius was powerless to resist. In this precarious situation, Vahram was simply too dangerous to cross.

Tarquinius hated having no idea how his friends were doing. All his guards had been threatened with dire punishments if they said a word. Combined with their deep-seated fear of his abilities, it meant that the haruspex lived in virtual solitude. Even the servants were too frightened to speak with him. Yet the silence was not as troubling as the isolation. Tarquinius thrived on knowledge of what was going on, and now he was being denied any.

The patch of sky over Pacorus' courtyard rarely afforded much information: apart from the occasional snowstorm, there simply wasn't enough to see. He had no hens or lambs to sacrifice either. Without realising it, Vahram had curtailed Tarquinius' capacity to prophesy. Virtually the only method left was to study the fire in Pacorus' bedroom. This was best done very late, when the commander was sleeping and the servants and guards had retired for the night. Letting the logs burn down to mere embers occasionally provided some useful snippets. Frustratingly, the haruspex could see little that referred to his friends. Or his own prospects. This was the random and infuriating nature of prophecy: to reveal little when it seemed important, and much when it did not. Sometimes it disclosed nothing at all. Tarquinius' doubts about himself resurfaced with a vengeance.

After giving Pacorus his last medicine of the evening, it had become his ritual to hurry to the brick fireplace in the room. No chance to divine could be missed. Tarquinius was now desperate to know something – anything – about the future. It was perhaps this eagerness that caused the slip in his normal attention to detail one night. The instant that the Parthian commander's lids closed in sleep, Tarquinius tiptoed away from the bed. But he forgot to bolt the door.

Squatting on his haunches by the fire, he sighed with anticipation. Tonight would be different. He could feel it in his bones.

There was one large log still burning. Surrounded by the charred shapes of others, it was glowing a deep red-orange colour. Tarquinius studied it carefully for a long time. The smouldering wood was dry and well-seasoned, with few knots: just the type he liked.

It was time.

An all-too-familiar feeling took hold. Recognising it as fear, Tarquinius gritted his teeth. This could not go on. He inhaled deeply, then again. Feeling calmer, he reached down for a poker and tapped the piece of timber with it. His action released a torrent of sparks. They wafted up the chimney in lazy streams, singly and in groups. The smallest went out very quickly, but bigger ones continued to glow as they were carried upwards by the hot air. The haruspex' pupils constricted as he studied their pattern, counting his pulse to judge the time each took to disappear.

At last, an image of Romulus.

Tarquinius' breath caught in his chest.

The young soldier looked troubled and unsure. Brennus was by his side, his normally jovial expression absent. Both were wearing their crested bronze helmets and dressed in full chain mail; their *scuta* were raised and a javelin was ready in each man's right fist. Plainly they were nowhere near the security of the fort. Around them, the scenery was unclear, any distinctive features covered in snow. There were other legionaries present too, at least one or two centuries.

Tarquinius frowned.

A fast-moving flash of red contrasted against the white landscape. Then another.

The shapes were gone before he could decide what they were. Battle standards? Horsemen? Or just his imagination? The haruspex was left with a lingering sense of unease. He leaned closer to the fire, concentrating hard.

And jerked back, repulsed.

A barrack-room floor awash with blood.

What did it mean?

The image disappeared as the log broke in half. Gentle crackling sounds rose as the two pieces fell. The fire's heart flared brighter as it seized control of the new fuel, and a new wave of sparks was released.

Tarquinius had long ago learned to let unclear, disturbing scenes go. Often they could not be interpreted at all, so there was little point in remaining anxious. He relaxed, pleased by the movement in the fireplace. There would be something useful in this. Lips moving silently, he focused his entire attention on what he was seeing.

A Parthian warrior sat astride a horse, which was panicking as an enraged elephant charged it. The man's face was turned away, so he could not be recognised. Behind him a battle raged between Roman legionaries and a dark-skinned enemy armed with all manner of strange weapons.

The haruspex was intrigued by the rider and the host's alien appearance. Intent on gaining an understanding of what was being shown, he did not hear the door open behind him.

'Vahram?' he muttered. 'Is it Vahram?'

'What sorcery are you up to?'

Tarquinius froze at the sound of the *primus pilus'* voice. The realisation that he had not locked the door crashed down on him. Complacency can kill, he thought grimly. It was something he had taught Romulus, yet here he was, doing the same himself. Without looking back, Tarquinius shoved the poker hard against the chunks of wood, pushing them down into the ash at the bottom of the fireplace. Starved of air, they would go out fast. No more sparks. 'I was just tending the fire,' he replied.

'Liar!' Vahram hissed. 'You said my name.'

Tarquinius stood and turned to face the *primus pilus*, who was accompanied by a trio of muscular warriors carrying spears. And ropes. Tonight, Vahram meant business. 'Pacorus will wake,' he said loudly, cursing the fact that he had not kept his thoughts silent.

'Leave him be.' Vahram smiled, but there was no humour in his face. 'We don't want to trouble him unnecessarily.'

He's making his move, thought the haruspex with alarm. And my comment has given him more ammunition. 'It's been a long day,' he said, raising his voice even further. 'Hasn't it, sir?'

Their commander did not move a muscle.

Tarquinius moved towards the bed, but Vahram blocked his way.

'Don't play it smart with me, you arrogant son of a whore!' The barrel-chested Parthian was incandescent with rage now. 'What did you see?'

'I told you,' answered Tarquinius earnestly, keen that the *primus pilus* should believe him. Who knew what he was really capable of? 'Nothing.'

Vahram went icy calm. Everyone in the whole camp knew that the haruspex was no charlatan. Pacorus and Tarquinius had both been careful not to tell anyone about the lack of results from his haruspicy. In the *primus pilus'* eyes, this was obstruction, pure and simple. 'Fine,' he said, his anger at last outweighing his fear. He snapped his fingers at the warriors. 'Tie him up.'

Tarquinius flinched.

Swiftly his wrists were bound together; a leather gag was wedged into his mouth and tied around the back of his head. Is this what was different about tonight? Tarquinius thought bitterly. There had been no inkling that this would happen. The thick cords tore at his flesh, breaking the skin, but he breathed into the pain, letting it wash over him. This was just the start. What was to come would be worse.

It was then that Pacorus stirred under his blankets. His eyes, heavy-lidded from the sleeping draught that Tarquinius had given him, opened.

Not totally confident in his authority, Vahram paused. His men did likewise.

The haruspex sent up a prayer to Mithras. *Wake up!*

Pacorus' lids closed again and he rolled over, turning his back to them.

The *primus pilus'* face twisted with pleasure and he jerked a thumb at the door.

Feeling incredibly weary, the haruspex let himself be dragged outside. Even Pacorus' guards had disappeared from their posts. The gods were in a cruel mood. There would be no easy divination tonight: just pain, and possibly death.

Initially, Vahram didn't even ask any questions. This was about revenge as well as information-gathering. He waited patiently as his men tied Tarquinius' wrists to an iron ring positioned high up on a pillar in the courtyard. Then he made a simple gesture with his hand. The beating that followed lasted for a long time. The three warriors changed places when their right arms grew tired from wielding the whip.

After a hundred lashes, Tarquinius lost count of the total. He lapsed in and out of consciousness, his tunic and flesh torn to tatters by the long, thin strip of leather with its weighted iron tip. Thick lines of blood ran down his back and on to his legs, congealing around his feet. Tidal waves of agony swamped his whole body. If the gag hadn't prevented him, he would have bitten through his bottom lip. But he could not stop the involuntary shudders racking him, which made Vahram laugh.

'Where's your power now, soothsayer?' he taunted.

Only the icy wind blowing through the courtyard provided Tarquinius with some relief, numbing his wounds somewhat. But its effect was also deadly. Through the haze of pain, the haruspex knew that if the ordeal continued for much longer, the cold and his injuries would kill him. Without the thick clothing that his tormentors were wearing, no man could last more than a few hours outside.

Vahram knew it too.

Dimly, Tarquinius felt himself being taken down and carried inside. Without ceremony he was dumped by the fire, which released fresh torrents of suffering. While one of the guards stoked the blaze, the others rubbed

his feet and arms with blankets until he could feel them again. The haruspex'
extremities tingled and stung as sensation returned to them, and his spirits
sank. The ministering that he was receiving proved that his suffering was
not over. Vahram was obviously desperate for information and would not
stop until he got it.

'Ready to talk now?'

Tarquinius opened his eyes to find the *primus pilus* by his side. Vahram
undid the gag so that he could speak. 'What do you want to know?' he
whispered.

Vahram's lips curved upwards in triumph. 'Everything,' he replied.
'About my future.'

'Your future?' Tarquinius croaked. 'And that of Pacorus?'

Nodding, the *primus pilus* grew bolder. 'Who should lead the Forgotten
Legion now?' he murmured. 'Surely not that cripple in the bed?'

In that instant it was all clear. The haruspex swallowed, his mouth bone
dry. With the increasing possibility that Pacorus might survive, Vahram's
hopes were beginning to disappear. His hand was being forced and now
the ambitious *primus pilus* wanted a sign so he could seize command of the
Forgotten Legion. If Tarquinius gave it to him, Pacorus would die. And
if he did not . . .

Behind the squat Parthian, the blaze was coming back to life. With new
logs to consume, flames darted back and forth, searching for the best place
to climb upwards.

Following the haruspex' gaze, Vahram's face grew eager. Neither spoke
for some moments.

In the white light, the rider whom Tarquinius had seen before reap-
peared. This time, he got a clear look at his visage. It was definitely Vahram.
Missing his right hand, he looked terrified. With huge effort, the haruspex
kept his expression blank. He could not reveal this without losing his own
life. Vahram's temper was ferocious.

'Well?'

His sensed dulled by the pain, Tarquinius could not think of a good
response. He shook his head.

Snarling with rage, the *primus pilus* smashed him full across the face
with a clenched fist.

The haruspex felt his nose break. Blood filled his mouth and he coughed up a great gobbet on to the carpet. 'It is unclear,' he muttered, his teeth stained red. 'Lately I have been able to see nothing.'

Disbelief twisted Vahram's face.

In his bed just a few steps away, Pacorus slept on.

'Take him outside again.'

The warriors hurried to obey. Hauling Tarquinius upright, they dragged him towards the door.

'Wait!' They heard the distinctive noise of a dagger being unsheathed. There was a long pause.

Looking over his shoulder at what Vahram was doing, one of the guards laughed.

Nausea filled Tarquinius. The *primus pilus'* cruelty knew no bounds. Measured steps came closer. When the heated blade touched the deepest of the cuts on his back, the haruspex could help himself no longer. A moan ripped free of his mouth.

Pacorus stirred and Vahram realised that he had gone too far inside the chamber. Taking his hand away, he ushered his guards and their burden through the door. Tarquinius was tied to the iron ring once more.

And the red-hot tip was pressed into his flesh over and over again. Vahram leaned in constantly, whispering in the haruspex' ear. 'Tell me, and I'll stop.'

Desperate to end his own suffering, Tarquinius could not. Except for two details, his normally acute mind had gone blank. Previously he had seen that Pacorus' role in his and his friends' future was vital, and tonight the fire had shown that the *primus pilus'* life might be in danger. Revealing either of these to Vahram was foolish in the extreme, and he could come up with nothing else. So the torture would go on.

Thankfully the freezing temperature cooled the dagger quickly.

But the *primus pilus* went straight back inside to the fire.

Weakness overcame Tarquinius and he sagged down, unable to hold himself upright any longer. The rope binding his wrists tightened cruelly, but by now he didn't even feel that. The pain from the whipping and his burns was threatening to overwhelm him.

Content to wait until their master returned, the guards lounged nearby, chatting idly.

The haruspex' eyes opened, unfocused. He could feel his strength departing with each heartbeat.

A gust of cold wind hit his face, and he looked upwards.

The night sky of earlier had changed: any sign of the moon and stars had disappeared. Great threatening banks of cloud were building. Deep inside them, flashes of vivid light flared, portents of the storm to come. Loud rumbles could already be heard and the air was heavy with expectation.

A rush of adrenalin coursed through the haruspex' veins.

Witnessing thunder and lightning was one of the best ways to see the future. The ancient Etruscan books that he had studied so many years before dedicated many volumes to just this type of natural phenomenon. Perhaps he would see something that would pacify the vengeful *primus pilus*. And save his own life.

Faster than the eye could see, a blinding bolt of light shot out of a cloud bank directly overhead.

His eyes opened wide with shock as a succession of images shot before them.

Scythian riders annihilating a much smaller Roman force.

Five legionaries with raised swords in a circle around Romulus and Brennus.

A corpse hanging from a cross.

A pair of men rolling and tussling beside the dim glow of a fire. In one's hand was an arrow with a hooked point. Their unknowing companions slept on alongside. The second struggling figure was Romulus.

Light spilled from the bedroom as Vahram emerged, the heated knife clutched in his right hand. He swaggered closer, knowing that Tarquinius could not take much more.

'Ready to talk?' he asked softly.

Deep in a trance, Tarquinius did not answer.

Vahram's lips peeled back with fury and he laid the blade against Tarquinius' left cheek.

The smell of burning flesh filled the air.

Tarquinius' lungs filled with air and he screamed. Using the last of his energy, he soared upwards towards the lightning, which was now flashing from the clouds every few moments. Before the end, he had to know.

The arrow threatening Romulus was Scythian. It was covered with *scythicon*.

The *primus pilus'* voice came from a long way away. 'I'll give you one more chance,' he said. 'Should Pacorus die?'

Romulus' face contorted with effort, but the other man was stronger. Slowly, the hooked point was pushed down towards his unprotected neck.

His energy utterly spent, Tarquinius plummeted down to earth.

It was over. All his predictions had been wrong. Romulus would not return to Rome.

Vahram had had enough. Lifting his dagger to the haruspex' throat, he moved in until only a finger's breadth separated their faces.

Bizarrely, Tarquinius smiled. Olenus had been wrong also. His journey would end here too, in Margiana.

The *primus pilus* lifted an enquiring eyebrow. Tarquinius' response was to spit in his face. 'Die, then,' snarled Vahram, drawing back the blade.

Chapter X: Defeat

Margiana, winter 53/52 BC

'Scum,' hissed Optatus, his teeth clenched. 'How dare you join the army?'

Romulus could not take his eyes off the arrow tip. If it even scratched his skin, he would die in screaming agony.

'Death's too good for you,' whispered Optatus. 'But at least this way will be painful.'

The burly veteran was using his right hand to push towards Romulus' jugular, which meant that the young soldier's weaker left arm had to try to prevent him. Stopping him from crying out, Optatus' other hand was clamped over Romulus' mouth. Even his sword arm could not remove it. And his enemy's greater strength meant that the arrow's hooked point was moving towards his neck with a slow, dreadful inevitability. Romulus struggled not to panic. If he did that, his life would be over. Faced with certain death, his desire to survive suddenly became overwhelming.

Bending his right leg with a jerk, he tried to knee Optatus in the groin.

'Got to do better than that, boy,' sneered the veteran, twisting his hips and avoiding injury.

Frantic, Romulus turned his head from side to side. His sword was just out of reach, as was the fire.

Optatus grinned viciously and leaned down on the arrow.

Desperation filled every fibre of Romulus' being. By stretching out, it might be possible to kick over a burning log, and the noise of that might wake Brennus. He would hurt himself badly, but he could think of nothing else. Marching with burns to one foot could be no worse than death, Romulus thought grimly. The notion of staying alive until at least dawn was enough. Managing to hold the barbed point a few fingers' width from his neck, he wriggled around, reaching out with his left sandal. It was no use, and terror filled Romulus once more.

Sensing this, the big veteran grimaced with effort and put all of his strength into stabbing Romulus with the lethal metal tip. Then his face changed. In a heartbeat, it went from surprised to relaxed, and he slumped down on top of Romulus, a dead weight. The arrow point buried itself in the ground less than a hand span from the young soldier's left ear.

Staring at the shaft, Romulus' eyes bulged with horror. Death had been so close.

Optatus was pulled off with a great heave to reveal Brennus' grinning face crouched over him. 'Looked like you needed a little help,' he whispered, wiping blood off the hilt of his longsword.

'You've only knocked him unconscious?' whispered Romulus, aghast at Brennus' restraint. 'This is a Scythian arrow! The bastard was trying to kill me.'

'I know,' replied the Gaul with an apologetic shrug. 'But we need all the men here to have a chance of breaking out.' He kicked Optatus. 'Even him.'

The veterans might not know it, but Brennus was right, thought Romulus bitterly.

Checking that Darius and the officers were still asleep, they dragged Optatus' bulk back to the space he was sharing with Novius and the others.

Shaken, the little legionary jumped up as they dumped Optatus' body beside their fire. 'Wake up!' he hissed at Ammias and Primitivus.

Their faces befuddled by sleep, his comrades jerked bolt upright.

Romulus and Brennus used their swords to cover both.

Novius regarded the pair warily: now it was they who had the advantage. Two against three, but he was the only one ready to fight.

'He's not dead,' said Brennus coldly.

Novius' face registered surprise, then shock. He knelt and laid a hand to Optatus' neck. Finding a pulse, he nodded at Ammias and Primitivus. Both looked very relieved.

'The scumbag should be though,' added Romulus, throwing down the Scythian arrow. 'This is what he came visiting with.'

Ammias flinched and Romulus saw that they had all known about it.

Novius' expression turned calculating. 'Why didn't you kill him?'

Romulus and Brennus did not answer.

'Whatever it was won't save your skins,' Novius sneered. 'Being nice doesn't entitle you to mercy.'

'Dirty slaves,' said Primitivus contemptuously.

Brennus growled deep in his throat, wishing he had not held back.

Romulus' anger boiled up, but he did not respond. Keeping silent about the possible Scythian attack was about the only advantage they had. 'Might as well get what rest we can,' he said to Brennus. He turned and walked away silently, the Gaul by his side.

'Fools,' said the little legionary with a smirk of satisfaction. 'They'll be dead before we get back to the fort.'

While it was still dark, Darius had the men stand to. The moon had set, but the crystal-clear sky overhead was bright with stars. In the freezing air, no sound could be heard from the enemy camp. A party was sent out to gather as many javelins as possible. Although the Roman *pila* often bent on impact, some inevitably failed to find a target. With the Scythian sentries either asleep or unaware of the creeping soldiers, the mission was a qualified success. Thirty legionaries soon had a second *pilum* again.

Grateful that the long night was over, the two centuries waited for Darius' orders. Brennus and Romulus took the time to stretch and rub their chilled muscles thoroughly. Many who saw them did the same. It was techniques like this which gave men the edge in combat.

Darius was in a better mood as he addressed his soldiers. 'Leave your yokes behind. Without them, this should be simple,' he whispered. 'We'll use a wedge formation to smash through to the track west. Remember your comrades who died here.' He pointed at the barracks. 'Kill as many Scythians as you can, but don't stop.'

Teeth flashed in the darkness as men smiled wolfishly. They stamped their feet in anticipation.

'Once through their lines, we double time it until I say stop.'

'That won't be long then, sir,' piped up Gordianus from the safety of the ranks.

There was muffled laughter at his joke. Beside the fit, lean legionaries, Darius was a portly figure.

The senior centurion had the grace to smile. 'I can run when needs must,' he answered.

Romulus was pleased. This was more like the leader he was used to.

'We wait for no one,' said Darius fiercely. 'Anyone who falls is to be left behind. Including me. Is that clear?'

Everyone nodded.

'Good.' Darius strode into the middle of the men, his guard by his side. 'Form up outside the gate.'

Making as little noise as possible, the legionaries walked out of the fortlet. Without fuss, they positioned themselves into a large V-shape, with Romulus and Brennus at the apex. Not even Novius had protested when the pair demanded this honour; he did not realise it was to show the other soldiers that the two friends were no cowards. The wedge was a useful attacking formation and with men like these at the front, it had more chance of success. Once moving, it was extremely hard for an enemy to stop. But the point was also the most dangerous place to be. Being killed was very likely.

By now, their eyes had adjusted to the dim light. Past the scattered corpses, it was possible to make out the shapes of sleeping men around a few small fires nearby. Groups of hobbled horses stood behind, moving gently from foot to foot. Steam rose from the beasts' thick coats. Still not a sound reached them from the Scythians.

Romulus grinned. Just like Darius' refusal to believe in his vision, these warriors could not imagine an attack in darkness. It would be the reason for their death.

'Ready *pila*,' whispered the senior centurion from their midst.

Silently they obeyed.

'Forward.'

Caligae crunched slowly on the frosty ground, but soon picked up speed. In a few heartbeats, the soldiers were at a trot. Icy air rushed into their faces, chilling their nostrils and throats with each inhalation. No one spoke a word. Every man knew his task, had practised it a thousand times before on the training ground. Shields held high to protect their bodies, they grasped their javelins loosely in their right hands, ready to stab downwards. The charge was all-important. If they broke through, freedom beckoned. Failure would mean death.

Momentarily forgetting the threat from Novius and his comrades, Romulus bared his teeth.

It was thrilling.

Terrifying.

Within fifty paces, they were on the enemy.

Preparing himself, Romulus drew back his *pilum*. Stooping low, he plunged it into the side of a sleeping form, and jumped over without checking to see if the Scythian was dead. Right now, injuring was good enough. Beside him, Brennus kept pace, stabbing the man's companion in the chest as he went by. Two more warriors were dispatched similarly and then they were past the first fire and on to three terrified sentries. Dark eyes opened wide with shock. The trio, who had been muttering quietly to each other, were suddenly confronted by an armoured mass of running legionaries, bloodied javelins in hand.

Screams of terror filled the air. They were rapidly cut off, ebbing away into bubbling whispers. But the noise woke the other Scythians. Wrapped in their thick cloaks and blankets, most had been sleeping comfortably. Waking to the sounds of men dying, the startled warriors jumped up and grabbed for their weapons. All was confusion and disorder.

There was no need for silence any longer. Brennus threw back his head and let out a blood-curdling battle cry; in response, the legionaries yelled a deafening roar of defiance.

The element of speed and surprise was vital, thought Romulus as they pounded on. The Scythians were still half-asleep and unable to fight back properly. It must have seemed as if demons had descended upon their encampment. They simply did not have a chance. Hobnailed *caligae* stamped down on upturned faces, breaking noses and splitting lips; *pila* stabbed down into soft, unprotected flesh, and were ripped free to use again. Legionaries used the iron rims of their *scuta* to smash down on enemy heads. It was most satisfying to revenge themselves for the deaths of the unfortunates in the fortlet. Nonetheless, they kept running.

Seeing the Scythians' horses reacting uneasily to the screams and cries, Romulus had a brainwave. 'Throw your javelins,' he cried, pointing left. 'They'll panic!'

The men immediately on his left needed no urging. Slowing down, they drew back and released their *pila* at the milling mounts. Romulus did likewise. It was impossible to miss: all of the missiles found a target. Rearing up in pain from the metal barbs buried deep in their backs, the injured horses kicked out with their front feet, spun in circles and barged their companions. That was enough. Ripping up the pegs which had tethered their lead ropes to the ground, the group of terrified horses turned and fled into the darkness.

Romulus whooped with glee. Now the Scythians could not pursue them.

'Good thinking,' cried Brennus.

Pleased, Romulus knew more still awaited. This was only the start – but it was a good one.

Soon the wedge had forced its way through the enemy camp. In its wake, it left utter mayhem. Scores of warriors lay in blood-soaked blankets, slain before they had even woken up. Others had belly wounds that would take days to kill, or badly cut limbs which completely disabled. Some had even been trampled by their own mounts. Those who were uninjured stood dazedly looking after the Romans, unable to respond.

Not a single legionary had been killed or wounded.

Romulus could not help but be proud. What other soldiers were capable of such a fast-moving manoeuvre in the dark? But this was no time to clap themselves on the back. They had to make as much ground as possible before dawn, and whatever fate that delivered to them.

Darius was in no mood to linger either. There was a moment to wipe their bloody *pila* on their cloaks and take a gulp of water, and then Darius bellowed, 'Double time!'

Romulus and Brennus took off, followed by their comrades. In case of pursuit, no change was made to the wedge for the moment. Thanks to the bright stars, following the track west was not difficult. The stones had been beaten down from the regular passage of legionaries, forming a wide, easily discernible stripe across the landscape.

They ran for a long time, until it felt as if their lungs would burst.

Behind them, the sky began to lighten. As the sun climbed into view, it finally became possible to make out their surroundings. Nearby was an inscribed stone tablet.

They were exactly two miles from the fortlet.

Horseless, the Scythians had no chance of catching them now. Roman legionaries could march twenty-four miles in five hours, carrying full kit.

Without their heavy yokes to slow them down, the patrol would probably reach the safety of the main fort in less than four.

'Halt!' cried Darius, his sweating face purple with effort. To give him his due, the senior centurion had kept up with his men. 'Down shields. Take a breather.'

The delighted legionaries smiled at the command. Everyone had seen the mile marker and done the maths. They had earned a brief rest. As ordered, their *scuta* clattered down. Keeping the wedge formation, the soldiers sank to one knee, breathing heavily. Gulps were taken from leather water carriers, helmets and felt liners lifted to dry hair that was wringing with moisture. No one could complain of being cold now.

Romulus grimaced as he scanned the low slopes around them.

'Not happy?' asked Brennus under his breath.

'No.' There were large areas of flat ground beyond the top of the inclines on either side of the defile. 'A whole damn army could be waiting up there.'

The Gaul's gaze followed his. He too had been on many patrols through here and knew every dip and fold of the terrain. 'It opens out soon,' he said reassuringly. 'Get through this section and we'll quickly see any enemy.'

'That's not for nearly a mile,' Romulus muttered. He turned to see where Darius was. Pleasingly, the Parthian was moving among the men, muttering encouraging words. It was the mark of a good officer to praise those under his command when they had performed well. With the adrenalin rush of their escape subsiding, Darius now seemed unconcerned. Romulus' warning the day before had meant nothing. In the Parthian's mind, there was time for a respite before the long march home.

Romulus prayed that his vision had been wrong. But his instinct was jangling an inner alarm.

It was time to continue. Instead of the attacking wedge, the legionaries formed up in a more typical marching order. Each century was six wide, fifteen deep. Darius took up his position at the front, his faithful guard alongside.

As they moved off, Romulus' heart pounded in his chest. He could not stop his eyes moving from side to side. Brennus was similarly alert, but neither said a word to anyone.

Spirits had risen hugely because of their escape, and it wasn't long before Gordianus began his usual ditty about the legionary in the brothel.

This was too much for Romulus, whose nerves were fraying. There was no point warning any enemies nearby of their presence. 'Give it a rest,' he said. 'We've heard that a hundred times before.'

'Shut it, you filth,' Novius responded. 'We want to hear about your mother.'

'And your sisters,' responded Brennus as quick as a flash.

The others cheered at the jokes.

Novius flushed with anger but his retort was lost in the din as the whole formation responded to Gordianus' tune.

Romulus' jaw clenched with anger at the insult. A lowly house slave, his mother had still done her best for him and Fabiola. It had meant suffering Gemellus' sexual abuse nightly for years, but Velvinna had never complained. Tragically, her efforts had come to nothing when the merchant's debts reached a critical mass. The twins were sold to raise money. Romulus knew nothing more of his mother, which stung his heart.

Brennus leaned over and spoke in his ear. 'Don't listen to them. The poor bastards would laugh at anything right now. And keeping quiet won't prevent an ambush either. Singing keeps their spirits up.'

Romulus' anger dissipated. The Gaul was right. Happy soldiers fought better than miserable ones. And they might as well imagine a good time in a whorehouse than being slaughtered by Scythians. He opened his mouth and joined in.

After a dozen verses had been bellowed out, Romulus was feeling more relaxed.

It was then that the colour of the sky changed from blue to black.

Fortunately, he was looking upwards at that moment. Lulled by Gordianus' bawdy chant, Romulus did not immediately recognise the dense swarm of arrows. When he did, his warning cry was too little, too late.

To avoid being seen, the volley had been sent up in a hugely steep, curving arc. But already the metal points had turned to point downwards. In three or four heartbeats, they would land amongst the unsuspecting legionaries.

'Arrows incoming!' Romulus bellowed.

One heartbeat.

At the cry, Darius looked into the air, his face a picture of shock. Behind him, other soldiers too were staring up in a mixture of fascination and fear.

Two heartbeats.

Still the senior centurion did not speak. Death was looking him in the eye, and Darius had no answer.

Three heartbeats.

Someone had to act, or most of the patrol would be killed or injured, thought Romulus. 'Form testudo!' he roared, breaking all kinds of rules by shouting an order.

Training instantly took over. The men in the middle squatted down, lifting their heavy *scuta* over their heads while those on the outside formed a shield wall.

Whirring through the air, the hundreds of wooden shafts came to earth. It was a soft, beautiful and deadly noise. While many sank harmlessly into the silk covers or the ground around the soldiers, plenty of others found the gaps between shields that were still coming together. There was a brief delay and then Romulus' ears rang with the cries of the injured. Soon he could hear little else. Legionaries cursed and screamed, clawing frantically at the barbed points that had sunk deep into flesh. The dead slumped against their comrades, their shields falling from slack fingers. Although many men were still obeying orders, the testudo had virtually fallen apart.

Biting back a curse, Romulus glanced towards Darius.

The jovial Parthian would never shout an order again. Pierced by half a dozen arrows, he lay motionless ten steps away. A thin line of blood was running from the corner of his mouth, while his right hand reached out towards them in a futile, supplicating gesture. Darius' bodyguard was sprawled carelessly nearby. Both their faces were frozen in a rictus of shock.

But the attack had just started. More arrows shot up into the sky from either side of them.

At last came a quick response. 'Form testudo!' The voice belonged to one of the *optiones*.

For the second time, the armoured square took shape. This time, though, it was much smaller. Fortunately, both junior officers were experienced men. Screaming orders and with liberal use of their long staffs, they forced the able-bodied men away from the uneven footing that was the injured and slain. It made no sense to trip up on one's comrade and end up dead as a result. Romulus could not look at the pathetic sight of those they left behind. Yet the *optiones* knew what they were doing. The plaintive cries for help from the blinded and maimed had to be ignored. In the heat of battle, the best action to take was that which preserved the lives of most.

Knowing what was about to happen, some of the wounded grabbed their shields and tried to cover as much of their bodies as possible. It wasn't enough: they still died when the second volley landed. By the time the last arrows had fallen, there was nothing more than a bloody pile of feathered corpses beside the testudo.

Brennus did a quick head count. 'This is not good,' he said, scowling. 'Lost nearly fifty men already.'

Romulus nodded, watching the slopes on either side. Any moment now, he thought.

As if answering his call, hundreds of warriors emerged into view. Clad in the same manner as the riders the Romans had butchered early that morning, these were also Scythians. There were infantry, archers on foot and on horseback.

My dream was accurate, Romulus thought with bitter amazement. This force was more than enough to annihilate what remained of the two centuries. What little trust he had had in Mithras withered away.

'We're fucked,' cried Novius, who was still unscathed.

An inarticulate moan of dread rose from the men.

It was hard to argue, but Romulus was damned if he would just let himself be killed. 'What now, sir?' he bawled at the older of the two *optiones*. By virtue of his years served, he was now the commander.

The junior officers looked uncertainly at each other.

The legionaries waited.

Brennus' smile had disappeared, to be replaced by a steely-eyed, fixed stare. Is this my time? he wondered. If it is, great Belenus, grant protection to Romulus. And let me die well.

The young soldier knew Brennus' look from experience. It meant that Scythians would die. Many of them. But even the huge Gaul could not kill all the warriors who were swarming down around the testudo, blocking off any escape avenue.

'Form wedge!' cried the senior *optio* at last. What had worked before might do so again. 'Drive through them and we've got a chance.'

His men needed no prompting. If they did not act fast, they would be surrounded completely.

'Middle ranks, keep your shields up. Forward!'

The desperate soldiers obeyed, instinctively moving at double time.

A hundred paces in front, Scythian foot soldiers were already forming up in deep lines. Romulus eyed the dark-skinned enemy warriors, who were lightly armed compared to the legionaries. Mostly wearing felt hats, few had chain mail or metal helmets. Their only protection was the small round or crescent shields they carried. Armed with spears, swords and axes, they would pose little obstacle to the fast-moving wedge.

'Those won't stop us,' Brennus panted. 'They're just light infantry.'

His friend was correct. Confusion filled Romulus. Perhaps his dream did not mean their annihilation after all? If they broke through, nothing stood between them and the fort. What kind of trick was Mithras playing?

They closed in on the Scythians, who immediately launched their spears. The man to Romulus' right was too slow in lifting his *scutum* and the next instant, a broad iron blade had taken him through the neck. Without making a sound, he dropped, forcing the men behind him to jump over his body. No one tried to help him. The wound was mortal. Other casualties were similarly ignored. Now, as never before, speed was of the essence. The legionaries loosed a volley of *pila* at twenty paces, causing dozens of casualties. On they ran.

Romulus fixed his gaze on a bearded, tattooed Scythian with a domed iron helmet.

Twenty steps separated them, then ten.

'For the Forgotten Legion!' roared Brennus. 'FOR-GOTTEN LE-GION!'

At the top of his voice, every man answered back.

It was the unifying cry for all of them, thought Romulus. They were truly Rome's lost soldiers, fighting for their very survival at the ends of the earth. Did anyone at home care about them now? Probably not. All they had was each other. And that wasn't enough. Gritting his teeth,

Romulus took a better hold of his horizontal *scutum* grip. With its heavy iron boss, the Roman shield was a good battering ram.

His target shifted uneasily, suddenly aware that the point of the wedge was heading straight for him.

It was too late.

Romulus punched upwards with his *scutum*, smashing the Scythian's nose. As he reeled back in agony, Romulus' *gladius* took him in the chest, and the warrior fell from view. The ranks behind were ready, however, and Romulus' vision was immediately filled with snarling, bearded faces. Lowering his shield again, Romulus let the wedge's momentum carry him forward. Although he could only make out Brennus and another legionary on either side, there were about a hundred men pushing behind them.

Swinging his sword wildly, a screaming Scythian threw himself at Romulus, who took the blow on the metal rim of his *scutum*. As his enemy raised his arm to repeat the blow, Romulus leaned forward and shoved his *gladius* deep into the man's armpit. He knew the damage it would cause – sliding between ribs to slice lungs and large blood vessels, perhaps even the heart. The Scythian's mouth gaped like a fish and a gush of arterial blood followed the blade out. Romulus grimaced with satisfaction as the corpse fell to the ground. Two down, he thought wearily. A few hundred to go. Yet, judging from the loud roars of encouragement from the men at the back, the wedge was still moving forward.

He pushed on.

A pair of similar-looking heavy-set men, brothers possibly, threw themselves at Romulus next. One grabbed the edge of his shield with his bare hands, pulling it down while the other stabbed forward with a long dagger. Romulus twisted to one side, barely avoiding the blade. A powerful slash followed, sliding off the cheek piece of his helmet and opening a shallow cut under his right eye. The first Scythian was still trying to wrest the *scutum* from him, so Romulus just let go. He couldn't fight two enemies at once. Staggering under the unexpected weight of the heavy shield, the man was unbalanced and fell backwards.

That left his brother with the dagger, who smiled now that Romulus had no *scutum*. Dodging forward, he angled his blade at the young soldier's unprotected lower legs. Romulus had to react fast. The Scythian was too close to stab with his *gladius*, so he used his shield hand, his left, to punch the other in the side of the head. As the man went down, half stunned, Romulus reversed his grip on the *gladius*. Gripping its bone hilt with both fists, he turned the blade and plunged it into the Scythian's back. Iron grated off his ribs as it slid through to pierce a kidney.

An animal scream of pain rang out and Romulus stooped, twisting the blade slightly to make sure.

Struggling to his feet, the second warrior saw his brother writhing on the ground. Rage distorted his face as he threw himself bodily at Romulus. It was a fatal mistake. Using one of Brennus' moves, Romulus let go of his sword with his left hand and stood, smashing the Scythian across the face with a stiff forearm. It bought him enough time to regain his *gladius* and step forward, dispatching his swaying enemy with a simple forward thrust.

Romulus turned his head, checking the situation on either side. On his right, Brennus was wading through Scythians like a man possessed. His sheer size intimidated before he even came to blows with each warrior. But the Gaul also possessed great skill with weapons. Romulus watched with awe as Brennus barged into a large Scythian, pushing him back several steps and knocking over two men in the ranks behind. While the warrior tried to defend himself, Brennus stabbed him in the belly. The Scythian fell and the Gaul leaped over him, cracking the bottom of his shield off the head of another man. Knocking the warrior unconscious, the blow also opened a deep cut in his scalp. Romulus knew exactly why. There was no end to Brennus' tricks. As in the *ludus*, the rim of his *scutum* had been sharpened.

'We're nearly through!' yelled Gordianus from his left, pointing with a bloody *gladius*.

Romulus grinned. Just three ranks stood between them and the road west.

They redoubled their efforts. After a few moments of cut and thrust, the last Scythians in their path had been dispatched. On the sides of the wedge, their comrades were still fighting past warriors, but the spirit had gone out of their lightly armed enemies. As the opposition melted away, the legionaries came to a gradual halt. Seven had fallen, twice that number had minor flesh wounds, but there were still nearly ninety men who could march. Chests heaving, faces purple with effort, they stopped to savour the view.

'A bare track never looked so inviting,' said Gordianus, wiping his brow. 'Well done, lad.'

Full of gratitude at the other's acceptance, Romulus did not reply.

Gordianus saw Brennus' worried look. 'What is it?' he asked.

Above the screams of the injured and the battle cries of the Scythian infantry to their rear, Romulus heard the sound of pounding hooves. His skin crawled, remembering Carrhae.

'Cavalry,' he said in a monotone.

Alarmed, Gordianus' eyes darted back to the track in front, which was still empty.

Questions from the other legionaries filled the air, but Romulus ignored them.

They could all hear it now.

Brennus stood calmly, thinking of his wife and son, who had died without him being there to defend them. Of his uncle, who had died saving him. Of his cousin, whose life Brennus had failed to save. Only death could assuage the guilt he felt over these losses. And if he saved Romulus' life while doing so, he would not have died in vain.

When the first horsemen came into view, Brennus actually smiled.

They were followed by at least two hundred more. Wearing polished scale armour that covered their bodies right down to their thighs, the Scythians were armed with lances, short-headed axes, swords and recurved composite bows. Maximising the full dramatic effect of their appearance, the riders reined in their red-coloured horses and stopped. About two hundred and fifty paces of snow-covered ground separated them from the battered Roman soldiers. Enough distance to reach a full charge.

I have accurately predicted the future, thought Romulus bitterly. But I did not see this.

Nearby, Novius blanched. What chance had they now?

He was not alone in his reaction. Finally taking in what awaited them, Romulus' spirits plummeted. The divination was my best. And last. We will surely die now. With infantry and archers about to engage them from behind, and the cavalry blocking their way forward, there was nowhere to go. Except to Elysium. From somewhere, Romulus summoned the dregs of his faith in the warrior god. *Mithras! Do not forsake us! We are worthy of your favour.*

'How did those bastards get here?' shouted the older *optio*. Scythia lay to the south-east, with a long range of mountains between it and Margiana. The communicating passes would be blocked by snow for months.

There was only one answer.

'They came around the peaks, sir,' replied Romulus. Only that could explain the Scythians' presence in midwinter.

'Why now?' demanded the *optio*.

'To catch us unawares,' Brennus said. 'Who would expect an attack of this size at this time of year?'

'The gods must be angry,' spat Gordianus, making the sign against evil. Without anger, he glanced at Romulus. They were now comrades again. 'Have we some hope?'

'Hardly any,' he answered.

Fearful mutters rose as this passed back through the ranks.

'Let's hope that Darius' riders made it back then,' said Gordianus. 'Or the whole legion could be in danger.'

Behind the wedge, the massed ranks of Scythians were closing in. Simultaneously, the lead cavalryman flicked his reins, forcing his horse into a walk. The trot would be next, followed by the canter.

Their fate was about to be sealed.

'What are your orders, sir?' asked Romulus.

The *optio* looked uncertain. Normally there was a centurion present to tell him what to do.

'If the horses get any speed up, they'll cut us to pieces, sir,' said Romulus.

The *optio*'s eyes flickered from side to side. On the heights were yet more warriors, with archers ranked behind. Escape that way meant fighting uphill, while being showered with arrows.

'Let's hit them quickly, sir,' said Romulus. 'That way, there's a chance of smashing through.'

'Charge them?' queried the *optio* disbelievingly.

'Yes, sir.' Romulus glanced back at his frightened-looking comrades. Being hit at the gallop by the approaching horses would undoubtedly break them. And if that happened, the Scythian infantry would soon finish the job. 'Now,' he urged.

Unused to such pressure, the *optio* hesitated.

Brennus' grip on his sword tightened. Romulus' idea was the best, the sole, choice. If their erstwhile commander did not act, he would intervene. Lethally, if necessary.

Ignoring the confused junior officer, Gordianus turned to his comrades. He too thought Romulus was right. 'We've only one chance,' he shouted. 'There's no way back or on either side.'

'What should we do?' cried a voice a few ranks back.

'Charge those fucking horses,' cried Gordianus. 'Before they reach top speed.'

The men looked dismayed, but did not protest.

Gordianus seized the moment. 'Let's do it!'

A defiant roar rose into the air. Novius and his cronies alone looked unhappy.

Romulus did not delay any longer. 'Form wedge!' he screamed. 'Charge!'

The dull-witted *optio* had no time to respond. Desperate to survive, the legionaries launched themselves forward, carrying him with them.

Romulus kept his position at the front of the wedge. Brennus was pounding along on his right and Gordianus on his left. Soon they were running at full tilt, their shields held high against Scythian arrows. Those behind could not run and hold their *scuta* over their heads, which meant speed was vital. Once the mounted archers started releasing, the men in the middle would begin to die.

The Scythians responded to the Roman charge by urging their horses into a canter. All had arrows already fitted to their bowstrings. To a man, they drew back and prepared to release.

Less than a hundred paces separated the two sides.

Arrows shot up in graceful arcs and whistled down amongst the legionaries. The man directly behind Brennus went down, shot through the cheek. More shafts thumped into Romulus' and Gordianus' shields, making them awkward to carry, but there was no chance to rip them out. The veteran began muttering a prayer to Mars, the god of war.

Sweat ran down Romulus' face and into the cut below his right eye. The salt stung, and he used the pain to focus himself. Some of the legionaries still had javelins left, he thought. Hit any of the Scythians and they'll fall off. Open up the formation. Maybe give us enough room to get through. *Mithras, protect us. Give us the strength to survive.*

Fifty paces.

'Ready *pila*,' he yelled. 'At my command, loose at will.'

Brennus smiled proudly. Romulus was turning into a leader.

Used to obeying orders, all those with javelins cocked their right arms back. Throwing while running was something they had all been trained to do.

Another flurry of arrows landed. Men made soft, choking noises as metal points skewered their throats; they screamed as eyeballs ruptured. Others were hit in the lower legs where their shields left them exposed. The falling bodies tripped up those immediately behind, and the legionaries at the rear had to just trample over them regardless. Injured, dying or simply winded, it was every man for himself now.

Thirty paces. Good javelin range.

'Aim at the front riders,' shouted Romulus one more time. 'Loose!'

It was difficult enough to aim a *pilum* accurately when standing still. At the run, it was much harder. At Romulus' command, eight or ten flew forward at the approaching horsemen. Most landed short. Just two found their mark, both striking the tattooed lead rider in the chest. Killed instantly, he toppled sideways and fell off. His body was trampled at once by the horses behind.

Gordianus cheered.

As Romulus had hoped, the dead man's mount turned away from the Roman wedge, eager to escape. Now there was a small gap in the enemy ranks. He aimed straight for it.

But the other Scythians kept up a relentless fire of arrows. At twenty paces, they were hardly able to miss the unfortunate legionaries. With every step, men dropped into the snow, their blood staining it a deep red.

Someone tried to speak, but the words were unintelligible. Romulus turned his head. Gordianus had been hit at the top of his left shoulder, just above where his chain mail shirt ended.

The veteran's face was stunned. He tried again to speak, but couldn't. His hand rose to the wooden shaft protruding from his flesh, then fell away. Gordianus knew that pulling out the arrow would only kill him quicker.

Grief filled Romulus, but there was nothing he could do. Gordianus was a dead man.

Dropping his *gladius*, the veteran leaned over and firmly gripped Romulus' shoulder with his right hand. His lips framed two silent words: 'My friend.'

With a leaden heart, Romulus nodded.

With the last of his strength, Gordianus pushed him away. As he did, a Scythian spear took him in his exposed left side. At such close range, it punched straight through the chain mail. Gordianus' eyes opened wide and he slumped to his knees.

Unable to watch, Romulus turned away.

'Steady, lad,' Brennus shouted. 'I'm still here.'

But the battle was not going well. Horsemen were sweeping down the sides of the shrunken wedge, loosing arrows from point-blank range. Their effect was terrifying and devastating. There was no let-up in the onslaught either. With a tight turning circle, the horses were simply riding around, repeating their attacks time and again.

By now, the wedge had ground to a halt. With every casualty, another gap was created in the shield wall, making it even harder to stop the Scythian arrows and spears. Romulus judged that fewer than forty legionaries remained uninjured. And they were rapidly losing the will to fight.

Then he saw why. A horde of infantry was closing in from the rear to seal their fate.

Romulus shook his head. Mithras had turned his face away. Of Jupiter there was no sign. This was where they would die. 'It's over,' he said wearily.

'It's never over,' roared Brennus. Grabbing a *pilum* from a dead soldier at his feet, he hurled it at an approaching rider. His effort was magnificent, hitting the Scythian in the chest with such force that he was thrown backwards off his mount.

Almost immediately another replaced him.

The Gaul scowled; to Romulus it just seemed another example of how the gods had discarded them.

Brennus' mouth opened in a sudden warning. His hand reached up to grab the hilt of his longsword.

There was a heavy impact and Romulus' vision doubled. Blinding pain filled his head and his knees crumpled, letting him fall to the ground.

'No!' cried Brennus. 'You stupid bastard!'

It was the last thing Romulus heard.

Chapter XI: The Warrior God

Rome, winter 53/52 BC

Although angered by Secundus' response to her question, Fabiola wisely kept her counsel. Her safety was quite fragile. 'I apologise,' she muttered.

An awkward silence fell, and Fabiola turned to see how Sextus was doing. His treatment was nearly over. Once Janus had removed all dirt and metal fragments from the eye socket, he had washed it out with *acetum*. Now there was a neat cloth bandage in place over the gaping hole. His face clean, Sextus was drinking from a small clay cup.

Janus saw her looking. '*Papaverum*,' he said, cleaning his hands in a bowl of water. 'One of the most powerful painkillers.'

'How is it made?' Fabiola had little idea what went into the strange concoctions made by apothecaries; theirs was a trade which guarded its secrets jealously.

'By crushing the seeds of a plant with small red flowers,' the orderly explained. 'We add a few other ingredients and boil them into an infusion. Dulls even the worst pain.'

'You mean physical pain.' Nothing can take away grief, thought Fabiola bitterly. Except revenge.

Janus helped Sextus to the nearest bed. 'Sleep,' he ordered.

There was little protest. Sextus collapsed back on to the straw mattress, letting himself be covered with a woollen blanket. 'Lady?' Secundus had moved to the door. 'We must leave him here for the moment,' he said curtly.

Nodding her thanks at Janus, she followed Secundus back to the front entrance, and then down another corridor. Soon Fabiola found herself seated by a table in the stone-flagged kitchen. It was similar to the one in Gemellus' house. There was a solidly built brick oven in one corner, long work counters along the walls and wooden shelves stacked with typical black and red clay crockery and deep sinks. As in all houses of the rich, lead pipes carried running water to wash food and plates; drains carried away the waste liquid. Yet there were no slaves here; Secundus had served her himself, refusing the offer of help as he awkwardly hacked slices off a loaf with his *pugio*. Cheese and fish was offered to accompany the bread, which Fabiola gratefully accepted. The day's events had left her feeling famished. As she ate, she ignored the mixture of curious and surly stares from the many veterans present. She and Sextus were under Secundus' protection; she doubted any of the scarred men would actually harm them.

When Secundus left, Fabiola reflected on her near escape from Scaevola. On what he had done to the fugitive and poor Corbulo at the *latifundium*. Closing her eyes, the young woman prayed as she had not done since she was sold into prostitution. Until today, those had been the hardest hours of her life, when only her faith and innate determination had allowed her to endure. Now, the guilt of Corbulo's and her guards' deaths weighed heavily on Fabiola's shoulders. Nearly being raped by a dozen men was also a trauma she would not soon forget.

A discreet cough broke her reverie. It was Secundus again. 'We've prepared a room for you, lady.'

'I am tired,' Fabiola admitted. A rest would do her good.

He managed a stiff smile. 'Follow me.'

Passing out of the kitchen, they walked in silence to the corridor opposite that which led to the *valetudinarium*. Not far from the statue of the god, they passed a half-open door. Wavering light from a single torch lit the interior. The room was empty apart from a trapdoor in the floor.

Seeing her glance inside, Secundus instantly shut the door. He continued down the passage without explanation. Fabiola followed without protest, but her pulse quickened. It was surely the entrance to the Mithraeum. Until this moment, she had not been aware that it would be underground. Few, if any, other shrines were built like that.

Secundus guided Fabiola to a simple bedchamber, which had little more in it than her room in the Lupanar, where she had lived for nearly four years. Yet a low bed, a wooden storage chest, a bronze oil lamp and a three-legged stool with a neatly folded man's tunic on it sufficed. Fabiola smiled: she did not have expensive tastes. The blankets looked clean and inviting. She suddenly felt more tired than she had in an age.

'You can sleep without fear tonight,' Secundus said in a more kindly tone. He pointed to a small bell on the floor. 'Ring if you need anything.' Without another word, the veteran was gone.

Fabiola needed little encouragement. Shutting the door, she blew out the lamp and took off her torn dress and sandals. Then she fell on to the bed. With the blankets pulled tight around her, she soon warmed up. A fit of shaking struck, delayed terror at the thought of what Scaevola had done to her life. And he would not give up. Other than Docilosa and the wounded Sextus, Fabiola was alone in the world. The fear was overwhelming but her exhaustion was greater. She fell into a deep sleep. Thankfully there were no bad dreams.

Yet when she awoke, it was with a real sense of panic. Wondering where she was, Fabiola sat up. Memories flooded back in a succession of disturbing images. Clodius' corpse being displayed in the Forum. The ensuing riot. Ambush by the *fugitivarii*. Her men's deaths. Scaevola. What had happened at the *latifundium*. Fabiola shuddered, trying – and failing – to forget.

Somehow she knew that night had fallen. The house was deathly silent, and the air around her was pitch black. Fabiola listened carefully for a long time, but could hear no activity. People tended to go to bed not long after sunset. The veterans were probably no different. Immediately the plain room with its trapdoor came to mind. Like all forbidden fruit, its appeal was great. Easing herself off the bed, Fabiola donned the man's tunic and tiptoed to the door.

Not a sound from the other side.

Turning the handle gently, she pulled it open a crack. No cry of alarm. A glimmer of light from an oil lamp further down the corridor revealed that no one was about. Barefoot, Fabiola slipped out of her room, closing the door. From the chamber beside hers came the loud sound of a man snoring. It was echoed in the others that she passed. Yet her tension grew and grew. If she was discovered, the veterans' reaction would not be pleasant. The thought stopped Fabiola in her tracks. She had had two lucky escapes already that day. It was pushing her luck to continue.

Down the dim passageway, in the *atrium*, she saw the large statue of

Mithras, cloaked and mysterious. The bull he was crouched over had its head raised and was looking straight at her, knowingly. Disconcerted, Fabiola shivered. Then curiosity, and a reluctance to admit defeat, got the better of her. Involuntarily, her feet began to move again across the cool mosaic floor. Soon she had reached the door which Secundus had closed. A quick glance to either side was enough to tell Fabiola that no one had heard her. The sole witness was the bull, and it did not speak.

Thankfully the portal was not locked. Nor did its hinges creak as she pushed it open. Inside the room was totally dark. Yet Fabiola did not dare to find flints to ignite a lamp. Once she was in the Mithraeum perhaps, but not before. If any of the veterans happened to see a light burning in here, her game would be up. She pushed the door to, almost closing it. Just the slightest glimmer from the corridor came through the tiny crack that she left between its edge and the frame. Fabiola hoped it would be enough. Sliding her bare feet cautiously across the tiles, she moved to where the middle of the chamber should be. On her hands and knees in the utter blackness, she searched with her fingertips. To her frustration, only the finest irregularities between the tiny pieces of tile which formed the mosaic were apparent. When Fabiola stopped, the only sounds were her own breathing and her rapid heartbeat. It was unnerving, and she had to pause a number of times to calm herself. For what seemed like an eternity, she found nothing.

At last her fingers closed on an iron ring. Careful probing revealed that it was attached to the middle of a rectangular stone slab. A rush of relief flooded her, yet goosebumps rose on her skin as she lifted the trapdoor, allowing a current of cool air to rise from the depths, bringing with it the smells of stale incense and men's body odour. This was hallowed ground, and she was forbidden from entering it.

Yet even if she had wanted to, there was no going back now. The draw of what she might find was too much. Mithras awaited. Taking a deep breath, Fabiola slid her legs over the edge, praying the drop would not be far.

It wasn't.

The staircase was steep and narrow, each step carved from a single piece of smooth stone. As long as Fabiola took care, she would not fall. It was just a case of descending into the utter darkness. Running her fingertips along the wall, she could feel no plasterwork. It was extremely difficult to determine where the joints between each slab were, if there were any at all. Whoever had built the hidden structure had been a master of engineering.

Only the faint slap of Fabiola's feet on the stone broke the silence. It felt quite terrifying, just as she imagined a descent into Hades might be. Keeping her mind occupied by counting the steps, Fabiola had reached eighty-four by the bottom. The Mithraeum was deep underground. The walls had not opened out at all either, meaning she was in a narrow passageway. It led forward, beyond her touch. Now Fabiola's fear grew too great to continue without illumination. Who knew what lay down here? She searched along the wall for a metal bracket or an oil lamp. When her fingers closed on the familiar shape of a bronze bowl, Fabiola almost cried out with relief. Beside it, in a little alcove, she found two sharp pieces of stone. Striking them off each other, she used the sparks generated to ignite the lamp's wick.

After so long in the dark, the light which flared felt blinding. Wisely, Fabiola looked away, letting her eyes grow accustomed. The first thing she noticed was the ornate mosaic floor beneath her feet. She had seldom seen tiny tile pieces as delicate, or designs as well executed. It would have taken a workman of great skill many weeks to lay the surface. With a plain stripe of dark colour running along the walls, the passage centre was divided into seven panels, each of which was filled with various symbols. It was immediately clear that what she was seeing was of huge importance.

The first depicted a black bird with a powerful beak, a *caduceus*, the symbol of commerce, and a small cup. Fabiola was delighted by the raven's image. And yet the majestic bird, one of her favourites, only represented the first stage.

The second square contained an oil lamp and a diadem. She walked forward, her eyes soaking in the wealth of information on the floor surface. There followed a lance, helmet and sling bag, and then a fire shovel, a rattle and Jupiter's thunderbolt.

Already a deep sense of reverence and of belonging had calmed Fabiola's initial nervousness. The panels clearly represented symbols sacred to the worshippers of Mithras. She longed to know what they meant.

The next stage was represented by a sickle, a dagger and a crescent moon with a star. Second from the end was a square filled with a torch, a whip and an ornate seven-rayed crown. The last had in it a Phrygian cap, a staff, a libation bowl and a large sickle. The cap was the same as that worn by the statue of Mithras in the *atrium* above.

Air moved over her face, telling her that the passageway had opened out. Moving slowly forward into the darkness, she lifted her lamp to light others in brackets on the wall. Their yellow glow revealed a long, rectangular room, its slatted roof supported by regularly placed wooden posts which had been driven into the floor. Low stone seating ran the entire length of both side walls. Covered in inscriptions, three small stone altars dominated the far end of the chamber. Above them, on the back wall, was a massive, brightly painted representation of the tauroctony. Crimson blood spurted from the wound in the bull's neck, and Mithras' dark green cloak was covered in bright dots of light that could only be stars. A male figure stood on either side of the god, each bearing a torch, one upright and the other pointing downwards. Positioned around him were animals and objects: Fabiola made out a raven, a cup and a lion. There was also a dog, a scorpion and a snake. More images covered the plaster panels to her left and right. Her mouth dropped at their quality and detail.

There were men feasting around a table, waited on by others bearing drinking cups and plates of what looked like bread marked with an 'X'. In others she could see Mithras in his Phrygian cap holding hands with an imposing golden figure wearing the seven-rayed crown. Was this the sun? The same god-like creature was in many of the pictures, seated with Mithras behind the dead bull's body, standing in a horse-drawn chariot, accepting gifts from lesser mortals. Even the floor was decorated. Its tiles were divided into twelve squares, depicting a variety of animals and symbols: twin children, a ram, a bull, a scales and a scorpion among others.

By now, Fabiola was reeling with the wealth of information she had just been exposed to.

She tiptoed across the mosaic, beginning to feel very self-conscious. Although there was no one else in the chamber, it felt as if there were. Her nerves returned, making her palms sweaty. Standing before the trio of altars, Fabiola looked up at Mithras. Had a woman ever stood here in this way? Should she leave? Blood pounded in her ears, but nothing struck her down.

Her eyes were caught by a small phial which was standing on the central plinth. Made of expensive blue glass, it had a delicately wrought top in the shape of a lion's head. Her hand reached out and picked it up.

This is the moment of truth, Fabiola decided, pulling out the stopper. She lifted the bottle to her nose and inhaled. She smelt a faint, attractive odour and instinctively knew that the contents were there to be drunk during rituals. This is my sacred time, Fabiola thought fiercely. Mithras will understand. Or he will poison me. It was time to place her trust completely in the warrior deity. Her heart raced for a few beats, but Fabiola allowed the sensation of calm that pervaded the chamber to regain control once more. Surely the god had brought her here? Who was she to resist? After the day's dramatic events, she had nothing to lose. Tipping back her head, Fabiola poured the liquid into her mouth. It tasted light and sweet, with a powerful undercurrent of unfamiliar flavour.

Replacing the phial on the altar, she swallowed.

For a long time, nothing happened. She began to feel disappointed.

Then it seemed to Fabiola that drums began to pound, a simple, repetitive beat which drew her in and down, its rhythm mesmeric. Instead of feeling alarmed, she felt euphoric. Mithras was here, in the room. She could feel him.

The drums' speed increased, rising to a crescendo of sound that shook the walls. Unaware of where she was, Fabiola stood motionless, absorbing the energy. Gradually the pounding died away, to be replaced by another, quieter sequence. She felt herself falling, falling, but there was no impact of the hard floor against her back. More hypnotic drumming followed, bringing Fabiola seamlessly into another world, an incredible place where she saw through the eyes of a flying bird. Blinking hard and trying to bring back the small chamber made no difference. If she now turned her head, Fabiola could see shiny black feathers sitting perfectly arranged on powerful wings. Had she really become a raven? Strangely, she felt no terror. Instead there was only joy.

It seemed completely natural to soar high in the sunlit sky, riding currents of air that allowed her to reach great speeds or to hang motionless, scanning the ground below. For long moments Fabiola revelled in just being, rejoicing in the freedom that flight granted and the view of the earth laid out as she had never seen before. Rivers wound sinuously through the landscape; hills and ice-capped mountains ran in short, stubby lines or immense, jagged ranges. The green stain of forests covered parts of the vista. Human settlements were scattered here and there; the dirt roads joining them appearing as mere ribbons. Where was she?

Movement on a great plain drew her attention and she flew lower, unseen by the two armies that were regarding each other from a safe standoff range. Along one side of the battlefield ran a river, wider than any she had ever seen. Now Fabiola was sure that it wasn't Italy. This place was far from anywhere that she knew.

Combat would commence soon, but for the moment the generals were trying to gauge their enemy's strengths and weaknesses, while their soldiers prayed and wiped the sweat from their clammy foreheads. Before long though, men would begin to die. Judging from the flat terrain and good weather, Fabiola knew that it would be in large numbers.

In the ranks of the host directly beneath her, sunlight sparkled off metal. Eyesight far more powerful than she normally possessed instantly focused on its source. What she saw was so incredible that it seemed beyond belief. There, among the massed ranks of soldiers, Fabiola saw a solitary silver eagle.

Here in an alien land, a Roman standard.

There was nothing else it could be. With powerful, outstretched wings, talons gripping a golden thunderbolt and borne by a man wearing a wolf-skin headdress, this was the talismanic symbol that led every legion into combat. Fabiola studied the figures around the silver eagle, seeing now the rounded bowls of their crested bronze helmets, the elongated, oval *scuta* they bore, the neat lines in which they stood. Surely these were Roman legionaries? But not everything about them fitted. Instead of *pila*, many men carried long, heavy spears, and their metal shield bosses were obscured by fabric. The officers standing to the side of each unit also looked out of place, carrying bows and wearing odd-looking conical hats and embroidered tunics and trousers. If these were legionaries, they were like none that she had ever seen before.

Confused, Fabiola had begun to climb away from the forces beneath her when a powerful image of a huge, pig-tailed warrior suddenly came to mind. He was flanked by a slim, blond-haired man who carried a double-headed axe. Memories stirred in the depths of the young woman's soul, struggling to emerge into the raven's consciousness. Then it was clear. *The Gaul was here. With another guide.* Fabiola's heart sang with joy.

Romulus might be alive!

But there was no time to search for him.

'What are you doing here?' cried an angry voice.

Someone took hold of Fabiola, turning her wing into a hand once more.

No, she thought desperately. *Leave me here! Great Mithras, let me find my brother. See him, in the flesh.* Fabiola pulled away, resuming her shape and swooping down on a fortunate draught of air. Free for a dozen heart-beats, she shot across the open ground in the plain's centre, horrified to see that the other army outnumbered the Roman one many times. Infantry armed with every weapon under the sun were flanked by skirmishers carrying slings and bows. There were thousands of archers, both in char-iots and on horseback. Worst of all, three squadrons of enormous grey, armoured creatures waited in the enemy's midst, flapping ears, long trunks and fearsome tusks tipped with metal adding to their fearsome aura. They had to be elephants, Fabiola thought. Each carrying two or three bowmen on their broad backs, these animals were the hammer blow that would drive terror into the hearts of the bravest soldiers. Who in the world would stand against them? Fabiola glanced back at the Roman soldiers, who had looked so brave and prepared as she had soared over their heads. Now, before the imposing host with its vast beasts, they appeared puny and insignificant. There could only be one result once battle was joined.

Overcome with grief, Fabiola did not believe that the god could be so cruel. To let her discover that Romulus might be alive and then to show her the instrument of his destruction in the same moment was more than she could bear. Her response was immediate, instinctive. Pulling her wings in tightly, she dropped her head and pointed her beak downwards, aiming straight for the lead elephant. Air whistled past Fabiola, streamlining her shape even further.

Down, down, down she dived.

Fabiola was soon close enough to see the wrinkles in its thick skin and the deeply curved bows carried by the men on its back. Perhaps she could take out an eye and send it off on a trail of death amongst its own men. The fall was immense – potentially fatal – but Fabiola did not care any longer. Anything was better than this pain. Plummeting like a black stone, with rage burning brightly in her heart, she consigned herself to oblivion.

This time, she was grabbed by both arms. Shouts filled her ears.

Fabiola could not help herself. Despite her frantic attempts, the plain covered in armed men disappeared. Crying tears of frustration and despair, she opened her eyes.

She was back in the underground chamber, which was now packed with veterans. Two were pinioning her arms while Secundus stood a couple of paces away, shaking with anger. 'What have you done?' he shouted. 'We save your miserable hide and you repay us by desecrating our temple?'

Fabiola looked at the men holding her. Both their faces wore the same furious look. What had been suspicion earlier was now rightful outrage. 'I'm sorry,' she whispered, her misery brimming over.

'That's not nearly enough,' Secundus replied grimly. 'You must be punished.'

His men growled in accordance.

'And there is only one penalty.'

Chapter XII: Pacorus

Margiana, winter 53/52 BC

'Hold!'

The shout reverberated in the confined space of the courtyard.

Surprised, Vahram paused and turned his head. Only half aware of what was going on, the haruspex followed his gaze.

Ishkan was framed in the entrance. Torches held aloft by his men illuminated the gory scene. The snow around Tarquinius was stained red. The thin, middle-aged senior centurion looked disgusted at the sight. 'What are you doing?' he snapped.

'Flogging this snake for information,' Vahram replied, furious that he had been disturbed. 'He's plotting against us.'

'Did the commander order this?' asked Ishkan.

'Naturally,' blustered Vahram.

'And he said to kill the haruspex?'

'If necessary, yes,' growled the *primus pilus*.

Ishkan raised his eyebrows. 'Where is Pacorus, then?' He looked around. 'I would have thought he'd watch.'

'He's not well enough to be outside for long,' said Vahram icily. 'And I am his deputy.'

'Of course you are, sir,' Ishkan answered, suspicion flaring in his eyes. 'But let's just check with him, shall we?'

Realising that his ruse would be discovered the instant that Ishkan woke Pacorus, Vahram panicked. Stepping away from Tarquinius' limp body, he blocked the doorway to the bedchamber.

The dark-haired senior centurion frowned. He lifted a hand and immediately his followers raised their weapons.

Vahram's trio of men looked to him for directions, but there were at
least a dozen warriors with Ishkan, all of whom were armed with bows.
Unless they wanted to die, there was nothing to do but see how the
standoff panned out. They relaxed, keeping their hands away from their
sword hilts.

Outmanoeuvred, the *primus pilus* scowled and stood to one side.

Leaving his warriors to watch Vahram, Ishkan opened the door. He was
not gone long.

Covered by a blanket and supported by the senior centurion, a shivering
Pacorus emerged into the light.

Vahram cursed under his breath. Things were getting out of control.
He should have just killed the damn haruspex.

Pacorus regarded Tarquinius' bloodied face and body with a mixture
of emotions. He cared little for the haruspex' health, but valued his abilities. Moreover, he did not like his inferiors acting without his direct
authority. Anger finally dominated on the commander's thin, grey face.
'What have you to say about this?' he snapped at Vahram.

The *primus pilus*' eyes flashed to Tarquinius. Although his word was
worth more, Pacorus would be highly suspicious of him if the haruspex
mentioned his plans.

Barely aware of the delicate situation, Tarquinius forced out an incoherent moan and let some bloody spit dribble from his lips.

Unsure of himself, Vahram made a snap decision. Hopefully, Tarquinius
was in no state to talk. 'I came in to see how you were, sir. Found the
whoreson crouched over the fireplace muttering your name.'

Aware that he had slept through whatever Tarquinius had been doing,
Pacorus sucked in a nervous breath. He had first-hand experience of the
haruspex' frightening powers. 'Has he said why?'

'No, sir.' Vahram shook his head angrily. 'Not a word.'

'Yet you did not think to check with me?' responded Pacorus. 'And
tried to prevent another senior centurion from bringing the matter to my
attention?'

'I didn't want to disturb you,' Vahram said weakly.

With a dismissive snort, the commander shuffled over. He was followed solicitously by Ishkan.

Tarquinius lifted his head to stare Pacorus in the face. Grey rings of exhaustion had formed under his dark eyes, and his broken nose had swollen beyond all recognition. The burn on his cheek was red raw and oozing clear fluid. Remarkably, in spite of his injuries, there was still an air of mystery about him.

Pacorus flinched at the haruspex' appearance. This was the man who had saved his life, and he was not ungrateful for that. Yet there was no trust between them. 'Well?'

Tarquinius jerked his head, indicating Pacorus should come closer.

Ishkan frowned warily but did not intervene. Tied-up, the half-dead haruspex posed no threat. Yet Vahram looked most unhappy.

'It was *his* name I was saying,' whispered Tarquinius. 'The *primus pilus* immediately wanted to know why. If I had told him, he would have killed me.'

'Looks like he was going to do that anyway,' Pacorus answered drily.

'Yes, sir,' gasped the haruspex. 'And I was just about to break when Ishkan arrived. Do not trust him.'

Pacorus looked back at Vahram, who instantly affected not to be interested. 'Why not?'

'He wants to lead the Forgotten Legion.'

The commander stiffened. 'Have you proof of this?'

Tarquinius was still able to raise his eyebrows.

Pacorus tapped a finger against his teeth, thinking. It was no surprise to him that the *primus pilus* might want to usurp his position. But it was also an easy way for Tarquinius to sow the seeds of doubt and distrust among his captors.

The drained haruspex read his mind. 'Where are your men?' he asked quietly.

Alarm filled Pacorus as he scanned the courtyard, seeing none of his bodyguards. This was the most significant detail so far.

'Vahram sent them away.'

Pacorus said nothing in response to Tarquinius' intimation, but the muscles in his jaw bunched. What was the best thing to do? Vahram was a popular figure among the Parthian garrison, and executing him out of hand could prove risky. Obviously Ishkan was loyal, but could he rely on all the other senior centurions? Still not fully recovered, he was just beginning to understand how easily he could have been killed. Concealing his emotions, Pacorus turned to the *primus pilus*. 'It was foolish to go this far,' he barked. 'He's useful in his own way.'

'Sorry, sir.' Vahram waited to see if there was more.

'I want you supervising sentry duty for the next three months,' the commander ordered. 'Consider yourself lucky not to be demoted.'

Vahram saluted, delighted that his punishment was so light. Tarquinius had revealed nothing and now he could continue to plot against Pacorus.

They were interrupted by the sound of running feet in the avenue outside. A sentry's challenge rang out, and was answered. Then the front gate creaked open.

Pacorus stared at Ishkan, who shrugged. Vahram looked similarly puzzled.

Above, the storm had abated. Tarquinius could determine nothing of relevance in what he saw. They were all in the dark.

A few moments later, a cloaked legionary emerged into the courtyard, accompanied by one of the Parthian warriors who guarded Pacorus' quarters. Both saluted and stood to attention.

'What is it?' cried Pacorus impatiently.

'This is one of the sentries from the main gate, sir,' said the Parthian. 'Some of Darius' men have returned.'

A cold sweat broke out on Tarquinius' forehead. Like him, Romulus and Brennus served in Darius' cohort. Where had they been?

Confused, the commander turned to Vahram.

'I sent out a patrol two days ago, sir,' explained the *primus pilus*. 'There had been no word from the fortlet to the east.'

Satisfied, Pacorus indicated that the legionary should speak.

'Three men have just got back, sir,' he faltered.

'Messengers?'

'No, sir.' There was a pause. 'Survivors.'

All the senior officers gasped. Tarquinius managed to stay silent, but his gaze was locked on the sentry.

'When they got to the fortlet, the garrison had already been massacred, sir. More Scythian raiders, apparently.'

Tarquinius' mind was suddenly filled with the image he had seen of a barrack-room floor covered in blood. And of the red flashes against the snowy landscape. Scythians always rode red-coloured horses. His misery deepened.

'They said that Darius sent two riders back with the news,' the soldier went on.

'We've heard nothing,' interrupted Vahram.

'They'll have been intercepted,' said Ishkan grimly.

Nervous, the sentry waited.

'Go on,' demanded Pacorus.

'Same lot attacked the patrol, sir. Annihilated it at dawn the next day as it was trying to retreat here.'

'Leaving three soldiers out of . . .'

'Two centuries, sir,' answered Vahram.

'And Darius? Is he here?'

The sentry shook his head. 'No, sir.'

Pacorus scowled. Nearly one hundred and sixty men dead, and now Darius. One of his best officers. 'How many Scythians?' he asked.

The question had to be repeated.

'They said a few thousand, sir,' said the fearful sentry at last.

All the colour left Pacorus' face. 'Mithras above,' he muttered, wishing he were fully recovered.

'It's the middle of winter,' Vahram ranted. 'The mountain passes to Scythia are blocked with snow!'

'Where are they?' Pacorus demanded. 'These survivors?'

'The duty *optio* sent them to the *valetudinarium*, sir,' replied the sentry. 'They're suffering from exposure and frostbite.'

'I don't give a damn!' screamed the commander, his face going puce. 'Bring them here at once!'

The sentry and the Parthian warrior scuttled from sight, grateful not to have been punished.

'This cannot go unanswered,' Pacorus growled, waving Vahram and Ishkan into his chamber. Almost as an afterthought, he looked back at Tarquinius. 'Cut those ropes,' he ordered Ishkan's men. 'Carry him in here.'

The haruspex gritted his teeth as he was borne none too gently inside and laid by the fire for the second time. While his body was torn and bruised, and his mind exhausted, he was anxious to hear all the news from the returned legionaries. Yet every breath, shallow or deep, hurt. Using all his powers of concentration, Tarquinius managed to keep himself alert while the Parthians waited. Pacorus quickly sat down on his bed, while Ishkan and Vahram took their places on stools alongside. Their low muttering filled the air. Some response would have to be made to the Scythian incursion. And fast. Although it was not campaigning weather, the tribesmen could not be left to ravage the area unchecked.

Tarquinius only cared about whether his friends had been on the ill-fated patrol or not. Everything else, even his own life, paled into insignificance.

After what seemed an age, there was a heavy knock at the door.

'Enter!' cried Pacorus.

A trio of legionaries shuffled in, their faces chapped and feet still blue with cold. They looked distinctly intimidated at being in the presence of the Forgotten Legion's commander. Most low-rankers never came face to face with Pacorus, except to be punished. And unless their story was plausible, that was a distinct possibility. Pushed forward by a number of warriors, the men reluctantly moved to stand before the Parthian officers. They did not notice the bloodied man lying in a heap by the fire.

Tarquinius recognised them at once, and his heart sank. Novius, Optatus and Ammias were from his own century, which meant that Romulus and Brennus were dead. He lay back, rare tears welling in his eyes. After years of protection, Tinia had utterly forsaken him and those whom he loved. And Mithras, the god whom he had begun to trust, was no different.

'Make your report,' ordered Pacorus.

Naturally it was Novius who spoke. He related the story of the patrol with minimal emotion. Like many legionaries, he spoke little Parthian, so Ishkan translated. After Darius, he was the senior centurion who spoke most Latin. Apart from an occasional interruption from Pacorus or Vahram, the story was delivered to a silent, horrified audience. The final battle was particularly emotive for Tarquinius, who could almost see his friends dying beneath the showers of poisoned Scythian arrows.

Having related the two centuries' fate, the little legionary paused. His life and that of his comrades hinged upon what transpired next. Cowardice was not tolerated in either the Roman or Parthian armies. Soldiers who ran from a battle were liable to be executed out of hand. Their reasons for surviving had to convince their commander.

And Tarquinius.

Pacorus knew exactly why Novius was uneasy. 'How is it,' he said, picking his words very carefully, 'that you three escaped without any wounds?'

Ishkan translated.

'The gods were smiling on us, sir,' Novius replied at once. 'It wasn't as if we were the only ones not to be hit. When the testudo collapsed at the end, two other lads broke free with us, but they were struck by arrows as we ran.'

Optatus and Ammias grimaced in unison.

'Then they both stayed to fight a rearguard action, sir,' said Novius, bowing his head. 'Saved our lives.'

Tarquinius studied the little legionary's face intently, searching for evidence of lies. So far, his story sounded genuine. But he had noticed that Novius' eyes kept flicking up and to the left. And malice oozed from him like bile from a cut gall bladder. The injured haruspex was unsure why, but he did not like Novius. Or trust him.

'I see.' Pacorus said nothing for a few moments. 'And there were no more survivors?'

Novius glanced uneasily at his companions.

Vahram seized upon the look like a cat on a mouse. 'There were!'

Ammias gave Novius the faintest of signals, as did Optatus.

The haruspex frowned at their move, which seemed rehearsed. Perhaps because they did not speak fluent Latin, the Parthians appeared not to notice. Had the trio fled the patrol before the final encounter, and watched from a hidden vantage point as their comrades were massacred? Tarquinius waited.

'We were obviously done for, sir,' the little legionary admitted. 'Some men ran. It happens.'

'Yet you did not,' said Pacorus.

Novius was shocked. 'Of course not, sir.'

Partially satisfied, Pacorus looked at Ishkan and the *primus pilus*. They briefly convened in a huddle to decide if they believed Novius' account.

It appeared they did, thought Tarquinius bitterly. He did not.

'I need the names and ranks of any men who fled,' said Pacorus at length.

Silence.

'Unless you want a cross each.'

The commander's threat hung in the air.

'Forgive us, sir,' grovelled Novius, genuinely afraid now. 'We're loyal soldiers.'

'Names,' said Pacorus. 'Now.'

Novius swallowed hard. 'I only got a good look at two, sir. Both plain legionaries, but not Romans.'

The commander glared. To him, the nationality of the men under his command was irrelevant.

'Romulus, sir,' said Novius hurriedly. 'And a big Gaulish brute by the name of Brennus.'

Tarquinius bit back the retort which sprang to his lips. He would have given Novius the benefit of the doubt about any other men in the century. Now, though, it was certain that he was a liar. *My friends would never run.*

Pacorus swelled with anger. How could he forget the young soldier who had refused to give him his shield? It was the last thing he remembered before being struck by the Scythian arrows. 'Cowardly scum,' he growled.

'I know those men too, sir,' Vahram hissed. His gaze strayed to Tarquinius, who instantly pretended to be unconscious. 'They're treacherous bastards. Friends of his.' He jerked a thumb at the haruspex.

Novius understood enough Parthian to turn his head and see the figure lying by the fire. He smiled in malevolent recognition. It was their own non-Roman centurion, who had been left behind while they went on the patrol. Tarquinius' battered appearance told its own story. 'That's right, sir,' he said viciously. 'And the centurion was always showing them extra favours.'

'Did they escape?' asked Pacorus.

'Not sure, sir,' answered the little legionary. 'It was right in the middle of the fight, you see.'

Optatus and Ammias shook their heads in agreement.

The commander bared his misshapen, yellow teeth. 'Let's hope that the Scythians find the mangy dogs. Or that the gods deliver them to us once more.'

Novius bobbed his head ingratiatingly, concealing the gleam of triumph in his eyes.

The haruspex' intuition told him the true story. It was the three ragged soldiers who had run from the massacre. Then, at the end, they had seen Romulus and Brennus fight their way free. He did not know whether to rejoice or to cry. His friends might be alive, but they were alone in the frozen wilderness with no supplies. Even if they managed to escape the Scythians, certain death now awaited them if they reached the fort.

And he could do nothing about it.

Utter helplessness swamped Tarquinius, and weakened by his wounds and the cold, he succumbed to unconsciousness.

Chapter XIII: Betrayal

Margiana, winter 53/52 BC

R omulus' first awareness was of the terrible pain that filled his head. Great waves of it washed over him, utterly draining his energy. Then there would be a short lag phase before another hit. After an age, he felt able to move again. By gently wriggling them, Romulus could feel his fingers and his toes. They were not warm, but at least they still functioned. Aware that he was lying flat on a rough stone floor, the young soldier gingerly opened his eyes.

There was a low roof almost within hand's reach. It was a cave. Turning his head, the first thing Romulus saw was Brennus' muscular back, bending over a small fire. Relief filled him. They were still free. Mithras had saved their lives after all.

'Where are we?' Romulus croaked, his throat dry with thirst.

The Gaul spun on his heel, a wide grin splitting his blood-covered face. 'Belenus be thanked!' he cried. 'I wasn't sure if your skull had been cracked.'

Romulus lifted a hand to the back of his head and probed gently. 'Don't think so,' he replied, wincing as his fingers found a fist-sized lump just above the hairline. 'Damn painful though.'

'Thankfully this took the worst of it,' said Brennus, lifting a battered lump of bronze which Romulus vaguely recognised as his helmet. 'I had difficulty getting it off.'

'What happened?'

'It was Primitivus,' revealed Brennus, his breath visible in the chill air. 'Crept up and hit you from behind. I slew the fool immediately, but you had already gone down.'

The veterans would stop at nothing. Romulus shook his head in confusion, releasing another wave of agony. 'Are you injured?'

'No,' said the Gaul. 'This is Primitivus' blood.'

Romulus was very relieved. 'How in Hades did we get away?'

'With Primitivus gone, Novius and his mates tried to make a break for it. Two or three others ran too,' said Brennus. 'It distracted many of the Scythians. The remainder were busy attacking what few of our lot weren't killed or injured. Somehow I was sure that it wasn't my time to die. I wasn't sure you were dead either, so I fell down and pulled Primitivus on top of me. The enemy cavalry drove forward, leaving us on open ground. The fighting went on for some time, and no one was looking back. It was just a matter of carrying you over the nearest rise and out of view. After taking a breather, I went up into the broken ground. Found this cave about half a mile away.'

The young soldier could only marvel at his friend's strength. The distance Brennus had mentioned so casually would have crippled any other man. 'What about the rest?'

The Gaul's face darkened. 'Gone,' he said heavily. 'I looked back once and there were maybe fifteen men still standing. But the Scythians were swarming around them like rats. They had no chance.'

Romulus closed his eyes. Even though the legionaries had recently made them outcasts, he felt genuine grief. They had been serving in the same century for over six months, and in the same army for over two years.

'It wasn't for nothing,' growled Brennus. 'They bought us enough time to escape.'

'That makes it even worse.'

'Our burden is heavier because of it,' Brennus agreed, remembering his uncle's sacrifice.

'And just think what the Scythians will do to the bodies.'

'Don't think about that. Our getting away means that the gods have not totally forgotten us. We live to fight another day.'

'True,' admitted Romulus. 'What about Novius and the others? Did they make it?'

Brennus' face darkened. 'I don't know,' he said. 'Let's hope not.'

*　*　*

Without blankets, food or equipment, the friends had no choice but to leave the small cave behind. All it provided was shelter and slight relief from the bitter weather. And news of the Scythian incursion had to be carried back quickly. The raiders would attack again soon, perhaps even at the fort. Using the bright stars to guide their path, they tracked steadily west. There was no sign of the enemy, meaning their escape had probably gone unseen. It was just as well. Brennus had retained his longsword, but all Romulus had to defend himself with was his *pugio*. Neither had shields. An encounter with the fierce warriors would have only one outcome.

The rest in the cave did not sustain Romulus for long on the freezing, difficult march. With his pounding headache, the young soldier was very grateful for Brennus' broad shoulder to lean on. As time passed, his strength returned somewhat, as did his determination. Besides, marching was the best way to keep even slightly warm. Under their cloaks, their chain mail was an icy deadweight, while their exposed lower legs were chilled to the bone. Sweat condensed instantly on their brows, and the air was so cold that every breath hurt.

When the outline of the crucifix finally appeared, Romulus felt great relief. Reaching it meant that their suffering was nearly over. But by starlight, the frozen body was even more terrifying. It was impossible not to stare at it as they walked past. Flesh now picked from his bones, the legionary was little more than a skeleton. Even his internal organs had been consumed by the hungry vultures. Teeth grinned from a lipless mouth; empty eye sockets seemed to watch their every step. This time though, Romulus saw nothing beyond the bare bones. But the memory of what he'd seen before burned brightly in his mind. And Tarquinius had seen a path home. Mithras, he prayed. Help me return to Rome.

Brennus made the sign against evil. 'Not a good way to go, eh?'

Romulus shook his head, making his headache worse than ever. 'No bastard is ever going to do that to me.'

'Nor me,' swore Brennus.

Yet crucifixion was one of the punishments they might receive on their return. It was impossible to predict how the volatile *primus pilus* would react to their cataclysmic news. 'What should we do?'

'Trust the gods,' Brennus advised. 'Tell the truth. We've done nothing wrong.'

Romulus sighed, unable to think of anything else. Brennus' faith carried him through situations like they were in now. Normally Romulus struggled with this simple approach. Here in god-forsaken Margiana, death seemed the only certainty in life. But they had survived the ambush, and he gave Mithras the full credit for that. Otherwise Brennus would have fought to the death. Afterwards, both of them would have been beheaded by the Scythians.

They tramped on in grim silence.

By the time the fort's reassuring shape came into sight, the sky was lightening. This time, a vigilant sentry challenged the pair long before they reached the main entrance. Brennus' bellowed answer, his simple horse-hair-crested helmet and their obvious Roman uniforms were enough to see the gate opened. They had reached safety.

Or so they thought.

The pair received none of the welcome they might have expected when the portal creaked ajar. Instead the waiting faces were full of anger and contempt. The instant they had passed within, a ring of legionaries formed around them, their *gladii* and shields raised threateningly.

'Hold on a moment,' bristled Brennus. 'What's going on?'

'The Scythians out there are the damn enemy, not us,' added Romulus.

'Really?' spat a grizzled soldier with one eye. 'Cowards!'

'What?' responded Romulus disbelievingly. 'Brennus fought his way free. He saved my life!'

'Liar,' shouted another sentry.

'You ran and left your comrades to die,' cried a third.

'Novius got back before us,' Romulus whispered to Brennus, horrified. 'The scabby shitbag!' And Brennus escaped because the gods told him to, he told himself.

The Gaul gave him a resigned nod. Things were going from bad to worse.

'Of course they fled,' said the one-eyed man viciously. 'They're fucking slaves.'

'I've never run from anyone,' began Brennus angrily. Then an image of his burning village came to mind. *I left my wife and child to die.* The memory was a weeping sore in his soul. He fell silent.

A chorus of sneers met his weak protest and the Gaul hung his head.

Romulus was about to say more, but one look at the hard, closed faces all around was enough for the words to die in his throat. His pounding head made it even harder to concentrate, so he sealed his lips. Do not desert us, Mithras, Romulus thought desperately. Not now.

'We should just kill them,' shouted a voice from the back. 'Get it over with.'

At this, the friends gripped their weapons and prepared to fight to the death.

'Quiet!' barked the *optio* in charge. 'Pacorus wants to see this pair immediately. He'll have something tasty for them up his sleeve, no doubt.'

Cruel laughter filled the air.

Romulus and Brennus looked at each other numbly. It seemed that their commander had survived, which meant that Tarquinius was still alive. Given their hostile reception, though, they might never see him again.

'Take their weapons,' said the *optio* briskly. 'Tie their arms.'

Eager to obey, men swarmed in and stripped the friends of longsword and *pugio*. Neither fought back. Defenceless, their wrists were tightly bound behind their backs with thick rope. Urged on with kicks and taunts, they were frogmarched towards the headquarters.

The fort was just beginning to come alive for the day. A cock cried repeatedly from his roost near the stables for the mules. The smell of baking bread reached them from the ovens. Legionaries were emerging from their barracks, yawning and stretching. Throats were being cleared; phlegm spat on the frozen ground. Queues formed outside the latrines; men joked and laughed with each other. Few took any notice of the small party going past.

Until the one-eyed soldier took it upon himself to let everyone know.

'Look who it is, boys!' he roared. 'The escaped slaves!'

The *optio* turned and glared, but it was too late. The harm had been done. Sleep-filled faces twisted with anger and insults were hurled through the air. More than one gob of spit flew in their direction. Over and over, the same phrases were repeated and Romulus burned with anger and shame to hear them.

'Cowards!'

'You left your friends to die!'

'Crucify them!'

Men swarmed on to the Via Praetoria, surrounding the *optio* and his men. Jostling and shoving, they tried to reach the prisoners. The sentries did not put up much resistance.

Romulus shrank away from the mauling hands. Having survived the horror of the patrol, it was utterly demoralising to be on the receiving end of such vitriol. But dying at the hands of a lynch mob held even less appeal. Brennus, his shoulders slumped, barely seemed to notice. This is my reward for running from my family, he thought. The gods' final revenge. There will be no cleansing redemption in battle.

'Stand back!' ordered the *optio*, using energetic swipes of his staff to beat the enraged legionaries on their arms and shoulders. 'Anyone who harms them gets fifty lashes!'

Sullenly the soldiers moved away, allowing the group to continue its journey to the Praetoria. Even the Parthian guards there looked down their noses at the two friends. The reaction of those inside the imposing gate was exactly the same. The doorways of the offices and storerooms positioned on three sides of the square forehall soon filled with disapproving faces. The nerve centre of the fort, this was where the quartermaster and a host of junior officers and clerks worked to keep the Forgotten Legion running smoothly. Few of them ever saw combat, but their attitude was just as extreme as the other soldiers. Desertion during combat was one of the most cowardly acts a legionary could commit. Death was the only punishment.

Their lives depended on Pacorus as never before.

They were taken inside the large chamber which directly faced the entrance. The *optio* made his report to the centurion who had been in charge of the fort overnight. Immediately a runner was sent to fetch Pacorus and the senior centurions.

Romulus found himself looking over at the shrine, where the legion's silver eagle and its other standards were kept. Positioned to one side of the main offices, it was guarded night and day by a pair of sentries. Heavy curtains obscured the standards from view. He longed to prostrate himself before the metal bird and ask for its help. Here, in the centre of the fort, was where its power was strongest. But it was a faint hope. No one was about to let a slave accused of running from the enemy pray to the most sacred item belonging to the legion.

Instead, Romulus pictured the silver eagle in his head. With its protectively outstretched wings, it was a powerful symbol of Rome. He did not cease praying to Mithras though. Surely the god would understand the importance of the bird to him? He was a Roman soldier and followed the legion's symbol with fierce pride. That did not diminish his belief in the warrior god who regarded all men in the same light. Equally, Romulus felt that the eagle would value his courage over the fact that he was a slave.

'So!' Pacorus' voice reached them first. 'The cowards have returned.' Accompanied by Ishkan, Vahram and all the other senior officers, the legion's commander stalked into view. A large party of warriors trotted behind them. Only Darius was missing. The early hour had not stopped any of the Parthians from wanting to be present. Romulus was struck by how ill Pacorus still looked, but twin red points of anger marked his hollow cheeks. Rage was giving him the energy to be here.

There was no sign of Tarquinius, the man whose hard work had brought Pacorus back from the brink. Disappointment swamped Romulus. Another mountain had been placed in their way. If the haruspex had been restored to favour, they might have stood a better chance.

When the officers had come to a halt, the *optio* and his men shoved Romulus and Brennus forward.

'What have you to say?' demanded Pacorus harshly.

'Before you are crucified,' added Vahram with a cruel smile.

'Scum,' said Ishkan.

Romulus looked at Brennus and was shocked to see dumb acceptance of their fate. 'This is my destiny,' whispered the Gaul. 'I deserted my own family and people when they needed me.'

'No,' hissed Romulus. 'It wasn't your fault! Your journey is not over.' But there was no time to persuade his friend. He was on his own.

The *optio* struck Romulus heavily across the shoulder blades with his staff. 'Answer the commander!'

He clenched his teeth to stop himself wheeling around and attacking the junior officer. The Parthians would know the truth at least. 'It wasn't us who ran, sir.'

Vahram threw back his head and laughed. Pacorus and the others just looked incredulous.

'It's true.' Romulus took a deep breath and tried to stay calm. Somehow he pushed away the pain in his head, focusing instead on their critical situation. It was vital that he persuade the Parthians of their story. 'Where are the liars who accused us of running, sir? At least let us hear the accusation from their mouths.'

Pacorus was taken aback.

'That's fair enough, sir,' said Ishkan.

'Why bother?' protested Vahram. 'Look at them! It's obvious that the dogs are guilty.'

The commander gave his senior centurion a measured stare before lifting a hand. An *optio* ran off to do his bidding.

Thank you, Mithras. Romulus breathed a small sigh of relief. Obviously all was not well between Pacorus and the *primus pilus*. If he could utilise that factor to their advantage, there might be some hope yet.

'Tell us what happened then,' ordered Vahram curtly. 'While we wait.'

Romulus did as he was told. By the time he had finished, Ishkan at least appeared to believe him. But Pacorus, and particularly Vahram, seemed utterly unmoved.

Despairing, Brennus was of no help. He stood beside Romulus, looking at the floor.

The Parthians began to speak quick-fire in their own language. From the gesticulations and arm-waving, it was obvious that the *primus pilus* wanted them both dead. Ishkan was more measured, speaking in a deep, calm voice, while Pacorus stood with eyes narrowed, pondering.

At length the *optio* returned. Novius, Optatus and Ammias were two steps behind him. They had clearly been asleep until a few moments earlier. But all weariness fell away when they saw Romulus and Brennus. Novius' face twisted with hate, and he muttered something to his companions.

'This young soldier says that you were lying,' announced Pacorus without preamble. 'That in fact you and your comrades were the ones to run.'

Furious, Optatus opened his mouth to speak, but Novius laid a hand on his arm.

'Of course he does, sir,' the little legionary said smoothly. 'But his word can't be trusted. He and his friend are damn slaves. Not citizens like us.'

Optatus and Ammias nodded righteously. In Rome, slaves' testament was only valid if it had been obtained by torture.

Pacorus seemed confused, so Ishkan leaned over and whispered in his ear. He had heard about the two friends' isolation in the days preceding the patrol.

'Idiot,' the commander snapped. 'You are all my prisoners. Who or what you were before Carrhae is irrelevant.'

'Not to us, sir,' replied Novius fiercely. 'It's very important.'

'That's right,' added Ammias. 'Sir.'

Shrewd enough to see how much it meant to the legionaries, Pacorus turned to Romulus. 'Is it true?' he demanded. 'You are slaves?'

There was little point in lying. This was all about who was telling the truth. 'We are,' he said heavily.

Brennus shot him an alarmed glance, but Romulus stayed calm.

'I knew it!' Novius crowed with delight. His friends looked similarly jubilant.

Pacorus waited.

'That doesn't mean I ran away,' Romulus growled. 'Courage belongs to all men.'

'True,' Pacorus answered. 'But I cannot tell which of you is lying.' He turned to the *primus pilus*. 'The whole damn thing is far more trouble than I need. Crucify them all.'

Vahram saluted with gusto. This would be a duty he would take great pleasure in. It was of little matter to him how many legionaries who went up on crosses. And, as friends of Tarquinius, he deeply distrusted the huge Gaul and his protégé. The *primus pilus* waved his hand and the Parthian warriors swarmed around Novius and his companions.

They looked terrified.

Pacorus frowned at the three veterans' reactions. They were very different to those of Romulus and Brennus, who seemed accepting of their fate. 'Wait,' he said. 'I've changed my mind.' The commander pointed at Novius, Optatus and Ammias. 'You lot will fight the slaves,' he said. 'To the death.'

The little legionary looked uncertainly at his comrades.

Three against two, thought Romulus. Those odds aren't too bad. Even the Gaul lifted his head. But Romulus eyed Pacorus with suspicion. Why this sudden change of heart?

Suddenly Vahram, who had been visibly disappointed, grinned. He guessed what was coming.

Pacorus wasn't finished. 'Slaves are not soldiers,' he went on. 'They should not bear weapons. It will be three swords against two pairs of bare hands.'

Romulus' mouth opened while Novius could barely conceal his glee.

'The gods will decide who is telling the truth,' said Pacorus.

'When?' asked Ishkan.

The commander rubbed his hands together. 'Right now,' he answered. 'Why not?'

Brennus' shoulders lifted at last. This way I can die fighting, he thought.

Romulus clenched his jaw, determined to die like a man.

The gods had granted them another faint chance.

Without further ado, they were marched out to the *intervallum*. Pacorus wanted as many men as possible to witness the combat, so the centuries from the nearest barracks were hastily assembled as well. The soldiers needed little encouragement. They poured out into the dawn air, eager to watch the unscheduled entertainment. Instead of the rope square used in the *ludus*, or the wooden enclosure of the arena, the fighting space was formed by dozens of legionaries, holding their *scuta* before them. Parthian warriors were stationed at regular intervals around the perimeter, their bows drawn. Another group stood protectively around Pacorus and the senior centurions.

Romulus and Brennus were untied and left to stand in one corner. Rubbing their wrists to restore the circulation in their hands, the two friends paid no attention to the curious stares of the men around them. The insults that filled the air were harder to ignore. These were their former comrades. Romulus burned to deny the charges being thrown at them, but he saved his energy, every scrap of which would be needed in the next few moments. Diagonally opposite were Novius, Ammias and Optatus. The veterans' armour and weapons had been fetched, and the three were busy donning their mail shirts and bronze helmets. With his left thigh still strapped, Caius was near his friends, his face full of relief that he was not part of it.

Romulus racked his brains for their best option. Somehow at least one of them had to arm himself. Quickly. It would not take their experienced enemies long to injure and kill two unarmed men.

'We split up,' whispered Brennus.

Romulus could not believe his ears. 'Our only hope is to stick together,' he protested.

'I'm bigger. Two of the bastards will go for me,' said the Gaul confidently. 'That gives you the chance to take a weapon from the third.'

It didn't seem much of an option.

'What will you do?'

'I'll manage,' Brennus answered grimly. 'Just get a sword.'

Romulus had no better alternative, and he had no time to think of one.

The veterans had armed themselves. With chain mail, shields and *gladii*, they were now a fearsome prospect.

'Begin!' shouted Pacorus.

There was a pause.

The commander bellowed an order and his men raised their bows. 'They will loose on the count of three,' he said. 'One . . .'

Fury filled Romulus. In the *ludus*, Memor's archers had forced him to fight a vicious Goth called Lentulus. That combat had also been to the death. But at least then I was armed, he thought. His heart pounded in his chest. What chance had they?

The three legionaries rushed to stand side by side. Drawing their swords, they brought their *scuta* together to form a small shield wall.

'Two.'

They began to advance, their faces grim and set.

Satisfied, Pacorus fell silent.

This is better than crucifixion, thought Brennus, adrenalin pumping through him. 'Now,' he muttered and darted away to one side.

Obeying, Romulus shot off in the opposite direction.

Pleasingly, Novius' and his comrades' faces were the picture of surprise. But they regained their composure fast. After the slightest pause, Novius and Ammias followed Romulus. Rolling his shoulders, Optatus went for Brennus.

Romulus cursed. The Gaul's plan had not worked. The veterans also planned to take down the weaker man first.

Him.

'Can't even fight with each other, eh?' Novius sneered as they drew nearer.

'We're not the ones who ran,' retorted Romulus. 'You are. Damn liars.'
Ammias actually looked guilty.

'Shut your mouth,' hissed Novius, lunging forward with his *gladius*.
'Filthy slave.'

Angering the little legionary might provide a chink of opportunity,
thought Romulus, dodging to the left. A quick thrust from Ammias followed
and desperately he shuffled backwards. Gloating, Novius and his comrade
split up.

Romulus had a brief moment before he was assailed from in front and
behind. Novius was the more dangerous of his opponents, and might see
through the only trick he could think of. The young soldier acted immediately. He ran forward and at the last moment, threw himself down on
the ground just in front of Ammias, rolling forward to collide with his
legs. The risky plan worked, and the veteran fell forward, cursing. Laden
down with weapons and his chain mail, he was momentarily helpless.
Wriggling free, Romulus jumped to his feet and delivered a huge kick to
his enemy's unprotected groin. Ammias screamed and dropped his sword.

It was the opportunity he had been praying for.

Romulus leaned over and grabbed the veteran's *gladius*. But there was
no chance of getting the shield as well. He pulled back to avoid a lethal
thrust from Novius, who had swept forward to aid his friend. Romulus
moved away, sliding his sandals carefully to make sure he did not lose his
footing on the icy ground. The little legionary did not pursue him, instead
helping up Ammias, who looked more embarrassed than anything. Romulus'
manoeuvre had been something only a novice would fall for. Wincing in
pain, Ammias pulled out his *pugio* and waved it at him.

'Ready to feel this in your guts?' he cried.

'Come and try,' sneered Romulus, holding up the *gladius*.

The two veterans made for him at the trot.

Romulus breathed deeply, filling his lungs with cold air. His situation
was only a fraction less critical than it had been. He glanced over his
shoulder to see how Brennus was doing. To his relief, the Gaul was still
unhurt. He was dancing around Optatus, ducking and weaving away from
thrusts of the big soldier's sword.

Again Romulus' enemies split up, preparing to hit him simultaneously
this time.

His fingers closed tightly around the sword's bone hilt as he watched them approach. It was times like this which separated cowards from the courageous. There was only one thing to do, thought Romulus. Go on the attack. If he waited until they reached him, it would be over in a few heartbeats. Which one? It took a mere instant to decide. Novius. It was Novius who was smaller.

Romulus charged straight at the little legionary, whose eyes widened at his audacity. Preparing himself, Novius ducked behind his *scutum*, protecting himself from his neck to his lower legs. The curved shield's size meant that it was almost impossible to deliver a fatal blow to the man holding it. But that was not Romulus' intention. Closing in, he feinted to one side, letting Novius think that he was attacking from his right. The legionary raised his *gladius*, ready to strike. At the last instant, the young soldier danced the other way and dropped his left shoulder. With an almighty heave, he barged into Novius' *scutum*, using his superior body weight to drive the legionary backwards. Used to having a comrade on his left side to defend him, Novius was caught unawares. Then his *caligae* slipped on a patch of frost and he fell, landing on the flat of his back. The impact drove the air from his lungs, winding him.

Romulus acted fast. Pulling the heavy *scutum* up and out of the way, he thrust his sword into his enemy's throat. Novius' pupils dilated with shock as the sharp iron blade sliced through soft flesh to grate off the vertebrae in his neck. Bright red blood gushed from the wound, staining the ground beneath. Novius' mouth opened and closed, like a fish out of water. Two heartbeats later, he was dead.

It was a quick end for the malevolent little legionary, thought Romulus. Too quick.

He looked back. Pelting in, Ammias was only a few paces away. His voice was distorted in a scream of fury. Again Romulus had to retreat without a shield. But his opponent was able to pick up a *gladius* as he stepped over Novius' body. They shuffled around, trading blows, each searching for weaknesses in the other. Twice, Ammias shoved his gilt shield boss at Romulus' face, but the young soldier was ready for the classic move and dodged backwards both times. Frustrated and angered by Novius' death, the veteran's attacks grew more frenzied.

Stay calm, Romulus thought. He'll make a mistake eventually. They always do.

From behind him came the unmistakable sound of a man crying out in pain.

Romulus couldn't help himself. He turned to see what had happened. Optatus had sliced Brennus across his left arm, opening a long cut from his elbow to his wrist. As blood welled from the wound, the Gaul desperately retreated, trying to avoid further injury.

Too late, the young soldier remembered Ammias. In slow motion, he spun back. His enemy's shield boss hit him full in the chest and Romulus heard a dull crack as two of his ribs broke. Used like this, the Roman *scutum* was an excellent offensive weapon. Stars cascaded across Romulus' vision and he landed heavily, dropping his sword.

At once Ammias kicked it out of reach. Snarling with rage, he stooped over Romulus. 'You killed my friend,' he growled. 'And the Gaulish bastard did for Primitivus. Now it's your turn.'

Romulus clenched his jaw in an effort not to cry out. Sharp needles were stabbing him with every breath. Sensing his weakness, the grinning veteran kicked him viciously.

He nearly passed out from the pain.

'Like that?' gloated Ammias. 'Slave scum.'

Romulus could not answer. Through slitted eyes, he saw his opponent's *gladius* rise up.

Roars of approval came from the watching legionaries. The unexpected entertainment was proving to be hugely enjoyable. It was all the better if one of their comrades was victorious.

Enjoying his moment of victory, Ammias paused.

Romulus knew that death was an instant away. When the sword came down, his life would be over. A procession of thoughts flashed through his mind. Now there would be no chance to help Brennus. Or Tarquinius. No possible return to Rome. No reunion with Fabiola. And no revenge on Gemellus.

Had Jupiter and Mithras protected him for so long, only for him to die like a dog?

Scrabbling with his fingernails at the hard earth, Romulus managed to scoop up a small handful.

Grimacing, the veteran thrust downwards.

Ignoring the agony from his ribs, Romulus rolled to one side, sweeping up his arm at the same time. Ammias' move brought him within reach, and at the last moment, the young soldier opened his hand. Particles of dirt filled his enemy's eyes and his *gladius* plunged into the ground, missing Romulus by a handbreadth.

Blinded, Ammias cried out in agony.

Romulus seized the moment and punched him in the solar plexus, badly bruising his right fist against the veteran's chain mail.

Letting go of his sword hilt, Ammias went down, his mouth open in an 'O' of surprise.

A shocked silence fell over the assembled soldiers.

Holding his ribs with his left hand, Romulus got to his knees.

Beside him, Ammias was rolling around, trying to find his *gladius*.

Romulus got there first. Pulling it free with a grunt of effort, he smashed the flat of the blade across his enemy's face. There was a sound of cartilage breaking, which was followed by a strangled cry. Ammias reeled backwards, clutching his ruined nose. Blood poured from between his fingers; his eyes were inflamed and full of grit. He was no longer capable of fighting. Romulus briefly considered killing him. After all, Ammias was one of the men who had tried to murder him on multiple occasions, had been instrumental in turning the whole legion against him. But he was unarmed and unable to defend himself. Ripping Ammias' *scutum* from his grip, Romulus stood.

He was no cold-blooded murderer. And Brennus needed his help.

With his opponent already weakened by blood loss, Optatus was doing his level best to kill the Gaul. It was only Brennus' huge strength that had allowed him to continue resisting the legionary's skilful attacks. When Optatus saw Romulus running over, his efforts redoubled. Punches with his shield were followed instantly by thrusts of his *gladius*. It was a deadly one-two combination and difficult to resist for long.

Ignoring the waves of pain from his broken ribs as best he could, Romulus neared the pair. Finally Optatus had to turn and face him.

'On your own now,' said Romulus, buying time. 'How do you like that?'

Optatus could see the young soldier's sides heaving, could imagine why he was winded. 'Two injured slaves,' he replied, his top lip lifting with contempt. 'I'll kill you both!'

It was a bad mistake. While they were talking, Brennus had retrieved Novius' sword and shield. Despite his injury, the Gaul was now a second deadly opponent.

A moment later, the friends were poised on either side of the big legionary.

Optatus was no coward. He made no attempt to surrender or to run. Instead, he turned this way and that, wondering who would attack first.

But Romulus and Brennus held back. Both were reluctant to kill Optatus. Sensing their indecision, the veteran lunged forward at Romulus.

He moved back a step, taking the blow on his shield. Optatus did not let up, thrusting again and again at Romulus' face with his *gladius*. Without doubt, he was the toughest of the legionaries. If he could overcome the young soldier, there was a chance of his beating Brennus.

The Gaul could not stand by any longer. As Optatus drew back another time, he leaned in and sliced the veteran's left hamstring with his blade.

Optatus collapsed with a loud groan, instinctively holding up his shield to protect himself. Still he asked for no quarter. Yet, lying on his back, he now had no chance at all.

Grudging admiration filled Romulus at his bravery. He looked to Pacorus for a similar reaction. Brennus did likewise.

It was not forthcoming. The commander's face was creased with anger. Novius and his cronies had lied to him. Romulus' and Brennus' clemency to the veterans clearly demonstrated that. He snapped out an order and his archers raised their bows.

Romulus realised what was about to happen. 'No!' he cried.

Brennus closed his eyes. He had seen things like this all too often.

A dozen arrows hummed through the air. Six pinned Optatus to the ground, while the remainder spitted Ammias through the chest and abdomen. Both were killed instantly.

Silence fell over the *intervallum*. Reaching into their quivers, the warriors fitted new shafts to their bowstrings.

'So die all those who lie to me,' shouted Pacorus, the veins in his neck bulging. 'I am the commander of the Forgotten Legion!'

Unwilling to meet his furious stare, the audience of soldiers looked down. Even Vahram avoided Pacorus' eyes.

Romulus and Brennus moved closer together, uncertain how the volatile Parthian would react next.

Another order from the commander rang out.

At full draw, the archers' bows swung to cover the two friends.

Chapter XIV: A New Ally

Rome, winter 53/52 BC

'Only devotees may enter the Mithraeum,' said Secundus in a hard voice. 'And death is the penalty for those who break that rule.' Fabiola trembled. In this, the centre of his power, she saw him in an entirely different light. Now Secundus was a tall, powerful figure, his authority exuding from every pore. Produced from a wooden chest, a golden staff had appeared in his left hand and a red Phrygian cap sat on his head. This was no impoverished army cripple, begging for a coin to feed himself. The face that Secundus gave to the world outside was a complete façade.

Ringing them angrily, his men shouted in agreement.

'Take her up to the courtyard,' Secundus ordered. 'Make it quick.'

Without a chance to explain herself further, Fabiola was bundled towards the passageway to the stairs.

By entering the Mithraeum, she had unknowingly crossed an invisible line. Mithras had shown her where Romulus might be, but now she was going to die. As her brother would, if he was present at the battle she had seen. If the vision was real at all, Fabiola thought bitterly. What had the strange-tasting liquid done to her mind?

Curious to know before the end, she threw a question at Secundus. 'What's in the phial?'

The veterans holding her faltered.

'Wait!' snapped Secundus. His face had gone pinched. 'You drank from this?' he said slowly, lifting the blue glass from the altar top.

She nodded.

Seeing that it was empty, Secundus' nostrils flared with fury.

Swords slid from scabbards at the new outrage, but he raised a hand to stop any hasty action. 'Did you see anything?' he asked quietly.

Fabiola tensed, aware that everything hinged upon her answer. Faced with death, she wanted life.

'Answer me,' muttered Secundus, 'or, by Mithras, I will slay you here and now.'

Fabiola closed her eyes, asking the warrior god for his help. The truth, she thought. Tell the truth. 'I became a raven,' she said loudly, thinking that the men listening would laugh. 'Flying high over a strange land.'

Disbelieving gasps met her comment. She heard the word 'Corax' whispered repeatedly.

'You're sure?' Secundus barked. 'A raven?'

Fabiola stared into his eyes. 'I am.'

He looked confused.

'How can this be?' demanded one veteran.

'A woman as a sacred bird?' cried another.

The chamber resounded with questions.

Secundus raised his arms for quiet. Remarkably, his men obeyed. 'Tell me everything you saw,' he said to Fabiola. 'Do not leave out a single detail.'

Taking a deep breath, she began.

No one spoke as Fabiola recounted her vision. When she had finished, there was a stunned silence.

Secundus moved to stand before the three altars and the depiction of the tauroctony. Kneeling, he bent his head.

No one spoke, but the grip on Fabiola's arms relaxed slightly. A sidelong glance at the veterans holding her revealed fear, and awe, in their expressions. She did not know what to think. If they believed in her vision, did that mean it could be relied upon?

After a few moments, Secundus bowed from the waist and got to his feet.

All his men tensed, eager to hear if the god had spoken.

'She is not to be harmed,' Secundus said, his eyes moving steadily around the room. 'Anyone who drinks the *homa* and then dreams a raven is favoured by Mithras.'

The faces around Fabiola registered shock, disbelief and anger.

'Even a woman?' said the guard who had admitted them earlier. 'But it's forbidden!'

More dissenting voices joined in.

Secundus raised his arms for quiet, but the clamour grew louder.

'This is blasphemy,' shouted a figure near the back.

'Kill her!'

A knot formed in Fabiola's stomach. These tough ex-soldiers would show as little mercy as Scaevola's *fugitivarii*.

Secundus watched without reacting. Eventually there was a brief lull in the noise.

'I am the Pater,' he announced in a firm voice. 'Am I not?'

Men nodded their heads. The angry mutters died away, leaving a sullen silence.

'Have I led you astray before?'

No one answered.

'Well then,' said Secundus. 'Trust me now. Release her.'

To Fabiola's amazement, the veterans holding her arms let go. They moved away awkwardly, avoiding her gaze.

'Come here.' Secundus, the Pater, was beckoning to her.

Feeling relieved yet scared, she moved to his side.

'Back to your beds,' ordered Secundus. 'I will take charge of her.'

With plenty of backward glances, the hard-faced men did as they were told. A few moments later, Fabiola and Secundus were the only ones left in the underground chamber.

Fabiola raised an eyebrow. 'The Pater?'

'In the eyes of Mithras, I am their father,' he answered. 'As the most senior member of this temple, I am responsible for its security.' Alone, Secundus seemed even more intimidating. He regarded her sternly. 'You breached our trust to come in here without permission. Consider yourself lucky to be alive.'

Tears formed in Fabiola's eyes. 'I'm sorry,' she whispered.

'It is done,' said Secundus in a more forgiving tone. 'Mithras works in strange ways.'

'You believe me?' she asked, her voice trembling.

'I see no deceit in you. And you dreamt a raven.'

Fabiola had to ask. 'Was my vision real?'

'It was sent by the god,' he replied evasively. 'Yet the *homa* can take us far away. Too far sometimes.'

'I saw Roman soldiers. And my brother's friends,' she protested. 'About to fight a battle that no one could win. No one.' Fat tears rolled down Fabiola's cheeks.

'What you observed may never happen,' said Secundus calmly.

'Or it has done so already,' she retorted, filled with bitterness.

'That is true,' he acknowledged. 'Visions can show all possibilities.'

Fabiola hunched her shoulders, trying to hold in the grief.

'It is remarkable to have such a powerful dream after drinking *homa* for the first time,' said Secundus. 'And surely a sign from the god.'

'Your men don't seem convinced.'

'They will obey my orders,' said Secundus, frowning. 'For the moment.'

Fabiola was somewhat relieved.

His next words were startling. 'The first step in Mithraicism is to become a Corax. A raven. Many initiates never even see one.' He stared at her. 'Your vision means that we have met for a purpose.'

'How do you know?'

'Mithras reveals many things to me.' Secundus smiled, infuriating Fabiola. She felt as if he was playing with her. 'What are your plans?'

Fabiola reflected for a moment. She had originally intended to return to the *latifundium*. That was now impossible. So was staying in Rome. The uncertain political situation was proving to be even more dangerous than she had imagined and Scaevola was still at large in the city. Denied twice, the *fugitivarius* would not give up his pursuit of her now. Fabiola had no doubt about that. Yet without protection, where could she go? 'I don't know,' Fabiola replied, eyeing the figure of Mithras hopefully.

'You can't stay here,' he said. 'My men wouldn't stand for it.'

Fabiola was not surprised. She had broken one of the veterans' most sacred rules, and the threats shouted at her would not go away.

'More than one wants you dead for what was done here tonight.'

She was at his, and Mithras', mercy. Closing her eyes, Fabiola waited for Secundus to go on.

'Your lover is in Gaul with Caesar,' he said. 'Trying to quell Vercingetorix's rebellion.'

Her heart rate quickened. 'He is.'

'Brutus can protect you.'

'It's hundreds of miles to the border,' Fabiola faltered. 'Even more beyond that.'

'I will guide you,' he announced.

She controlled her shock. 'Why would you do this?'

'Two reasons,' grinned Secundus. He bowed towards the tauroctony. 'One is that the god desires me to.'

'And the second?'

'Caesar needs all the help he can get in Rome,' he answered with a sly wink. 'We'll see what he says to the offer of more than fifty veterans' swords. If he agrees, we'll get the recognition and pensions we deserve.'

It was a shrewd plan, thought Fabiola.

Years of absence from Rome had allowed Julius Caesar to write himself an undeniably impressive *curriculum vitae*: the conquest of Gaul and the immense wealth it yielded. Following this came incursions to Germania and Britannia, short but forceful campaigns to hammer home Rome's military superiority to the natives of those areas. Kept up to date with every victory by Caesar's messengers, the plebeians loved him for his dash and his martial tendencies.

Yet it was not enough: he was not daily on the ground in the city, pressing flesh, showing his face to the public, courting powerful nobles' and senators' favour. Bribes and the work of his minions could only do so much. Caesar still needed the influence of his surviving partner in the triumvirate: Pompey Magnus. Who, delighted by Crassus' death in Parthia, was paying lip service to his erstwhile ally while simultaneously making friends with every little faction in the Senate. Few of these loved Caesar, Rome's most illustrious general. As someone who had flouted the law before, he was too real a threat to the Republic. And now, with the political situation in real flux and anarchy threatening, Caesar was bogged down in Gaul for the foreseeable future. The offer of tough men in the capital would be tempting indeed.

'You have my thanks,' Fabiola said gratefully. 'But there will be bandits on the way. And Scaevola and his *fugitivarii* might follow us.'

Seeing her involuntary glance at his stump, the veteran laughed. 'It won't just be me. We'll have whatever comrades I can persuade.'

It only took Fabiola a moment to decide. The road north would be full of danger, and the situation in Gaul even more perilous. But what real option did she have?

Fabiola extended her arm in the man's fashion. Secundus smiled and accepted the grip.

Leaving the city turned out to be a wise plan. The sun had barely risen before plumes of smoke filled the sky. Yet more buildings were going up in flames. The mob was making the most of the fact that the Senate was paralysed by a combination of corruption, indecision and infighting. As civilian politicians, the senators were unprepared for, and rightly fearful of, such blatant, armed insurrection. The Republic's military was almost never needed within Italy itself, and to avoid attempts on power, legionary garrisons were prohibited within many miles of Rome. This rule left the city vulnerable to precisely such civil unrest. Now, having burned down the capital's most important building, Clodius' men were brimming with confidence. And when Milo's gladiators regrouped, they would want only one thing. Revenge.

Chaos had descended on Rome.

More violence was as inevitable as dusk followed dawn. Only trained soldiers could quell the bloodthirsty mobs, could bring safety to the warrens of dangerous streets and alleyways. Secundus and his men were too few to bring the situation under control. Crassus was gone to Hades and Caesar was far away. Without Pompey Magnus' involvement, Rome's future looked very bleak indeed. Unless they wished to see more public structures such as the markets and law courts, or even their own homes, burned down around their ears, the senators and nobles would have no choice but to ask for his help.

As they left the city walls behind, Fabiola remembered Brutus' prediction of this exact manoeuvre by Pompey. This was the man who had outwitted Crassus to take the credit for quelling the Spartacus rebellion, and then done the same to the general Lucullus, after he had almost crushed Mithridates' uprising in Asia Minor. Pompey was not about to be beaten to the ultimate prize. Bringing armed legionaries into the Forum Romanum for the first time since Sulla would give Pompey physical control of the Republic itself.

Yet the Senate had no other choice.

Five days later, it was as if the violence had never been. The screams of people caught up in the rioting had been replaced by birdsong, the creaking of the litter and the muttering of Secundus and his men. Leaning her head out of the litter's side, Fabiola peered into the distance. Docilosa clicked her tongue disapprovingly, but Fabiola ignored her. Horrified at what had happened to Fabiola on the street, her middle-aged servant had refused point blank to be left behind. Glad to have the female company, Fabiola had not put up much protest. Now though, after bumping up and down for hours on end, she was bored. Snatching an occasional glance outside was perhaps not wise, but Fabiola needed to do so to stay sane.

The other person who had declined to stay in Rome was walking directly alongside. Despite his horrific wound, Sextus had insisted he accompany Fabiola north. The one-eyed slave followed her like a shadow; it was a most comforting feeling. Apart from Docilosa, no one was allowed within three steps of her without his nod of approval.

Passing between rows of empty fields, the paved road stretched on to the grey horizon. Far from the nearest town, there were few other travellers in sight. Those that were abroad generally hurried past with the hoods of their cloaks turned up. With no official force to protect ordinary citizens in Rome or outside it, the Republic's roads were dangerous, by day or night.

The countryside was regularly dotted with *latifundia*, their lands lying fallow until the spring. Like Fabiola's, each was made up of a central building complex with the obligatory vineyards, olive groves and fruit trees. Dense groves of oaks and cypresses grew near the entrances; large packs of guard dogs ran loose around all the properties. Secundus and his men had frequently been obliged to throw stones at the fierce animals. Gangs of armed men in grubby tunics also lounged at the gates to many of the villas: protection against robbers. In these dangerous times, rich landowners guarded their estates even more closely than normal.

The parties of unshaven heavies eyed the litter and its accompanying guard of twelve men with suspicion, but dared not delay their passage, even when their hounds were stoned into submission. The distinctive bronze crested helmets, the thigh-length mail and army weapons marked out the tough-looking figures as veterans. They were all equipped with bows to boot, which made any attempt to rob them especially perilous. At these times, Fabiola was careful not to show her face. Presuming the passenger in the litter to be a wealthy nobleman or merchant, the thugs sullenly stood back.

In this fashion, they had travelled without trouble. Every night, Secundus chose a place for their camp as far from the road as possible. Avoiding attention was their main aim. Once he was happy with their position, the tents were swiftly put up. It did not take Secundus' eleven followers long to hammer the iron pegs into the ground and erect them. Until this journey, Fabiola had never seen the eight-man leather tents used by legionaries on the march. She and Docilosa had one to themselves, the men shared two others and the four slaves who carried the litter slept in a fourth. Refusing all other offers, Sextus spent every night wrapped in a blanket at the entrance to Fabiola's. Inside, the women's sleeping arrangements were simple: the bedding consisted of cushions and blankets from the litter. The Spartan decoration was still more than she was used to from her childhood. As then, there were few opportunities to bathe. This did not trouble Fabiola either: the weather was so cold that washing did not appeal much.

There had been no sign of Scaevola since they had left Rome. Fabiola prayed daily that the malevolent *fugitivarius* had not managed to regroup his men sufficiently to mount a pursuit. So far, her prayers had been answered. If their run of good luck continued, the main problems to overcome would be the Pompeian forces that lay to the north, and any rogue tribesmen in Gaul.

Although spring was around the corner, the days were still short. Finding a suitable spot to stop for the night, Secundus called an early halt to their march that afternoon. Sticking his head inside the litter, he beckoned to Fabiola. 'It's safe to come out now,' he said.

Gratefully she emerged into the cold air. Being able to stretch her legs in daylight was a real pleasure. Today Secundus had picked a secluded location by a river. Although it was only a hundred paces from a bridge over the fast-flowing water, it was protected by a grove of trees. Despite their bare branches, they provided plenty of cover. With darkness about to fall in the next hour, their camp would remain well hidden overnight.

'Don't go far,' Secundus advised.

Fabiola had no intention of doing so. Even with Sextus at her back, she did not feel safe unless there were plenty of armed men in view. They walked to the river, which swept past, swollen by winter rainfall in the Apennine Mountains. Huge pieces of wood spun in lazy circles, revealing the immense power of the water carrying them by. Like most Romans, Fabiola could not swim. Falling into the torrent would mean certain death by drowning. She shuddered at the thought and turned away. Anxious to lift her sombre mood, she looked up at the sky.

Clouds were scudding across it, illuminated from beneath by the setting sun. The strong wind was from the north, and it promised more snow. Fabiola knew this from the grey-yellow colour of the clouds, and from the biting chill that numbed her fingers and toes. Their journey was going to get even more difficult, she thought wearily. Unease sneaked over her, and Fabiola hurried back to the tents, eager to get away from the threatening weather. Sextus followed, also glancing unhappily into the darkening air.

The wind speed increased through the evening, until it had become a shrieking voice that drowned out all sound. Extra pegs had to be placed to hold the tents securely to the ground. Secundus ordered the sentries doubled, positioning them close enough so they could see each other. Chilled to the bone, Fabiola and Docilosa went to bed fully dressed and even earlier than normal. It was rare to stay up past sunset anyway. What was there to do by the light of guttering oil lamps now, other than brood? Which is what the young woman found herself doing anyway.

Even if they reached Gaul without further mishap, who knew if they would find Brutus amid the carnage and mayhem? With the whole country in revolt against the Romans, travel had become more dangerous than in Italy. Bands of brigands competed with dispossessed tribesmen for whatever pickings could be found. While the men accompanying her were solid veterans, they would not be able to withstand a large Gaulish war party.

Fabiola sighed. What point was there in worrying about the future? Right now, surviving from one day to the next was enough to deal with. Tomorrow was another day. Trying to keep this sentiment to the forefront of her mind, she finally fell asleep.

Cries of alarm roused her from a deep slumber. Thankfully, the howling wind had died away. Dull light penetrated through the tent fabric, telling Fabiola it was early morning. Throwing off the thick blankets, she pulled her *pugio* from under her pillow. Never again would Fabiola be overcome as she had been on the street in Rome.

Docilosa was also awake. 'What are you doing, Mistress?' she asked, looking alarmed.

Without answering, Fabiola moved to the door and partially unlaced the flap, which allowed her to see the area in front of their tent. 'Sextus is gone.'

'It could be dangerous,' warned Docilosa. 'Stay here.'

Ignoring her, the young woman stepped into the morning air. To her relief, Sextus was only a few steps away. Clutching his *gladius* with white knuckles, his gaze was fixed on the blood-soaked figure which lay in the thick snow just beyond the next tent. Fabiola joined him.

Secundus and two of his men were crouched over the body.

It was one of the sentries. And his throat had been cut from ear to ear. The frozen snow around him had turned red, a shocking clash of colours in the dawn light.

'What happened?'

'Don't know, Mistress,' answered Sextus grimly. 'I've heard nothing all night.'

Noticing Fabiola, Secundus turned to face her. His face looked older than she remembered. His hands were covered in blood.

'His name was Antoninus,' the veteran said heavily. 'He served with me for ten years.'

Fabiola's heart went out to him. 'Who did it?'

Secundus shrugged. 'The same bastards who killed Servius, I guess.'

Shocked, she looked at him questioningly.

'There's another one over there,' he revealed. 'Both were covered in snow, so it must have happened during the storm. Any footprints have been well covered.'

Fear clenched Fabiola's stomach. 'Bandits?' she asked.

'Could be,' said Secundus angrily. 'Damn smart ones though, to get so close without any of us knowing. Antoninus and Servius were good men.'

Fabiola went white. She knew a man who was a real expert at tracking. Scaevola.

Chapter XV: A New Threat

Margiana, winter/spring 53/52 BC

The archers stared down their arrow shafts at Romulus and Brennus, waiting for the command to release. Despite the friends' chain mail, the short distance between them meant that the barbed iron points would tear their flesh to pieces.

Romulus' pulse was pounding in the hollow of his throat.

Resignation filled Brennus. The pain of Optatus' sword cut was as nothing compared to having the satisfaction of victory taken away and replaced with the threat of summary execution. Again. As a gladiator, at least he had been applauded after winning a fight. Here, he was an expendable piece of meat. If he was to die, Brennus wanted it to be as a free man, not as a prisoner or a slave.

Pacorus was about to speak when one of the sentries on the rampart bothered to glance out eastwards. Like his companions, the soldier had been totally absorbed by the combat being fought below his position. His hoarse cry of alarm drew everyone's attention away from the pair of sweating figures standing over the legionaries' corpses.

'A messenger comes!' he roared. 'He's signalling that an enemy is near.'

As with all units on guard duty, there was a trumpeter standing by. Quickly he put his bronze instrument to his lips and blew a short, sharp series of notes that everyone recognised.

The alarm.

Pacorus' mouth twisted with apprehension. Before they came within shouting range, riders could raise their right arm to warn their comrades of danger. This was clearly what the sentry had seen. 'Get to the gate,' he barked at Vahram. 'Bring him to me at once!'

The squat *primus pilus* snapped off a salute and trotted away.

Pacorus turned back to Romulus and Brennus, who were still being covered by his archers. 'How many did you see out there?'

'One to two thousand, sir,' answered Romulus confidently. 'Perhaps more.'

'Mostly infantry?' asked Pacorus hopefully. A much weakened people compared to their heyday centuries before, the Scythians were still feared opponents of any army. Especially their skilled horsemen.

'About half of each, sir.'

Grey-faced, their commander sucked in a ragged breath. His forces were nearly all foot soldiers. 'Five hundred to a thousand horse,' he muttered to himself. 'Mithras damn them all.'

The friends waited.

So did the Parthian bowmen.

The *primus pilus* arrived with a warrior on a lathered mount a few moments later. His words confirmed those of Romulus. But instead of advancing further towards the fort, the Scythians were heading north again – in the direction of their own lands and the other fortlets. Satisfied for the moment, Pacorus muttered an order to his men, who finally lowered their bows. Suddenly there were more important things on the commander's mind than the execution of two ordinary soldiers.

The tension in Romulus' shoulders began to dissipate, and he let out a long, slow breath.

'Present yourselves to the *optio* in the first century of the *primus pilus*' cohort,' Pacorus snapped. 'He can keep an eye on you there.'

'Gladly, sir,' said Vahram, leering at them. 'There'll be no question of desertion while I'm around.'

Romulus imagined the punishment duties that the sadistic Parthian would come up with. And yet they were alive, he thought gratefully. Brennus nudged him and they ran off, both trying not to let their injuries show. It was best not to wait for Pacorus to reconsider, and what the volatile *primus pilus* might do later scarcely seemed to matter.

Behind them, they heard Pacorus speak to Vahram. 'I want the whole legion ready to march in an hour. Have all the long spears issued as well.'

'Sir.'

'The silk-covered shields should withstand their poison arrows,' he went on. 'And the spears will break their charge.'

It was the last thing that Romulus heard. Rounding a corner on to the Via Principia, they trotted along, ignoring the curious stares thrown in their direction. Soon they found themselves at their new barracks. The most important cohort in the Legion, the First was under Vahram's personal command. Being the *primus pilus* was in fact two jobs: running his own unit of six centuries, as well as being the ranking senior centurion in the Forgotten Legion.

The *optio* of the first century was a dour Capuan called Aemilius and they found him standing in the narrow corridor, yelling orders at his men. He looked surprised to see the pair, as did the legionaries present. Everyone in the camp had heard Novius' malicious gossip, and sour comments immediately filled the air.

Ignoring them, Romulus relayed their orders and saluted.

'Pacorus himself sent you?' Aemilius repeated.

'Yes, sir,' answered Romulus, stiffening to attention again. Brennus did likewise.

If it was humanly possible, they had to get on Aemilius' good side from the start. Otherwise the two most senior officers in the century would be out for their blood. And that was before the legionaries became involved.

Aemilius rubbed his chin, thinking. 'Escaped slaves, eh?'

All the men listening craned their heads to see.

There was no point denying it any longer. 'Yes, sir,' Romulus replied, although he no longer felt like one. Training as a soldier, fighting battles and surviving this far had given him a seasoned confidence beyond that of an ordinary slave.

Slavery had never sat easily on Brennus' broad shoulders, but he held his tongue too. Here, remaining silent was the same as agreeing with Romulus.

While the nearby soldiers hissed with disapproval, Aemilius did not react. Romulus hid his surprise at this. It was a tiny spark of hope.

'You were on Darius' patrol?'

Both nodded.

'And what they say,' said the *optio*, his stare piercing, 'is it true? Did you run away?'

'No, sir,' protested Romulus fiercely.

'The men who did are lying dead on the *intervallum*, sir,' added Brennus. 'We just bested the three of them, unarmed.'

Gasps of disbelief filled the corridor. The First Cohort's barracks was beside the Praetoria, a long distance from the front gate. Busy with routine duties, none here had witnessed the dramatic duel.

Aemilius' eyebrows rose. 'Did you, by Jupiter?'

'Ask any of the other officers, sir,' urged Romulus.

'We're no cowards,' said Brennus.

Something told Romulus that the *optio* was a fair-minded man. He threw caution to the wind. 'The gods helped us.'

The Gaul shook his shaggy head in agreement. After what they had been through, it did seem that way.

Superstitious mutters rippled between the legionaries.

Aemilius looked dubious. 'I've seen you two on the training ground before,' he said. 'You're good. Very good. More likely that's why you're standing here now.'

Romulus kept silent, breathing into the waves of pain from his ribs.

Aemilius relaxed. Then, noticing the deep cut on Brennus' left forearm, he frowned. 'You can't hold a shield with that.'

'Bit of strapping and I'll be fine, sir. Don't want to miss the fight,' answered Brennus stolidly. 'There are some deaths to be avenged.'

'Whose?'

'The men of our century, sir,' Romulus interjected.

A slow smile appeared on the *optio*'s face. These two soldiers were brave at least. Time would tell if they were liars or not. 'Very well,' he said. 'Have it seen to in the *valetudinarium*. Your young friend here can go to the armoury for kit and weapons.'

Romulus and Brennus hurried to obey.

There was a battle to fight.

In the event, the expected clash with the Scythians did not occur. Realising perhaps that the response to their attack would be rapid and ruthless, the nomadic warriors had pulled back from where they had been spotted by the Parthian rider. Pacorus' order for the men to carry enough supplies for several days turned out to be a fortunate one, as the legionaries marched fruitlessly after an enemy which had the advantage of being many miles away at the start of their pursuit. The exercise proved to be nothing more than an extended training march in winter conditions. Naturally, the soldiers were not pleased by this, but they had to obey.

After three days, with his men's food running low, the Parthian commander was forced to call a halt. But he was determined not to give up. Upon their return to the fort, six cohorts were immediately provided with enough rations for a month and sent out again. Much of the winter passed in this fashion: searching an empty, frozen landscape for a wraith-like enemy. There were occasional skirmishes with the Scythians, but nothing decisive.

Like all the others, Romulus and Brennus took part in the sorties, marching alongside Aemilius and his men. Forced to join a *contubernium*, they had achieved grudging acceptance from the six legionaries with whom they lived, slept and ate every day. Yet there was no friendship and the other men in the century shunned them entirely. It was no better amongst the rest of the cohorts. Like Romulus and Brennus, Caius had fully recovered from his wound, and he was ceaseless in his efforts to foment bad feeling against the two friends. No one made direct attacks on them, but the threat was always there. They could not leave each other's company, even to visit the latrines or baths.

It was an extremely wearing existence, and Romulus grew heartily sick of it. He and Brennus could not fight the entire legion. Desertion was their one option, although there was virtually nowhere to go. Well over a thousand miles of barren wilderness lay between the fort and the city of Seleucia in the west. It was hundreds more beyond that to Roman territory. To the north and east were unknown areas, populated by savage tribes like the Sogdians and Scythians. The land of Serica, where silk came from, lay even further eastwards, but he did not know where. Romulus had a single idea: to head south, through the kingdom of the Bactrians. Occasionally some of the Parthian warriors mentioned a great city called Barbaricum, where a mighty river met the sea. Romulus had seen it once on the *Periplus*, Tarquinius' ancient, annotated map. He knew that Barbaricum was a bustling trade centre, where precious items such as spices, silk, jewels and ivory were bought and sold. From it, ships apparently sailed to Egypt, carrying goods that were worth a king's ransom in Italy and Greece.

But Romulus had no idea how to reach it: the only possible route home.

And he would not leave without Tarquinius. Neither would Brennus. There was still no sign of the haruspex anyway. He was alive, yet, as before, he was kept under close guard in Pacorus' quarters. Any attempt to free him would doubtless end in disaster, and so the pair watched, waited and endured for many cold months. All they could do was pray to the gods.

Spring arrived, and the six cohorts which were out on patrol surprised the Scythians in their camp. Utilising the dusk for an unusually timed attack, Vahram led his men to a stunning victory. Almost the entire force of raiders was annihilated in one short, brutal encounter. With little threat remaining, the *primus pilus* hurried back to the fort the next day. He was doing everything in his power to regain Pacorus' approval. A pair of riders was sent on in advance to relay the good news.

When they returned, Pacorus was waiting at the fort's main entrance with a party of his warriors. He called Vahram to his side and exchanged a few words with him before indicating that the legionaries should enter. As the ranks of the First Cohort began passing by, the commander dipped his head in acknowledgement. He seemed genuinely pleased by their victory.

Anger filled Romulus at the sight of the swarthy Parthian in his richly cut cloak, the picture of arrogant superiority. He longed to plunge his javelin into his chest, but of course he wouldn't: he might gain his vengeance, but Tarquinius would still be a prisoner. The young soldier dared not act. He and Brennus had been fortunate to escape with their lives and avoid the commander since. He hoped that Pacorus had forgotten them for now. With Mithras' blessing, it would stay that way. All the two friends could do was keep their heads down.

The First Cohort came to an abrupt halt and Romulus almost walked into the soldier ahead of him. Confused, men stood on tiptoe to see what was happening. A loud commotion came from the front. Angry shouts were met by a low, insistent voice which held one's attention.

Recognition tickled the edges of Romulus' memory.

Taller than nearly everyone, Brennus raised a hand to his eyes.

'See anything?' asked Romulus.

'No,' came the annoyed reply.

'What's going on?' snarled Pacorus impatiently at the nearest centurion. 'Move on!'

The officer scurried to obey, using liberal strokes of his vine cane on his men, but no one would budge.

A stooped figure wrapped in a heavy blanket emerged from the gateway. Shuffling rather than walking, it limped towards Pacorus. Superstitious gasps rose from the soldiers as they saw who it was.

Positioned on the outside of the rank, Romulus could see more than the Gaul. Sadness and euphoria filled him at the same time.

All the colour drained from Brennus' face. 'Is it . . . ?' he began.

'Yes,' answered Romulus simply.

They had not seen him for months, but only one person in the camp had the ability to cause such confusion.

Angry that his order had not been obeyed, Pacorus snapped out another. Two of his men ran to stand before the figure, challenging it first in Parthian and then in bad Latin. There was no answer.

Another command rang out and one warrior stepped forward, roughly pulling away the blanket from the newcomer's head. Obviously weak, he tottered backwards and nearly fell. Somehow he regained his balance and stepped forward. The Parthians blocked the move at once, but the man stood proudly, staring at Pacorus across their outstretched arms.

As Tarquinius' face was revealed to those nearby, Romulus bit back the cry of horror that sprang to his lips. The haruspex had aged ten years. There were grey streaks in his long blond hair and new worry lines furrowed his entire face, giving him the appearance of an old man. The blanket had slipped away from his now bony shoulders, exposing his flesh, which was beaten and badly bruised. But the worst thing of all was the red, recently healed burn on Tarquinius' left cheek. It was the shape of a knife blade.

'They've tortured him,' hissed Romulus, moving out of rank.

The Gaul's great hand gripped his right arm, stopping him.

Romulus' protest died away. 'Each man's fate is his own' was one of the haruspex' staple sayings. It was not his place to intervene. And Tarquinius had engineered this situation.

'You!' said Pacorus with a sneer. 'Come to see what my troops have done without you?'

His warriors laughed.

Tarquinius licked his dry, cracked lips and Romulus' heart ached.

'Enough!' barked the commander. 'Move on,' he shouted at the centurions.

'Hold.' Tarquinius' voice was not loud, but every man heard what he said. Remarkably, no one moved.

Pacorus swelled with fury, yet the two Parthians holding the haruspex also seemed less certain.

'The Scythians have been defeated,' said Tarquinius. 'That danger is gone.'

Pacorus could not stop the smirk that formed on his lips. He raised his arms in triumph, and his warriors cheered. Even the legionaries looked pleased.

Tarquinius waited until they had all stopped. 'What of the Indians though?' he asked softly.

Shock replaced the happiness in men's faces. The five words hung in the air, which had suddenly turned clammy. Romulus glanced at Brennus, who shrugged.

'The Indians?' Pacorus laughed, but it rang hollow. 'They would have to defeat the Bactrians before coming anywhere near Margiana.'

'They have already done so.'

Pacorus' complexion turned pale grey. 'Spring has only just started,' he retorted.

'A hundred miles to the south, the snows have melted early,' came the instant response. 'And Bactria's army has been crushed.'

The commander was visibly deflated.

'A huge army is on the move towards us,' Tarquinius continued. 'The Indian king Azes desires more land. Unchecked, he will sweep through Margiana.'

Pacorus' miserable expression spoke volumes. Tarquinius had mentioned this once, a long time ago. 'How many?' he asked.

'Thirty thousand infantry,' intoned the haruspex. 'And perhaps five thousand cavalry. Battle chariots too.'

Shouts of disbelief rose into the air from the nearest legionaries.

'A small threat,' growled Pacorus, trying to shrug it off.

Tarquinius' eyes were dark pits. 'There are also elephants. One hundred of them at least.'

Now the soldiers began to look scared and the Parthian's shoulders slumped.

Romulus' joy at seeing his mentor again began to dissolve. This was the doom of the Forgotten Legion. And of his friends too. He knew it. Wrapped in new misery, he did not notice Brennus' reaction.

There was a long silence before Pacorus finally regained control of his emotions. 'Back to barracks. At once!' he muttered. Morale would be affected if even more was revealed, but judging by the unhappy voices among the ranks of the First, that was already happening.

The centurions and *optiones* hurriedly obeyed. With kicks and curses, and blows from their vine canes, they got the men moving.

'We must talk,' the commander said to Tarquinius.

The haruspex gravely inclined his head. Despite his horrific injuries, there was still an air of gravitas about him.

Romulus and Brennus marched on. Tarquinius' head turned as they came alongside. Romulus' eyes and his met, before Tarquinius' gaze moved to Brennus. He grinned at them, and it was impossible not to respond. The greatest threat to their lives might lie ahead, but they were all still alive.

And then they had tramped past, under the arched gateway and the sentries on the ramparts. A maelstrom of emotions could be felt in the First's ranks. The legionaries' elation at their stunning victory had been utterly diluted by the haruspex' ominous words. After Novius' accusations, Tarquinius had automatically been tarred with the same brush as Romulus and Brennus. Being incarcerated, no one could accuse him of being an escaped slave, yet he was guilty by association. But kinder memories of the terrible march east from Seleucia were also vivid. That was when Tarquinius had become widely known, nursing the sick and wounded. Moreover, his prophecies invariably came to pass, which had earned him huge respect throughout the Forgotten Legion.

If Tarquinius said that an invasion was imminent, few men would argue.

They would soon need all the luck Fortuna was prepared to throw their way.

Pacorus had indeed taken Tarquinius' words to heart. That evening, all centurions were ordered to the Praetoria. There it was announced that the legion would march south the next day. Only a small group of warriors and those who were unable to march would be left behind. Every single *ballista* made by the bored armourers during the quiet winter months was to be taken. Fortunately the tough mules which had accompanied the prisoners east from Seleucia were well fed. Theirs would be a tough job too. As well as food, spare equipment and the engines of war, the pack animals had to carry hay for themselves, the long spears and the tents.

The announcement was quickly disseminated by the grim-faced centurions. Although Parthian, they too were dismayed by Pacorus' decision. Going on campaign this early in the year was not an appealing prospect. Yet the news wasn't of much surprise to the weary legionaries. They had been looking forward to celebrating their victory over the Scythians, and the pleasure of sleeping in their own beds. Instead, they were brooding over Tarquinius' words, which had already been repeated a dozen times in every barracks. One perilous battle was to be followed by another, yet more ominous. As darkness fell, thousands of prayers rose up into the empty, windless sky. Few men slept well.

Romulus in particular lay awake for much of the night, considering his future. It seemed utterly hopeless. Everyone was out for their blood: Pacorus, Vahram, Caius and now the Indians. For every danger that he survived, two more seemed to spring up. As ever, deserting seemed pointless, while trying to rescue Tarquinius was tantamount to suicide. Marching to face the Indians was the only option. South, into the unknown, to a battle that no one could win. A dense gloom enveloped Romulus. But Mithras had seen fit to keep him alive this far, and Tarquinius would be travelling with the legion. Perhaps there was a faint chance.

Brennus did not like talking much. Instead he had fallen asleep and was snoring contentedly nearby, a tiny smile playing on his lips.

Wrapped up in his own troubles, Romulus still did not notice his friend's relaxed manner.

And in the courtyard of Pacorus' quarters, Tarquinius studied the stars filling the heavens. Try as he might, the haruspex could not see past the battle that lay ahead.

As at Carrhae, the slaughter would be immense. Too many men would die to allow the paths of three single individuals to be discerned on their own.

But where were the visions that had showed the possibility of returning to Rome? Had Olenus, his mentor, been wrong?

Tarquinius too was filled with unease.

As Romulus and Brennus emerged from the confining sides of the narrow pass and the men in front began to descend, they were granted a view of the land that awaited them. Eleven days had passed and the Forgotten Legion was about to complete its traversal of the mountains to the south of its fort. With Pacorus' expert knowledge of the area, the legionaries had marched safely through a narrow defile, well below the snowline.

'Great visibility,' said the Gaul, pointing due east. 'I'd say fifty miles at least.'

It was hard to disagree. With a cloudless sky overhead, the crystal-pure air allowed them to see every tiny detail below them. Rivers thundered down from the peaks to divide the landscape into huge, irregular portions. This was more fertile land than that to the north. Small villages were dotted throughout, their patchwork fields spread unevenly around the houses. On the foothills that ran down from the mountains were thick clumps of trees. Unlike the Romans, the Parthians and Bactrians did not build roads, but plenty of well-worn tracks joined the areas of human inhabitation. It was not dissimilar to parts of southern Italy.

Pleased mutters rose from the other soldiers: there was no sign of a huge host.

Romulus sighed. He did not know which was worse – the expectation of doom, or the actuality of it.

Brennus threw a comforting arm around his shoulders. 'We're all still alive,' he said. 'Breathe the air. Enjoy the view. You might as well.'

He managed a small smile.

From the following dawn, they advanced steadily, covering a good fifteen miles before dark. The next day it was twenty, and the day after that, a few more. No one knew exactly where they were going, but the rumour was that their destination was the River Hydaspes.

This was proved correct when, after nearly a week's march, an enormous watercourse eventually halted the Forgotten Legion's progress. Running almost directly north–south, it was at least a quarter of a mile wide. A less imposing barrier than the mountains, the river still acted as a formidable natural border.

* * *

Tarquinius sat astride his mule, watching the water glide past at speed. Around him were Pacorus and many of the senior centurions on their horses. A ring of dusty warriors stood ready at their backs, secretly relieved to rest. To get a better view, the commander's party had advanced to the river's edge. Low trees and heavy vegetation grew right down to the water on both sides, restricting the view of the far bank.

'The Hydaspes,' announced Pacorus, gesturing expansively. 'The eastern limit of the Parthian Empire.'

'Alexander's army finally came to a halt not far from here,' said Tarquinius. 'Because his troops would go no further.'

'They were wise men,' the commander answered. 'Since deepest antiquity, the Indian kings have fielded huge armies. Far bigger than that damn Greek might have had.'

That damn Greek had more military talent in his little finger than you do in your whole rotten body, thought the haruspex.

'Nothing has changed then,' added Vahram drily.

'Where are they, though?' asked Ishkan.

Nervous eyes turned to Tarquinius.

'The gods help you if this was a wasted march,' growled Pacorus.

Vahram gripped his sword hilt, always keen to administer a quick revenge.

Tarquinius did not answer immediately. Surviving the *primus pilus'* torture had, if anything, helped him to consider everything for longer. Raising his head, the haruspex smelt the air. His eyes never still, he searched the sky.

Over the previous week, the weather had improved steadily. Spring was now well under way. In the fields belonging to the settlements that they had passed, the new wheat and barley was sprouting pale green shoots. Away from the colder climate of the mountains, the plants and trees were beginning to bloom. The river level would have fallen from its winter highs, the haruspex thought. It was about two months before the monsoon began. A perfect time for an army to cross safely.

Vahram was growing impatient, but Pacorus sat quietly astride his black stallion. Although he hated it, he had grown used to Tarquinius' contemplative manner. Waiting for a few moments more would not change the course of their fate.

Tarquinius' gaze was drawn to a solitary huge vulture flying over the far bank. Its appearance was striking, and unusual. Black circles dramatised its eyes; the rest of its head was white, while the neck and body were a pale brown colour. Even its long, diamond-shaped tail was distinctive.

Its presence had to be of significance.

Clutching a large tortoise in its talons, the vulture was climbing steadily into the air. When it had reached a height that he judged to be at least two hundred paces, it simply let go. The tortoise plummeted to the ground, its rigid shell guaranteeing a certain death. It was followed in a more leisurely way by the bird.

A striking example of intelligence, Tarquinius thought. A good lesson, when the odds seemed insurmountable.

In the eastern distance, over the trees, he glimpsed banks of massing thunderclouds. Tarquinius gave silent thanks to Tinia and Mithras. Since Vahram's torture, divining had become more difficult. But his talents had not completely disappeared. 'We're late,' he said. 'There are shallows two days march to the south. They're already crossing there.'

Ishkan's tanned face paled. He knew where the ford was, but there was no way that Tarquinius could have: none of the Parthians would have mentioned it.

This was more proof that Tarquinius' abilities were indeed real, thought Vahram. It was good that he had not killed the haruspex. Yet, he reflected, what faced them was as ominous as the fate which awaited any who killed such a man. A week earlier, the Forgotten Legion had abandoned the easily defendable pass through the mountains. The plan had been to reach the Hydaspes before the enemy, to deny them the crossing, or at least to make them pay dearly for it. Now, the realisation that the Indians were already on this bank hit home. And on the open ground by the river, their situation seemed even more vulnerable.

Pacorus set his jaw. A brave man, he was not about to run from his duty. Better to die honourably in battle against Parthia's enemies than suffer an ignominious end at the hands of King Orodes' executioners. He looked searchingly at Tarquinius. 'Well?' he said.

'There is much to be done.'

Vahram sneered. 'What can we possibly do, except die?'

'Teach the Indians a lesson they will never forget,' growled Pacorus.

* * *

Tired and footsore after yet another long march, the legionaries were unhappy at having to erect a marching camp a good mile from the river. The distance meant that those on water-hauling duty would spend far more time driving the mules to and fro than normal.

Romulus wasn't concerned by the camp's location. He had seen the Parthian horsemen take off at dawn, and knew that something was up.

When it was announced that every man would have to work the next day as well, the grumbling grew even louder. No one dared to question the order, however. Opening one's mouth guaranteed severe punishment. Besides, it made sense to build defences.

The following dawn, they started. Brennus took to the task with gusto. In his huge hands, a shovel looked like a toy. But the amount of earth that he moved proved otherwise.

The Hydaspes was to shield the Forgotten Legion's left flank. Under Tarquinius' direction, the soldiers dug lines of deep curved ditches parallel to the riverbank, but about eight hundred paces away. This was the approximate width of the legion in battle formation. Branches were cut and trimmed, and dug into the bottoms of the defences. Facing outwards like one half of a circle, the trenches would protect the right flank. Without significant numbers of cavalry, this was the haruspex' way of improvising. Inside the ditches, hundreds more sharpened wooden stakes were buried at an angle in the ground, jutting forward like so many crooked teeth in a crocodile's jaws. In between them were scattered the caltrops, their iron spikes sticking jauntily into the air.

The dozen *ballistae* were split up, half facing forward along the line, and the rest placed to cover the area in front of the ditches. If necessary, they could be turned to cover the rear as well. The men that could be spared from other duties searched out suitably sized rocks by the river, and used the mules to haul them back. Pyramidal piles of this ammunition were built up beside each catapult. They varied from the size of a fist to lumps bigger than a man's head. Aimed and fired correctly, all were deadly. Romulus had watched the artillerymen practising on many occasions and knew that the *ballistae* would play an important part in the battle.

The last, unexplained task was to dig a narrow yet deep trench from the river; it crossed right in front of where the Forgotten Legion would stand. Scores of long side channels were also excavated, until the ground looked like a field with too many irrigation channels. The final part of the trench, which would allow the Hydaspes to pour in and reach all its tributaries, was finished last. As the final clumps of soil were dug away, the trickle soon became a minor torrent, filling the channels to the brim.

With their purpose made obvious, there were weary smiles all round. By the morning, the area would be a quagmire.

The day of intense physical labour was over, allowing the legionaries to dwell on morbid matters — such as their future. And the battle that loomed ever nearer.

The remnants of Pacorus' horsemen arrived back that evening, bloody and battered. They had been attacked by a far greater force of Indian cavalry, suffering heavy losses. And they reported that the army that followed in their wake was as large as Tarquinius had predicted. Or larger. It would arrive the next day.

A deep despondency fell on the legionaries. The haruspex had been proved correct yet again. Every single man in the Forgotten Legion but one wished the opposite.

Romulus knew now that he could not escape his fate. He felt it rushing in as if borne on the wings of doom itself. Thoughts of returning to Rome seemed utterly futile, a waste of valuable energy. Better to save it for the fight the next day, when death would find them all on this green plain, by the River Hydaspes. Seventeen seemed too young to die, he thought sadly.

A strange sense of complacency filled Brennus. Word had spread that they were not far from where Alexander's incredible advance had been halted. 'This is the end of the world,' muttered many men as they sat around their fires that night. 'Even if they could, who would want to travel any further?'

Their unknowing words reverberated deep in the core of the Gaul's being.

A journey beyond where any Allobroge has gone. Or will ever go.

After nine long years, the gods were finally beginning to reveal their purpose to him.

Chapter XVI: The Road to Gaul

Northern Italy, winter 53/52 BC

Seeing her fear, Secundus moved closer. 'Tell me.'

'It's the *fugitivarii*,' Fabiola whispered. 'I know it.'

'This would be their style,' he said with a scowl. 'And they'd be wary of my men. So they creep in like thieves and kill them unawares.'

'To even the numbers.'

'Exactly.' Secundus scanned the nearby trees and bushes. 'The bastards will have been tracking us since we left.'

'Should we go back?'

He barked a short, angry laugh. 'Whoever it was murdered these lads will find it easier to recruit more men there than if we keep moving. Besides, the rioting has spread. Rome is no place for any of us right now.'

'And it'll take weeks for Pompey's legions to arrive,' said Fabiola. If the rumours sweeping the city as they left were correct, the sole consul would by now be dictator for the year. Nervous of the situation, the Senate had finally acted. But Pompey's armies were scattered throughout the Republic; most were in Hispania and Greece, while others were dispersed across Italy.

'Time we don't have,' Secundus declared. 'Best move on.'

'Fast,' added one of the others.

Sextus bared his teeth in agreement.

Fabiola did not argue. The graphic evidence of what might happen if they did nothing was still lying before her.

Despite the frozen soil, it did not take the veterans long to bury their comrades. Fabiola was struck by their efficiency as she watched them swiftly shovel out a pair of deep holes, inter the blood-soaked bodies and cover them with earth. Their weapons were also buried. Everyone stood around while Secundus said a few words. But there was no time to carve a wooden grave marker. Servius and Antoninus had disappeared as if they had never existed.

Yet the plain graves were still more than most slaves got, Fabiola thought sadly. Like the excess city waste and the bodies of executed criminals, they were simply discarded in stinking, open pits. After a battle, a similar fate awaited the dead soldiers of the losing side. Like Romulus, at Carrhae. Or wherever the battle she had seen in her vision would take place.

She climbed miserably into the litter, followed by a stone-faced Docilosa. Secundus barked an order to move out.

Nothing further happened that day and Secundus made sure that the party reached a town by nightfall. Not wanting others to know their intended route to Gaul, it had been his aim to avoid human contact where possible. The night attack had changed things; safety now lay in numbers. Secundus hurried them to the best inn to be found, a low-roofed timber affair with a bar room full of unsavoury types and a muddy yard enclosed by stables. Curious glances followed the two women as they quickly descended from the litter, raising the hoods on the dark-coloured military *lacernae* which Secundus had provided. They had been reduced to skulking like thieves.

Once a simple meal had been provided for Fabiola and Docilosa in their room, Secundus left two men outside their door with Sextus. He and the others shared the neighbouring chamber, but regularly came to check on them. With Docilosa in bed early, there was time for him to talk to Fabiola in private. Secundus seemed increasingly convinced of her right to become a Mithraic devotee, and had begun revealing fascinating details about the secretive religion, including its central beliefs and rituals. Keen to be part of a cult which recognised slaves as equals, Fabiola soaked it all up.

Eight more days passed in this fashion: journeying without pause, followed by a poor night's sleep in a flea-ridden, uncomfortable bed. By the morning of the ninth day, Fabiola was beginning to wonder if her fears had been overreaction. The violent storm and the sentries' murders had sent her mood into the black depths. Perhaps now though their deaths could be put down to bandits: a random event that would not be repeated. The border with Gaul was a week's march away, and the thought of seeing Brutus again filled her with joy.

Even Secundus and Sextus seemed happier. Only Docilosa remained in bad spirits. Not even the prospect of better weather could please her. All along the roads, the frost was melting. Snowdrops were already poking free of the short grass beneath. When the sun emerged from behind the clouds, there was a new warmth in its rays. Spring was coming at last. Birds sang in the trees, alerting the world to the fact. Fabiola could not stop herself from smiling at Docilosa's continued grim demeanour as the litter bumped and creaked along.

Later, she would regret not paying more attention to it.

Their choice came in the afternoon, not long after the road had entered a narrow valley. Tall trees hemmed in the way ahead, their bare lower branches reaching out threateningly at head height. Entering, the bright sunshine all but disappeared, leaving a small strip of sky visible overhead. Between the closely positioned, gnarled trunks on either side were huge boulders covered in moss, the remnants of an ancient rock fall. Few birds or animals were visible, leaving a deathly silence over the wood. It was most unwelcoming.

Unusually, Sextus had left Fabiola's side to check out the way ahead with two men acting as scouts. Secundus conferred with them upon their return while Sextus stood alongside, nodding his head. According to the three, there was little choice but to press on. The alternative route around the defile would set them back a day or more.

'My lads saw no sign of anyone,' Secundus announced. 'And this section only lasts for a short distance before opening out again.'

Unsure, Fabiola chewed her lip.

'They both have noses for trouble like a hound on the scent,' Secundus went on. 'We'll be through it in half an hour. No more.'

Sextus grinned encouragingly.

The temptation was too much for Fabiola. If Sextus, her good-luck talisman, was happy, then it must be safe. Ignoring Docilosa's grumbles, she nodded her assent.

A trio of Secundus' men led the way, bows at the ready. Next came the litter, borne by the sweating slaves, flanked closely on either side by a pair of veterans. The narrowness of the road and the sweeping branches meant that these men were forced to stoop regularly as they walked. Taking up the rear were Sextus, Secundus and the last two of his followers. It was far from an ideal way to continue, thought Fabiola as she peered out and almost lost an eye to the sharp end on a half-decayed branch.

Time dragged in the semi-darkness. In an effort to lift the mood, Fabiola tried engaging Docilosa in conversation about the possibility of finding Sabina, her daughter. The child had been taken from her at the tender age of six, sold as an acolyte to one of the temples. It was a bad choice of topic. Docilosa's sour expression deepened, remaining unchanged no matter what Fabiola said. She determined to try and track down Sabina if she ever got the chance. It would be worth paying good money just to see Docilosa smile.

Docilosa sensed it first. 'What's wrong?' she asked sharply.

Deep in thought, Fabiola did not react.

The litter came to an abrupt halt, jolting her into awareness.

There was silence for a moment, and then the air filled with terrifying screams. They came from all around them, and Fabiola froze.

'Fabiola!'

She came alive at the sound of Secundus' voice.

Soft hissing noises were followed by thumps and shouts of pain. Arrows, thought Fabiola. An ambush. Would the gods never leave her alone?

'Get out! Quickly!'

Docilosa looked terrified, but Fabiola took her arm and forced her to follow. Death awaited them if they stayed put. Pulling aside the curtain, she forced her way through a dense clump of branches to the ground. Muttering to herself, Docilosa came too. Sextus was waiting, and protectively ushered them forward. He looked shame-faced.

Ducking down, Fabiola moved to the front of the litter. Three of Secundus' men were crouched there, holding their shields together to form a protective screen. Alarm filled her. The road ahead had been blocked with a combination of large rocks and pieces of fallen deadwood, completely preventing the slaves from carrying the litter past. And from behind the barrier's protection, cloaked figures were firing volleys of arrows at the ex-legionaries. Thanks to the low-hanging branches and the poor light, their faces were obscured. Whatever their ambushers' identity, they had moved fast to set the trap after the scouts had returned.

Her head turned this way and that, trying to assess the situation.

There was only one body in clear sight, that of a veteran. An arrow jutted from his open mouth, a fatal shot that would have given an instant of blinding pain before total oblivion. She couldn't see the remaining five, or Secundus.

'Where is he?' she asked.

'On the other side of the litter,' replied one of the ex-soldiers grimly. 'Kneeling behind his *scutum* like us.'

'We can't stay here,' protested Fabiola. 'They'll pick us off one by one.'

Reinforcing her point, two barbed shafts thumped into the litter just over their heads. The slaves moaned in fear. Jeers and insults from their attackers followed.

Sextus and the three veterans stared at her mutely. Fabiola realised that low-rankers were used to following orders, not initiating them. They would hardly obey her either – a woman whom they did not trust. Fabiola was therefore very relieved when Secundus appeared behind her. Given the choice of whether to bear arms or protect himself, he had opted for the safer option of using a shield. He was accompanied by five others, one of whom had a broken arrow protruding from his left arm. It meant that the sole fatality so far was the unfortunate lying in front of the litter.

They all waited to see what Secundus would say.

'There's only one way out,' he said. 'And it isn't by retreating.'

'Why not?' asked Fabiola. At least they knew the route that lay behind. Who knew what was ahead?

'I heard voices back there.'

'So did I,' added the oldest of the group.

This was met with uniform scowls.

'Another group waiting to butcher us if we run,' said a sallow-faced veteran with pockmarked cheeks.

'There are more of them than we thought,' muttered Secundus. Crouching down, he beckoned.

His men immediately huddled closer and, knowing she had to be guided in such situations, Fabiola did the same.

'We charge the fuckers,' declared Secundus confidently. 'Go straight across the barrier.'

'Just like old times,' interjected the sallow-faced man.

There were fierce nods of agreement. Faced with death yet again, the

veterans felt the familiar thrill of battle. Along with the pumping adrenalin and the knot of fear in their bellies, it felt good. None of them had
ever shirked their duty; they would not do so now.

'Does the first one over the summit get a *corona muralis*?' asked another.

Everyone except the two women laughed.

Secundus saw their confused look. 'It's the golden crown given to the
first man on top of an enemy wall,' he explained.

'What shall we do?' asked Fabiola, keeping her voice as calm as possible.
'Tell us.'

Docilosa moved closer and clutched her mistress' hand; alongside Sextus
snarled silently.

Pleased by their willingness, Secundus smiled. 'We'll form a small wedge.
There are few men who can withstand it,' he said. 'These dogs will be no
different.'

'We have no shields,' said Fabiola stoutly. 'Does that matter?'

Respect filled the one-armed veteran's eyes. 'Don't worry,' he replied.
'Both of you will be in the middle.'

'And on the other side?'

'We make a run for it. If enough of them are dead, they'll have lost the
stomach for a fight. Otherwise, there's a small settlement not far beyond
the trees which should provide safety.'

'Should?' Fabiola enquired archly.

Secundus shrugged. 'If the gods are smiling on us.'

'And the slaves?'

Secundus grimaced. 'They're untrained and unarmed. Have to take their
own chances.'

'We have no spare weapons. Save yourselves,' Fabiola ordered the four
slaves. 'Run into the trees when we attack. With luck, they'll never find
you. Head back to Brutus' house in Rome if you can.'

A couple of them nodded fearfully.

Then mistress and servant stared at each other; Docilosa's face full of
uncertainty.

Another volley of arrows hit the shields of the veterans at the front.

'Give me a dagger,' said Docilosa abruptly.

'That's the spirit,' grinned Secundus.

One of his men tugged a *pugio* from his belt and handed it over.

They did not delay any longer. Keeping their helmeted faces low behind their *scuta*, the ex-soldiers moved away from the protection of the litter. Fabiola and Docilosa scuttled behind them, with Sextus by their side. The sallow-faced man assumed the lead position, while three others formed each side of the wedge. Ushering Sextus and the two women within, Secundus and the injured veteran closed up the rear.

Cries of alarm rose as their ambushers saw what was about to happen. More arrows flew through the air.

'Now!' cried Secundus.

Mud squelched underfoot as they broke into a run.

Twenty paces and the ground began to grow uneven. The wedge's speed slowed dramatically as each person had to look where they placed their feet. Fabiola concentrated hard on staying upright, knowing that a fall would probably be fatal.

'Don't stop!' yelled Secundus. 'Keep moving!'

Clambering over rough logs with protruding branches that ripped and tore at their lower legs, the veterans pushed up on to the barrier. They were close enough now to make out the faces of their enemies. In between helping Docilosa find her footing and managing not to lose her own, Fabiola scanned the shouting ruffians, searching for any she might recognise.

Two men hurled themselves at the sallow-faced veteran who led the wedge's point. The first got a shield boss full in the face and went down screaming. Wary now, his comrade slowed down a trifle. Then he lunged viciously at the ex-legionary's foot with his curved knife. As the thug bent down, the next man in line leaned over and stabbed him through the chest with his *gladius*. A gush of blood spattered on to the rocks; now two of their ambushers were out of action.

The wedge advanced slowly up the barrier, arrows and small rocks banging off the shields. Several more thugs slammed into it, trying to reach the veterans. They met swift ends from efficient sword thrusts. All that needed to be done was disable the enemy, Fabiola realised. It was not necessary to kill each one. After a *gladius* blade had opened a man's belly or sliced deep into the muscles of his arm or leg, he wasn't about to pose any further problem. Respect and a little hope filled Fabiola as they continued. It was terrifying, and incredible, to witness. She could easily imagine how an enemy might be punched apart using the 'V' shaped formation in a battle.

Then everything became a blur.

A ruffian with long, greasy hair shoulder-charged the smallest veteran on the wedge's left side. The impact and the uneven ground were suffi-cient for the short ex-soldier's *caligae* to skid on a rock. Stabbing the thug through the chest as he fell, he also collided with the comrade on his left. This in turn caused the last man to stumble, and the wedge broke apart. With more men, they might have managed to haul each other up again, but there simply weren't enough. Their heavy *scuta* were now a hindrance rather than a help, leaving the fallen completely at the mercy of their enemies. With roars of triumph, more ambushers swarmed in, spitting the three helpless veterans like boys might spike fallen apples with sticks.

Fabiola's eyes opened wide with horror. There was no one between her and the ruffians now; the nearest ones were clearly visible. Fabiola recog-nised none, but was dismayed to count at least six. And there were more attacking the other side. Then Fabiola's heart stopped. Twenty paces away stood a familiar figure, directing the attack with waves of his long spear. The stocky build, the silver bracelets and four long scabs on his cheek from where she had scratched him. It could be no one else. Scaevola.

Their eyes met.

Making a filthy gesture, Scaevola grinned at her. 'I wanted to finish our date,' he shouted.

Fabiola felt sick.

'Keep going, Mistress!' Docilosa's voice hissed in her ear. 'It's our only chance.'

Dumbly, she obeyed.

Secundus and one of the others swung around to try and close the gap left by their fallen comrades. Sextus darted forward as well, an over-keen thug immediately dying beneath his *gladius*. Secundus gave another a great shove in the chest with his *scutum*, sending him reeling back into the men behind.

At the front, the sallow-faced veteran had reached the top of the barrier. 'Come on,' he yelled. 'We can make it!'

They were the last words he ever spoke.

Scaevola's spear hurtled through the air, striking him in the neck, below the cheek guard of his bronze helmet. The leaf-shaped blade sliced through the veteran's flesh to emerge blood-red on the other side. Without a sound, he toppled forward on to the road, ten steps below.

Next to die was the man with the arrow wound. He was followed by another on the wedge's right side, who was simply overwhelmed by weight of numbers. Secundus, Sextus and just two more were the last men left. Scrambling frantically down over the boulders and logs, the party reached the flat ground beyond. A trio of thugs were waiting for them, weapons raised, while the rest came charging in pursuit.

'You fools! Don't let them escape!'

Above the clash of arms, Fabiola recognised Scaevola's voice.

'Five *aurei* to the man who captures the good-looking bitch!'

His desperation meant that they had a chance.

'Run!' Fabiola cried. Lifting her dress, she raced forward, through the trees.

Eager to win the huge prize, the *fugitivarius*' men tore after them.

'Form rear guard,' Secundus ordered his two remaining followers. 'Now!'

Disciplined to the last, they immediately obeyed. Both slowed down and turned to face the enemy. Standing shoulder to shoulder, their shields clunked together in a final sound of defiance.

'Mithras protect you,' shouted Secundus.

Without speaking, the pair lifted their *gladii* in salute.

Looking back, Fabiola saw what would happen. 'NO!' she screamed.

'They are soldiers,' said Secundus proudly. 'It is their choice to die this way.'

She had no time to respond. Sextus had taken her arm in a vice-like grip and was propelling her onward. Secundus ran on Fabiola's other side. With her face fixed in a rictus of terror and rage, Docilosa protected her back.

Just three thugs stood between them and the road north.

Sextus killed the first with a no-nonsense thrust to the chest.

Secundus feinted to the left at another. Unaware that his enemy could not follow through, the ruffian dodged backwards to avoid the expected sword thrust. His feet slipped on a piece of moss and he fell heavily to the ground, dropping his axe.

The last swept around Sextus and came face to face with Docilosa. Shocked to see a woman bearing a weapon, he hesitated.

Docilosa did not. With teeth bared, she buried her *pugio* to the hilt in his belly.

Grievously wounded, the thug folded over and was gone.

The four survivors had broken clear.

But Scaevola and the rest of his men were closing in. There were nearly a dozen cursing figures running along the road behind.

With fear giving them an extra turn of speed, they pelted along between the thinning trees. And then they were out, bright sunlight falling on their sweating, desperate faces. The valley had opened out, its slopes falling away to meet the open plain beyond.

A plain which was now occupied by a Roman legion.

Fabiola could not believe her eyes.

A wide protective screen of legionaries was standing guard while their comrades toiled behind them, digging with their shovels. Using the earth from the defensive *fossae*, they would next erect the marching camp's ramparts. Safe in the knowledge that there were few if any enemies in Italy, most of the soldiers on watch were chatting to each other.

But it would not be long before they were spotted.

Scaevola had seen the troops too. Calling his men back to the protection of the trees, the *fugitivarius* watched in helpless rage as Fabiola and her companions moved beyond his reach.

Sextus and Docilosa were delighted, but Secundus swore out loud. And Fabiola's face turned thunderous.

'Who are they?' asked Docilosa, confused by her mistress' reaction.

'Pompey's men,' Fabiola replied in a flat tone. 'Marching south to Rome.'

The shouts of eager sentries reached them at last. *Bucinae* rang out, and a half-century of men under an *optio* swiftly formed up to come and guide them in.

Fabiola searched the sky for a sign. She could see nothing. Not even a raven, Mithras' bird, which was common in hilly areas.

Misery overcame the young woman, and a sob escaped finally escaped her lips.

One bitter enemy had been exchanged for another.

Chapter XVII: The Final Battle

By the River Hydaspes, India, spring 52 BC

When day broke, the rising sun lit the eastern horizon with a deep shade of crimson. The blood-red tinge actually seemed quite apt to the poorly rested, irritable legionaries. With a sky that colour, Hades could not be far away. Fervent prayers were uttered as men made their last requests of the gods. As always, wives, children and family were high on the list. While those in Italy had no doubt given them up for dead, the soldiers of the Forgotten Legion had survived partly by thinking of home. Now, for the last time, they asked the deities to protect their loved ones. They themselves had little need.

Those who could face it had a light breakfast; they weren't many. More important were their water bags, which were full to the brim. Combat was thirsty work.

Not long after dawn, Pacorus had them march to their position parallel to the riverbank. Positioned about half a mile away, the temporary marching camp with their tents and spare equipment was simply abandoned. It did not need to be defended. If by a miracle the Forgotten Legion was victorious, its contents would be safe. If not, it did not matter what happened to their yokes, clothes and few valuables.

With the most experienced veterans, the First was positioned in the centre of the line. It was flanked by five more on each side, with seven cohorts and Pacorus' remaining horsemen held in reserve. His warriors were also kept back, surrounding his position behind the First. A group of Parthian drummers and Roman trumpeters waited on one side, ready to pass on Pacorus' commands. That was also where the *aquilifer* was placed:

far enough back to protect the silver eagle, but close enough that every man could see it if he turned his head.

Every single tiny scrap of advantage was to be wrung out.

The first five ranks of legionaries were armed with the long spears, while nearly two-thirds had a silk-covered shield. The precious fabric obtained from Isaac, the Judaean merchant they had encountered en route to Margiana, only covered five thousand shields or so. It would have to suffice. At the sides and rear, the soldiers manning the *ballistae* turned and twisted their machines, making sure the mechanisms were well oiled, the washers tightened to the maximum and the thick gut strings sufficiently taut. Arcs of fire were checked repeatedly, as were the piles of stones alongside. The old hands among the artillerymen had already paced out the ground in front, marking each hundred paces with a distinctively shaped rock or a stake driven almost completely into the earth. It gave them exact range markers, and would make their volleys far more lethal.

Finally, a party was sent to dig out even more of the trench near the river, allowing more torrents of water to pour through and causing all the carefully dug channels to overflow. Then the entire area was covered with small branches, concealing the digging that had gone on. Seeing the result helped to lift the men's sombre mood a fraction.

They all waited.

It was a beautiful clear morning. The ominous red colour had lightened and then faded away, letting the sky turn its usual blue. The only clouds visible were groups of delicately shaped lines, very high up, but they still managed to dull the bright sunlight and kept the temperature pleasingly cool. The air was calm, and filled with a rich variety of birdsong from the trees along the riverbank. In the distance, a group of wild asses moved through the long grass, flicking their tails to keep flies at bay.

Romulus had already seen Tarquinius standing beside Pacorus, pointing here and there as they discussed the best battle strategy. There was no chance of talking with the haruspex, and Romulus had to hope that he and Brennus would be with him if the end came.

When it came, Romulus thought bitterly. He needed no ability to prophesy here, for the army that came to meet them was vast.

The Indian horsemen were the first to arrive. Riding small, agile ponies, the turbaned warriors carried a variety of weapons from javelins and bows to short spears and round or crescent-shaped shields. Bare-chested, dark-skinned, few wore any armour at all. Instead, a simple loincloth sufficed. Carefully keeping out of arrow range, they watched the Romans with dark, inscrutable eyes. These were skirmishers, highly mobile troops similar to the Gauls who had accompanied Crassus; their versatility could turn the course of a battle. There were at least five thousand of them, while Pacorus had perhaps two hundred and fifty horsemen remaining. Knowing this, many of the enemy confidently rode their horses down to the river to drink.

But they made no attempt to attack the Forgotten Legion. In their eyes, there was no need.

Pacorus kept silent, saving his men and the stones from his *ballistae*. Every single one was now more precious than gold.

Next to arrive were the battle chariots. Pulled by pairs of horses, they were larger than any Romulus had ever seen. Built from hardwood, and richly decorated with silver and gold inlay on their sides and solid wheels, they were essentially raised, enclosed battle platforms containing a driver and two or three warriors armed with spears and bows.

Romulus counted nearly three hundred of them.

As the chariots joined their cavalry comrades, shouts and jeers were hurled at the Roman lines. More and more voices joined in, until the mighty din filled the air. The exact words of the insults were unclear, but the meaning was crystal clear.

Following normal Roman tactics, the legionaries remained totally quiet. After a while, this had the effect of silencing the Indians and a strange peace reigned as the two sides watched each other warily. Some time later, the air filled with a low thunder.

The legionaries peered upwards, but there were no ominous-looking clouds in sight. Then it dawned on them that the noise was from the sheer number of infantry approaching. As the horizon to the south filled with the shapes of marching men, Romulus gradually picked out groups of archers, slingers and ordinary foot soldiers. The variety of weapons they carried was enormous: it seemed that no two men were armed the same. He saw axes, short swords, spears, even longswords like Brennus' mighty one. There were pikes, spiked maces and knives with angled blades similar to those used by Thracian gladiators. Like the cavalry, most of the Indians wore no protective clothing at all. Some had leather armour and helmets and carried small, round shields. Just a few were wealthy enough to have mail or scale coats, but all were more lightly protected than the legionaries, with their heavy *scuta* and thigh-length chain mail. It didn't matter.

There were at least thirty thousand of them.

The enemy numbers were bad enough, but this was not what had the Roman soldiers shifting uneasily from side to side. The low rumbling sound was not just from the men who drew ever nearer. It was being made by animals. Above the enemy ranks loomed the shapes of great, grey beasts.

Elephants.

There were dozens of them, guided by a mahout wielding a short staff topped with a sharpened hook. Each was wearing on its back a thick red fabric caparison, which was held in place by a band of leather that ran around its broad chest. Two or three archers and spearmen perched on this carpet, gripping tightly with their knees to stay in place. Every tenth beast carried a single passenger who was positioned above large drums hanging on both sides: these men's sole purpose was to relay orders during battle. The animals' small ears flapped from side to side as they lumbered along, giving them a deceptively gentle appearance. This contrasted with the heavy layers of moulded leather covering their heads and shoulders. To protect the mahout, a protective fan of the same material protruded upwards from the nape of the neck. As they drew nearer, it was possible to see that many of the elephants' tusks were tipped with points or swords. A number even had spiked iron balls on chains dangling from their trunks.

They looked unassailable. Invincible. Romulus' heart sank further, and even Brennus was dismayed; on either side of them, the legionaries looked downright terrified. The junior officers and Parthian centurions shuffled their feet uncertainly.

By now, the use of elephants in the arena was reasonably commonplace. There they killed or maimed at will. Even if he had not seen it for himself, every Roman knew of the huge beasts' capacity to tear apart men like fire-wood. The Nubian king Jugurtha had used them in his fight against Rome, and no one ever forgot King Pyrrhus or the Carthaginians, enemies who had used elephants against the legions with devastating effect. It had given them a place in legend. And while Roman allies had used the great beasts alongside legionaries for many years now, most men here had never trained or fought with them.

Elephants were the ultimate battle weapon, able to smash aside almost any opposition – and the Indians knew it.

Romulus could almost sense their confidence as he watched the laughing, chattering men opposite. They were happy to delay the battle until all their forces had arrived.

Fearful muttering began in the Forgotten Legion's ranks. Prayers and curses mingled in equal numbers. The whole pantheon of gods and goddesses were named: Jupiter, Mars and Minerva. Fortuna and Orcus. Neptune, Aesculapius and Mithras. Even Bacchus got a mention as every possible divine being was called upon. It made no difference. They were alone on the plain.

The solid lines of legionaries began to waver back and forth like reeds in the wind.

'We're doomed,' shouted one.

His cry was infectious.

'It's Carrhae all over again!'

Fear changed at once to panic.

Romulus glanced at the terrified faces around him. Despite the cool air, they were sweating. If something was not done fast, the legionaries would flee. And if they did that, he knew exactly what would happen. The Indians would simply run riot. The plain truly would become another Carrhae.

He could see that Brennus thought the same, but neither man knew what to say to their comrades.

'Take courage,' shouted a familiar voice.

Heads turned in surprise.

Pushing his way through the ranks, Tarquinius emerged to stand before the frightened soldiers. Pointedly turning his back on the enemy, he held up his hands for silence.

A hush fell over the Forgotten Legion.

'This is a long way from Italy,' the haruspex began. 'A whole world away.'

Nervous laughter met his comment.

'But that does not mean you should forget who you are. Look behind you,' he urged. 'At the silver eagle.'

The legionaries obeyed.

'It is watching your every move,' Tarquinius announced loudly.

Sensing the moment's importance, the *aquilifer* raised his wooden pole high. Rays of sunlight lit up the metal bird, and the golden thunderbolt in its talons glittered and flashed. No one could fail to be impressed by its imperious stare, thought Romulus, taking heart. Even elephants could not scare the eagle.

Their pride stirred, men looked to each other for reassurance.

'You are Roman soldiers!' Tarquinius cried. 'Who do not run!'

This raised a ragged cheer, but many remained unconvinced.

'What can we do against those monsters?' shouted a man near Romulus.

'The fucking Parthians are no use,' said another. 'Their mounts will be terrified.'

Uneasy murmurs met the comment. As many knew, the musty smell of elephants made horses panic. They had to be trained to accept the presence of such strange creatures.

'We haven't got any flaming pigs to set among them either,' Aemilius quipped.

There was a burst of laughter from those who got the joke. One of the more successful tactics employed against the Carthaginians' elephants had been to coat swine in grease and pitch before setting them alight and driving the screaming creatures into the enemy's midst.

If only we had axes, thought Romulus. Another historical method used to disable the great beasts was to run underneath and hamstring them. But Tarquinius possessed the only such weapon in the Forgotten Legion.

'We haven't.' Tarquinius smiled thinly. 'But Alexander's hoplites learned to defeat them long ago,' he revealed. 'Near this very spot.'

Hope appeared in some faces. Despite all her previous glories, Greece was now under Rome's control, its formerly invincible phalanxes no match for the legions. Surely they too could equal what a conquered people had done?

'More recently than that,' Tarquinius went on, 'Roman legionaries learned to fight the elephants of Carthage and beat them. Without pigs.'

'Tell us how,' shouted Aemilius.

Romulus and Brennus roared in agreement and a more determined air settled over the Roman soldiers.

Tarquinius looked pleased. 'Use the long spears,' he said. 'Keep them bunched together. Aim at the elephants' sensitive spots: their trunks and eyes. They won't advance if it's too painful to do so.'

The nearest legionaries nodded keenly.

'And every man with *pila*,' cried the haruspex, 'yours is the most important job of all.'

The ears of those at the rear pricked up.

'The mahouts control these beasts. They sit on the shoulders, just behind the head, and wear little or no armour. All that protects them is the fan of leather in front,' Tarquinius explained. 'Kill them, and the elephants will turn and flee.'

Determination began to replace some of the fear.

'Then it's just the rest we have to deal with,' joked Aemilius. 'No problem, eh?'

It was the right thing to say. Men grinned at each other, taking strength from the knowledge that they had been through hell together before. They even laughed, slapping each other on the shoulders. They accepted that death was likely, but they would not run. That was what cowards did.

High overhead, a raven croaked. It was a good omen, and everyone's eyes lifted to the sky.

Glancing up with the rest, Romulus watched the black bird swooping through the air from behind their position, controlling its flight with astonishing precision. Its head turned, taking in the legionaries arrayed beneath it. Bizarrely, Romulus had a real sense that it was assessing the battlefield. He could not shake off the feeling.

Seeing him look, Tarquinius also lifted his gaze as the raven crossed into no-man's-land. Even some of the Indian troops began to stare upwards.

As it flew over the enemy lines, the bird croaked again, a raw, angry cry that pierced the air. It was if the Indians' presence offended it in some way. Without further warning, the raven pulled in its wings and dived towards the lead elephant. Like a black stone, it hurtled downwards, aiming its powerful beak straight at the beast's head.

Brennus had seen too. 'What's it doing?'

Awestruck by its suicidal bravery, Romulus did not answer.

More and more legionaries began pointing and gesticulating.

'The raven is helping us,' cried Tarquinius. 'It's a sign from the gods!'

Finally a cheer of approval left the men's throats.

Even Pacorus and his warriors were watching, agog. 'Mithras is watching over us,' a number of warriors shouted. 'He has sent his Corax to help!'

Delighted by this revelation, Romulus threw up a prayer to his new favourite deity.

Gradually the mahout on the front elephant realised that something was up. When he saw the raven plummeting towards him, he cried out in fear. His shout was enough to unsettle the massive creature; it raised its trunk and blared an alarm. Its companions' response was immediate. Loud bugles of distress echoed up and down the Indian line, and the mahouts struggled to control their mounts. The response of their infantry and cavalry was most pleasing: to a man they looked terrified.

'See?' shouted Tarquinius. 'They're frightened of their own beasts! If we can panic them, they will turn and run.'

Now a rousing cheer went up from the legionaries.

When it was less than twenty paces above the elephant's head, the raven suddenly pulled out of its dive and banked up into the sky again. Scores of Indian archers shot arrows at it, to no avail. Their shafts flew up in dense shoals and fell back to earth, wasted. Flapping strongly, the raven had soon climbed far out of range. Without further ado, it flew off to the west, its odd action a complete mystery.

It's heading towards Italy, thought Romulus sadly. For some reason, a powerful image of Fabiola struck home, and he took heart.

He missed Tarquinius' dark eyes upon him.

The black bird left unsettled elephants, angry mahouts and a less confident Indian host in its wake. The lead beast was still most unhappy, and had barged backwards out of line. Screams carried through the air as some of the closely packed infantry were trampled to death.

'If a raven can scare an elephant like that, imagine what a dozen spears in the face will do!' Tarquinius raised a clenched fist. 'The Forgotten Legion!'

Proud of the name he had originally coined, Brennus echoed the cry.

A passionate roar followed the haruspex' words. Swelling as it rolled through the ranks, the legionaries' response was fuelled as much by desperation as it was by bravery. As at Carrhae, there was nowhere to run. Nowhere to hide. They had to stand and fight, or die.

The men's reasons did not matter, thought Romulus. As he knew from the arena, courage was a mixture of many emotions. What mattered was the belief that there was a chance of survival, however slim. He gripped his spear shaft tightly and held on to the tiny spark of hope in his own heart, gathering himself for the titanic struggle. Mithras, watch over us, he thought.

The Indian leader did not delay his attack any further. There was no reason to. The raven's odd behaviour had already handed a small advantage to his enemies. The sooner they were crushed, the better. His first mistake was to send in the battle chariots.

Their wheels creaking loudly, they rolled towards the Roman lines at the speed of a man walking fast. Hundreds of infantry accompanied them, filling the spaces between to form a great wall of men and weapons. Musicians played drums, cymbals and bells, and the soldiers chanted as they came on. The noise was incredible. Used to smashing apart enemy formations with this initial charge, the Indians were full of confidence.

Then the chariots reached the covered water channels.

Which had turned the earth into a mud bath.

Simultaneously, all the lead chariots' solid wheels sank deep into the morass. Cumbersome, hard to manoeuvre and immensely heavy, the battle platforms were not made to travel on anything other than flat, firm ground. The frustrated charioteers whipped on their horses. Valiantly obeying, the steeds pulled a few steps further. Now the chariots sank to the axles, and the attack stalled before it had even come near the waiting legionaries.

Pacorus' response was instantaneous. 'Loose!' he roared at the soldiers manning the *ballistae* that covered their front.

The grizzled *optio* in charge had been waiting for this moment, and had already marked the Indians' distance from his position. It was less than two hundred paces, a good killing range. He barked an order and the six powerful machines twanged as one, hurling pieces of stone bigger than a man's head in a graceful arc over the Roman lines.

Romulus watched in awe. He had not seen *ballistae* used much since before Carrhae. The pitched battles fought by the Forgotten Legion were never large enough to require them. Today though, every shot counted. What mattered was causing maximum enemy casualties. Through this was their only chance of victory.

The volley was a good start.

The *optio*'s range marking was precise. The sixth stone merely smashed the front wheel of a chariot, immobilising it, but the rest found human targets. Men's heads were cleanly ripped off, chests smashed in, limbs pulverised. The horrified companions of those hit were covered in a red mist of blood from spraying carotids. Their energy still unspent, the boulders went on to tear holes in the chariots' sides or injure more soldiers before they fell to the ground, throwing up great splashes of mud and water.

The stunned Indians had barely time to react before the *ballistae* fired again. Yet more chariots were torn asunder, their crews killed or maimed. With his next barrage, the *optio* had his men load smaller stones and aim at the infantry. It was like watching heavy rain knock down a field of ripe wheat, thought Romulus. Gaping holes opened up in the Indian ranks as the projectiles landed, taking out far greater numbers than the previous volleys. It was a complete slaughter.

'Stop them with the mud, then massacre the poor bastards,' said Brennus, grimacing. 'Very efficient. Very Roman.'

'They'd do the same to us,' retorted Romulus.

'True,' replied the Gaul. 'And there'll be plenty left.'

Keen to conserve the catapults' rapidly dwindling store of ammunition, Pacorus signalled the *optio* to cease firing. Their volleys had pulverised the Indian attack. Already the enemy infantry were fleeing in blind panic towards their own lines.

The *bucinae* signalled that the First and Third Cohorts should advance at once. Leaving their heavy spears behind, they trotted forward, their *caligae* squelching through the mud. Romulus gritted his teeth. Their purpose was to kill the survivors.

The gruesome task did not take long. It was a necessary evil, reducing enemy numbers and badly affecting their watching comrades' morale. Fearful and in disarray, the main Indian force looked on as the unfortunates left behind were dispatched by the legionaries. Soon the only living figures in the muddy area were those of Roman soldiers. Indian infantry lay scattered in piles while other bodies festooned the stationary battle platforms, hanging half-in, half-out as if still trying to escape.

The signal to withdraw rang out.

Concerned about the dozens of horses tethered by their traces and struggling in the mud before the immobilised chariots, Romulus was busy chopping through as many leather straps as he could. It was also a way to avoid killing injured, helpless enemy soldiers. He had set free a number of teams when Brennus grabbed him.

'Come on!' urged the Gaul. 'You can't help them all.'

Romulus glanced at their comrades, already halfway back to their own lines. On the other side, the enraged Indian leader had signalled his mahouts to move forward. With ponderous steps, the now calm elephants began to advance.

'We don't want to be caught here when those arrive,' said Brennus.

Adrenalin pumping, they both laughed at the absurdity of two men fighting an army of elephants. They turned and ran.

Their Parthian centurion glared furiously at them as they reassumed their position. But it was not the time or place to punish minor infractions like this. It was enough that hundreds of Indians had been killed with no Parthian casualties at all.

Buoyed up by the combined success of the water channels and the catapults' volleys, the legionaries' demeanour was much steadier as they watched the elephants approach. The enemy infantry had finally been rallied by their officers and were marching between the grey beasts, using them as protection from attack.

Romulus took in the Indians' tactic at a glance. The elephants would try to smash apart the Roman shield wall and then the foot soldiers could pour into the gaps. If that happened, the Forgotten Legion would quickly be overwhelmed. He grimaced. It was vital that they used their long spears as Tarquinius had said.

Whooping loudly, the Indian cavalry broke away from their army and cantered off to the west. There was no point trying to charge through the mass of abandoned chariots and corpses, so the Indian leader had ordered a probing attack around his enemies. Romulus was not worried by this. Thanks to the defensive ditches, any attempt to flank the Forgotten Legion would not work. And he doubted the lightly armed horsemen could break through the reserve cohorts either. At least a thousand of the long spears had been held back to use in this exact scenario.

Romulus shifted from foot to foot, trusting in the soldiers at his back, just as they were depending on him and Brennus. Perhaps if they survived, their status as escaped slaves would not be such a badge of hatred for the other legionaries. In his heart, Romulus doubted that would happen. It seemed that in the eyes of citizens and free men, there was an inescapable stain on the character of a former slave. The knowledge left a sour taste in his mouth. He longed to be accepted for what he was – a good soldier.

Using their short staffs to guide their mounts, the mahouts manoeuvred between the stranded chariots full of corpses. The obstacles slowed up their progress, and it bunched the elephants closely. Together with their enormous size, it made them excellent targets.

'Loose!' roared the optio by the *ballistae*.

More stones flew through the air, striking the elephants on their heads and bodies. Some hit the warriors on their backs, hurling them to the ground. The projectiles were not powerful enough to badly injure the huge beasts, but, better than this, they created fear and confusion. Ignoring their frantic mahouts, many elephants immediately whirled around and stampeded into the distance. Any Indian infantry in their path were trampled underfoot without regard.

A pair began fighting fiercely, battering each other with their iron-tipped tusks in an effort to wound or disable. Another barrage of stones landed; one beast was struck in the eye and also ran away, trumpeting in pain. But the rest, better trained, continued tramping forward.

Close behind marched the tightly packed Indian infantry, allowing the Romans to study them properly for the first time. Many men sported cloth turbans, and they wore an incredible variety of garments from loincloths to leather armour and chain mail. Large numbers carried round shields while others carried tall ones fashioned from animal skin. Romulus saw crescent shields similar to those carried by the Scythians, as well as rounded triangular ones. The foot soldiers were armed with spears, long and short swords, axes and knives. Like *retiarii* in the arena, some even carried tridents. Romulus did not even recognise a number of the weapons: leaf-shaped double-ended blades with a short handle in between, and lengths of thick wood wrapped with bands of iron.

But none of the men struck fear into Romulus' heart as the elephants did. They were now very near. Terrifyingly, the closest one had a spiked metal ball on a chain attached to the end of its trunk. Romulus could already imagine its destructive power. Suddenly the long spear in his hands, made from Margianian iron and so successful against enemies on horseback, seemed puny.

Following orders, half the legionaries had slung their *scuta* from their shoulders by their leather carrying straps. Only a two-handed grip on their spears would suffice. To combat the enemy foot soldiers, every second man retained his shield and drew his sword.

Soon the elephant's musky odour reached their nostrils. It was strong but not unpleasant; Romulus thought he could smell alcohol too. Lines of coloured paint had been drawn around the beast's eyes, while an ornate silver headdress covering the head completed its exotic and fearsome appearance. Dangling its lethal ball, the prehensile trunk swayed from side to side, its tip scenting the Romans' alien smell. The mahout shouted and used his goad, forcing the elephant into a shambling run. High above on its back, the warriors readied their bows and spears. Hastily released arrows shot past Romulus, one plunging deep into a legionary's eye.

His screams did little for the soldiers' nerves. There were grey faces everywhere now. Men rubbed lucky phallic amulets, cleared their throats nervously and spat on the ground; others whispered prayers to their favourite deities. At least one legionary vomited, his courage frayed to breaking point. The acrid smell of bile mingled with those of the elephant and men's sweat.

Romulus glanced at Brennus. The Gaul was eyeing him proudly and he ducked his head, embarrassed. A tickling worry began at the back of his mind. Something Tarquinius had said, a long time ago. Could that moment be now?

'Raise your spears!' bellowed Aemilius, his nerves still steady. 'Those at the back, ready *pila*.'

Wooden shafts clattered together as the front ranks obeyed. Behind them, line after line of right arms swung back, pointing barbed javelin heads upwards. Indian arrows hummed through the air, but the legionaries just had to ignore them. Some struck home, creating small gaps in the line. More shafts followed, accompanied by a volley of stones from the enemy slingers.

Twenty paces separated the two sides.

Screaming blood-curdling battle cries, the Indian infantry broke into a full charge.

A cold sweat broke out on Romulus' forehead, but his spear tip did not waver. Oddly, Brennus began to laugh, a strange jarring sound coming from deep in his chest. His blue eyes lit up with battle rage; he looked terrifying. Romulus was very glad that the Gaul was fighting with, not against him.

'Hold steady, lads!' Aemilius shouted.

To the legionaries' credit, they did not break.

Blaring with anger from the mahout's blows, the lead elephant reached the forest of spears. Bending like twigs, half of them simply snapped in two.

Romulus' vision was entirely filled with flashing metal-tipped tusks, a swinging trunk and the beast's open, angry mouth. He could see streams of thick, pungent-smelling liquid pouring down the sides of its face, but did not realise their significance. He would find out later that it meant the bull was full of breeding 'rage'. But all he could do right then was react. And use his spear.

'Aim at the head!' screamed Aemilius. 'Loose javelins!'

A flurry of *pila* shot up, striking the elephant in the face and wounding the mahout in the right arm. Two of the warriors on its back fell off, injured or killed, but the last continued to fire arrows at the legionaries. Bellowing with rage, the massive creature swung its head and the spiked metal ball spun forward on its chain, sweeping aside more of the long spears as if they were brushwood. As it swung back, the deadly weapon carried a trio of soldiers into the air, crushing the skull of the first and badly injuring the others.

Leaning down towards his mount's ear, the mahout shouted encouragement.

Around came the ball again, tearing the front ranks apart.

The man next to Romulus had his shoulder smashed into pieces by a glancing blow. With rings of chain mail mashed deep into his flesh, he collapsed in a heap, screaming.

Relieved it had not been him, Romulus stabbed at the elephant's head. It made no difference at all. The beast's destructive power was matched by the sheer terror it caused. All the Romans' efforts were in vain: it was like trying to kill a mythical monster. Even Brennus' powerful thrusts seemed to have little effect. Romulus was beginning to despair when a lucky javelin took the mahout through the chest. Hurled by a legionary several ranks behind, its pyramidal iron head punched through his ribs. Mortally wounded, he toppled sideways from his position.

'Now's our chance!' cried Romulus, remembering Tarquinius' advice. 'Attack it!'

The soldiers' spirits rallied and a dozen long spears were shoved up into the elephant's neck and shoulders, penetrating its leather armour. Blood streamed from multiple wounds. Bellowing in pain and no longer guided by the mahout, it turned and pounded back into the Indian ranks, trampling men like ripe fruit.

Before the legionaries could even cheer, the enemy infantry slammed into their lines.

Brennus jumped forward. With a huge slice of his *gladius*, he took off the head of the first man to reach him.

Frantically, Romulus dropped his spear and unslung his *scutum*. All around him, his comrades were doing the same, but it was too late to form a complete shield wall.

Short and wiry, the dark-skinned soldiers swarmed into the gaps, thrusting and stabbing.

Plunging his shield boss into a bearded Indian's face, Romulus felt the man's cheekbone break against the metal. As he reeled back, Romulus thrust his sword into his unprotected midriff. It was a disabling blow and he ignored the Indian as the blade pulled free. Concentrate on the next enemy, he thought. Stay focused.

Even as he killed another man, Romulus knew that the Indians' attack was too powerful. He fought on regardless. What else was there to do? Like a machine, he cut and thrust with his *gladius*, always mindful of the soldiers on either side. Beside him, Brennus bellowed like a lunatic, dispatching every Indian who came near.

At last, thanks to good discipline, the shield wall began to re-form in their section of the line. Without the elephants to back them up, the lightly armed Indian foot soldiers were unable to break the First's formation. Peering around desperately, Romulus could see that their centre was holding fast, but the cohorts on each side were buckling badly under the pressure.

Then the left flank gave way.

Trumpeting in a combination of triumph and rage, a trio of elephants barged forward, followed by hundreds of baying warriors.

Seeing them, Romulus was swamped by a tide of hopelessness. The end was near. The Indians were simply too many. Even the reserves could not stop this.

He and Brennus exchanged a significant look. It said many things to both. Love. Respect. Honour. Pride. But there was no time to vocalise any of them.

Sensing victory, the Indians facing the First Cohort redoubled their attack. Soon half a dozen more men had died beneath Romulus' and Brennus' blades. Then it was ten, but the enemy no longer quailed at the danger. The scent of victory was in their nostrils. Screaming incoherently, they pushed forward, uncaring that a certain death awaited those at the front.

As Romulus' *gladius* pulled free from the chest of a thin man with prominent ribs, the din of battle suddenly dimmed. From behind him came a voice.

'Time to go.'

With Romulus' dying enemy falling in slow motion, there was a moment of safety before another replaced him. He turned his head.

The haruspex was two steps to his rear, his battleaxe gripped in both hands. Amazingly, there was a new energy about him. Gone was the stoop, the age-old weariness. Instead the figure looked more like the Tarquinius of old.

Romulus was stunned. He felt joy and confusion in equal measure at Tarquinius' reappearance. 'Leave our comrades?' he faltered.

'We cannot run.' Brennus glanced angrily over his shoulder. 'You said I would face a battle that no one else could fight. This must be it.'

The haruspex regarded him steadily. 'It is not over yet,' he said.

The Gaul stared at him, then nodded once.

Romulus' face twisted with anguish. He could not bear it: his hunch was correct.

Before Romulus could utter a word, Tarquinius spoke again. 'We must leave at once, or our chance will be lost. There is safety on the far bank of the river.'

Their gaze followed his outstretched arm to the other side, which was completely deserted. To reach it, they would have to fight their way through the bitter hand-to-hand struggle between the elephants and the doomed legionaries of the left flank.

'If we stay?' Romulus asked.

'Certain death. You must each choose,' the haruspex replied, his dark eyes inscrutable. 'But the road to Rome lies over there. I saw it in the Mithraeum.'

Mithras has kept faith with me! Grief and joy were tearing Romulus in two. He wanted to return home, but not at this price.

Brennus gave him a huge shove. 'We're going, and that's final.'

Almost of their own accord, Romulus' feet began to move. He felt numb.

With great difficulty, they managed to turn and shove their way through the packed ranks, ignoring the objections that followed. Romulus found it hardest to meet the legionaries' angry stares.

'Where are you going?' demanded one.

'Cowards!' cried another.

'Typical fucking slaves,' added the man to his right.

Romulus flushed with shame at the familiar insult.

More rained down before the most vocal soldier's voice came to an abrupt, choking halt.

Brennus' right hand had taken an iron grip on his throat. 'The haruspex here has told us we must follow our destiny to the left flank,' he snarled. 'Like to join us?'

The legionary shook his head dumbly.

Satisfied, Brennus released him.

No one else dared to speak, and the trio ducked their heads, pushing on. When they reached the edge of the First Cohort, it suddenly became easier to move. The narrow gap between it and the next unit which allowed manoeuvring in battle was still present. Tarquinius darted down it, away from the front line. The two friends followed. In less than a hundred paces, they were clear.

Behind the cohorts was a small open area. It was here that the *ballistae* stood.

And it was also where Pacorus, Vahram and the last of the reserves were gathered.

Romulus threw a hate-filled glance at the *primus pilus*, whose eyes somehow locked with his.

Barely taking time to notify Pacorus, Vahram whipped his horse into a gallop. 'After them!' he screamed at the nearest warriors. 'A talent to the man who brings me any of their heads.'

The amount of gold mentioned was worth more than a lifetime's pay for the average soldier. Every Parthian who heard responded, charging wildly in pursuit.

Thankfully, within twenty steps they had been subsumed into the heaving confusion of men and beasts that was the left flank. The cries of injured soldiers and shouted orders from the officers mixed with loud trumpeting and the metallic clash of arms. The only discernible detail was that the Roman lines were being inexorably, inevitably, driven backwards. Throwing in the reserve cohorts had failed, and shields and swords could only withstand the weight of angry elephants for so long. Craning his head, Romulus saw that the nearest behemoths were almost within javelin range. If they did not hurry, they too would meet the same fate as the legionaries at the front. Judging by the screams, it was not a pleasant way to die.

On they went, occasionally having to use the flat edges of their weapons to create a space. Romulus no longer felt dishonour at this. Theirs was a primeval struggle for survival, and since Optatus' discovery of their status, none of these men had done anything but show hatred towards them. The last comments by the soldiers of his own cohort said it all. Romulus' comradeship with the Forgotten Legion was dead. And Tarquinius had seen a possible road to Rome for him. It was time to take what the gods had offered.

They emerged near the river soon afterwards. A narrow band of ground was clear of combatants; the risk of falling in and drowning kept both sides away.

Romulus' spirits began to lift. They were all three still alive and unscathed. His chest heaving, he peered at the muddy, roiling water. It flowed swiftly by, impervious to the noise and to the blood being shed only a few steps away. It was a long way to the far side. Branches and other debris swept past, revealing the river's massive power. Crossing it would be no easy task, especially in heavy armour. He cast his eyes up and down the shore, hoping against hope that he might see a boat.

There were none.

'Nothing for it but to swim,' grinned Tarquinius. 'Can you manage it?'

Romulus and Brennus looked at each other grimly; then they nodded.

Instantly the pair began stripping off their mail shirts. Whatever chance they had would be greatly increased by their removal.

Tarquinius knelt down, shoving his map and other precious items into a pig's bladder. It had served him well on their arrival in Asia Minor two years before.

Unseen, Vahram waited until Romulus and Brennus were both in just their tunics. Driven by his hatred, the *primus pilus* and his horse had also emerged unharmed from the fray. Still armed with his recurved bow, Vahram calmly drew a shaft from the case on his hip and fitted it to the string. Spooked by the sudden blare of a wounded elephant, his mount jumped as he released.

The move deflected his arrow a tiny fraction.

Romulus heard Brennus gasp as if shocked. In slow motion, he turned to see a barbed metal head protruding from the muscle of his huge friend's upper left arm. Although it was not the mortal wound that Vahram desired, swimming the river might now be too much for the Gaul. Romulus knew immediately who was responsible. Spinning around, he took in the *primus pilus* in a blink. Dropping his chain mail, Romulus snatched up his *gladius* and charged forward. 'You bastard!' he screamed in rage.

Vahram panicked and loosed too soon.

His next arrow flashed past, burying itself in the ground.

And then Romulus was on him. Memories of Felix' anguished face flashed across his vision, lending him superhuman strength. Focusing his anger, Romulus reached up and took hold of Vahram's right hand, which was frantically reaching for another shaft. With a powerful downward slice, he lopped it off.

The *primus pilus* screamed in agony and blood gushed from the stump, covering Romulus in a mist of red droplets. With true battle frenzy consuming him for the first time in his life, he did not care. Just one thing was important: killing Vahram. But before he could complete the task, the Parthian's terrified horse skittered away on dancing hooves. Spinning in a tight circle, it trotted back towards the battle.

Romulus cursed. Even now he was being denied his revenge for Felix' death.

It was then that a wounded bull elephant emerged into view, one tusk snapped clean away and the other red-tipped with gore. Every few steps, it blew out its ears and raised its trunk, letting out a piercing bugle of anger. Romulus was not the only being affected by battle rage. Its mahout was still in place, occasionally managing to direct his mount towards any legionaries within range. A solitary warrior remained on its back; he was firing arrows as well. The bull's armoured head and neck bristled with bent *pila*, thrown by the legionaries in a vain attempt to bring it down. Yet what had done most damage was the lucky javelin that had pierced its left eye, half blinding it. The remaining eye now gleamed with a piggy, intelligent fury.

Unused to elephants, Vahram's horse froze with terror.

Instantly the archer loosed a shaft, which took the Parthian through his left arm and rendered him totally unable to guide his mount away to safety. A cruel smile played across the Indian's face.

Romulus paused, overcome with awe at what he was about to see.

And Tarquinius gave thanks to Mithras for granting him the strength not to reveal this during his torture.

Moving with surprising speed, the great bull swept forward, wrapping its trunk around Vahram's body.

A thin, cracked cry left the *primus pilus'* throat as he was lifted high into the air.

It was the last sound he ever made.

Dashing him to the ground, the elephant immediately knelt down, crushing Vahram beneath its front legs. Then, grabbing the Parthian's head with its trunk, it decapitated him.

Romulus closed his eyes. He had never seen a man die more brutally, yet somehow it felt quite apt. When he looked up again a single heartbeat later, the bull was making straight for him.

Romulus felt his heart hammer in his chest. Without chain mail and armed only with a *gladius*, his life was over too.

A massive hand covered in blood pushed him to one side. 'This is my quarrel, brother,' said the Gaul quietly. 'A time for Brennus to stand and fight.'

Romulus stared into the other's calm blue eyes.

'I will run no more.'

The words brooked no argument.

Ever since he had gained an insight into Tarquinius' abilities, this moment was what Romulus had dreaded. Now it was here. Fat tears of grief welled up, but his protest died away. In Brennus' gaze he saw only bravery, love and acceptance.

And the gods had decreed it. Mithras had brought them here.

'Return to Rome,' Brennus ordered. 'Find your family.'

His throat closed with lead, Romulus could not answer.

Like a hero of old, the pigtailed Gaul stepped forward, his longsword ready. Without his chain mail, he was a magnificent sight. Huge muscles rippled and tensed under his sweat-soaked military tunic. Runnels of blood covered his left arm, but he had snapped off and drawn out the Indian shaft.

'You were right, Ultan,' Brennus whispered, looking up at the magnificent beast now rearing above him. Bunching his left fist, he breathed into the pain that radiated from his arrow wound. 'A journey beyond where any Allobroge has gone. Or will ever go.'

'Romulus.' The voice was insistent. 'Romulus.'

The young soldier let Tarquinius lead him the few steps to the edge. He did not look back. Holding only his weapon, Romulus jumped into the river with Tarquinius.

As the cold water closed over his head, his ears rang with Brennus' last battle cry.

'FOR LIATH!' he roared. 'FOR CONALL, AND FOR BRAC!'

Chapter XVIII: Pompey's General

Northern Italy, spring 52 BC

By the time that the legionaries reached them, Fabiola had regained control of her emotions. The forty men clattered to a halt, shields and *pila* at the ready. Sextus and Docilosa were very careful not to raise their bloodied weapons. Any perceived threat would result in a volley of javelins. Yet the soldiers' disciplined appearance was infinitely more appealing than that of Scaevola and his crew. There would be no out-of-hand rape here. Ignoring the soldiers' eager stares, Fabiola took her time, fixing her hair back into place with a couple of decorated ivory pins and lifting the neck of her dress to a more modest level. Then she beamed at the *optio* in charge, who had made his way to the front. Brazening their way out of the situation might yet be possible.

'Centurion,' Fabiola purred, deliberately giving him a higher rank. 'You have our thanks.'

While the *optio* flushed proudly, his men tittered with amusement.

He threw an angry glance over his shoulder and they fell silent. 'What happened, my lady?'

'Those ruffians you saw,' Fabiola began, 'they ambushed us in the woods. Killed almost all my slaves and bodyguards.' Not entirely acting, she let her lip tremble at the memory.

'The roads are dangerous everywhere, lady,' he muttered in sympathy.

'But they ran when you appeared,' said Fabiola, batting her eyelashes. Embarrassed now, the *optio* looked down.

Secundus hid a smile. As if the *fugitivarii* would have attacked them in front of an entire legion, he thought.

Awed by her beauty, the *optio* said nothing for a moment. A short man with a scar across the bridge of his nose, he carefully considered the four figures, their clothes torn and covered with bloodstains. 'Might I ask where you are bound?' he asked eventually.

'Ravenna,' lied Fabiola. 'To see my aged aunt.'

Satisfied, he nodded.

Fabiola thought she had succeeded. 'If we might proceed then?' she said. 'The next town is not far. I will be able to purchase more slaves there.'

'That won't be possible, lady.'

'Why ever not?' she demanded, her voice rising.

The *optio* cleared his throat awkwardly. 'I have my orders.'

'Which are?'

'To take you in,' he said, avoiding her eyes. 'The centurion said so.'

Fabiola looked at Secundus, who gave her a tiny shrug.

The *optio*'s superior might want them questioned further, but they could not exactly refuse.

'Very well,' she said, acceding gracefully. 'Lead on.'

Pleased, the junior officer barked an order. Parting smoothly in the middle, his men positioned themselves on either side of Fabiola and her little party.

Before walking away, she glanced at the trees. Nothing. Scaevola and his *fugitivarii* had disappeared.

Fabiola knew that it would not be the last time that they met. She'd have to kill the merciless slave-catcher on the next occasion, or he would do the same to her.

In the event, Fabiola's fear about not being allowed to continue her journey proved correct. The centurion who greeted them nearer the marching camp was no less impressed by her beauty than the *optio*, but he was far more assured in his manner. Fabiola's request to proceed was brushed aside with a courteous yet firm refusal.

'There aren't many travellers about, lady,' he said, tapping his nose. 'I'm sure the legate would appreciate a chat with you. Find out what's going on. Offer some advice, maybe.'

'He'd hardly bother with me,' Fabiola protested.

'On the contrary,' came the reply. 'The legate is a man of fine taste who would want me to offer you his hospitality.'

'That is most gracious,' said Fabiola, bowing her neck to conceal her dread. 'And his name?'

'Marcus Petreius, lady,' the centurion answered proudly. 'One of Pompey's best generals.'

Again the *optio* took charge.

The walk to the temporary camp did not take long. Never having seen one constructed before, Fabiola watched the working soldiers with interest. Three deep *fossae* were already finished, their bottoms decorated with caltrops. Now the legionaries were finishing off the ramparts, which were the height of two tall men. Tamping down the earth with flattening blows of their shovels, they formed a firm surface to walk upon. Stakes chopped from freshly felled trees decorated the corners, forming protective areas for the sentries. As with a permanent fort, one entrance was being situated in the middle of each side. With the legion on the march, there were no wooden gates to use. Instead, one wall angled just in front of the other where they met, forming a narrow corridor. Fabiola counted twenty paces as they passed through it. Piles of cut branches were being stacked nearby; these would be used to fill the gap once night fell.

Inside the camp, leather tents were being erected in long, neat lines. There was minimal fuss as hundreds of men worked side by side. Their officers watched, vine canes at the ready for anyone who slowed down. Secundus explained to Fabiola what was going on as they walked by. A simple standard marked the spot where every centurion's tent stood. Each *contubernium* then set up theirs alongside by turn, in the same place as their room in a permanent barracks would be.

Fabiola marvelled at the organisation being displayed, and her sense of unease was slightly dispelled. She noticed Secundus enjoying the scenes that he must have partaken in so many times in his army career.

A wide path led straight from the entrance to the centre, where even bigger canvas pavilions already stood. This was the legion's command post, and to one side stood the luxurious quarters of its legate, Marcus Petreius. As the most important officer, his tent had been erected immediately after the headquarters were thrown up. A red *vexillum* had been stabbed into the ground by the entrance. At least twenty hand-picked legionaries stood guard outside it, while messengers ran to and fro, relaying Petreius' orders to his senior centurions. A pair of saddled horses were tethered nearby, happily eating from nosebags. The couriers who rode them stood idly by, gossiping with each other.

The *optio* led his men straight to the main tent. Coming to a halt near the centurion in charge of the guards, he saluted and stood to attention.

The officer smiled when he saw Fabiola. This was far more pleasing than some fat, balding merchant come to beg assistance. Swallowing a piece of bread, he strolled over.

There was a brief conversation as the *optio* reported his news.

'My lady,' said the duty centurion with a courteous bow. 'No doubt you will wish to clean up before meeting the legate.'

'Thank you,' replied Fabiola gratefully. It was vital that she make a good impression.

'Come inside.' He indicated she should follow him. 'Your slaves can find somewhere to sleep with the mule drivers and camp followers.'

Secundus bit back his retort. This was no time to draw attention to himself.

But Fabiola bridled with anger at his dismissive attitude. 'They are my servants, not slaves,' she said loudly.

Sextus' eyes widened, and pride filled his face.

The centurion stiffened, and then inclined his head. 'As you say, lady. I will have a tent prepared for them among the soldiers of my own cohort.'

'Good,' answered Fabiola. 'Like myself, they will require hot water and food.'

'Of course.' He could not protest further.

Docilosa unsuccessfully tried to hide her smirk.

Curtly ordering one of his men to accompany Fabiola's companions, the centurion made to lead her into the tent.

Secundus stayed by her side.

Surprised, Fabiola turned to him.

'You still need protection, lady,' he muttered.

'Don't worry,' she said, touched by his loyalty. 'Mithras will protect me.'

Fabiola's answer satisfied Secundus and he stood back, watching as she followed the centurion inside. A silent prayer of his own went up to the warrior god. The beautiful young woman would have to be very careful what she said. If Petreius got even the tiniest whiff that they were heading north to join with Caesar, there would be little mercy shown. He had heard the legionaries talking as they walked into the fort. Outright hostilities had not yet commenced, but Caesar was already regarded as an enemy.

Ushering Fabiola to a large partitioned room, the centurion bowed. 'I will have hot water and drying cloths brought, lady,' he muttered. 'We have no women's apparel, I'm afraid.'

'Of course not,' Fabiola laughed, trying to put him at his ease. 'A wash will suffice until my dress can be cleaned.'

Discomfited, he ducked his head and left.

Fabiola looked around, pleased at the level of luxury on offer. Being on campaign did not mean that Petreius had to do without any of life's necessities. Thick carpets and animal skins covered the floor, while richly patterned wall hangings concealed the canvas of the tent's sides. The roof was high, supported by a network of long poles. From these hung ropes suspending elegant bronze oil lamps overhead. Yet more stood on decorated stone plinths, illuminating the chamber well. A weapons rack near her held a number of *gladii* with beautifully carved wood and bone hilts. Even their sheaths were ornate, the beaten gold on their surfaces depicting scenes from Greek mythology. Occupying a central position was a well-carved bust of Pompey. Having seen him in Rome, Fabiola recognised his bulbous eyes and mop of curly hair.

Iron-bound wooden chests had been placed around the periphery, while a heavy desk sat in the centre, a comfortable-looking leather-backed camp chair behind it. Tightly rolled scrolls lay scattered on the desktop, and Fabiola's heart quickened. This was Petreius' private working space, and vital information about Pompey's plans might be included in the cylinders of parchment in front of her.

She longed to understand them. Like most slaves, or former slaves, Fabiola was illiterate. Gemellus had seen no value in educating those who served him. Only Servilius, his bookkeeper, had known how to read and write. And Jovina, the wily crone who owned the Lupanar, actively discouraged the prostitutes from learning. Uneducated women were far easier to intimidate and coerce. At Fabiola's request, Brutus had started teaching her, but there had been so little time before he was called away.

Her thoughts were interrupted by a pair of young, shaven-headed slaves who silently delivered a large cauldron of steaming hot water, drying cloths and a beaten bronze mirror on a stand. Also offered was a metal tray with small vials of olive oil, a curved *strigil* and two finely carved boxwood combs laid upon it. The embarrassed slaves bobbed their heads and withdrew, avoiding Fabiola's gaze all the while. Having a beautiful young woman to serve rather than soldiers was clearly too much for them.

Fabiola stripped and washed herself down with warm water, before rubbing oil all over her skin. Lastly she used the *strigil* to take off the grime and dirt that covered her body from the ambush and pursuit. Although not as relaxing as a bath, it felt good to wash. All that was missing was a phial of perfume, but like all her possessions, such things were lying back in the litter. While Scaevola would have no use for these items, there would be no opportunity to go back for them either.

Pulling on her damp, sweaty dress once more, she grimaced at its feel against her skin. At least there weren't too many spots of blood on it. Smoothing back her hair, Fabiola looked into the mirror and combed it as best she could.

'Aphrodite herself has come to visit us,' said a deep voice behind her.

She jumped with fright.

A tall, brown-haired man in late middle age had entered the chamber. He was dressed in a well-cut thigh-length tunic; soft leather shoes covered his feet. A belt of gold links and a sheathed dagger confirmed his status as a soldier. High cheekbones and a strong chin were the most striking features in his rugged face. 'Forgive me, lady,' he said when he saw Fabiola's reaction. 'I did not mean to scare you.'

Wondering how long he had been watching her, Fabiola bowed. 'My nerves are a little ragged,' she replied.

'That's not surprising,' said the man. 'I have been told of the scum who ambushed you. What were they – deserters or just common bandits?'

'It's difficult to know.' Fabiola had no wish to reveal any details about Scaevola. 'They all look the same.'

'Indeed. I'm sorry for even mentioning it,' he said reassuringly. 'Try to forget the whole episode. You're safe now.'

'Thank you,' said Fabiola, her relief only half acted. Delayed shock was beginning to set in, draining her energy when she needed it most. It was crucial that she divulge nothing about her journey while somehow persuading the general to let her party continue unhindered. Mithras, *Sol*

Invictus, help me, Fabiola thought. Asking help from the warrior god felt appropriate when faced with this military threat.

'Allow me to introduce myself.' He bowed deeply. 'I am Marcus Petreius, legate of the Third Legion. You are welcome in my camp.'

Returning the gesture, she smiled radiantly. 'I am Fabiola Messalina.'

Unaffected by her wiles, Petreius came straight to the point. 'I find it most unusual for a beautiful young woman to be travelling alone,' he said. 'The roads are so dangerous.'

She feigned surprise. 'I have – had – servants and slaves with me.'

He raised his eyebrows. 'No father or brother to accompany you?'

It was usual for unmarried noble women to travel with a male relation or chaperon of some kind: the lies had to start now.

Fabiola took a deep breath and began. 'Father is long dead. And Julianus, my eldest brother, was killed in Parthia last year.' The tiny shred of hope left in her heart stopped her naming Romulus as the fictional sibling who had died. But it was still the likely reality. Fabiola lowered her gaze, real tears pricking her eyes.

'You have my sympathies, lady,' he said respectfully. 'But what about the rest of your family?'

'Mother is too frail for such a long journey and Romulus, my twin, is out of the country on business,' protested Fabiola. 'Someone had to visit my widowed aunt in Ravenna. Poor Clarina does not have long.'

He nodded understandingly. 'Yet these are troubled times. It's very unwise to travel without a large party of guards.'

'It is no better in Rome,' cried Fabiola. 'The mobs are burning nobles alive in their own homes!'

'That is true, the gods curse them,' said Petreius, his jaw hardening. 'But I will soon stop that.'

She gasped in apparent surprise. 'Are you marching to the capital?'

'Yes, lady, with all speed,' the legate replied briskly. 'The Senate has appointed Pompey Magnus as sole consul for the year. His main remit is to restore law and order, and the Third will do that by whatever means necessary.'

Fabiola looked suitably shocked. The use of troops in Rome was one of the Republic's abiding nightmares. Forbidden by law, it had last happened more than a generation before. Sulla, 'the butcher', had ordered it and then assumed total control of the state. In the minds of most, that was not a time to be repeated.

'This is what it has come to,' sighed Petreius. 'There is no other way.'

She could see the legate believed in what he was saying. 'Has no one protested?'

'Not a single senator,' he said wryly. 'They're all too worried about their houses being looted.'

Fabiola smiled, remembering how many of her clients had been obsessed with nothing more than increasing their own wealth, regardless of how it was obtained. Yet when the poor tried to take something for themselves, the rich were the first to condemn them. Although Rome was nominally a democracy, in reality for generations the fate of the Republic had been governed by a tiny elite class of nobles, the vast majority of whom were only out to line their own pockets. Gone was the ancient founding spirit that had seen successful generals relinquish their commands and return home to eat from plain earthenware bowls; in Rome now just a few ruthless men wrestled for ultimate riches – and ultimate power.

Which is why there was a legion camped outside.

It was appalling.

'Caesar won't be happy when he hears about this, but there are more pressing things on his mind.' Petreius' lips lifted into a mirthless grin. 'Like survival.'

Fabiola concealed her alarm. She knew nothing of recent developments. 'I'd heard there was renewed rebellion in Gaul, but nothing more,' she said brightly.

'Things go very badly for Caesar, which is good news for Pompey.' His expression changed, becoming more pleasant. 'Enough of politics and war. Those are no subjects for a lady. Would you honour me with your company for dinner?'

With little choice but to accept, she bowed. 'It would be my pleasure.'

Fabiola was terrified. She was walking a fine line between deception and discovery, with no option other than to continue. And what about the others? Hopefully no one would ask much of Docilosa or Sextus, she thought, and Secundus would know to keep his mouth shut. His status as a supporter of Caesar was as good a reason to remain anonymous as hers.

Petreius guided her to another part of the enormous tent, where three reclining couches were positioned closely around a low table, leaving one side free for food to be served. Typically, each couch was able to accommodate up to three people. The level of opulence here was the same as the area where Fabiola had washed, and equalled most banqueting halls in Rome. Even the table was a piece of art, with an inlaid surface of gold and pearl and wonderfully carved legs in the shape of lions' paws. Light from the huge candelabra hanging overhead bounced off large platters of Arretine ware, red glazed pottery with intricate designs in relief. There was fine glassware in a range of colours, a silver salt cellar and spoons with delicate bone handles. A trio of slaves sat in one corner, alternately playing the pan pipes, lyre and cithara, a large stringed instrument with a sweet sound. Others stood by, waiting to serve food and drink.

Hoping there would be more guests, Fabiola looked around.

Petreius met her glance with a wink. 'Normally I dine with my tribunes, but not tonight.'

She managed to return his smile, but a flutter of unease rose from her stomach. After her time in the Lupanar, Fabiola could read men like a book.

'Please.' Petreius was indicating where she should lie. It was the place of honour, directly adjoining his position.

Her mind in a turmoil, the young woman sat down. Taking off her shoes, she placed them on the floor beneath the seat before reclining.

Thankfully the legate took the central couch rather than sitting right beside her. He waved a hand at the nearest slave, who hurried over, pouring *mulsum* for them both.

Fabiola took the proffered goblet gratefully. After her near escape from Scaevola, the mixture of wine and honey tasted like nectar to her. Without thinking, she drained the lot.

The glass was refilled at once.

Sipping his, Petreius fixed his gaze on Fabiola. 'Tell me of your family,' he said warmly.

She searched his face for signs of deception, but could see none. Praying again to Mithras, and to Jupiter, Fabiola began constructing an elaborate life history. She was one of three children of Julianus Messalinus, a deceased merchant, and his wife, Velvinna Helpis. The family resided on the Aventine, a mainly plebeian area. To make her story more authentic, Fabiola wove much of her own life into it. Where she had grown up was unremarkable; like anywhere in Rome, patricians lived there too. Naming her mother correctly somehow felt right, as did mentioning a twin brother. Julianus, the oldest, had joined the army as a bookkeeper and been killed with Crassus in Parthia. At this point, Fabiola's voice wobbled and she stopped for a moment.

Petreius looked suitably sympathetic.

Nervously, Fabiola went on. While it increased her danger to invent living people who could never be traced, she wanted to feel that she had some kin still, instead of being alone in the world. So Romulus, her twin, now ran the family business, but was often out of the country on trading ventures. Unmarried, Fabiola lived in the ancestral home with her mother and their retinue of slaves. To avoid Petreius asking why she was still single, Fabiola mentioned a number of regular suitors. So far, none had met with Velvinna's approval.

'All mothers are the same,' laughed the legate.

The young woman was amazed by her own inventiveness. Yet it was not difficult for her to come up with a completely fabricated existence. As a child in Gemellus' *domus*, she had observed much about Roman society. Although he came from impoverished roots, the cruel merchant had achieved a certain level of public recognition because of his riches. He had dealings with all levels of society, and had often entertained his clients at his home. Fabiola had an excellent understanding of the way the trading classes dealt with each other.

She paused, her throat dry from talking. Another swallow of the *mulsum* helped her to continue.

Petreius listened carefully, long fingers cupping his jaw.

Easy targets because of their awkward table manners or poor social etiquette, former slaves were frequently the butt of cruel jokes. Determined that this would not happen to her if she was ever freed, Fabiola had also absorbed every little piece of information that came her way in the Lupanar. Many of her customers spent large amounts of time in her company, during which they poured out their life stories to her. As the most popular prostitute, she had encountered numerous members of the Roman elite, the senators and *equites*. Other clients had been prosperous merchants or businessmen. All were men who lived at the pinnacle of Roman society, in a world far removed from that of the average slave, and one which Fabiola had only recently been admitted to. She was careful, therefore, to portray herself as being from the middle class of Roman society rather than the upper.

Petreius did not appear upset that Fabiola was from trading stock rather than noble. If anything, he looked pleased by her revelation.

Her initial story also seemed to satisfy him. To take the focus away from herself, she quickly went on the offensive.

'I am so unimportant,' Fabiola said. 'Whereas you are the commander of a legion.'

Petreius made a modest gesture of denial, but she could see he was pleased.

'You must have fought many wars,' she said encouragingly. 'And conquered many peoples.'

'I've seen my fair share of combat,' he replied with a shrug. 'Like any who do their duty for Rome.'

'Tell me,' Fabiola requested, her eyes shining with false excitement.

'I was one of those who defeated the Catiline conspirators,' he said. 'And among other things, I helped Pompey Magnus to quell the Spartacus rebellion.'

Fabiola gasped in apparent admiration, holding back the riposte that it had in fact been Crassus who was responsible for putting down the uprising. Tellingly, Petreius had just shown himself to be a liar. As the informed knew, Pompey's role had been only minor; his defeat of five thousand slaves who had fled the main battle a helping hand rather than a decisive thrust. Yet he had managed to claim all the credit by sending the Senate a letter informing them of his victory. The stroke was one of Pompey's finest, and clearly Petreius had jumped on the bandwagon of his master's success.

Fabiola noted this chink in the legate's armour. If only the Thracian gladiator had not failed, she thought sadly. Romulus and I might have been born free. Had completely different lives. Instead, outmanoeuvred and surrounded by the legions, Spartacus had failed. Now slaves were more rigorously controlled than ever before.

'Of course the uprising never really posed much threat to Rome,' Petreius sneered. 'Damn slaves.'

Fabiola nodded in seeming agreement. How little you know, she shouted inwardly. Like many nobles, Petreius regarded slaves as little more than animals, incapable of intelligent thought or action. She fantasised about grabbing the *pugio* on his belt and sticking it in his chest, but quashed the idea on the spot. While appealing, it would not help her get out of this situation. Any such action would also endanger the lives of the people in her care: Docilosa, Sextus and Secundus. What other options were there? Escaping from the massive camp without the legate's permission would be impossible. Sentries watched all the entrances day and night, and no one came or left without being challenged.

A sinking feeling began to creep over her.

Like her previous clients, Petreius hadn't noticed Fabiola's momentary lack of attention. By simply smiling and nodding her head, the beautiful young woman could keep men absorbed for hours. Her previous profession had taught Fabiola not just how to physically satisfy men, but also the skilful art of making them think that they were the centre of the world. While pretending to enjoy their conversation, she also tantalised and teased. The promise of pleasure was sometimes more effective than actually providing it. Throaty laughs, a flash of bosom or thigh, fluttering eyelashes – Fabiola knew them all. Fuelled by the wine and her despair at what to do, she now found herself making more of these suggestive gestures than planned. Later, she would wonder if there was anything else she could have done.

'I also served in Asia Minor,' Petreius went on. 'Mithridates was a very skilled general. It took more than six years to defeat him. But we did.'

'You fought with Lucullus then?'

Although Lucullus had not struck the final blow, Fabiola knew that the able general had been largely responsible for bringing the warlike king of Bithynia and Pontus to heel. Yet Pompey, the leader sent by the Senate to finish the job, had taken all the credit. Again.

Petreius coloured. 'At first, yes. But after he was replaced, I continued the campaign under Pompey Magnus.'

Fabiola hid a knowing smile. That's how it works, she thought. Pompey had stripped Lucullus of his command, but let his friends keep their posts. 'And now you find yourself leading men again,' she purred. 'To Rome.'

The legate made a diffident gesture. 'Merely doing my duty.'

You're bringing the Republic to the brink of civil war at the same time, thought Fabiola. Caesar could regard Pompey's actions of sending troops to Rome for nothing less than what it was: a blatant show of force. The man who restored peace to the capital would become an instant hero. In addition, having legionaries stationed in the Forum Romanum would place him in a powerful position indeed. And its timing was masterful. Stuck in Gaul, fighting for his life, Caesar could do nothing to prevent it.

'I'm hungry,' announced the legate. 'Would you care for some dinner, my lady?'

Fabiola smiled her acceptance. Lining her stomach was a good idea. It might slow down the rate at which the *mulsum* was going to her head. She was not used to drinking much alcohol.

Petreius clicked his fingers and two slaves hurried over with bowls of steaming water and drying cloths. While they washed their hands, the others left, returning at once with a multitude of platters. There were various types of salted fish. Sausages in porridge sat alongside plates of freshly cooked cauliflower and beans. Sliced hard-boiled eggs and onions were served with piquant sauce.

Fabiola stared at the surface of the low table, which was now covered in food. As a child, hunger had been a constant feature of her life. Now it was the opposite, which seemed ironic.

Muttering a brief request to the gods for their blessing, Petreius leaned over and began. In the Roman fashion, he mostly used his fingers to pick up his food; occasionally he used a spoon.

The young woman breathed a slow sigh of relief. His attention had been diverted for the moment. Picking on some fish and beans, she tried to gather her thoughts through the fog that the *mulsum* had induced. She had a little while: the legate was obviously hungry. Clearing his plate, he indicated that the unfinished foods should be removed. After they had washed their hands again, the second course was brought in.

It felt so decadent to Fabiola as yet more serving dishes arrived. Sow's udder in fish sauce, roasted kid and more sausages. Baked fish: bream, tunny and mullet. Pigeons and thrushes baked on a tray. Chestnuts and cabbage sprouts, and the inevitable onions. It was far more food than two people could ever eat. Marcus Petreius' athletic stature belied his appetite.

She was sure that Brutus would not approve. Her lover ate sparingly, preferring to spend his time at the table in good conversation.

A slave slipped past and filled clean glasses with watered-down wine. Being lighter, *mulsum* was served with starters.

'Drink,' encouraged Petreius. 'It's a very good Campanian. From one of my *latifundia*.'

Fabiola took a swallow, but she was careful not to finish all of the richly flavoured red wine. It had a deep, earthy taste, which was only marginally reduced by its dilution.

They made more polite small talk over the main course. Nothing was mentioned about Fabiola's journey or Petreius' mission to Rome. When he had eaten enough, the legate waved at the slaves again. One immediately laid out a selection of food, beside which he poured a little pile of salt. A cup of wine was placed beside this, the traditional dinner offering to the gods.

Petreius bent his head, his lips moving in silent prayer.

Fabiola did the same, fervently asking not just for Mithras' and Jupiter's blessing upon their meal, but for their assistance. She still had no idea what to do.

The final course consisted of all kinds of pastries, hazelnuts, and preserved pears and apples. Not wanting to appear rude, Fabiola helped herself to a few small portions and took her time eating.

More wine was poured for both of them.

'Your aunt in Ravenna,' said Petreius out of the blue. 'What was her name again?'

'Clarina,' replied Fabiola. 'Clarina Silvina.'

'Where exactly does she live?'

Unease filled Fabiola. What did he care? 'Not far from the Forum, I think,' she lied, picking a location that could fit any town in Italy. 'Off the street that leads to the south gate.'

'Is her house large?'

'Not especially,' she said. 'But Mother says that it is well appointed. Aunt Clarina has good taste.'

He said nothing for a moment.

Fabiola's heart began to pound in her chest and she busied herself with another piece of dried fruit.

'The southern quarter of the city was where fire broke out last year,' Petreius announced in a hard voice. 'Almost all the houses were burned down.'

Fabiola felt her cheeks flush bright red. 'Clarina mentioned that in a letter,' she responded, her voice a trifle too high. 'Hers escaped with light damage.'

'The only ones to be left unharmed were those near my *domus*,' the legate said coldly. 'Thankfully my slaves managed to soak the nearby roofs with enough water to ensure that they did not catch fire and thus spread it to mine.'

She watched him dumbly, a sick feeling in her stomach. How could she have known that Petreius had a residence in Ravenna?

His next words were like the strokes of doom.

'The residents were so grateful that they came to pay their respects. I don't recall an elderly lady by the name of Clarina Silvina.'

Fabiola's mouth opened and closed. In that time, he had moved to her couch; they were now close enough to touch. Petreius' eyes were slate grey, and distinctly unfriendly now. 'I . . .' Fabiola was uncharacteristically lost for words.

'You have no aunt in Ravenna,' the legate said harshly. 'Have you?'

She did not answer.

'And one of your companions is a crippled veteran. What use is he to anyone?'

Fabiola's heart rate shot up. Petreius must have been watching from his tent when they arrived, and recognised Secundus' military bearing. It was difficult not to.

'Secundus? I found him on the steps of Jupiter's temple,' Fabiola protested, angry that Petreius had no respect for the casualties of Rome's wars. After all, similar things happened to his men. 'I took pity on him. He's proved very reliable.'

'Really? How did he survive the ambush when all the others were killed?' the legate demanded.

Fabiola flinched before his practised interrogation. 'I don't know,' she whispered. 'Perhaps the gods spared him.'

'There's far more to this than meets the eye.' Petreius sat up. 'We'll see what your servant says to a taste of hot iron. That makes men sing like canaries.'

'No!' cried Fabiola. 'Secundus has done nothing.'

She was not being totally altruistic. Few individuals could resist torture, especially at the hands of the experienced soldiers that Petreius would have available. If Secundus revealed Fabiola's real destination, all hope of reaching Gaul would be gone. Who knew how the legate would react if he found that out? Disposing of four ragged travellers would pose no problem. No one would ever know any different.

Fabiola's heart sank. In comparison to the likes of Petreius, she really was a nobody.

He turned back, leaning in so close that the musky mix of *mulsum* and wine from his breath filled her nostrils. 'Unless another solution might be found,' he said, lightly squeezing one of her breasts. 'A much more pleasurable one.'

For a heartbeat, Fabiola hesitated. She felt faintly sick. It was an old, familiar feeling: the one she used to get in the Lupanar when a client had just chosen her from the line of prostitutes.

Had she any other choice?

Rather than pulling away, she drew him towards her.

Chapter XIX: Alesia

Northern Italy, spring/summer 52 BC

Trying to reduce Petreius to a sweating, drained shadow of his former self, Fabiola had used every trick of her previous trade when coupling with him. All the time she was driving the legate mad with lust, she was racking her brains for a way out of the situation.

How could she rejoin Secundus and Sextus and safely continue north to Gaul?

Petreius would have no particular reason to set Fabiola free. A nubile bed companion like her would make his journey to Rome far more pleasurable. And there was nothing she could do if he did decide to keep her by him. With almost five thousand soldiers at his beck and call, the ruthless legate could behave as he pleased.

The possibility of staying and becoming Petreius' mistress had entered her mind. He was not a bad-looking man, and seemed personable enough. Far away in Gaul, Brutus would be able to do nothing about it. Fabiola decided not to make this choice for two reasons. The first was that it meant changing allegiance to Pompey's side. That felt like a bad idea. Her instincts told her that Caesar's former partner in the triumvirate was not the man to back. And the second, more important, reason was that becoming Petreius' lover – and therefore siding with an enemy of Caesar – would probably mean that she would never meet the nobleman who might be her father.

A more callous thought also occurred to Fabiola. She could simply wait until the legate fell asleep and then kill him. But even if she left his tent without being discovered and managed to find Docilosa, Secundus and Sextus, their next task would prove impossible. There was no reason to think that any of Petreius' disciplined soldiers would just let her and her companions leave without permission. Fabiola had no desire to be crucified or tortured to death, one of which would surely be the punishment when his body was discovered.

What in the name of Hades was she to do?

Thinking that she had tired him out, Fabiola was surprised when Petreius found the energy to take her again a short time later. Kneeling on all fours, she encouraged his deep thrusts with loud moans. When the legate had finished and sagged back on the sweat-soaked sheets, Fabiola climbed off the bed. She desperately needed time to think. Naked, she walked a few steps to a low table that had a selection of food and drink arrayed upon it. Filling two cups with some watered-down wine, the young woman turned to find Petreius admiring her.

'By all that is sacred,' he said with a satisfied sigh. 'You look like a goddess come to tempt a mere mortal.'

Fabiola batted her eyelashes and flashed a practised smile.

'Who are you?' he asked, intrigued. 'No merchant I've ever met would have a daughter like you.'

She laughed throatily and spun in a slow circle, drawing a loud groan of desire from him.

But the question would be repeated, of that there was no doubt. Fabiola tried to quell the panic rising in her breast. Petreius was no satiated customer to be ushered out of the door when his time was up. This was a man used to getting his own way, a powerful noble experienced in commanding soldiers and fighting wars. Completely at his mercy, on his territory, her feminine wiles would only go so far.

Like all sleeping chambers, Petreius' had a small shrine in one corner. Most Romans prayed to the gods on rising and retiring, to request their guidance and protection during both day and night. The legate was no different. As Fabiola's gaze passed idly over the stone altar, her attention was drawn back to it. Prominently displayed in front of deities such as Jupiter and Mars was a small, cloaked figure that looked familiar. Fabiola's breath caught in her chest as she recognised Mithras. The delicately carved statue was portrayed in the same manner as the large sculpture in the Mithraeum in Rome. Wearing a Phrygian cap, the god was crouched over a reclining bull and plunging a knife down into its chest while looking away.

Fabiola closed her eyes and asked for his divine help.

Was this her chance?

Petreius was a follower of Mithras. She had been inside the god's temple and had drunk the sacred *homa*. Importantly, Fabiola had had a vision as a raven. The fact that she had done so without permission, outraging most of the veterans in the process, was irrelevant right now.

A daring idea began to take root in Fabiola's mind. It was all she could think of, so it had to work.

A low laugh came from behind her. 'Lucky I have no statue of Priapus to beg my case,' Petreius said. 'Otherwise I'd keep you awake all night.'

'We don't need him,' Fabiola answered, moving her legs apart slightly and bowing from the waist towards Mithras.

The view this afforded drew a shocked, lustful growl from the legate.

With a subtle rolling motion, Fabiola turned back and strode towards him, her full breasts moving gently. The light from the oil lamps coloured her flesh, giving it an alluring amber glow. She knew from long experience that looking like this, no man could resist her. Placing the wine on the floor by the bed, Fabiola put her hands on her hips.

'You look like a woman who means business,' Petreius said.

She laughed and arched her pelvis towards him. 'Do I?'

Little do you know.

Unable to take any more teasing, he reached out for her – but she stepped away, out of reach.

The legate frowned.

Quickly Fabiola moved closer again, allowing his eager fingers to grasp her buttocks.

'Who needs Priapus?' he muttered, rolling to the edge of the mattress in a desperate attempt to get closer. 'I'll fuck you again right now.'

Fabiola smiled to herself. This was where she wanted him: crazy with lust. Turning, she stared down as Petreius pressed his face into her groin. 'You have a statue of Mithras, I see.'

'What?' His voice was muffled.

'The warrior god.'

He pulled back, looking faintly irritated. 'I began following him during my time in Asia Minor. What of it?'

Aware that she had to act with the utmost delicacy, Fabiola fell silent.

Stooping, she gently rolled him over and began stroking his erect member.

Enjoying what she was doing, he relaxed again.

There was silence as Fabiola climbed on to the bed and lowered herself down on him.

When he came, Petreius gasped in ecstasy, gripping her hips with his hands. Then he flopped back on the sheet and closed his eyes.

Satisfied that the legate was now as vulnerable as she would ever see him, Fabiola threw the dice. 'I have heard that Mithras' followers honour and respect each other greatly,' she said. 'They give help to one another when it is needed.'

'If we can, we do,' he replied in an already sleepy voice.

'What if the situation is awkward or difficult?'

'All the more reason to be of assistance.'

'And most of you are soldiers,' Fabiola said, changing tack.

'Yes.'

'But some are not.'

'No,' he answered, sounding confused. 'There are men of many trades and professions in our religion. Even some more worthy slaves. We are all equal before the god.'

The seed had been planted, thought Fabiola. It was time to act.

'I have aided you tonight,' she murmured, climbing off him and lying down.

He chuckled. 'You have. Very much.'

'Then will you help me?'

'Of course,' he replied, amused. 'What is it you want? Money? Dresses?'

Fabiola clenched her fists, hoping that the primary tenet of honour mentioned by Secundus so many times was also an important part of Petreius' belief system. There was no way of knowing unless she tried. 'More than that.' She paused, noticing that her hands were actually trembling. 'I need a letter of safe conduct and enough men to protect me on my journey north.'

He jerked upright, suddenly fully awake. 'What did you say?'

'I was the first woman to enter the Mithraeum in Rome,' she said. 'To become a devotee.'

'That is forbidden under all circumstances,' Petreius stuttered. 'I know the provinces are a bit backward when it comes to new traditions, but this? On whose authority was it allowed?'

'Secundus,' she replied. 'The one-armed veteran who was with me when your troops rescued us.'

'A low-ranking cripple?' he scoffed. 'Sounds like he's getting ideas way above his station. Does he want to screw you?'

It was unsurprising, Fabiola thought, that a man of Petreius' status would look down on someone as lowly as Secundus. 'It's nothing like that,' she said firmly. 'And despite what you may think, he admitted me to the Path. My rank is that of Corax, which makes me a comrade of yours.'

'You'll be telling me next that he is the Pater of the temple,' sneered the legate.

'Correct,' Fabiola replied. 'He is also my guide.'

Petreius' nostrils flared, but he let her continue without further interruption.

'After drinking the *homa*, I became a raven,' she said quietly. 'And was granted a vision, in which I saw the survivors of Crassus' army. Secundus decreed that it was sent by the god himself.'

'Wait. This is too much to take in.' Rubbing a hand through his close-cropped hair, the legate stood up and walked over to a tall swan-legged bronze ewer. Bending his neck, he vigorously splashed cold water over his entire head and neck a number of times. Pulling a cloth from a wooden stand, he dried himself and donned a clean robe.

Fabiola sat on the bed, waiting patiently.

'Start from the beginning,' he ordered, sitting beside her. 'Tell me exactly how you met this Secundus.'

Fabiola kept it simple, keeping her original fabrication the same, but accurately recounting how she had met the veteran on the steps of Jupiter's temple in Rome. Her rescue was simplified to take place on the fringes of the riot over Pulcher's death. There was no point complicating matters by mentioning Scaevola and the *fugitivarii*.

'That's all very touching,' Petreius said when she had finished. 'But saving a pretty girl's life doesn't mean that the Pater would just invite you to become one of us.' His face turned hard. 'Tell me the truth.'

This was a crucial moment.

'I have done. Most of my guards were killed well before the veterans arrived,' Fabiola said. Acting modestly, she looked down. 'It was a case of defending myself or being raped on the spot. Perhaps the gods helped, but I managed to kill three or four of our attackers.'

'By Jupiter!' exclaimed the legate. 'Has someone trained you to fight?'

'No.' She stared at him, wide-eyed. 'I only ever saw my father and brothers practise in the yard of our *domus*. It was sheer desperation, I suppose.'

He regarded her slender arms with new respect.

She dared a bit more. 'Secundus said that he had rarely seen such bravery, even on the battlefield.'

'If what you say is true, I'm not surprised,' agreed Petreius emphatically. 'With soldiers like you, we would have little to fear from Caesar.'

Pleased by his praise, Fabiola flushed.

A rigorous interrogation about Mithraic practices and rituals followed. Petreius listened intently, showing no emotion at Fabiola's responses. This made her even more nervous, but by taking her time, the young woman was able to answer every question correctly.

When the legate had finished, there was a long silence.

'You know a lot about Mithraicism,' he admitted. 'Only an initiate should know these things.'

A great wave of relief washed over her, but her ordeal was not over yet.

'Perhaps an old lover tried to impress you by revealing Mithraic secrets,' he ventured, his eyes narrowing. 'If you're lying to me . . .'

'I am telling the truth,' Fabiola said as calmly as possible.

Resting his chin on one hand, Petreius drummed his fingers against his cheek.

He was a tough customer, thought Fabiola, a bad enemy to make, but she had committed herself now.

'Secundus is the man to ask,' he said at last. 'No Pater would lie about something like this.'

Fabiola quailed mentally at the idea of this trial, which would truly test Secundus' belief in her.

The legate called in one of the legionaries standing on guard outside his tent, ordering him to bring Secundus before them.

An uncomfortable silence reigned as they waited. After Fabiola's revelation, Petreius seemed almost embarrassed by what they had done together.

Worried that Secundus would reveal what had really happened in the Mithraeum, Fabiola was unable to keep up her usual bright chatter. She took the opportunity to have a wash, get dressed and tie up her hair. Secundus would draw his own conclusions about what had gone on here, but she still wanted to look her best.

Of course the legate was too smart to talk to Secundus in front of her. When the legionary returned with him a short time later, Petreius asked Fabiola to remain in the bedchamber. All she could do was comply.

The low murmur of voices soon came from the main part of the tent. Fabiola could make out Secundus' tone, answering questions. In an agony of nerves, she knelt before the stone altar and studied the statue of Mithras. Forgive me, great one, she thought. I have lied in your presence about what happened in the Mithraeum. But that does not mean I do not believe in you. Help me now, and I swear to be a faithful follower of yours for ever. The magnitude of what she was promising was very great, but Fabiola knew her situation was desperate. If Secundus' version of events did not tie in neatly with hers, then it would be Orcus, the god of the underworld, whom she had to deal with, rather than Mithras. For dishonouring his religion, the legate could easily have her killed.

She was still praying when Petreius re-entered the room. His voice made her jump.

'Secundus is a good man,' he said. 'And no liar.'

Bile rose in the back of Fabiola's throat, and she turned to face him.

'Neither am I,' she whispered, sure that Secundus had denounced her.

'The Pater has corroborated everything.' Petreius smiled. 'He feels sure that your remarkable vision was sent by Mithras.'

'So you believe me?'

'I do,' he replied warmly. 'I will give you the help you asked for. The god would want it.'

Fabiola nearly fainted with relief. Her gamble had paid off.

Petreius moved behind her, and she felt his warm breath on the back of her neck.

'I've never bedded another follower of Mithras before,' he said.

Fabiola closed her eyes. There was a further price to pay, she thought bitterly. Would it always be so?

Cupping her breasts with his hands, he pushed against her buttocks.

Fabiola's hand reached around to his groin. Dawn could not come too soon for her.

Petreius had not even asked where Fabiola was going. Naturally his men would tell him upon their return, but the magnanimous gesture was a remarkable example of honouring one's principles, Fabiola thought. Aid was being given freely, just because it had been asked for. She smiled wryly. Petreius' help had not been completely free, of course. But even though he had slept with her, the legate had also shown himself to be a cut above the average by respecting one of the central tenets of his faith. From her considerable experience of men, Fabiola doubted that many would have acted in the same way. Despite the fact that Petreius was one of Pompey's officers, she wished him well.

It seemed apt that the *optio* and half-century of legionaries who had driven off the *fugitivarii* should accompany Fabiola and her companions north. And by the end of the first day, she was very glad to have them marching stolidly around the litter that Petreius had provided. As Rome grew further away, so the rule of law grew lighter upon the land. The party regularly encountered army deserters, bandits and impoverished peasants, any of whom would have been capable of robbing and murdering four people travelling on their own. None, however, were prepared to tackle forty well-armed soldiers, and the journey proceeded without incident for more than two weeks.

Following the Roman road along the coast and thereby avoiding the Alps, they crossed the border into Transalpine Gaul. It was the first time that Fabiola had ever left Italy and she was gladder than before to have plenty of protection. Although citizen farmsteads were dotted throughout the countryside, it was clearly a foreign land. Even the presence of regular army checkpoints failed to allay her fears. Most Romans knew that the population of Gaul was made up of fierce tribes, peoples who would rise up at the slightest provocation. And the sullen-looking inhabitants of the miserable settlements and villages that they passed through appeared downright dangerous to Fabiola. The long-haired, moustached men dressed in baggy patterned trousers and belted tunics, very different to Roman wear. Silver adorned their wrists and necks, and practically every single one carried a longsword, hexagonal shield and spear. Even the women carried knives. This was a fighting nation, and they resented their masters.

Fabiola had no chance to explain that as an ex-slave, she had no quarrel with them, and had no part in Rome's aggressive foreign policy. To those who saw her, she was just another rich Roman passing by.

But, as the *optio* told her, there had been little fighting in this area. Much of Transalpine Gaul had been under the Republic's control for over a century, and fortunately the tribes here had not answered Vercingetorix' call to arms. Thus Fabiola's unease grew even greater as they travelled further north, towards the regions affected by the uprising. Gossip from the legionaries in the regular outposts and garrison towns did little to reduce this. Caesar had suffered a major setback at Gergovia, during which he had lost hundreds of soldiers. Emboldened by this victory, Vercingetorix had pulled his army back to the fortified town of Alesia, there to await his enemy's arrival.

And the titanic struggle was still going on.

Despite the reluctance of Petreius' *optio*, Fabiola insisted they continue their journey. His remit had been to follow her orders, and she wasn't about to let him forget it. She and Secundus had consulted an oracle in one of the towns near the border, and the omens had been promising. False or not, the prophecy had merely gilt-edged Fabiola's determination. At this point, she felt there was no going back. Her stubborn pride prevented it. But it was not just that. If Caesar lost the battle at Alesia, all of her plans would have come to nothing. In that case, the young woman did not care what happened to her. With her mother dead and Romulus probably so, she might as well die too.

If Caesar had been successful however, his ambition, and that of Brutus, would know no bounds. Moreover, the public would adore him for it. Pompey's suppression of the rioting in Rome would hardly compare with a victory over hundreds of thousands of fierce warriors. The citizens would appreciate such a crushing blow all the more because of the Romans' historical fear of Gaul. The sacking of their capital by the tribesmen over three centuries before had left a lasting scar on the national psyche. Caesar *had* to win, because then Fabiola could continue her quest to find Romulus and discover her father's identity.

They travelled on.

The escape from Scaevola had been the most frightening and hair-raising part of Fabiola's journey so far. That was, until they neared Alesia. The horror continued for mile after mile. And yet the threat was not living. Just a dozen miles from the last legionary outpost, the countryside was filled with burnt villages and fields of torched crops. Herds of cattle and sheep lay slaughtered, their bloated corpses stinking in the early summer sunshine. Vercingetorix' men had been hard at work, their aim to deny food and supplies to Caesar's army. Any living creatures remaining were wild animals and birds. There were no people – everyone had either fled, or joined Vercingetorix in Alesia. It was a sign of how desperate the struggle had been, Fabiola realised. Surely a chieftain would only order the destruction of his own people's livelihood in the worst of circumstances? Now large tracts of the Gauls' land lay in waste, which meant there would be no food for the coming winter. Long after the soldiers on both sides left, innocent women and children would starve to death. This extra blood price was chilling.

But what was she supposed to do? One woman could not change the aggressive nature of the Roman Republic, or of one of its best generals. As usual, Fabiola's practical side took control. The people of Gaul were beyond her aid. She would help those she could, such as her slaves. Furthermore, she resolved to locate the boy who had been pursued on to her land by Scaevola. The memory of what the *fugitivarius* had done to him afterwards still tortured her.

Fabiola had little time to dwell on it.

Beyond the devastated farmland lay even more graphic evidence of Caesar's war. By the time they were within a few miles of Alesia, there were dead and dying Gauls lying all along the wayside, men who had fled the battle or been evacuated by their comrades and then left to die when they could no longer keep up. Thankfully, there was no sign of any able-bodied warriors, but the *optio*'s fears had grown so great that he refused to continue. Red-faced with determined embarrassment, he insisted that Fabiola and twenty men conceal themselves in a large copse several hundred paces from the road. She could only watch in frustration as he and the other legionaries headed off to find out what they could.

The *optio* was not gone for long.

'It's all over,' he shouted jubilantly when within earshot. 'Caesar has done it!'

Whispers of excitement passed between the hidden soldiers.

Fabiola breathed a long sigh of relief, while Secundus grinned from ear to ear. Impatient, they waited until the junior officer had reached them.

'The battle finished yesterday, apparently. By all the gods, you should see it,' he said, waving his arms with excitement. 'Caesar's legions have built miles of fortifications all around the town to prevent any break-out.' He paused. 'And another set facing outwards to stop any attempt at relieving the siege.'

Fabiola could not conceal her surprise. 'They were being attacked by two armies?'

The *optio* nodded vigorously. 'Caesar had ten legions, yet he must have been outnumbered by at least five to one. There are thousands of dead Gauls everywhere, but they say it's even worse north-west of the battlefield.'

'Is that where the battle was decided?' asked Secundus, his face alight.

'Yes. The enemy warriors almost broke through the defences there. Caesar sent reinforcements led by Decimus Brutus, but they were nearly overwhelmed.'

Fabiola blanched.

'Then Caesar rallied the soldiers and turned the tide!'

'You're one of Pompey's men, remember?' joked Secundus.

'I follow orders just like anyone,' grumbled the *optio*. 'Doesn't mean I can't appreciate a great general.'

'Is Brutus alive?' interrupted Fabiola.

'Yes, lady. I asked.'

'The gods be thanked,' she cried. 'And is it safe to continue?'

'It is. I can guide you to him.' He grimaced. 'But we'll need to travel straight across the battlefield.'

'Lead on.' Sure that she had seen the worst of it, Fabiola could wait no longer. She had to see Brutus.

The *optio* paused, unsure.

'The danger is over,' she snapped. 'You said so yourself.'

The junior officer glanced at Secundus, who shrugged. He tried one more time. 'It's not a sight for women.'

'I'll be the judge of that.'

Used to her domineering nature by now, the *optio* snapped off a crisp salute. Signalling the men to follow, he led the way down to the road.

Over a small rise, the battlefield proper began. A strange, unquiet air hung over the whole area. It was in marked contrast to the frantic mayhem of the previous days, which Fabiola struggled to imagine. Clouds of ravens and crows swooped and dived overhead, their harsh cawing the only sound. Like a forest of small trees, countless spears jutted from the ground, any gaps in between filled by the smaller, feathered shapes of arrows.

But it was the number of dead that drew her eyes, again and again.

Fabiola was utterly horrified. Nothing could have prepared her for it, not even the bloodshed she had witnessed in the arena. The ground was littered with more bodies than seemed possible: this was death on an unreal scale. Here was a glut of food that even the flocks of birds could not deal with. And now the corpses were Roman as well as Gaulish. They were heaped in huge piles, draped over each other like sleeping drunks at a feast. There was blood everywhere – on the slack faces, oozing from the count-less gaping wounds, on the discarded swords and spears. Pools of it lay clotted around soldiers who had bled to death. Underfoot, the grass had been trampled down from the passage of men, churned into a red, gluti-nous mud that stuck to the legionaries' sandals. A faint buzzing sound permeated the still air, made by the clouds of flies that clustered on every exposed piece of flesh.

Groups of legionaries could be seen moving methodically through the dead, stripping them of weapons and valuables. Occasionally enemy warriors were found alive, but none were being spared. By now, the only ones to remain living on the field were those who could not flee. Badly injured, the Gauls were therefore of no use as slaves. From time to time swords flashed in the sun, and short choking cries bubbled away into nothing.

The number of bodies soon made it impossible for the slaves carrying the litter to continue. Alighting, Fabiola raised a hand to her nose, vainly trying not to inhale. The cloying smell of rotting flesh was already sticking in the back of her throat. She could imagine how bad it would be after two or three more days under the hot sun.

Hastily, the *optio* directed a number of men to march in front of Fabiola, clearing the way. The walk was still like having to traverse the underworld, but she wasn't going to stop now. Finally, Brutus was within reach. She would be safe once more.

The Roman circumvallation came into sight, dragging Fabiola's eyes away from the carnage around her. No one could fail to be impressed by the scale of the engineering And all these features had been constructed in duplicate, on the other side.

Fabiola was astonished by Caesar's sheer determination. He truly was the amazing general that Brutus had described. A dangerous man. A rapist?

On a large plateau above the fortifications, stood the object of Caesar's attention: Alesia.

Trying to break through from either direction would have been a suicidal task, Fabiola thought. And defending the ramparts, utterly terrifying.

The *optio* had not been exaggerating about the scale of the slaughter. It was far greater here than what they had left behind. Her gorge rose, and she struggled not to vomit. Is this what Hades looked like? Had Carrhae been this bad?

Cries of pain drew her attention away from one horror to another.

A short distance away, a group of legionaries was gathered around a moaning, prone figure: an old man, in a robe.

Fabiola watched, horrified, as they drew nearer. He was unarmed, and probably just unfortunate enough to have strayed within their reach.

Javelin tips probed forward, drawing blood and fresh screams. Studded army sandals stamped down on unprotected flesh. Fabiola was sure she heard one of his arms snap. Turning her head made no difference. Cruel laughter filled her ears. Again and again her attention was drawn back to the dreadful scene. The torture went on until the soldiers grew bored. First one man drew his *gladius*, then another.

Fabiola was moving before she even realised it. Pushing past her surprised legionaries, she shouted at the top of her voice. 'Stop it!'

'Come back,' shouted Secundus from behind her. 'You cannot intervene.'

She ignored him, unwilling to watch such a summary execution. It reminded her too much of what might have happened to Romulus. Fabiola also had a powerful feeling that she should get involved.

Her screams had the desired effect. A couple of the legionaries stopped what they were doing and looked around. Leering unpleasantly, they nudged their comrades.

Ignoring their lustful reactions, Fabiola stalked closer.

Intimidated by her confident manner, the nearest men moved back. But the ringleader, a hardbitten-looking soldier with rusty chain mail and a battered bronze helmet topped by a simple horsehair crest, did not budge one step. Instead, he licked his lips suggestively at the beautiful young woman who had interrupted their sport.

Fabiola went straight on the offensive. Perhaps shame could help. 'How brave you are to torture an old man like this,' she hissed. 'Have you not seen enough killing?'

Laughs of derision met this question.

Scanning the tough, scarred faces around her, Fabiola realised these were some of Caesar's veterans. After six years of constant campaigning in Gaul, war and death was all they knew.

Secundus arrived, followed closely by Sextus and the *optio*. All three were careful to keep their hands away from their weapons.

'Who the fuck are you to order us about?' demanded the ringleader. 'And what business of yours is it anyway?'

His comrades grinned and, as if to prove a point, one of them kicked their victim.

'How dare you speak to me in that manner?' screamed Fabiola. 'I will have you all flogged!'

Confused looks met this outburst.

'Why wouldn't we kill him?' asked a thin soldier.

Peering closer, Fabiola took in what, in her rage, she had not noticed before. Although the old man's robe was threadbare, there was a sickle slung from his rope belt. A worn leather pouch had been opened and its contents scattered on the ground. Dried herbs lay on small stones polished by long use; beside these were the tiny bones of a mouse. A short dagger with bloodstains on its rusty blade provided the final piece of evidence. Now Fabiola understood why the soldiers were acting so cruelly.

Few figures provoked more fear in Roman hearts than the Gaulish druids. Members of a powerful group learned in ancient lore, they were revered and hated in equal measure by their own people. It was said that Vercingetorix himself relied on one to provide him with predictions of the future.

'See?' said the thin legionary. 'He's a damn druid.'

'Not for much longer, he isn't,' quipped their ringleader.

There was more laughter.

Moving forward, Fabiola saw that while most of the old man's wounds were superficial, one was not. Through his clutching fingers, large amounts of blood had soaked through his robe over his belly. Her intervention had come too late. It was a death wound.

And gazing at the druid, she saw that he knew it too.

Bizarrely, he smiled. 'Some of my visions were true, then,' he said to himself. 'A beautiful, black-haired woman who seeks revenge.'

Fabiola's eyes widened.

Behind her, Secundus was paying keen attention.

No one spoke for a moment.

'You are close to one beloved of Caesar,' he rasped suddenly.

The watching legionaries exchanged worried glances. Fabiola's threat had not just been an empty one. Without further protest, they let her kneel by the druid's side.

Horrified by the whole situation, Fabiola was also intrigued. Here was a man with more power than any of the charlatans to be found at Jupiter's temple in Rome. Yet he was dying. She had to find out what else he knew before it was too late.

The druid beckoned to her. 'Do you still grieve as before?' he whispered.

An involuntary sob rose in Fabiola's throat, and she nodded. *Mother. Romulus.*

He grunted with pain, and Fabiola instinctively reached out to grip one of his gnarled, bloody hands. There was little else she could do.

His next words rocked her world.

'You had a brother. A soldier who went to the east.'

It was all Fabiola could do not to break down completely. 'Have you seen him?'

He nodded. 'On a great battlefield, fighting against a mighty host with massive grey monsters in its midst.'

Romulus was in my vision! Fabiola glanced around at Secundus.

Unsurprisingly, he was beaming. Mithras *had* spoken through her.

Exultant, Fabiola calmed herself. 'Is he still alive?'

Her words hung in the sultry air.

'Rome must beware of Caesar.'

Angry snarls met this comment, and the legionaries pressed forward with ready swords. But the old man's expression had already gone glazed, his eyes unfocused.

'Is Romulus alive?' Fabiola squeezed his fingers, to no avail.

A last rattling breath escaped the druid's lips, and then his body went limp.

'Good riddance,' growled the ringleader. 'Our general is the only man fit to lead the Republic.' He hawked and spat, before skulking off. His comrades did likewise. There was no sport left here, and by leaving quickly, they would escape punishment. Finding nondescript legionaries like them amidst an army was almost impossible.

Uncaring, Fabiola sagged down, drained of all energy.

There would be no revelation about Romulus.

How was she to bear it?

Chapter XX: Barbaricum

Barbaricum, on the Indian Ocean, summer 52 BC

S quatting by the edge of the rough-hewn wooden dock, Romulus spat angrily into the sea. The journey south had aged him. There were dark rings of exhaustion under his blue eyes and a light growth of stubble covered his jaw. His black hair had grown longer. Although he did not know it, Romulus was now an imposing sight. His military tunic might be ragged and dirty, but his height, heavily muscled arms and legs and sheathed *gladius* marked him out as a man not to cross.

Tarquinius' gaze fell away from the men he had been watching. He took in Romulus' mood at a glance. 'Brennus chose his own fate,' he said quietly. 'You could not stop him.'

Unsurprised at his mind being read, Romulus did not answer. Instead he watched the mixture of objects floating in the water with a mix of curiosity and revulsion. Typical of any large port, there were rotting fish heads, broken pieces of timber, small pieces of discarded fishing net and over-ripe fruit bobbing about between the wooden hulls of the moored ships.

The shouts and cries of merchants, stallholders, slave-dealers and their prospective customers filled the warm, salty air. Just a hundred paces away was part of the immense market which formed the basis for Barbaricum's existence. Despite the oppressive temperatures and high humidity, the place was thronged. Bearded traders in turbans were selling indigo, different varieties of pepper and other spices from open sacks. Naked except for their chains, scores of men, women and children stood miserably on blocks, waiting like so many cattle. Neat piles of tortoiseshell were stacked higher than a man. Polished tusks lying in pairs were mute evidence that not every elephant became a beast of war. Trestle tables were covered in pieces of turquoise, lapis lazuli, agate and other semi-precious stones. There was silk yarn and cloth, cotton in bales and sheets of finely woven muslin. It was a veritable cornucopia.

But the ships that would carry all these goods away were of more interest to Romulus and Tarquinius. Tied up in their dozens, shallow-draughted fishing boats with small single masts knocked gently against larger merchant vessels with neatly reefed sails. Many of the craft were of unfamiliar shape to Romulus, but the haruspex had mentioned feluccas and native galleys. Here and there he saw sharp-prowed, lateen-rigged ships, their armed, unsavoury-looking crews eyeing each other warily. These were not honest traders. Without a bronze ram or banks of oars, the dhows still reminded him of Roman triremes. Of fighting ships.

It was a group of men from one of these that Tarquinius was studying intently.

But what did it matter anyway? Once more, Romulus' misery settled over him like a cloak. He briefly considered letting himself fall in, to sink beneath the slick, greasy surface. Then his guilt might end.

'It is not your fault that he died,' said the haruspex softly.

The words sprang to Romulus' lips unbidden. 'No,' he spat. 'It's yours.'

Tarquinius recoiled as if struck.

'You knew,' shouted Romulus, uncaring that men's heads were turning in their direction. 'Since that night after Carrhae. Didn't you?'

'I—' the haruspex began, but it did not stop Romulus' flow of rage. It had been pent up since the battle – since leaving Brennus to face an elephant on his own.

'We could have gone with Longinus and marched back to the Euphrates.' Romulus pressed his fists against his head, wishing that were the truth. 'At least they had a chance of escaping. But you said that we should stay. So we did.'

Tarquinius' dark eyes grew sad.

'And then Brennus died, when he did not need to.' Romulus closed his eyes and his voice tailed away into a whisper. 'He could have escaped.'

'And left you?' Tarquinius' voice was low but incredulous. 'Brennus would never have done that.'

There was a long silence, during which the onlookers grew bored and turned away.

Even that was probably part of Tarquinius' plans, Romulus thought bitterly. Avoiding attention was always a good idea. At that very moment, however, he did not care who saw or heard their conversation.

Several weeks had passed since their journey from the battlefield, yet now, as then, Romulus was consumed by one thing. Had the haruspex known about, or planned, their whole experience since joining Crassus' army? Had he and Brennus been nothing more than unknowing pawns, acting out an already written script? It was a question that Tarquinius repeatedly refused to answer. Overcome with grief after Brennus' heroic sacrifice, Romulus had simply gone along with him. Swimming across the Hydaspes was an ordeal in itself, and the passage south that had followed was even more arduous. Without helmets, chain mail or shields, with only their *gladii* and Tarquinius' battleaxe for protection, the two weary soldiers had been forced to travel mainly by night. Otherwise their pale skins and inability to speak the local languages would have marked them out as foreigners, easy prey for even the ignorant villagers whose land they passed. Strangers such as they might carry money or riches.

Fortunately, their combined skills had been sufficient to hunt or steal just enough food to live on without often being detected. It was trying to avoid centres of human population that was hardest. The fertile land near the River Indus, which the Hydaspes had joined, was densely inhabited. Most communities were situated close to the river, the main source of water for agriculture and life in general. And the pair had no choice but to follow its course. The grief-stricken Romulus had no idea which way to go, and even Tarquinius knew only to head south. The *Periplus*, the ancient map given to him by Olenus, had sketchy details for this part of the world. Consequently, they had to creep their way around all the villages in pitch darkness, risking discovery each and every night. More than once, dogs had raised the alarm, forcing them to retreat and wait for another chance, as lurking thieves do.

The process was mentally and physically exhausting for both, and five days later they had made the decision to steal a small boat from a fishing hamlet. It had proved to be the riskiest but most profitable move of the entire journey. None of the sleeping denizens had noticed until it was far too late, and those who did awaken were not foolish enough to pursue the pair along the river in the pitch black. Romulus' and Tarquinius' new boat had two crudely made oars, which meant that they could travel whenever they chose. They stayed close to the shore, only risking the strong current mid-river when other vessels were encountered. The ragged nets on board had allowed them to fish daily, providing a simple, if boring diet.

Conversation had been limited after Romulus had accused Tarquinius of failing to prevent Brennus' death. Taking the haruspex' refusal to answer as a confession, Romulus had lapsed into a furious silence that was only broken by questions about food or their direction of travel. As a result, their arrival in the exotic metropolis of Barbaricum had been muted, but neither could deny that it was an important milestone. Cities had become an alien place to them.

It was more than a year since they had been paraded through the streets of Seleucia, the capital of Parthia. Margiana, where the Forgotten Legion had served as a border force, held nothing more than a few towns and the tiny settlements along the Indus were scarcely more than hamlets. In contrast, this massive city was protected by strong walls, fortified towers and a large garrison. As in Rome, most inhabitants were poor labourers or shopkeepers, but instead of living in blocks of cramped flats, they dwelled in primitive one-storey mud huts. There was no sign of a sewage system: rubbish and human waste lay everywhere on the muddy streets.

Barbaricum also lacked the proliferation of huge temples that existed in Rome, but it was still an impressive sight. Flashy palaces abounded, the homes of wealthy nobles and merchants. And the enormous covered market near the docks was a sight to behold. The portion near them formed just a tiny fraction of the whole bazaar. Romulus had been awestruck by the variety of goods, living or inanimate, human or animal, on offer there. Yet this was one of India's main trading centres, a seaport where every kind of merchandise under the sun came to be bought and sold before being transported away to far-off lands. It was living, breathing proof that Rome was only a tiny part of the world.

As if reminding him of that, a line of heavily laden porters emerged from the maze of narrow alleyways that opened on to the harbour. Led by a self-important-looking man in a short, belted robe who was carrying a bamboo cane, they pushed through the clamouring crowds, eventually reaching a large merchantman with two masts which lay alongside the main dock. Following close behind the column was a group of guards armed with spears, swords and clubs. They fanned out protectively as the valuable merchandise was lowered to the ground. There was a brief pause as the merchant conferred with the ship's captain and then the porters began the laborious task of carrying their loads up the narrow gangplank.

Romulus felt a thrill of excitement. From here, ships sailed westwards once a year, on the monsoon wind, to Egypt. And from there, a man could journey to Rome. All they needed now was to find a captain who would give them passage.

So much had happened to bring him here, thought Romulus. He and Tarquinius had survived the carnage of Carrhae and the epic march east, evaded murderous attacks by other legionaries and escaped annihilation by an Indian king's army, finally ending up in a place whence returning home was actually possible. It seemed incredible – a virtual miracle, in fact. But the price exacted was heavy: apart from the countless thousands in Crassus' army and the Forgotten Legion who had died, first Felix and then Brennus had lost their lives. The death of the man who meant more to him than anyone apart from his mother and Fabiola had been a particularly devastating blow. Guilt weighed down on Romulus' shoulders. Two friends had died to give him this opportunity and there was nothing he could do about it.

And the haruspex had known what would happen to Brennus all along. What else did he know? 'You played us both like a fish on a hook,' Romulus hissed, wishing that he could turn back time. 'Damn you to Hades.'

'It may be my fate to go there,' Tarquinius answered, moving to his side. 'That remains to be seen.'

'No man should die alone, facing insurmountable odds.'

Tarquinius thought of Olenus, and the manner of his death. 'Why not, if he chooses it?'

Unaware of the haruspex' past, Romulus bridled at his instant response. 'It would have been better for Brennus to have died in the arena.' Even as he said the words, he knew them to be untrue. The fate of gladiators rested with the fickle and bloodthirsty Roman mob. Instead, the Gaul had died as he had wished, under the bright sun with his sword in his hand. A free man, not a slave.

Romulus chewed a nail. How could he have forgotten the message that had burned so brightly in Brennus' eyes? His friend had come to accept his fate, which was more than most men ever did. Who was he to deny that? Which meant that the anger he had felt against the haruspex since their flight was being fuelled entirely by the guilt and shame savaging him inside. It was a startling realisation. A great gust of sorrow left Romulus' chest, emptying his lungs and leaving him with a feeling of total emptiness inside. Unbidden but welcome tears rolled down his cheeks at the memory of big, brave Brennus, who had died that he might live.

Tarquinius looked awkward for a moment, and then he put an arm around Romulus' shoulders.

It was extremely rare for the haruspex to display such emotion and, sobbing like a boy, Romulus wept for what it meant. Tarquinius was grieving for their friend too. At last his tears dried, and he looked up.

Their eyes met. For long moments they stared at each other.

There was an openness in Tarquinius' face that Romulus had never seen before. He was relieved to see no evil there.

Remarkably, it was Tarquinius who looked away first. 'I did know that Brennus would meet his fate in India,' he said in a low voice. 'It was written in the stars on the very first night we met.'

'Why didn't you tell him?'

'He did not want to know then, if at all,' answered the haruspex, regarding him steadily. 'You knew that too.'

Romulus flushed.

'Advising you both to retreat with Longinus would have been interfering with your destiny,' Tarquinius went on. 'Would you have wanted me to do that?'

Romulus shook his head. Few things angered the gods more than trying to change the course of one's life path.

'And I was not the first to predict Brennus' future. His druid had told him,' said Tarquinius. 'Believing that prophecy was what helped him survive for so long in the *ludus*. As well as Astoria and you, of course.'

The memory of Romulus' first real meeting with the big Gaul was still vivid. After killing a *murmillo* who was holding Brennus' lover Astoria hostage, Romulus had incurred the wrath of Memor, the brutal *lanista*. Facing a daunting single combat the next morning as punishment, and with nowhere to sleep, Romulus had begun to despair. Brennus was the only fighter to offer him refuge. Unsurprisingly, their friendship had grown from there.

'Apart from wanting the best for you, Brennus wished for just one thing.'

Romulus knew what Tarquinius would say next.

'It was to regain his honour while saving his friends.'

'As he had been prevented from doing before,' Romulus finished. 'With his wife and baby.'

'And his uncle and cousin.'

A surge of faith filled him. 'So the gods granted his final wish.'

'That is what I believe.'

Both men sat for a while, honouring Brennus' memory.

Below them, a fish jumped high in the air, catching a fly. There was a loud splash as it re-entered the water.

Romulus wrinkled his nose at the unpleasant smell which arose. Bizarrely, it reminded him of his former owner. The cruel merchant had bathed little. Abruptly he decided to test Tarquinius' honesty. 'What about Gemellus?'

The haruspex looked surprised. 'His recent business ventures have not gone well. More than that I do not know.'

Satisfied and pleased with this simple response, Romulus ventured another question. 'Are my mother and Fabiola still alive?'

This was his most deeply held hope, the burning ember of which he guarded like the font of life itself. For fear of the haruspex' possible answer, Romulus had never dared mention it before.

Tarquinius' expression changed, becoming sombre.

Romulus steeled himself.

'Fabiola is,' Tarquinius said at length. 'I am certain of it.'

Joy filled him, and he grinned. 'And my mother?'

The haruspex shook his head once.

Romulus' initial elation ebbed away, to be replaced by sadness. His mother's death was not a complete surprise to him, however. While not particularly old at the time of his sale to the *ludus*, Velvinna had been small and slight of build. And her children's sale would have finally broken her spirit. The incredibly harsh environment of the salt mines, into which Gemellus had promised to sell her, killed even the strongest of men within a few months. To expect that she would survive more than four years in such a living hell was unrealistic. Romulus had kept her alive in his imagination because it helped him with his own situation. Closing his eyes, he asked that the gods look after his mother in paradise.

'Where is Fabiola now?' Romulus nearly choked on his next words. 'Still in the brothel?'

'No.'

'Where, then?'

'I'm not sure,' said Tarquinius. 'If I see more, you'll be the first to know.'

Romulus sighed, wondering why, in his vision, Fabiola had been at the Forum. He would have to wait for the answer.

Overhead, the harsh keening of the gulls reminded them of their proximity to the sea: their possible route home. Romulus' heart sang with previously unthinkable ideas.

The timbers beneath them creaked as heavy footsteps approached their position.

The haruspex' eyes narrowed, and Romulus' fingers crept towards the handle of his *gladius*. In this exotic port, they had no friends – only potential enemies. The gravelly voice that butted in was a rude reminder of this fact.

Romulus did not understand the words, but the angry tone conveyed the speaker's meaning very well.

'He wants to know what we're doing on his dock,' whispered Tarquinius.

'*His* dock?' hissed Romulus incredulously.

The haruspex raised his eyebrows and he had to stifle a smile.

A brute of a man was standing over them, his hands on his hips. Dressed in a plain loincloth, his deeply tanned body was covered in scars. Thick cords of muscle stood out on his chest and arms; leather bands encircled both wrists. Greasy black hair fell in long braids on either side of the man's broad, unshaven face. A badly broken nose twisted his features, which were lumpen and crude. He repeated his question.

Neither of the friends answered, but they both got to their feet. Facing the newcomer, they moved a couple of paces apart.

A sword with a deeply curved blade jutted from a wide belt around the man's waist. Tiny brown discoloured pits in the iron revealed the newcomer was a sailor. Or a pirate. Only salt spray affected metal like that, thought

Romulus. The fool didn't know that oiling his weapon would prevent it from rusting. Or didn't care.

Raising his hands in a peaceful gesture, Tarquinius spoke a few words.

The response was an angry growl.

'I told him that we were merely resting,' the haruspex said in an undertone.

'That doesn't seem to be enough,' muttered Romulus, taking in the corsair's body language.

'No,' Tarquinius replied archly. 'He wants to fight.'

'Tell him we don't want trouble,' said Romulus. Doubtless this brute had friends.

Tarquinius obeyed.

Instead of standing aside, the man sneered and planted his trunk-like legs even further apart. Now he resembled some kind of deformed Colossus, standing astride the wharf.

Angered by the threatening move, Romulus took an involuntary step forward.

'Look,' warned Tarquinius.

Romulus peered over his opponent's shoulder to see that the rails of a predatory-looking dhow a short distance away were lined with grinning men. 'What should we do?'

The haruspex watched two screeching gulls fight over a juicy scrap. He was reasonably sure that they should offer their services as crew on a merchant vessel rather than get involved with pirates like those watching. But it was best to check.

Romulus waited, studying the big corsair.

A smile broke out on the haruspex' scarred face as, at the last moment, the smaller black-beaked gull boldly snatched a morsel from the beak of the larger bird.

And then things happened very suddenly.

Romulus' enemy lunged forward, attempting to seize him in a bear hug. Ducking underneath his swinging arms, Romulus planted an elbow in his back instead. The hefty blow elicited little more than a grunt of anger but produced gales of laughter from the onlookers. The pair turned to face each other once more. Tarquinius took the opportunity to move well out of range of the struggle.

Romulus grimaced. Once more events had been taken out of their hands. He wasn't going to let a random thug just beat him up, but the consequences might be serious. Be careful, he thought. Don't injure the brute.

The pirate approached more slowly this time. Clenching his jaw with anger, he slid his bare feet forward across the dock's warped and cracked planks. Romulus crouched, bending his knees and remembering the dirty moves that Brennus had taught him. He let the other come even closer. There was no room for error: few men were stronger than Brennus, but here was an example. If a single blow connected, Romulus knew he would go down and not get up again.

Two or three paces apart, they stared at each other.

The pirate's sunburned, cracked lips peeled back, revealing rows of brown, rotten teeth. His huge fists bunched, ready to strike. As far as he was concerned, Romulus was now within his reach. Victory was already his.

The young soldier feinted to the left, and as expected, his opponent moved away. But Romulus did not follow through with a punch. Quick as a flash, he kneed the other in the groin. He did it with all his strength, and the pirate's mouth opened in an 'O' of surprise and agony. Crumpling neatly, he dropped to the dock with a loud crash. A low, inarticulate moan emanated from his slumped form.

Romulus grinned and stepped away, pleased that he had not needed to badly injure the corsair.

With luck, his shipmates would also appreciate the restraint.

Glancing over, he could see that many of them were laughing. But a sizeable number seemed quite unhappy too. Angry fists were being shaken in his direction. A coal-black Nubian with gold earrings stood by, watching to see the outcome. More and more insults rang out, and a few men reached for their weapons. It was the beginning of a trickle effect. Realising that he and Tarquinius would have to run like cowards, Romulus cursed silently. Just like a rioting mob that pauses before lynching an innocent bystander, the pirates were still stationary, but it would only take one man to move for the whole lot to swarm over the rails.

Romulus waved Tarquinius forward, over the groaning heap. Once off the wharf and mingling in the crowd, they would be safe.

A large hand reached out and grabbed at the haruspex' ankle, almost tripping him.

Hearing Tarquinius cry out, Romulus spun on his heel and in reflex, stamped down on the corsair's head. A blow from the hobnailed sole of his army sandal was like being hit with a hammer, and the big man slumped down, unconscious. Rolling gently away, his huge weight gave him just enough momentum to reach the edge of the narrow dock and tumble over it. With an almighty splash, he hit the water, sinking immediately.

Aghast, Romulus peered down into the murky depths. Killing his opponent had not been his intention, but that would surely be the outcome now. Already he could see nothing more than chains of rising bubbles.

With an inchoate roar of rage, the entire crew of the pirate ship leapt overboard and sprinted towards them. They were on a parallel jetty, but it would not take long for the two friends' escape route to be cut off.

Tarquinius grabbed his arm. 'Let's go,' he hissed. 'Now!'

'But the poor bastard will drown,' protested Romulus.

'Do you think he'd care if it happened to you?' retorted the haruspex. 'His friends can save him.'

'It'll be too late by then.' He could not leave a man to die yet again. Romulus unbuckled his belt, took a deep breath and dived in. For the second time in as many moments, the water fountained into the air.

Horrified, Tarquinius stared after him. His moment of indecision cost him dearly. Several pirates had already reached the end of the wharf he was standing on. Leering with pleasure, they swaggered along the planks towards him, axes and spears raised.

Romulus knew none of this. Kicking downwards, he cast his eyes left and right. Fortunately, the visibility was good, much better than on the surface. But he could see nothing. Long fronds of seaweed straggled up from the bottom, threatening to entangle him. Romulus searched fruitlessly for what seemed an age, when a thick rope appeared before him, leading diagonally downwards. It had to be the anchor cable for one the ships above. Romulus took a good hold of it and pulled himself even deeper. If he didn't find the pirate soon, it would be too late.

Half a dozen heartbeats later, he reached an enormous stone anchor. Romulus was running out of air. Mithras, help me, he prayed desperately.

It was the braids of black hair that caught Romulus' attention. Like the seaweed around them, they were swaying to and fro in the current. He swam forward, finding the big man within arm's reach, flat on his back and completely motionless. Not a good sign, he thought. Grabbing hold of the long tresses with his left hand, Romulus placed his feet on the sandy bottom and bent his knees. Using the power of his muscular thighs, he pushed upwards with all his might. The surface seemed miles away, and the weight dragging down his left arm like a sack of lead. But he transferred his grip to the corsair's chin and, stroke by slow stroke, they ascended.

When two heads broke through the scummy water, great cries of relief went up.

Tarquinius' voice was among them.

With a sinking heart, Romulus saw that the haruspex had been disarmed and was surrounded by corsairs. But he had no time to think; although he could feel a pulse beneath his hand, the big man was limp in his grasp. His lungs could be full of water. Realising the same thing, his comrades quickly lowered a rope. Romulus tied it fast around the unconscious pirate's chest and watched as he was pulled up to the dock. Lying the big man on his front, a swarthy figure delivered a few sharp blows to the back of his chest. Nothing happened, and Romulus' heart sank. The procedure was repeated a number of times to no avail. Just when he thought his rescue attempt had been pointless, the hulk coughed violently before vomiting up a large amount of seawater.

His friends cheered with delight.

Again the rope was dropped, and Romulus eagerly swarmed up it, hand over hand. Surely he would be well received. After all, he had saved the man's life.

As Romulus reached out to pull himself up on to the dock, a pair of calloused black feet stepped in his way. He looked up, into the eyes of the Nubian with gold earrings. This had to be the pirate captain – and there was a large, wide-bladed cutlass in his right hand.

'Tell me why I shouldn't cut this rope,' the Nubian said in passable Parthian. 'Before my men kill your friend.'

Chapter XXI: Reunion

Central Gaul, summer 52 BC

After a long time, Fabiola managed to pull herself together. Muttering reassuring words, Secundus moved her away from the druid's body. Fabiola hardly noticed the gore any longer as the *optio* led his men towards the group of tents on a promontory overlooking the corpse-strewn ground. The terror of the previous few weeks had been overwhelming, and her encounter with the dying druid agonising. Fabiola shuddered. But with the aid of the gods, she had coped this far. Endured. She breathed deeply and imagined the reception she would get. Gradually Fabiola's mood changed to that of nervous excitement. She was about to see Brutus again! Nothing could be done about Romulus for the moment, and her deep-held worries about Caesar faded into the background. Her perilous journey was nearly over, and at last she would be able to relax a little. The prospect filled her with relief.

They climbed the slope, reaching a number of checkpoints manned by exhausted-looking legionaries. Many had bandaged arms, legs or heads; their armour and shields were battered and blood-stained. To a man, though, their manner was alert and watchful. At each, Fabiola declared her status and her mission, which saw them ushered through with surprised but respectful salutes. As she passed, the soldiers' heads turned in lust and awe at her beauty. But not one dared say a word within earshot. Who wished to incur the displeasure of Decimus Brutus, key right-hand man of Julius Caesar?

They came within range of the army's command post: this was also where the senior officers' quarters had been erected. Fabiola's pulse quickened. As well as the usual force of guards, messengers and trumpeters, there were men in gilded armour standing outside the largest tent, with a lithe, energetic figure gesticulating in their midst. It could only be Caesar. And where he was, Brutus would not be far away. She smiled, imagining her lover's response when he saw her.

'Caesar is the best general Rome has ever had,' Secundus declared. 'This is a victory like no other!'

Remotely associated with Caesar through Fabiola and Brutus, Docilosa swelled with pride. After surviving great dangers and threats to their lives, this was just reward.

'Look, lady.'

Secundus' words dragged Fabiola from her reverie. Her gaze followed his pointing arm. It was no surprise that Caesar had moved to this spot, she thought. The whole battlefield was laid out below them, allowing an appreciation of the scale of his achievement and the size of the force which must have opposed his ten legions. The view to the north-west was obscured by the rock face, but the fortifications stretched as far as the eye could see to the south-east, facing both ways, with lethal killing grounds in front and behind. There were blocks of wood with iron hooks to drag at passing men's feet and clothing, pits with sharpened stakes at the bottom and ditches filled with irregularly cut gravestones. Inside these were two deep trenches, one of which had been filled with water from a nearby river. Finally there was the palisade itself, which was reinforced by a layer of spiked branches poking forward below the battlements. Regular towers along it provided excellent fields of fire. Stores of *pila* were still stacked along the walkways, the last remnants of the thousands which must have been hurled at the Gauls as they advanced slowly through the death-traps. Fabiola could see that Caesar's defences had been tested to their limit. Corpses covered the ground between the circumvallation and Alesia, as well as on the other side. Many of the dead were clearly Roman, slain in counter-attacks and missions to retrieve undamaged *pila*, but the vast majority were Gauls – warriors in the prime of life, younger men, youths and even a few old men. Whole tribes lay here.

Fabiola's fearful admiration for Caesar soared. Her knowledge of warfare was limited, but no one could fail to appreciate the immensity of the struggle which must have gone on here. To win when so greatly outnumbered was incredible. Fabiola was glad that she had not decided to stay with Marcus Petreius. Even Pompey might not be capable of outwitting the general who had won this remarkable victory. If it came to it, was anyone? A tremor of fear ran through Fabiola. She suddenly felt very small and insignificant. Brutus had hitched his fate to a meteor, it seemed. And hers with it. Only time would tell if they both got burned.

'Fabiola? Is that you?'

The sound of the familiar voice made her stomach turn over. Fabiola turned her head, and saw her lover walking towards them. Nervously, she raised a hand. 'Brutus!'

With an excited cry, he broke into a run. Of average build, Brutus was clad in a typical senior officer's gilded breastplate, red cloak and transverse crested helmet. He held on to the ornate hilt of his sword, but the studded leather straps which protected his groin and upper legs jingled to and fro as he ran.

Fabiola longed to race to her lover, but in an effort to keep her composure, she remained stationary. Smoothing down her plain dress, she wished there had been time to buy more clothes and some perfume. Stay calm, she thought. This is not Rome, or Pompeii. There are no luxuries when on campaign. I am here: that is enough.

'By all the gods, it is you!' shouted Brutus as he drew near.

Fabiola gave him a radiant smile, the one she knew he loved.

Petreius' legionaries saluted and pulled apart smartly, forming a corridor.

Slowing, Brutus strode the last few paces, drinking in Fabiola's beauty as a thirsty man drains a cup of water. There was a tired grey sheen to his unshaven face, but he was unhurt. 'How in the name of Hades?' he demanded, beaming and frowning by turns. 'What are you doing in this godforsaken spot?'

She pouted. 'Aren't you pleased to see me?'

He took her hands in his and squeezed them hard. 'Yes! It's as if Mars himself has answered my prayers.'

Fabiola leaned forward and kissed him on the lips. Brutus met her passion with a burning intensity of his own, and enveloped her in his arms. Finally they parted, staring into each other's eyes, needing to say nothing. It was luxury for both to feel the other's body against their own. 'Gods,' Fabiola murmured at last. 'I've missed you so much.'

Boyishly, he grinned from ear to ear. 'And I you, my darling. How many months has it been?'

'Nearly nine,' she replied sadly.

'I'm sorry,' Brutus said, clasping Fabiola's fingers as if he thought she would disappear if he let go. 'This campaign has been like no other. We've done nothing but march and fight since the damn rebellion started. I couldn't leave Caesar's side.'

'Of course,' said Fabiola understandingly. 'I know.'

'How is it at the *latifundium*?' Seeing her expression change, Brutus frowned. 'Has something happened?'

At once tears formed in the corners of Fabiola's eyes. Poor Corbulo, she thought guiltily. He died because of my rash behaviour. So did the gladiators I hired. My slaves have been sold off to the highest bidder. And that poor boy, castrated just to satisfy Scaevola's pique.

Brutus gazed into her eyes, full of concern. 'Tell me,' he said gently.

It all poured out in a torrent of words. The runaway. Scaevola and his *fugitivarii*. Her humiliation of him. How her slaves had appeared in the nick of time.

'Crossing the *fugitivarius* was not very wise perhaps,' said Brutus. 'But I know how overbearing men like him can be.'

Nodding, Fabiola went on, relating how two slaves had been murdered in the fields. This had hastened her decision to travel to Rome, where she had met Secundus. She indicated the veteran to Brutus. No details were spared about Clodius Pulcher's death, the ensuing riots and the dramatic burning of the Senate.

'We heard about that even here. Where's the respect for proper order gone?' muttered Brutus darkly. 'Plebeian scum! They need the point of a sword shoved where it hurts.'

'That's probably already happened,' said Fabiola, inclining her head towards the legionaries around them. 'One of Pompey's legions will have reached Rome by now.'

The *optio* grinned proudly.

Understanding, Brutus did not ask more. 'Thank Mars that you weren't there for that,' he replied. 'Go on.'

Without mentioning Scaevola's powerful backer, Fabiola related the story of his street ambush and of what the *fugitivarius* had done to Corbulo and the others on the *latifundium*. Brutus' eyes bulged with anger, but he let her continue without interrupting. Upon hearing of Fabiola's near rape however, he swelled with outrage. 'What's his name again?'

'Scaevola.' To deliver the thunderbolt, Fabiola placed her lips by Brutus' ear. 'Apparently he's on Pompey's payroll. And we're not the first supporters of Caesar to be targeted.'

Brutus went icy calm. 'I see,' he said. 'Well, he needs to be made an example of. Finding an arrogant son of a whore like that shouldn't be much problem. Scaevola will pay for what he has done. Slowly, too.'

Relief filled Fabiola. Already the malevolent *fugitivarius* felt like less of a threat. To be sure though, she would have to stay by Brutus' side. 'Are you finished . . . ?' she began.

'Here?' Brutus indicated the heaped bodies below them. 'Perhaps. Vercingetorix is in chains and we have taken tens of thousands of his men as slaves.' He frowned. 'Many tribes may continue fighting though. But we will not stop until Gaul is truly part of the Republic. Until Caesar has won completely.' He raised his voice. 'Victory to Julius Caesar!'

The nearest of Caesar's legionaries cheered when they heard, while the soldiers who had accompanied Fabiola north looked distinctly uneasy.

Brutus turned next to Docilosa, bestowing a broad smile on her. 'Looking after your mistress well?'

'She's a godsend,' interrupted Fabiola. 'I'd have been lost without her.'

Docilosa's face went beetroot with pride.

'Your fealty will be rewarded,' said Brutus kindly. 'And who is this man here?'

'Sextus, Master,' the slave replied, bowing low. 'The last of the mistress' bodyguards.'

'He has the heart of a lion,' Fabiola declared. 'And fights like one too.'

'You have my thanks.' Brutus clapped Sextus on the shoulder.

'Master.'

'And this is Secundus?' asked Brutus.

'I am, sir.' Secundus clenched his fist and thumped it off his chest in salute. 'A veteran of thirteen years' service.'

'He and his comrades saved us from Scaevola,' said Fabiola. 'They gave us shelter and then guided us on our journey.'

Sextus nodded emphatically.

Brutus threw a grateful look at Secundus. 'Are these your men?' he asked with some confusion.

Secundus' face turned sad. 'No, sir. My comrades were all killed by the *fugitivarii*. Two weeks or so north of Rome, they ambushed us again. Caught us napping like raw recruits.'

'No,' cried Fabiola. 'With Mithras' help, you got us out of there. No one else could have.'

Secundus dipped his head in acknowledgement.

'Mithras, you say?' asked Brutus sharply.

'Yes,' Fabiola answered. 'Secundus and his men follow the path.' For the moment, she said nothing about her own involvement.

At once Brutus leaned forward. With a laugh, Secundus did the same and they shook hands firmly.

It was Fabiola's turn to be surprised. 'You worship Mithras too?'

'For the last few months. A senior centurion who served in Asia Minor introduced me to the religion,' Brutus explained with glee. 'And now, under Secundus' protection, the god has brought you to me. This calls for a generous sacrifice!'

Fabiola was delighted.

'So these legionaries . . .' began Brutus. 'Whose are they?'

'We got them thanks to Mithras too, sir,' said Secundus in a low voice. 'The *fugitivarii* fled when we encountered a Pompeian legion on its way to Rome. It was under the command of Marcus Petreius, who turned out to be a believer too.'

Fabiola beamed at him, overjoyed that a plausible explanation had been provided. She had been troubled about bypassing her involvement with Petreius since leaving the legate's camp.

Brutus' eyebrows rose. 'Mithras has truly blessed you, my love. Fortuna too, I think.'

If only you knew it all, Fabiola thought, thinking of her *homa*-induced vision. But that is best told in private. Except for what happened in Petreius' bedchamber.

'Fabiola has been safely delivered,' Brutus said to the *optio*. 'It was a job well done. Now you'll need to be getting back to your unit, I expect. But all of you deserve a good rest before setting off.' He whistled at the nearest of his men. 'Take these soldiers down to the camp. Find them some hot food and a bed for the night. Quickly!'

There were pleased grins all round as the *optio* and his half-century were led away. Secundus accompanied them but Sextus stayed by Fabiola's side.

'Let's walk to my tent,' said Brutus, taking Fabiola by the arm. 'You can relax there. Tonight, a feast to celebrate our victory is being held, and I'm sure Caesar would want you present. He's heard all about you.'

The moment that Fabiola had desired for an age was nearly here – and it was almost too terrifying to contemplate. During all that she had endured, she had never actually dared to imagine it. But, thanks to Mithras, it would come to pass, in the unlikely setting of a battlefield in Gaul. 'Wonderful,' Fabiola, concealing her jangling nerves. 'I will be honoured to meet your general at last.'

Helped by Docilosa, Fabiola was dressing for the evening. A table, mirrors, some jewellery and bottles of makeup and perfume had been produced from Alesia, as had a selection of dresses. Fabiola knew better than to ask where they came from. The clothing fitted her so well it could have been for her double, which felt poignant. Fabiola made a silent request of Mithras to protect the clothing's owner, whoever she was.

'You look stunning,' said Brutus, regarding Fabiola admiringly. He moved closer, caressing her shoulders with the tips of his fingers. 'Not trying to impress Caesar, are you?'

Docilosa pursed her lips with disapproval.

'If I do, it's for your benefit,' Fabiola reproached. 'You know that.'

'Of course,' Brutus replied, embarrassed. 'I'm sorry.'

If only you knew what I really want.

'Do you want me to change it?'

Brutus eyed her low cut silk *stola*, which exposed large amounts of creamy skin. 'No,' he said with a lustful grin. 'It looks good.'

Mollified, Fabiola sat down in front of the small bronze mirror on her table. Docilosa fussed behind her, tucking a few loose strands of hair behind her ears while Fabiola applied the finishing touches to her makeup. A small amount of ochre on her cheeks and the faintest dusting of antimony did the trick. By religiously keeping out of the sun, Fabiola had so far avoided the need to whiten her complexion with lead. She had decided to feel pleased about meeting Caesar at the feast. No doubt his attention would be taken up by his officers, allowing Fabiola to study him at her leisure. The men she met would also be potential sources of information about the shrewd general. Once more, Fabiola determined to use all her wiles in her quest for her father.

She looked Brutus up and down with a practised eye. Her lover had shed his military dress and *caligae* for soft leather shoes and a brilliant white toga of the finest wool. Never happy, his *vestiplicus*, whose job it was to arrange the garment's complex folds, fussed and bothered around him. Finally Brutus could take no more and dismissed the fawning slave.

Docilosa took the opportunity to fade into the background.

'Well?'

'Very handsome, my love,' Fabiola murmured, moving to his side and cupping his groin.

They had spent the entire afternoon coupling like rabbits, but Brutus' response was instant.

'Perhaps you could complain of a bad stomach,' she suggested throatily.

'Stop it,' he laughed. 'We can't miss the feast.'

'I wouldn't want to,' Fabiola replied, kissing him on the lips.

Blithely unaware of her motives, Brutus smiled proudly.

Great Mithras, she prayed. Give me a sign. I need to know if Caesar is the one.

A small guard of four legionaries and an *optio* brought them to Caesar's massive tent.

Sextus watched the pair go, a worried expression on his face. He did not like letting Fabiola out of his sight. Ever.

A balding major-domo was waiting for them at the entrance. 'Welcome,' he said, bowing from the waist. 'Please follow me.'

Full of sudden apprehension, Fabiola froze. Was she mad? Even if her suspicion was correct, to dream of harming one of Rome's most famous sons was tantamount to committing suicide. A wry smile twisted her lips. What did that matter? Although she had survived terrible dangers, her twin brother had endured far worse. Without Romulus, my survival is unimportant, thought Fabiola. Death is nothing to be afraid of.

Brutus had not noticed her reaction; he eagerly entered after the slave. Steeling herself, Fabiola hurried in too.

Normally where Caesar met daily with his officers, the spacious yet Spartan chamber had been redecorated with dining furniture. In customary fashion, a large reclining couch was placed on three sides of each table, with the fourth left open. The couple were only two of more than twenty guests for dinner. Legates, tribunes and senior staff officers relaxed in threes on each couch, while numerous serving slaves moved to and fro between them. There was no sign of Caesar himself yet, but the lively hum of conversation filled the air.

Heads turned and appreciative murmurs were made as Brutus led Fabiola past the outer tables. He nodded and bowed to many of the officers, while Fabiola smiled hesitantly. Reaching the central table, Brutus greeted the four men who were already reclining around it. Fabiola was delighted. This was clearly where Caesar would sit and to be invited to dine here was an honour of the highest kind.

'Marcus Antonius, Titus Labienus, Caius Trebonius and Gaius Fabius, good evening.'

The quartet murmured courteous replies, but all their eyes were on Brutus' companion.

'May I present Fabiola, my lover? To my utter surprise, she has risked her life through the wilds of Gaul just to come and see me.'

Antonius gave Fabiola a lingering, unpleasant stare, which she ignored.

'I'm not surprised,' responded Labienus appreciatively. He was a thin, grey-haired man in late middle age. 'You're one of Caesar's best officers. A fine catch.'

'Don't listen to him, my love,' Brutus demurred. 'Along with Caesar and Fabius, this man won the final battle. And those two' – he pointed at Antonius and Trebonius – 'saved our skins the night before with their cavalry.'

Antonius laughed at Brutus' comment. 'You did your bit,' he drawled, rubbing a hand through his curly brown hair. 'That's why you're here. Now sit.'

Brutus flushed and guided Fabiola to her seat at the end of the right-hand couch. He took the middle space, meaning they were separated by a bolster, and both faced Caesar's couch. It had been left empty for the general to occupy alone. Having learned the importance of the different places, Fabiola knew that only Labienus and Antonius were reclining in superior

positions to her lover. Pride filled her, but she was also worried by the
obvious animosity between Brutus and Antonius, Caesar's best friend: a
man with a wild and dangerous reputation.

Glasses of *mulsum* were served at once, but Fabiola had scarcely swallowed a mouthful before loud cheering broke out. Officer after officer
stood, and she realised that Caesar had entered the room.

Getting to his feet, Brutus turned to Fabiola with a smile. 'See how they
love him?'

She nodded.

'The legionaries are the same,' he said. 'They would follow him to Hades
and back.'

'Why?' she asked, trying to understand.

'Caesar always rewards his soldiers' bravery. For example, every single
one who fought here at Alesia is to receive a slave as bounty,' whispered
Brutus. 'But it's not just that. Caesar is also courageous, so they greatly respect
him. Whenever necessary, he leads from the front. Vercingetorix' warriors
were very close to winning yesterday, but Caesar rode out from the palisade
with our cavalry reserve and smashed into their rear.' He thumped one fist
into the other. 'All along the line our men were hard-pressed and about to
break, but when they saw Caesar in his red cloak galloping up and down,
they counter-attacked. The Gauls panicked and fled, and the battle was won!'

Soon the cheering and clapping had reached deafening proportions. The
nearest officers parted, revealing Caesar for the first time. A lean whippet
of a man, he had short, thinning hair, a narrow face with high cheekbones
and an aquiline nose. While not traditionally handsome, something about
him demanded attention. Fabiola could not put her finger on it. She noted
that the toga Caesar was wearing had a narrow purple border. This was
the mark of censors, magistrates and dictators. Few could doubt which
category Caesar fell into, she thought in admiration. But was he responsible for raping her mother? A striking resemblance to Romulus provided
new fuel for her suspicions.

'Welcome, sir,' said Antonius expansively. 'You grace us with your
presence.'

Caesar nodded at each of them in turn. He lingered most on Fabiola,
who flushed and looked down at her shoes. Meeting one of the most
powerful men in the Republic was intimidating.

Brutus clicked his fingers and a delicate goblet was placed in his general's hand.

'This must be the beautiful Fabiola,' said Caesar. His gaze was piercing and charismatic. 'At last we meet.'

'Sir.' She bowed deeply in response. 'I am honoured to be here, at your victory feast.'

He smiled, putting Fabiola more at ease. 'Please be seated.'

They all obeyed, and Fabiola looked on politely as the men became engrossed in a lively discussion. Naturally enough, they talked first about the battle. Fabiola's interest was aroused and soon she was listening to every word.

Caesar led the conversation, analysing every angle of their campaign. There was much to consider. His struggle against Vercingetorix might have ended at the walled city of Alesia, but the conflict had lasted for many months. It had begun with the besieging of a number of towns loyal to the rebel chieftain, including Cenabum and Avaricum.

'I've heard of Cenabum before,' said Fabiola.

'Probably because the townspeople massacred Roman traders who were living there,' explained Caesar. 'Of course we wanted revenge, so the siege did not take long.'

'What happened?' asked Fabiola.

'My forces set fire to the gates, burst into the town and sacked it.' He smiled thinly at her horror. 'Soldiers are wolves. They need the thrill of the hunt to stay keen.'

Fabiola nodded, remembering the adrenalin running through her veins as she fought alongside Sextus. She could also imagine the terror of the civilians inside Cenabum when the legionaries swarmed in.

'Besieging Avaricum was harder though. It was winter still and we ran very short of food,' continued Brutus. 'Foraging parties were sent out daily, but the Gaulish cavalry played havoc with them.'

'A dark few days,' agreed Antonius.

'So I gave my legions the option of lifting the siege . . .' said Caesar.

'Did they take it?' asked Fabiola curiously.

'They refused to a man,' he replied proudly. 'Said it would be a disgrace not to finish what they had started. So, with no corn left to make bread, my legionaries lived on beef and nothing else for several days.'

'At the same time, they were building an enormous embankment to fill the gully which protected the only way into the town,' Brutus went on, his face alight. 'And the Gauls were hurling sharpened stakes, massive rocks and boiling pitch down on us all the while.'

'Even when the timber base of the embankment itself was set on fire, the men did not lose heart,' said Caesar. 'The next day, despite heavy rain, they took the walls and then the town.'

Fabiola gasped admiringly. With *mulsum* coursing through her, she became more and more involved in the animated conversation between Caesar and his officers. Her desire to find out if he was her father became submerged beneath her fascination with the awe-inspiring details of the campaign. Losing her inhibitions, Fabiola even began asking detailed questions of Caesar himself. Alarmed, Brutus threw her an admonishing glance, but his general, appearing amused, tolerated this for some time.

With her cheeks aglow, Fabiola did not notice when Caesar began to appear impatient. Brutus was reaching over to whisper in her ear when she made an uncharacteristic mistake. 'If your men are so valiant, what went wrong at Gergovia?' she asked forcefully.

A shocked silence fell across the table. Caesar's face froze.

'Well?' Fabiola asked again.

No one answered her.

'Fabiola!' hissed Brutus. 'You exceed yourself.' She had never seen him so angry.

Suddenly Fabiola felt very sober. 'I'm sorry,' she whispered. 'It's none of my business – a mere woman.' *What have I said?* Her mind was in complete turmoil. Discretion and stealth were her watchwords. Asking Caesar about a defeat – however rare – that he had suffered was downright foolish. Mithras, Fabiola prayed, forgive me. Do not let this affect Brutus' friendship with his general.

There was a quiet chuckle.

The sound was so unexpected that for a heartbeat Fabiola did not recognise it. Looking up, she saw Caesar was watching her, and laughing. It was unnerving. Fabiola felt like a mouse caught between the front paws of a cat.

'What happened was that the men taking part in the surprise attack did not answer my recall,' revealed Caesar coldly. 'While some scaled Gergovia's walls, others pressed home to the gates. Seeing the legionaries were isolated from my main force, the Gauls inside and out regrouped and enveloped them completely.'

'You soon came to the rescue with the Tenth, sir,' said Brutus hurriedly.

'Not before we'd lost seven hundred men,' replied Caesar. The regret in his voice was obvious. 'And forty-six centurions.'

Fabiola bent her head, wishing that the floor would open up and swallow her. It didn't.

Brutus tried to make some small talk, but his attempt failed miserably. Sitting on the same couch, the three others began talking among themselves. It left Brutus and Fabiola facing Caesar, which was unnerving.

'Your young lover is blessed with an enquiring mind,' said Caesar loudly a few moments later. 'An intelligent one for a former slave. And whore.'

Their companions looked suitably surprised by this revelation.

Brutus clenched his jaw, but refrained from speaking.

Fabiola burned with embarrassment and shame. Yet it was to be expected that Caesar knew everything about her. She waited, wishing with all her heart that time could be turned back.

'Such ability is sometimes a good thing,' Caesar went on. 'But often it is not. Combined with such beauty, a woman might achieve much. Gain influence over powerful people.'

'I see, sir,' Brutus replied, avoiding eye contact.

'Keep the girl on a close leash,' Caesar said sourly. He turned his piercing gaze on Fabiola.

She quailed, but did not look away.

'Or I might be forced to.' With this, he fell silent. His granite-hard expression revealed more than any words could.

'Rome must beware of Caesar,' the druid had warned.

So must she.

Chapter XXII: News

More than two years pass . . .
Cana, on the Arabian coast, winter 50 BC

T he pirates were in pensive mood as the ship slipped between a pair
of imposing towers and into Cana's imposing stone-walled harbour.
The *olibanum* and tortoise shells they had plundered were hidden
in the hold, and their weapons were concealed underneath rolls of spare
canvas on the deck. Anything more than a cursory search, however, would
discover their status. Although well able to fight, the thirty corsairs were
vastly outnumbered by the soldiers patrolling the battlements above.

Eyeing the vigilant sentries, Romulus also felt uneasy. His feelings
weren't helped by the fact that, with one exception, neither he nor Tarquinius
trusted a single one of their comrades. Mustafa, the greasy-haired giant
who had nearly drowned by the dock in Barbaricum, was now his devoted
follower, but the rest were hard-bitten sailors or murderous ex-slaves from
India and the shores of the Erythraean Sea, every shade of brown and
black under the sun. The toughest and most treacherous of them all was
Ahmed, the Nubian captain. Unfortunately, he also held their fate in his
hands. Yet, through a combination of guile and luck, they had survived
this far.

Tarquinius nudged Romulus as they glided past the towers and anxious
muttering rippled among the crew. They all had good reason to be
concerned: a row of men's heads, bloodied and decaying, was prominently
displayed on spikes above the nearby battlements. It was a very pointed
warning by the ruling powers of Cana to all those who entered the port.

'Pirates probably,' said the haruspex in a low voice.

'Us, in other words,' replied Romulus, glancing his friend up and down and imagining how he must look himself. The burning hot sun had turned any exposed skin a deep mahogany colour. Like the rest of the crew, Romulus went about the deck in nothing but a loincloth, his feet hard and calloused. His hair had grown long and unkempt and lay in thick black waves, framing his handsome face, which was largely covered by a beard. He was now a fully grown, mature man of twenty. Powerful muscles rippled beneath his dark skin, revealing the scars of battle. On Romulus' upper right arm, covering the mark where his slave brand had been, was a tattoo of Mithras sacrificing the bull.

During their time aboard, Tarquinius had revealed many details about the warrior religion. Its tenets of courage, honour and truth appealed immensely to Romulus, as did the equality between devotees. He had taken to Mithraicism with gusto, finding it helped with his grief for Brennus. Romulus prayed daily now; having the tattoo was another way of showing his devotion. And if they ever reached Rome, it would hide the irregularly healed scar that had caused so much trouble in Margiana.

Rome, he thought longingly.

'We need to keep a low profile here,' said Tarquinius grimly, bringing Romulus back to Cana.

Ahmed also looked concerned, but weeks of sailing off the barren Arabian coast meant that their stocks of food and water were running low. The risk they were taking was a necessary one.

Dozens of dhows similar to their own were tied up side by side with larger merchant ships. Their sterns moved gently as they pulled on the anchors holding them to the sandy harbour floor. On a long quay, men scurried to and fro with bulging sacks, helping to load the vessels. Noises carried across the water: shouted orders from merchants; a woman laughing; mules braying with indignation.

Sitting at one end of the harbour was a menacing fortress, bigger than any they had seen since Barbaricum. Its walls were patrolled by even more soldiers in conical helmets and armed with spears and recurved bows.

'There must be plenty to protect here,' said Ahmed, jerking his head at the imposing structure. His gold earrings shook with the movement. The broad-nosed, full-lipped Nubian had a muscular build, and his ebony skin was covered with a fine latticework of whitened scars. A wide-bladed cutlass was shoved into his belt, its blade spotted with rust and darker stains.

'Cana is one of the main towns in southern Arabia,' replied Tarquinius. 'The *olibanum* grown for miles around is carried in by camel. Once sold, it is transported to Egypt.'

Egypt! Romulus struggled to contain the excitement bubbling up inside him. Reaching this port felt like a real milestone. They were nearer Rome now than at any time since Carrhae.

The Nubian's face also lit up. 'Plenty of vessels to take west of here, then.'

Tarquinius' dark eyes glinted with satisfaction at Ahmed's enthusiasm for continuing the voyage. Thank you, Mithras. You have brought us this far, he thought. Let our journey continue without mishap.

Offered the chance to join the pirates after Romulus' rescue of Mustafa, the two friends had accepted with alacrity. It had seemed like a ticket home, and compared to the other option – execution – had not been difficult to accept. But the reality of life aboard the dhow had been very different, and its range extremely confined. While the merchantmen, their prey, sailed hundreds of miles to and from India, the corsairs preferred not to stray far from their base, a swampy island in the Indus delta. Generally there was no need, with well-laden ships plying the seas around Barbaricum on a constant basis. After two long years, Ahmed had only sailed west with the monsoon because the pickings near Barbaricum had grown lean.

Romulus had been secretly ecstatic, and even the reticent Tarquinius was pleased.

As they drew close to the jetty, a stout man clad in clean white robes took notice and began shouting in their direction. Clutching a tablet and stylus in his hands, he impatiently waved the dhow into a mooring place.

'The harbourmaster,' said Tarquinius. 'A good source of information.'

'And lies,' advised Ahmed as they tied up alongside a broad-bellied merchant vessel. 'Watch what you say in this town. That goes for all of you.' He glared.

The crew nodded. They had already seen the summary justice on offer here.

'Once the harbour dues have been paid, the ship must be reprovisioned,' said Ahmed. 'I need six men for that.'

Reluctant to delay their excursion to shore, everyone looked at the deck.

Unperturbed, the captain simply picked the pirates nearest him; Romulus, Tarquinius and Mustafa were lucky enough to avoid the duty.

'The rest of you can do as you wish, but I want no trouble. Take no swords ashore. Only knives.' Ahmed held up a warning finger. 'Any man who isn't back one hour before nightfall will be left behind.'

Wide grins split the faces of those who were about to spend a day on dry land. It had been many weeks since they had drunk alcohol or visited a brothel. The fact that it was still early morning would not stop any of them. The pirates to be left on board looked suitably miserable.

Romulus considered wearing the mail shirt he'd bought in Barbaricum, but settled for just his ragged military tunic. Too much attention would be drawn to the rusty armour. Feeling naked without a weapon, he attached his dagger to his belt. Tarquinius did likewise. After a bout of sunstroke the previous year, he had finally stopped wearing his hide breastplate, but, stubborn to the last, the ageing haruspex still refused to exchange his leather-bordered skirt for a loincloth. Following the rest, the two friends pulled themselves on to the next boat and made their way towards the jetty. Like a faithful puppy, Mustafa followed. By now, Romulus did not even try and stop him.

Endless varieties of goods were piled on the timber dock. Bales of purple fabric were stacked beside heaps of tortoise shells, large sheets of copper and planks of hardwood. Rich smells wafted through the humid air from mounds of open-necked cloth bags. Prospective buyers dipped their hands in to taste and smell the spices and incense on offer.

'*Olibanum* and myrrh and cinnabar,' breathed Tarquinius, his eyes shining. 'What is sitting right there would make us wealthy beyond our wildest dreams.'

'There are no guards,' said Romulus in amazement.

'They've got that.' Tarquinius glanced at the fortress. 'And there was a chain at the harbour mouth that could be pulled up to stop ships leaving.'

Romulus felt his unease grow.

The haruspex seemed comfortable though, and he quickly forgot about it. After so long at sea, being in a town felt exhilarating.

They pushed their way off the quay and on to Cana's narrow dirt streets, which were lined with primitively built three- and four-storey-high mud-brick houses. The ground floors were occupied by shops, much as they were in Rome. Butchers plied their trade side by side with carpenters, barbers, metalworkers and sellers of meat, fruit and other food.

Except for half-dressed prostitutes beckoning suggestively from doorways, not many women were to be seen. The most numerous men were brown-skinned Arabs in their distinctive white robes, but there were many Indians in loincloths and turbans as well. There was a scattering of Judaeans and Phoenicians, and also some black men, noticeable for their aristocratic faces and high cheekbones.

Romulus nudged Tarquinius. 'They're very different looking to Ahmed.'

'They are from Azania, far to the south of Egypt. Their women are said to be incredibly beautiful.'

'Let's find a whorehouse with some then,' growled Mustafa. 'I haven't had a fuck in an age!'

'A tavern first,' said Romulus, his thirst winning out. 'Off the beaten track.'

Tarquinius nodded and Mustafa did not argue.

The trio made their way off the main streets, and the shop fronts soon became smaller and grimier. Brothels became plentiful, and Mustafa's eyes grew lustful. Urchins in dirty rags homed in, clamouring for coins. Keeping a hand on his purse, Romulus ignored them. Distastefully he picked his way past the human waste thrown from the windows above.

Tarquinius laughed. 'Just like Rome, eh?'

Romulus curled his lip. 'It smells the same all right.'

A moment later, they stumbled upon a dingy, open-fronted inn which would meet their purpose. Sand was scattered on the floor to absorb spilt alcohol, or blood. Small tables and rickety chairs were the only furniture. The dim light inside came from a few guttering lamps hanging from the low ceiling. Most of the customers were Arabs, although there was a smattering of other nationalities. Romulus fought his way to the wooden bar while Tarquinius and Mustafa secured a table in the corner. There were many curious glances, but nobody addressed him, which suited Romulus. Sitting down soon after, however, with a jug and three clay cups, he could feel eyes burning holes in the back of his tunic. Unobtrusively, Romulus loosened his dagger in its sheath.

Oblivious, Tarquinius tasted the wine. Instantly his face screwed up. 'Tastes like horse piss mixed with poor quality *acetum*.'

'It's all they've got,' retorted Romulus. 'Expensive too, so drink up.'

Mustafa laughed and drained his beaker in a single swallow. 'Finding a whore will be more productive. I'm going to check out those brothels,' he said. 'Be all right on your own?'

'We'll be fine.' Romulus glanced round the room, seeing no immediate danger. 'See you back here.'

Mustafa bobbed his head and vanished.

After a time, the wine began to taste a little better. Romulus raised his cup in a silent toast to Brennus. During his time on the dhow, there had been plenty of time to relive the Gaul's last gift to him. Over time, the pain had lessened and while Romulus still felt regret, he also recognised the great debt he owed to Brennus. He would not be sitting here now if his friend hadn't sacrificed himself. Romulus was sure that Mithras would have approved of Brennus' actions.

Thoughts of home also filled his mind. With a warm glow in his belly, Romulus imagined how he might feel at the sight of Rome and of Fabiola. And even of Julia, the barmaid he'd met on that last fateful night in the capital.

'Welcome to Cana,' someone said in Latin.

Romulus almost choked on a mouthful of wine. Red-faced, he looked up at the speaker.

A tall, long-jawed man with short hair had approached from a nearby table. His companions, three heavily built men wearing swords, remained seated.

'Do I know you?' Tarquinius asked coolly.

'No, friend,' said the stranger, raising his hands peaceably. 'We've not met before.'

'What do you want?'

'A friendly chat,' he said. 'Romans are very rare here in Cana.'

Romulus had managed to regain his composure. 'Who said we're Romans?' he growled.

The newcomer pointed at Tarquinius' leather-bordered skirt and Romulus' faded russet tunic.

Neither of the friends acknowledged his keen observation.

But he was not to be put off. 'My name is Lucius Varus, *optio* and veteran of the Seventh Legion,' he explained. 'I'm part-owner of a merchant vessel now, though. Every year, I sail between Egypt and Arabia, buying and selling.'

From the rich cut of his tunic and the large emerald ring on one hand, it was obvious that Varus was doing very well.

Romulus was curious now. 'What do you trade in?'

'Here they like Italian wine, olive oil, Greek statues and copper,' Varus replied. 'And *olibanum* and myrrh are always in demand in Egypt and Italy. Tortoiseshell and hardwood too.'

Rome, thought Romulus excitedly. This man has travelled recently from Rome.

'Are you not also traders?' Varus enquired.

He's fishing, thought Romulus. But surely there was no harm in a little conversation?

'No,' replied Tarquinius, putting him at his ease. 'We're on our way back to Italy.'

'How long have you been away?'

Romulus grimaced. 'Five years.'

'Really?' Varus exclaimed. 'Even a journey to India takes less than twelve months each way.'

Romulus and Tarquinius looked at each other.

'We fought for Crassus,' said Tarquinius slowly.

'Vulcan's balls!' Varus' mouth opened and closed. 'Are you deserters?'

'Watch your mouth!' Romulus snarled, thumping the table with his fist.

'Peace, friend. I meant no insult,' said Varus in a placatory tone. Alarmed, his companions stood, but he raised a hand and they sat back down. He then gave a knowing look to the barman and a jug of wine quickly materialised. Varus drank half a beaker first to show they had nothing to fear. 'Try some of this,' he urged. 'It's the best Falernian. Brought it here myself.'

Suspiciously, Tarquinius tried it. His frown disappeared, replaced by a broad smile. Reassured, Romulus reached for the wine himself, pouring himself a generous measure. It had been years since he had drunk anything that tasted better than vinegar.

'Not all of Crassus' soldiers were killed at Carrhae,' Tarquinius revealed. 'Ten thousand of us were taken prisoner.'

'Rome was full of the terrible news at the time,' exclaimed Varus. 'It was soon forgotten by most, though. What happened to you?'

'The Parthians marched us more than fifteen hundred miles into the east,' said Romulus bitterly. 'To a place even the gods have forsaken.'

'Where?'

'Margiana.'

Varus looked intrigued.

'We served as border guards,' Romulus continued. 'Constantly fighting the Parthians' enemies – Sogdians, Scythians and Indians.'

'A hard fate, by Jupiter,' muttered Varus. 'Especially as many of Crassus' legionaries had almost completed their army service.' He took a sip of wine. 'You two escaped, obviously.'

Romulus nodded sadly, remembering the cost of that escape.

Varus noticed his face. 'An arduous journey, no doubt.'

'Yes.' Romulus wasn't about to explain more. 'But eventually we reached Barbaricum.'

Like all merchants, Varus had heard of the large trading city. 'And then?'

'Joined a trader bound for Arabia with a cargo of spices and timber,' lied Tarquinius smoothly. 'Here we are.'

'By Jupiter, you've travelled the whole world,' said Varus in amazement. 'I thought you were just guards from another merchant ship.'

Still upset by the memory of Brennus, Romulus drew his dagger and held it flat on the table. At this range, he could stab Varus before his companions had even noticed. 'I don't like being accused of lying,' he hissed.

Tarquinius stared at Varus. 'We've been through a lot, you understand.'

'Of course,' he replied quickly. 'Your tale is remarkable.'

'Think what you like,' said Tarquinius mildly. 'It's true. And we're the lucky ones. If they're still alive, the other poor bastards are rotting in Margiana.'

Varus looked at them again. This time he saw the world-weary expressions, Romulus' threadbare military jerkin and the holes in Tarquinius' leather bordered skirt. Neither really looked like someone hired to protect a cargo of spices. 'I apologise,' he said, filling both their beakers to the brim. He raised a toast. 'To those under the gods' protection.'

Romulus sheathed his knife and they all drank.

There was silence for a time.

'You won't know about the situation in Rome, then?' asked Varus at length. 'It's not good.'

'We've heard nothing,' Romulus replied eagerly.

Tarquinius too gave Varus all his attention. 'Tell us,' he requested.

'Things between Pompey and Caesar began to sour about four years ago,' said Varus. 'It started with the death of his wife Julia, Caesar's daughter. You heard about that?'

Romulus nodded. It had been news when Crassus' army was in Asia Minor.

'Then Crassus was killed, and the whole balance of the triumvirate disappeared.' Varus frowned. 'But Caesar was busy campaigning in Gaul, so Pompey relaxed a little. Took a back seat for a while. Every politician on the Seven Hills jumped in, trying to get into office. They used intimidation, bribery or even force. Crime soared, and there were regular riots. The blame for that can be laid at the feet of Pulcher and Milo. Their gangs were clashing on a daily basis for control of the city. The streets became very unsafe, even in the middle of the day.'

'Sounds terrible,' Romulus said, hanging on to every word. Uneasy memories of his vision at the crucifix were beginning to surface.

'It was.' Varus made a face. 'The worst violence was after Pulcher was killed by gladiators working for Milo. Almost three years ago, that was.'

'Milo had been hiring fighters for some time, hadn't he?' Romulus could remember the external duty, which was much desired by those in the *ludus*.

'Indeed,' Varus replied. 'But they went too far by murdering Pulcher. His followers went crazy afterwards. There was a huge battle in the Forum Romanum, and hundreds were killed. The fuckers even burned down the Senate House!'

Romulus paled. His vision *had* been accurate. He looked to Tarquinius, who gave him a tiny, reassuring smile. It did little for his nerves.

Unnoticing, Varus warmed to his task. 'After that, the Senate had little choice. They made Pompey sole consul, with dictatorial powers. Under Marcus Petreius, one of his legions was brought in to quell the trouble.' Seeing their shock, he scowled. 'I know. Soldiers in the capital! But it calmed things down. And after Milo was exiled to Massilia, everything went quiet for a few months.'

Romulus tried to relax. According to Tarquinius, Fabiola had survived the riot in the Forum, so hopefully she was safe. Mithras, he thought, and Jupiter, Greatest and Best, look after my sister.

'But Cato and the Optimates were still on the warpath,' Varus continued.

'They wanted Caesar to return to Rome and stand trial for various things – using violence during his previous term as consul, exceeding his remit in the conquest of Gaul. Meanwhile, Caesar was eager to continue in office – it didn't matter which one – to avoid prosecution. His campaigns had made him incredibly wealthy, so to further his ends, he bought up every politician who'd take his money.'

'Shrewd,' said Tarquinius.

'Caesar's supporters repeatedly blocked the Optimates' attempts to corner him,' agreed Varus. 'As a result, there was often stalemate in the Senate.'

'And Pompey sat on the fence?' asked Romulus.

'Yes. He was often "sick", or missed crucial debates.' Varus shrugged. 'I think he was trying to stay out of trouble.'

'Or he knew what might happen,' added Tarquinius.

'You could be right,' agreed Varus with a heavy sigh. 'But for whatever reason, Pompey has finally joined the Optimates and all those who want Caesar's head on a plate. Nine months ago, it was only the veto of Curio, a tribune paid off by Caesar, which prevented the passing of a decree recalling him to face justice. More attempts have been made; it's just a matter of time before they succeed.'

'They're pushing Caesar into a corner,' said Romulus. It was all starting to make worrying sense. Things had changed dramatically in Rome since his departure. For the worse. If he did manage to return, what would happen to him? And to Fabiola? Suddenly there was more to worry about than just revenge.

Varus nodded resignedly. 'If they force the issue, he won't lay down his command meekly either.'

'You think it'll come to war?' queried Romulus.

'Who knows?' Varus replied. 'Yet that was all the talk on the street and in the bathhouses when I left.'

Romulus could not explain why, but he wanted Caesar to come out on top. Was it because of the cruel mass combat sponsored by Pompey that he and Brennus had taken part in? Unusually required to fight to the death, scores of gladiators had died that day. No, it was more than that, he decided. Unlike Crassus, Caesar sounded like an inspiring leader – a man to follow. And Romulus did not like lots of people ganging up on another. That was what had happened to him, in the *ludus* and in Margiana.

In contrast to Romulus, Tarquinius felt some pleasure at the Republic's plight. The state which had crushed that of the Etruscans, his people, was in danger of collapsing. Then he frowned. Although he hated Rome, perhaps this anarchic situation was not desirable. If the Republic fell, what would replace it? Olenus' voice rang in Tarquinius' head, clear as a bell, and a chill ran down his spine. 'Caesar must remember he is mortal. Your son must tell him that.' He glanced sidelong at Romulus. Was this why Mithras had preserved them thus far?

A blinding realisation struck Tarquinius. Why had he not thought of it before? He stared again at Romulus, who meant as much to him as a . . . son.

Then Tarquinius stiffened. There was danger nearby.

'We're all better off out of the army, that's for sure,' said Varus jovially. 'Who wants to fight other Italians?'

Neither of the others replied. Romulus was daydreaming again, lost in memories of Rome. Deep in concentration, Tarquinius' eyes were distant.

Suddenly Varus grinned. 'Why don't you come and work for me? I'll pay you well.'

Tarquinius turned to regard him. 'Thank you, but no.'

Disappointed, Romulus saw the faraway look on the haruspex' face which often presaged a prophecy. His protest died in his throat. Something was up.

Tarquinius drained his cup and stood. 'My thanks for the wine,' he said. 'May your trip be profitable. We have to go.' He jerked his head at Romulus.

Leaving the bewildered Varus behind them, the pair headed outside.

'What is it?'

'I'm not sure,' Tarquinius replied. 'A threat of some kind.'

They had gone only a few paces before the slap of sandals reached their ears. Reaching a larger thoroughfare, they saw Zebulon, a Judaean member of the crew, running past. One of the men chosen by Ahmed to help with the provisions, he beckoned to them urgently.

'What is it?' cried Romulus.

Zebulon slowed down, his chest heaving. 'Back to the dhow!'

'Why?' demanded Tarquinius. 'What's wrong?'

Zebulon sidled closer. 'Customs,' he whispered. 'All the ships are being searched.'

No more needed to be said.

Yet again, Romulus was amazed by the haruspex' ability. Then he remembered their companion. 'Mustafa!' he cried. 'Where is he?'

'There were at least a dozen whorehouses,' said Tarquinius. 'You can't search them all.'

Instinctively, Romulus looked up at the narrow band of sky that was visible between the closely built buildings. Nothing. Frustrated, he turned to Tarquinius. 'We can't just leave him.'

'There's no time,' the haruspex muttered. 'And Mustafa is master of his own fate. He'll find a place on any vessel.'

Zebulon was showing no inclination to look for his crewmate either.

Romulus nodded jerkily. It was not as if they were leaving Brennus behind. And after five years of hell, the last thing he wanted was to be caught as a pirate. Yet if the *olibanum* taken from the coastal villages was discovered, that is precisely what would happen. Then they would all be executed. The knowledge gave Romulus extra speed, and he soon outstripped Zebulon and Tarquinius, pushing through the throng. At full tilt, they made their way through the maze of streets.

Raised voices and shouts were coming from the quay, where a large crowd had gathered. Like people the world over, the denizens of Cana were happy to relieve the daily boredom of making a living by watching someone else's misfortune.

Halfway along the dock, Romulus saw the harbourmaster, accompanied by a number of officials and a group of heavily armed soldiers. The stout figure was gesticulating furiously at a man on a large ship tied up near the merchants' stalls. At his signal, his men notched arrows to their bowstrings.

Unhappy at the prospect of being searched, the captain stood his ground.

The harbourmaster pointed angrily. At once, the bows were aimed at the sailors on the ship. Loud gasps rose from the crowd. Finally the captain spat into the sea, acknowledging defeat. With a furious wave, he beckoned the officials on board. Full of self-importance, the harbourmaster clambered down first. Several soldiers followed. Still covering the crew, the others watched.

'Now's our chance,' Romulus urged. 'While they're busy with that one.'

Sauntering casually on to the quay, he began to weave his way between the onlookers. Tarquinius and Zebulon were close on his heels. Few people glanced at the trio as they passed by. The goings-on were far more interesting.

They found Ahmed uneasily pacing the dhow's deck.

'Seen any of the others?' he barked.

Romulus and Tarquinius shook their heads.

'Just the ones I sent back,' said Zebulon. 'And these two.'

'Gods above!' spat Ahmed. 'Three are still missing.'

It was hardly the crewmembers' fault, thought Romulus resentfully. They had been given permission to stay ashore until an hour before sunset. Zebulon had done well to find so many.

The stocky Nubian stamped up and down as the crew quietly prepared to leave. By the time the soldiers had finished checking the first vessel, he was growing increasingly nervous. Although there were two more ships to be searched before his own, Ahmed could take the pressure no longer. Losing three crewmembers was of less concern than the alternative.

'Cast off!'

His muttered order was immediately obeyed by the worried pirates.

Romulus could not help himself. 'What about Mustafa?' he tried one more time.

'He's a fool,' snapped Ahmed. 'And so are the others. They can fend for themselves.'

Romulus looked away, still feeling quite guilty about leaving the long-haired hulk behind. He sent up a swift prayer to the gods, asking them to watch over Mustafa, who had been a comrade of sorts for over two years.

Then he glanced at the rows of heads on the battlements above. Eyeless, nearly fleshless and with grinning teeth, they resembled demons of the underworld. Once they had been men though. Lawbreakers. Criminals. Pirates. A whiff of rotting flesh reached Romulus' nostrils. Stomach turning, he moved his gaze to the open sea.

Chapter XXIII: The Rubicon

Ravenna, northern Italy, winter 50/49 BC

Fabiola shivered miserably and moved closer to the fire. Hot wine, thick clothes, underfloor heating – even staying in bed didn't help. Nothing she did could get her warm. Snow lay thick on the ground outside and a biting north wind was rattling the red tiles on the roof, as it had all week. Fabiola's lips tightened. The new year might have begun, but the weather gave little sign of improving. Neither did her mood.

Naturally, there was more to Fabiola's bad humour than the cold. Yet there was much to be grateful for – she acknowledged that. She was still here, close to one of the men shaping the future of Rome. Despite this, she felt hollow inside.

Fabiola reflected on the two years which had passed since her reunion with Brutus. Her fond memory of falling into his arms would always be soured by what she had said at the feast a few hours later. The foolish gaffe had offended Caesar, shaken her confidence and deeply angered her lover. Brutus was extremely loyal to his general and it had taken Fabiola an age to repair the damage she had done. But, coaxed, pampered and tantalised, Brutus had eventually succumbed to her charms once more. Meanwhile, Fabiola determined never to repeat such a public embarrassment. After Caesar's thinly veiled threat, she kept a low profile, placing her quest to discover her father's identity on indefinite hold. In the security of Brutus' quarters, she did not have to worry about Caesar or Scaevola, or anyone else. Confused and scared, Fabiola buried her head in the sand. For a time, that was enough.

Outside, though, events were moving on.

After Alesia, Gaul belonged to Rome in all but name, and in response to Caesar's stunning victory, the Senate had voted twenty days of public thanksgiving. It also awarded him the rare privilege of standing for consul while still in Gaul, rather than being present in Rome as was the norm. Ushered in by Caesar's allies, this new law crystallised the issue which most troubled Cato and the Optimates. If Caesar moved seamlessly from the proconsulship of Gaul – his current position – to the consulship of the Republic, he would at no stage be a private citizen, open to prosecution. While this concerned the adoring public not at all, it enraged Caesar's enemies. Since the general's illegal actions during his first term as consul, when intimidation and violence were used against his co-consul and other politicians, they had been waiting for their chance to strike. Now it was to be denied them. The intrigue thickened. Plots were hatched, deals struck and impassioned speeches made. One thing was for certain: Cato would not take this lying down. If it took him the rest of his life, Caesar would face justice in Rome.

Camped in Gaul, Caesar heard all the news from the capital. Frustrated, he could do little about it. War beckoned once more. Despite Vercingetorix' overwhelming defeat at Alesia, some tribes had refused to submit to Roman rule. Twelve months of campaigning followed as the final reduction of Gaul took place. Accompanying Brutus and his general, Fabiola knew how angered Caesar was by the Optimates' attempts to disgrace and punish him. Her curiosity and interest had been aroused as she listened nightly to her lover's rants. Focusing again now on his arguments – although unassuming, Brutus was a convincing speaker – finally lifted Fabiola's black mood.

Did the Senate not know what Caesar had done for Rome? Brutus had exclaimed. The dangers he had endured in its name? The glory he had heaped upon its people? Was he supposed just to lay down his command and walk into the lion's den while Pompey retained all his legions? It was not surprising that Caesar refused to submit to the Optimates' demands, thought Fabiola. Placed in the same situation, she would not. She doubted that Pompey, his rival, would either.

But like a dog shaking a rat, Cato had not given up. Months passed and session after session of the Senate was taken up with endless debates about Caesar's command: the number of legions he should keep; how many legates he was to be allowed; when exactly he should give up his post. Many senators were won over to the Optimates by these arguments, but liberal donations of Caesar's Gaulish gold ensured that an equal number remained loyal to him. Curio, Caesar's paid-off and eloquent tribune, also vetoed every attempt to bring Caesar to bay in the Senate. With a dreadful inevitability, the house began to split down the middle. In the face of the Optimates' increasingly bitter campaign, staying neutral had become well-nigh impossible. Yet, for his own reasons, Pompey managed to do just that, appearing to agree first with one side and then the other. Worked on relentlessly by Cato and his allies though, he finally gave in. His comments started as veiled threats, but over the months, became more hard-line.

Fabiola looked out at the flurries of snow scudding past the window, and a chill struck her heart. She had imagined this day, but never thought it would truly come to pass.

Over a month before, guided cleverly by Curio, the Senate had passed a motion decreeing that Pompey's commands in Italy and Hispania should not be allowed to run on beyond those of Caesar. It was a neat example of skilled diplomacy in the face of looming conflict. And fair enough, thought Fabiola. But the unhappy extremists then succeeded in pressuring Pompey to declare his hand. Visited the very next day by one of the consuls, he was handed a sword and asked to march against Caesar to rescue the Republic. Whether they realised the significance of their actions or not, the Optimates were requesting the services of the only other man in Italy with a huge private army. And he had accepted. 'I will do so,' Pompey answered after a moment's hesitation, 'if no other way can be found.' This inflammatory remark was followed by the immediate mobilisation of his troops.

Caesar's response to this illegal action was typically fast. Two legions were summoned from Gaul to Ravenna, just twenty-five miles from the frontier, the River Rubicon.

For the first time in two generations, the Republic was on the brink of civil war.

Fabiola found herself firmly in Caesar's camp. As Brutus' lover, it was not altogether surprising. Her old, deep-rooted suspicion and more recent fear of Caesar had been submerged beneath a wave of resentful admiration. A consummate military leader, he had also acted intelligently throughout the political storm which had raged since. Even now, at this late hour, Caesar was offering diplomatic solutions to his impasse with the Senate. But the Optimates were having none of it. An offer by Caesar to surrender Transalpine Gaul immediately and his other provinces on the day of his election to a second consulship was rejected. So was a revived proposal to disarm at the same time as Pompey. Even Cicero's attempt to open negotiations had been stamped down. Three days before, a motion demanding that Caesar disband his legions by March or be considered a traitor had only been halted by the vetoes of Marcus Antonius and Cassius Longinus, the new tribunes. Both were Caesar's men through and through.

As Brutus said, Caesar was being boxed in from all sides. It was a bad place to put such a skilled general.

Utilising her only resource, Fabiola prayed daily to Mithras, asking for protection for herself and Brutus. And although she found herself supporting Caesar, Fabiola could not include him in her requests for divine help. Part of her just held back. Was it because of the druid's warning, which regularly returned to her? Fabiola wasn't sure. Besides, the man acted as if he did not care what the gods thought. Caesar chose his own fate. Time would tell what that would be.

There was a clatter of hobnails along the corridor; then the door opened, bringing with it a blast of cold air. And Brutus. His usually jovial face was thunderous.

'My love,' Fabiola exclaimed, rising to meet him. 'What is it?'

'The Optimates brought that damn motion before the Senate again,' Brutus replied indignantly. 'Demanding that Caesar relinquish his legions by March.'

Fabiola took his arm. 'But Antonius and Longinus have their vetoes.'

He barked a short, angry laugh. 'They weren't there.'

Her brow wrinkled. 'I don't understand.'

'The bastards warned both tribunes not to attend, "for the good of their health". They were forced to flee the city with Curio, disguised as slaves! The motion was passed without opposition.' Brutus swelled with outrage. 'And they accuse Caesar of acting illegally.' He broke away and paced the room like a caged animal.

Fabiola watched him for a moment. 'What will Caesar do?' she asked, knowing the answer.

'What do you think?' Brutus snapped back.

Fabiola flinched, only half acting.

Instantly his face gentled. 'I'm sorry, my love. But Caesar has been declared an enemy of the Republic. He is ordered to surrender to the Senate, and accept the consequences.'

'He won't do that, surely?' she asked.

Brutus shook his head emphatically.

Fabiola hardly dared say it. 'To the Rubicon then?'

'Yes,' cried Brutus. 'Tonight! The Thirteenth Legion is already on the near bank. They only await Caesar's arrival before crossing.'

'So soon?' Startled, Fabiola glanced at her lover. But he was not joking. 'What about Pompey's forces?'

His lips parted in a wolfish smile. 'The fool has none in the area, and the garrisons of Ariminium and other nearby towns have been bribed well.'

Fabiola was relieved. There would be no immediate bloodshed. 'What are his plans?'

'You know Caesar,' Brutus replied with a wink. 'Never happy unless he goes for the jugular.'

She paled. 'Rome?'

He grinned in acknowledgement.

Fabiola felt faint. This was far more than she had expected. Although it was not all here in Ravenna, Caesar's battle-hardened army was the most powerful ever controlled by one man in the Republic's history. Yet once assembled, Pompey's would be far larger. The impending clash over which of the two had ultimate power boded ill for the future of democracy and the rights of the ordinary citizen. How had things come to such a pass? 'And us?' she asked.

'This is when Caesar most needs support.' He smiled fiercely. 'We go with him.'

Fabiola's heart began to pound. Fear and dread blended with a strange excitement. She would witness a Roman leader commit the most treasonous act possible.

Crossing the Rubicon under arms.

Awe filled Fabiola. The druid had been right. If only he had revealed more about Romulus, she thought with a pang of anguish.

'You'll hear about it later,' Brutus revealed.

Fabiola looked at him enquiringly.

'Caesar's holding a banquet. We're invited.'

'Is he not meeting with you and the other officers?' she asked, confused.

'Quite the opposite. Relaxation before a battle is the best policy,' Brutus laughed. 'Just remember not to ask him about Gergovia.'

Fabiola giggled, then her face turned serious. 'Don't worry, my love. I won't ever let you down again like that.'

'I know.' Stepping closer, Brutus looked into her eyes. 'You, I can rely on more than anyone else.'

This comment lit up Fabiola's heart. It confirmed that Brutus was hers more than Caesar's. An important battle had already been won.

To Fabiola, that was more important than any of the ones to follow.

Fabiola had long ago lost her embarrassment when being introduced to nobility. By now most, if not all, of Brutus' colleagues knew her history. Unknown to her lover, one or two had even been clients in the Lupanar. Often, though, Romans were quite accepting of slaves who had been freed, which made her life much easier. As far as the military officers Fabiola encountered were concerned, she was a beautiful, intelligent young woman whom Brutus valued considerably. She suspected that many were some-what jealous and would have liked her for themselves.

At the feast that night, Fabiola was grateful for her acquired poise when introduced to Longinus, one of the new tribunes. Meeting him made Fabiola so nervous that she wanted to vomit, yet she controlled herself adroitly. Together with Antonius and Curio, Longinus had brought the news of the Senate's actions to Ravenna just a few hours before. But that was not what interested Fabiola most. This was the officer who had escaped from Carrhae with his honour and the survivors of his legion intact. He had also brought news of the terrible defeat to Rome. While it was like reopening an old wound, Fabiola could not help wanting to pick Longinus' brains, asking him not about his role in the impending civil war but his experiences in Parthia. All her hopes about Romulus had resurfaced with a vengeance the instant he appeared.

Longinus was surprised. 'Why would you want to know about that burning hell?' he asked, his scarred face confused. 'I try never to think about it.'

A quick glance over her shoulder told Fabiola that Brutus was not watching. She turned coy, a policy which rarely failed with men. 'Don't be modest, general,' she purred. 'I'm told that if you had been in charge at Carrhae, the outcome might have been quite different.'

Flattered, Longinus' grizzled features softened. 'I don't know about that,' he protested. 'But Crassus certainly wouldn't listen to my advice that day.'

She nodded understandingly. 'How bad was it?'

Longinus scowled. 'Beyond your imagination, lady. Nothing but sand as far as the eye could see. Temperatures hotter than Hades. Scant food and no water.' He sighed. 'And the damn Parthians. Little men for the most part, but by all the gods, they can ride and shoot arrows. Ordinary legionaries just can't fight them.' His face darkened. 'And thanks to the treachery of our so-called Nabataean allies, we had precious few cavalry.'

'They say that was Crassus' greatest mistake,' Fabiola threw in. 'Not having reliable cavalry.' She was pleased to see respect appear in his face. Longinus did not know it, but the sentiment was one Fabiola had heard Brutus utter before.

'True enough,' Longinus agreed. 'When our Gaulish horsemen were killed with Publius, Crassus' son, the rest simply fled. There we were on a flat, burning plain: thirty thousand infantry facing ten thousand horse, most of them mounted archers with an unlimited supply of arrows. You can imagine what happened next.' He fell into a grim silence.

While Fabiola had heard plenty of snippets and gossip about Carrhae, Longinus had painted a far more terrifying picture. A lump formed in her throat at the thought of Romulus being there. The horror was incalculable. Fabiola swallowed, taking consolation from her vision in the Mithraeum. To be present at the battle she had seen, her brother had somehow survived the devastation of Crassus' army. It had to be the gods who had saved Romulus, Fabiola thought desperately. And they would continue to look after him.

'My lady, what is it?'

Some of her inner turmoil must have shown, Fabiola realised. She was about to lie, and then saw that there was no point. Longinus knew of her origins. 'My brother was there,' she said simply.

'I see. Was he also a . . .' Longinus paused, looking uncomfortable.

'Slave? Yes, he was. And a gladiator,' Fabiola answered, without batting an eyelid. 'I think he joined a mercenary cohort as an ordinary soldier.'

Longinus failed to conceal his surprise. 'Their recruitment policies are, shall we say, a little more relaxed than the legions. Yet most of them fought very well. At one stage during the battle, twenty brave mercenaries who had been isolated with Publius were allowed to return unharmed to our lines. Not that it did them much good, probably. Rome lost so many good soldiers that day.' He looked her in the eyes. 'A few irregulars retreated to the Euphrates with my legion. Was your brother among them?'

Fabiola shook her head. 'I don't think so.'

He patted her arm.

'Romulus survived though,' she said stoutly.

Longinus gave her a disbelieving look.

'I'm sure of it.'

'I see. If he did, then . . .' Longinus flashed a false grin. 'Who knows?'

Fabiola smiled brightly at him. The grizzled tribune was trying to protect her from the brutal reality of the Roman survivors' fates. But he had not seen what she had after drinking the *homa*. Nor heard the druid's dying words. They had been cut short, which meant that there was still hope. While her fortunes continued to soar, Fabiola had to believe that those of Romulus stayed on an even keel at least. It was either that, or go mad.

'Fabiola?' It was Brutus' voice. 'Caesar has personally requested that we attend him.'

Longinus inclined his head and stood aside.

Murmuring her thanks, Fabiola followed Brutus, who seemed delighted. 'What does he want?' she asked nervously. Since Alesia, there had not been a private, face-to-face meeting. In public with other people around, yes. But like this, no.

'He's already done it with Antonius and a couple of the others,' replied Brutus. 'I think it's to toast our good fortune in the days ahead.'

At the entrance to a side chamber stood four smartly turned-out, tough-looking veterans. As the couple drew near, they stiffened to attention. An *optio*, the most senior, slapped a fist off his mail shirt and saluted.

Brutus languidly acknowledged the gesture. They passed inside, into Caesar's personal quarters. The man himself was alone, bent over a detailed map of Italy laid out on a nearby desk. Still unaware of their presence, he stabbed a finger down on to the parchment. 'Rome,' he muttered.

Brutus grinned.

Not for the first time, Fabiola was struck by how alike Caesar and Romulus were. She herself bore the same fair complexion, aquiline nose and piercing eyes. And while their stations in life were worlds apart, Fabiola felt the burning drive to succeed that she saw in Caesar. Here he was, unafraid to take on the entire institution of the Republic. A similar stubborn courage had burned in Romulus' heart; it did in hers too. And while Fabiola's task might be less ambitious than Caesar's, she would not stop until she discovered who had raped her mother. And taken revenge upon him. *Even if it is Caesar*, thought Fabiola fiercely. *I owe it to Mother. And Romulus.* At once doubt filled her. *Is he really my father? How in the name of all the gods can I know?*

Finally Caesar sensed their presence. Straightening, he gave them both a warm smile. 'Thank you for coming.'

'My pleasure, sir,' replied Brutus.

'And mine.' Fabiola bowed deeply.

He offered them both *mulsum*. 'To a swift victory,' said Caesar, raising his glass. 'Or to the Senate seeing sense.'

Smiling, they drank.

'This is a sad day for the Republic,' commented Caesar. His voice changed, growing angry. 'But they leave me no option. The most successful general in our history should not be treated like a dog.'

'Of course not, sir,' agreed Brutus indignantly. 'Pompey will not lay down his commands or disband his legions, so why should you?'

Fabiola murmured in agreement.

'Pompey is no raw recruit,' warned Caesar. 'I hope that he and the Optimates decide to negotiate, or this could be a long struggle.'

'Gaul only took seven years, sir,' said Brutus with a grin. 'What's another few?'

Caesar threw back his head and laughed before regarding Brutus steadily. 'My success has a lot to do with good men like you,' he said. 'I do not forget these things.'

'Thank you, sir,' replied Brutus.

Fabiola was delighted by this show of affection.

They made polite conversation for some time. Then Caesar reached into a drawer on his desk. 'I need you to do something important for me,' he said conspiratorially to Brutus. 'It won't take long.'

'Anything, sir.' Brutus looked eager.

A rolled parchment appeared in Caesar's hand. 'These are fresh orders for the troops in Ariminium.' He saw Fabiola's confusion and explained. 'I sent some there yesterday, dressed in civilian clothing.'

'You want me to travel on ahead, sir?' asked Brutus.

'No. Just deliver it to the *optio* who's waiting outside by my carriage. He knows where to go.'

Taking the parchment, Brutus hurried from the room.

Left alone with Caesar, Fabiola smiled uneasily. Had this been planned? For a short time, her worries seemed unfounded as Caesar asked solicitously about her wellbeing and hopes for the future.

'Will you bear him children?' he asked.

Fabiola coloured. 'If the gods will it, yes.' Using her knowledge of herbs from the Lupanar, she had avoided pregnancy this far. Consolidating her new position was far more important. Naturally, Brutus knew nothing of this. Trying not to look nervous, she fiddled with one of her gold and carnelian earrings.

Seemingly satisfied, Caesar took Fabiola into another chamber, where he showed off his gilded breastplate and red general's cloak. 'That's what I'll be wearing later,' he said. 'At the Rubicon.'

'You will look magnificent,' gushed Fabiola, listening out anxiously for Brutus. What was taking him so long? 'Quite the conquering hero.'

'You certainly know how to compliment a man,' said Caesar, leaning in close. 'Brutus is very lucky to have a woman like you.'

'Thank you, general.' There was a soft clunk, and Fabiola looked down. Something glittered in the carpet. It was her earring, which had now fallen off. Fabiola bent to pick it up, revealing rather more cleavage than she intended. When she stood, Caesar was eyeing her flesh greedily. Terrified, Fabiola froze.

'So young,' he murmured. 'So perfect.'

There was a new, predatory look in Caesar's eyes which made Fabiola feel very uncomfortable. She backed away a step, her fist clenching on the earring until it hurt.

He followed silently.

Retreating further, scared now, Fabiola collided with the wall. There was nowhere else to go. She tried not to panic. Where was Brutus?

Caesar stepped forward. Wine fumes filled her nostrils. 'You're a real beauty.'

Fabiola looked down, praying that he would go away. Instead he reached out and cupped her breasts. Next he began to lick her neck. Terrified and disgusted, Fabiola did not dare react. This was one of the two most important men in the Republic, while she was just a nobleman's mistress. A nobody.

At length, Caesar paused. 'You were a slave before.'

She nodded.

'Then you should be used to this,' Caesar hissed, lifting her dress.

Silent tears of fury ran down Fabiola's cheeks.

Breathing heavily, he pulled aside her underclothes and fumbled with her.

Mithras and Jupiter, she thought. Help me! But there was no divine intervention. Nor any sign of Brutus.

Caesar's efforts grew more frantic, and Fabiola felt his erection pressing forward against her thigh. 'No,' she cried. 'Please!'

One of the legionaries outside laughed, instantly arousing Fabiola's suspicions. Perhaps this was not the first time Caesar had assaulted a woman?

Hearing the noise, he stopped for a moment, listening.

Fabiola's heart leapt, but it was a false alarm. Instead of releasing her, Caesar twisted Fabiola's arm and forced her on to her knees with him. She moaned with fear.

'Be quiet, or I'll hurt you.'

Fabiola was unsure why, but the words struck a deep chord. Suddenly she knew. She just knew. Caesar *was* the rapist. He was her father.

'Take off your dress,' he ordered. 'I'm going to fuck you on the floor.'

An image of Velvinna flashed before her eyes. Naked. Helpless. Alone. Twenty-one years before, this man had done the same thing to her mother. Burning fury consumed Fabiola. 'No,' she snarled. 'I won't.'

Caesar drew back his hand to strike her.

And she prepared to fight back with all her strength.

'Fabiola?' Brutus' voice was not far away. 'Caesar? Where are they?'

There was an awkward silence.

'Answer me!' Brutus shouted.

'In the other room,' one of the sentries reluctantly muttered.

'Stand aside!'

Caesar cursed under his breath. Hastily rearranging his clothing, he got to his feet.

Fabiola was quick to do so as well. Brutus must not suspect anything. She knew his temper. Brutus was liable to lash out at anyone who had assaulted Fabiola in such a manner, even Caesar, his general. The consequences if he did that were far too grave to even consider. For both of them. She had to act as if everything were normal. Inspiration hit, and Fabiola opened the throbbing palm of her right hand. On it lay her gold and carnelian earring, now crushed. Overcome by terror, she had been unaware of her actions until that moment.

Brutus appeared in the doorway. 'There you are,' he said, relieved. His brow creased at the sight of Caesar and his lover standing so close together. 'What's going on?'

Caesar self-consciously cleared his throat.

'Nothing, my darling. The general was showing me his armour. Then I lost this,' answered Fabiola brightly, holding out her hand. Lamplight flashed off the mangled piece of jewellery, and she prayed he would not peer too closely at it. 'We were just looking for it.'

'I see,' Brutus answered, looking suspicious. 'The *optio* has left, sir.'

'Good. Time to make my excuses to the guests,' Caesar announced briskly. 'You should do so too. We need to reach the Rubicon by dawn at the latest.'

'Of course, sir,' Brutus replied.

'Until the next time.' Caesar bowed to Fabiola, an arrogant half-smile curving his lips at the double meaning only they understood. His secret was safe with her. A former slave, Fabiola would never dare say anything to Brutus. And if she did, he would simply deny it.

Fabiola graciously inclined her head in response, but her thoughts were all of bloody revenge.

Brutus led her outside. 'You look tired, my love,' he said, stroking her arm. 'You can sleep on the journey. I'll wake you when we get to the ford.'

Barely able to conceal her anger, Fabiola nodded.

'Rome awaits us,' called Caesar from behind them. 'The die has been cast.'

'And may Fortuna grant that it falls on a six,' answered Brutus, grinning.

Fabiola wasn't listening. You would even rape your own daughter, she thought furiously. Filthy bastard. A boiling rage consumed her, renewing all her energy. She would not rest again until Caesar had paid for his crime. And whether he knew it or not, Brutus would be the tool. Fabiola would work on the flash of suspicion that she had seen until it was a roaring flame of resentment and jealousy. And she would take her time.

Mithras, she prayed fervently. And Jupiter, Greatest and Best. Grant me just one more thing in my life.

The death of my father.

Chapter XXIV: The Erythraean Sea

Nearly eighteen months pass . . .
Off the Arabian coast, summer 48 BC

Ahmed and his pirates survived because they lived carefully. The Nubian captain kept the dhow in the waters around the horn of Arabia, which all ships rounded on the way to and from India. By day, they sailed along the coastline, searching for vessels that were small enough to overwhelm easily. Then, before dark every evening, Ahmed would seek out secluded coves and bays to anchor in. Wary since Cana of his crew being recognised as corsairs, he avoided any inlets with villages or towns unless absolutely necessary. In quiet anchorages, no prying eyes could watch them. And there they found brackish water in shallow streams, trickling down from the mountains that formed the backbone of southern Arabia.

The pirates' solitary lifestyle meant that for much of the time, their diet consisted solely of fish caught with hand lines. This was monotonous in the extreme, and at every opportunity, Romulus would go hunting with his bow, often returning with a small desert antelope. His comrades were delighted by his skills. They won no favours with Ahmed, however. From the first day on board, neither party had trusted the other in the slightest, but it suited both for the relationship to continue: Tarquinius had the *Periplus*, the ancient map which guided their voyage, and Romulus could fight like three men. Meanwhile, Ahmed kept sailing west, which took the friends closer to Egypt.

The area had proved to have plenty of passing ships, the majority heading west. Plying the lucrative route to the towns far to the north, most were large and carrying well-armed crew. These the Nubian steered well clear of:

there was no benefit in pointlessly wasting his valuable men. From time to time though, they would come across smaller, vulnerable merchant-men. Then they would strike.

The corsairs' tactics were simple. When a prospective prey was sighted, they would sail as close to it as possible. Pretending they had not noticed, the crew busied themselves about the deck with the old fishing nets kept for this purpose. Ahmed relied on the fact that his double-ended dhow with its triangular sail looked like any other off Arabia and Persia. Of course every captain knew that pirates were nearly as numerous as fishermen, and his approach rarely worked for long. Their victims would set off on a different course, keeping plenty of distance between them and the dhow.

As soon as their ruse began to fail, Ahmed would roar for the specially fitted oars to be manned. With ten men rowing on each side, the dhow could quickly catch slower merchant vessels over a short distance. After a short but bloody battle, the corsairs were inevitably victorious. Unless fresh crewmembers were needed, they took no prisoners. Romulus and Tarquinius took part in the attacks – they had to – but left the executions to other pirates. This restraint went unnoticed, thanks to their comrades' bloodthirsty natures.

After more than a year, they had taken a dozen ships, and the hold was bulging with the proceeds, even though only the smallest, most valuable goods were kept – mostly indigo, tortoiseshell and spices. What was now below decks was worth a huge fortune. In addition, they captured a number of unfortunate slave women, whom Ahmed ordered left alive to service the men's physical needs. On such a long voyage, it was important to keep morale high. Romulus found it very hard to ignore the abused women's constant weeping, but there was little he could do.

Inevitably perhaps, the Nubian began to get edgy. Journeying so far from India was an experiment that had paid off, royally. It had been done thanks to his daring, and Tarquinius' map. And the gods had been smiling upon his dhow. Like most men, Ahmed believed that the latter was some-thing that would not last forever. He began to talk about sailing home.

It was an alarming development. Egypt was so near, and yet still so far.

The friends' worries about Ahmed's desire to return to India grew considerably in the days that followed. Bizarrely, fewer small ships seemed to be travelling through. Three weeks went by without a successful attack.

In frustration, the pirate captain led his men on an assault on a large dhow with two large lateen sails like their own. But the merchant ship's crew were tough, experienced Egyptians who fought like men possessed, and the empty-handed corsairs limped away from the engagement with four dead and several wounded. Tarquinius was lucky not to lose an eye when an enemy arrow grazed his left cheekbone and glanced away into the sea. While he laughed it off, Romulus saw it as a sign of the haruspex' mortality. And the losses greatly reduced Ahmed's ability to attack any vessel at all.

The captain's foul temper was not helped by the discovery a day later of a minor leak in the hold, which had ruined some of the *olibanum*. This was the final straw.

'The gods are angry!' Ahmed said, pacing up and down like a caged beast. 'We must be grateful that the damn wind will change soon. It's time to set sail for India.'

The crew looked pleased. After this long away from their base, they were thoroughly homesick. Only Romulus and Tarquinius were dismayed by the captain's decision, and all their attempts to convince the Nubian to change his mind failed miserably.

They were beginning to contemplate deserting the dhow when Mithras smiled on them once more. Anchoring for supplies at a tiny, fly-ridden settlement, the Nubian heard exciting news. Adulis and Ptolemais, a pair of towns on the opposite shore of the Erythraean Sea, were good places to buy ivory. It was from these locations that the Egyptians set out to hunt elephants and other wild creatures. This fortunate discovery rekindled Ahmed's greed. There was still a short time before the south-west monsoon began, and it might as well be spent in pursuit of more riches.

Following his orders, the dhow turned and set sail on a westward course. A day later, it negotiated the passage into the narrow waterway which divided Arabia from Africa. In the cool light of dusk, Romulus saw the Ethiopian coast for the first time.

He had never felt so happy.

While he was pleased for Romulus, Tarquinius' emotions were mixed. The possibility of making landfall in Africa could soon become reality. Old memories welled up, but he did not let himself utter the name that Olenus had given Egypt so many years earlier. So it gnawed away at his mind constantly.

The mother of terror.

The very thought made Tarquinius feel uneasy. After more than two decades, Olenus' prophecy was being fulfilled.

He said nothing to Romulus.

The waters off the southern coast of Arabia had been calm, and the crew had stopped the normal routine of changing the heavy daytime sail for a lighter one every night. That evening was no different as the dhow moved through the water, scarcely making a sound. Phosphorescence sparkled in the bow wave. It was an effect that fascinated and confounded Romulus, and which he never tired of watching. Even Tarquinius had no explanation for the phenomenon, making the young soldier wonder if it was made by the gods themselves.

A myriad of stars filled the sky, illuminating the sea so well that the steersmen's task was made easy. Covered by a rough blanket, Romulus lay on the deck, unable to sleep. He wondered, for the thousandth time, who might have killed Rufus Caelius, the noble outside the Lupanar whose death had precipitated all his travels. After long consideration, Romulus was utterly convinced that it had not been him. He sighed. What chance was there of ever discovering the real culprit? Romulus' frustration at this could not dampen his spirits though. His situation now was better than it ever had been. After five long years of constant warfare and captivity, he was nearing a country where Rome's influence would be noticeable. This previously unthinkable situation filled Romulus with exultation. I am a free man, he thought fiercely. A slave no longer. And no one except Gemellus or Memor knows any different. With Mithras' help, his tattoo would suffice to protect him against men like Novius.

I am a Roman, first and foremost.

Romulus smiled.

What more proof did he need that the gods looked out for him? He stared up at the Perseus constellation, the symbol of Mithras, as it chased the stars that represented Taurus, the bull, across the sky. 'Let us both reach home safely, Great One,' he whispered. 'Even if there is a civil war going on.'

Tarquinius stirred, and Romulus looked over. Together with Brennus, the haruspex had shaped him into the man he was today. Loyal companions, the pair had become his two father figures – teaching and protecting him, always there to give advice when needed. Ultimately, Brennus had made the greatest sacrifice any man could for another. Now there was just Tarquinius, the enigmatic Etruscan, who knew so much. Too much? For himself, Romulus was glad that the future was often uncertain. Anticipating what would happen was a heavy burden, and wariness swamped him at the idea of divining seriously again. The memory of what he had seen at the crucifix in Margiana haunted Romulus still. Especially since the merchant Varus' news had backed it up.

Romulus was sure of another thing. He did not want to know when, or how, either he or Tarquinius might die. Suddenly anxious, he found it difficult to let this disturbing idea go. Could it be soon? He scowled. Only the gods knew. In the dangerous world they inhabited, death was a daily possibility. Nothing could change that. To each his own fate, Romulus thought. And no man should interfere with another's path.

Tarquinius twitched gently, deep in the throes of a dream.

It was an unusual role reversal, Romulus reflected. Normally it was the haruspex who lay awake for hours on end watching him. An adult now, he smiled.

As always, the rising sun woke him. Romulus opened his eyes to find Tarquinius sitting cross-legged on the deck beside him, chewing on some food.

'The coast is in sight.'

Romulus rubbed the sleep from his eyes and clambered to his feet. Along the horizon, he saw an unmistakable line of land emerging from the night mist. Other members of the crew were also lined up against the rails, pointing. Even at a distance, it was clearly much greener than the opposite shore.

He turned to the haruspex with a smile. 'It's not far.'

'No more than two hours.' Tarquinius felt cold. What had Olenus seen in the lamb's liver that day? He had never tried to ascertain the truth of it since. Although he occasionally predicted the deaths of others, Tarquinius was wary of doing the same for himself.

'I'll offer to hunt again this evening. We can just melt away into the bush,' muttered Romulus. 'They'll never find us once it gets dark.'

Concealing his unease, Tarquinius gave him a brief smile. 'Good idea.'

The dhow sailed closer as the sun climbed into the sky, and the Ethiopian coastline became clearer to the eye. There weren't many trees, but there were far more signs of life than in the Arabian desert. Birds wheeled in great circles above while a herd of unfamiliar-looking antelope drank from a stream a little way inland.

Following the breeze, Ahmed ordered the steersmen to set a course north. The sight of greenery had put the Nubian in good temper. Where there was vegetation, there were animals. And the men who hunted them. Hopefully, they might encounter a vessel full of ivory in these waters.

Romulus' mind was devising their escape when he heard a shout: 'Ship ahead!' He glanced around idly, and his heart leapt into his mouth.

About a quarter of a mile ahead lay a prominent headland. Emerging from behind it was the square sail and distinctive predatory shape of a trireme. He stared again. There was no mistaking the curved stern, the three banks of oars, and the enormous eye painted on the side of the prow to threaten the enemies it approached. Its decks were lined with marines, armed similarly to legionaries. Four deck catapults were already being loaded with massive arrows and stone balls.

Tarquinius also looked amazed. 'Romans on this sea?'

'Ship dead ahead!' came the cry again.

Romulus didn't know what to think. Previously, the Republic had always confined its naval presence to the Mediterranean. This new departure had to be an attempt to protect the valuable trade that the corsairs had been preying on. He grimaced. There was every chance that the dhow would not be viewed in a friendly manner. Which did not bode well for them.

Ahmed pointed in alarm. 'What in the name of all the gods is that?'

'It's a Roman fighting ship,' replied Tarquinius. 'A trireme.'

'Is it fast?'

'Very,' answered Romulus grimly.

The unmistakable sound of a drum carried across the waves. Its rhythm was rapid, triggering memories of the voyage to Asia Minor. They had been seen.

The rowers at the oars responded to the booming command, and the trireme's speed began to pick up. It surged forward, creating a large bow wave. The top of the bronze ram at its prow became visible, and even those who had never seen one could guess what the huge mass of metal would do to another vessel.

'Come about,' yelled Ahmed. 'Quickly!'

The two steersmen needed little encouragement. Frantically they leaned on the heavy steering oars, slowing the dhow in the water and beginning a wide turning circle.

Romulus clenched his jaw. It was slow, far too slow. He stared at the trireme's low-slung shape with morbid fascination. Even faster drumbeats filled the air. The Roman vessel was now in red-hot pursuit. By trying to flee, Ahmed had probably sealed their fate. There was little chance of escape.

From the look on the Nubian's face, he was thinking the same thing.

'Time to leave,' Romulus whispered to Tarquinius, who was muttering a prayer. 'Ready?'

'Of course.'

Hastily the two friends donned their armour and tightened their belts. Although Romulus' mail shirt and Tarquinius' hide breastplate were heavy, the protection they granted would be needed in the days to come. And it was only a few hundred paces to shore. That distance was nothing to worry about. After four years at sea, Romulus had learned to swim well and Tarquinius was a natural.

The haruspex shoved a water bottle into his hands and together they moved to the side of the ship. They had to act fast. The trireme was already moving significantly faster than their dhow, and over such a short distance, it posed a lethal danger. A hundred and twenty disciplined oarsmen rowing in unison could rapidly bring it to the speed of a running man. If the pirate ship did not complete its turn soon, it would be run down and sunk.

'You miserable bastard, Tarquinius! Look what you have guided us to!' shouted Ahmed. He spun round to deliver more abuse. 'Trying to escape now?' he screeched, drawing his sword. 'Kill them both!'

Men's heads turned, and their faces twisted with fury as they saw two of their erstwhile comrades about to jump ship.

'Come on,' urged Romulus, swinging himself up on to the wooden side rail.

The Nubian sprinted across the deck, waving his cutlass and screaming with rage. He was aiming straight for the haruspex – who tripped and fell awkwardly to one knee.

'Jump!' shouted Tarquinius.

As Romulus turned back to help his friend, he lost his balance and tumbled backwards – into the sea.

Chapter XXV: Pharsalus

Eastern Greece, summer 48 BC

Brutus reined in his bay horse, which was growing tetchy in the heat. The flies buzzing around its head were no help. 'Steady,' he whispered, patting its neck. 'It will soon begin.'

Around him were six cohorts of legionaries. Like all Caesar's units, they were understrength, but these were supremely fit, crack troops. Their obliquely angled position to the rear of Caesar's *triplex acies* formation belied the importance of their task, Brutus thought proudly. Hidden away, he and his men were Caesar's secret weapon.

After nearly a week of standoff on the plain of Thessaly, Pompey had finally decided to give battle. Moving away from the foothills to the north that morning, his eleven legions had formed up in three lines, the classic configuration; this was copied at once by Caesar's nine. Although Caesar's army matched the width of his enemy's, the difference in their sizes was already obvious. Weakened by their heavy losses in Gaul, his veteran cohorts were stretched painfully thin. In contrast, Pompey's were at full complement, meaning he had about forty-five thousand infantry to his opponent's twenty-two. His cavalry, swelled by volunteers from all over the east, outnumbered Caesar's by nearly seven to one. The figures were daunting, but Brutus' general was not about to avoid confrontation. While his army was much smaller than Pompey's, all Caesar's legionaries were seasoned fighters; in contrast, many of their opponents were raw recruits.

It was an interesting yet potentially disastrous situation, thought Brutus nervously. Would Caesar's gamble pay off? Only the gods know, he reflected, asking Mithras for his aid while there was still time. For battle would shortly commence. Both sides were ready now. Pompey's right flank was protected by the River Enipeus, which ran roughly west–east, while nearly all his superior horse was massed on the left. Today there was to be no classical pincer movement, using cavalry to encircle the enemy on both flanks.

Like any military officer with wits, Brutus knew what was about to unfold instead.

As the opposing legionaries went head to head, the Republican horsemen would drive through Caesar's small numbers of cavalry, opening up his rear. There they would wreak havoc, cause widespread panic and potentially win the battle. Unless Caesar's risky venture paid off.

Still nothing happened. The summer sun was climbing in the sky, and although the air was warm, it was nowhere near what it would be by midday. Almost unwilling to fight, the two armies watched each other in silence. When they finally met, Roman would face Roman in unprecedented numbers. Armed and dressed similarly, attacking in the same formations, brothers would fall upon each other while neighbours fought to the death. The momentousness of this confrontation was obvious to even the lowliest foot soldier.

Yet it was time that things were resolved, thought Brutus impatiently. More than eighteen months after Caesar's crossing of the Rubicon, the two generals had still not fought a decisive battle. Italy was not to be the battlefield, either. Shocked, unprepared for Caesar's daring, Pompey and most of the Senate had fled from Rome, foolishly leaving the treasury contents in the temple of Saturn. They convened at Brundisium, the main jumping point to Greece, where, furiously pursued by the newly enriched Caesar, they were nearly caught in March. But after an attempt to blockade the port failed, Pompey, his entourage and entire army had made the short crossing without harm.

Brutus smiled. As ever, his leader had not sat around for long.

Keen to secure his rear from the seven Pompeian legions in Hispania, Caesar marched north and west, besieging Massilia and its Republican garrison on the way. The city did not fall quickly so, leaving Brutus and Caius Trebonius to finish the job, he had continued to Hispania. After a frustrating campaign of four months, Pompey's forces there were finally defeated and assimilated into Caesar's own. Marcus Petreius and Lucius

Afrianus, their leaders, had been pardoned on the condition that they did not take up arms against him again.

Brutus scowled. He would not have been so merciful. 'Great Mithras, let me meet those treacherous dogs today,' he muttered. It was unlikely on a battlefield this large, Brutus thought, but he could hope. Petreius and Afrianus were *here*. The instant they had been released, the pair had gathered what troops they could and sailed to join their master. Two other men whom Brutus badly wanted to meet were Cassius Longinus, the tribune and ex-army officer, and Titus Labienus, Caesar's former trusted cavalry commander. In a surprise move, they had both switched sides to join the Republicans and were present on the field too. Traitors all, he thought.

Pompey in turn had not been idle while the conflict in Hispania went on, assembling nine legions of Roman citizens in Greece. Added to these were the two veteran legions from Syria, and allied troops numbering three thousand archers from Crete and Sparta, twelve hundred slingers and a polyglot force of seven thousand cavalry. Every city-state ruler and minor prince within five hundred miles had sent a contingent to join the Republican forces.

When Caesar had returned to Italy in December, he received the news of this, the host that was awaiting him in Greece. Keen to prevent further bloodshed, he made several attempts to open negotiations with Pompey. All were swiftly rebuffed. The Republicans had decided that they would settle for nothing less than their enemy's total defeat. Caesar's response was to carry the war to Greece without delay. Now Brutus laughed out loud, uncaring that his men looked at him strangely. Caesar had ignored all his officers' advice and set sail from Brundisium. At the time, it seemed like utter madness: seven under-strength legions sailing at night, in the middle of winter, across a strait controlled entirely by the Pompeian navy. Like so many of Caesar's daring tactics, though, it had worked; the next day his entire host landed unopposed on the western coast of Greece.

Caught napping by this, the wily Pompey then avoided battle for months, knowing that his supply situation was far superior to that of Caesar's. With limitless ships to provide food and equipment to his army, he could afford to march up and down the land while his opponent could not. Boring the tactic might seem, but Pompey knew that Caesar's men could not live on fresh air. They needed grain, and meat. It was during this lean time that

Brutus really grew to respect their opponent. If the rumours were to be believed, Pompey was under constant pressure from the numerous senators and politicians he had in tow. The Optimates, Brutus thought scornfully. There isn't a real soldier among them. Already resentful of Pompey's position as supreme Republican commander, these hangers-on wanted a pitched battle and a quick victory.

So did Caesar, and when Pompey would not give it to him, he attempted to force the issue at Dyrrachium. Although by then his forces had been augmented by four more legions, it was a painful memory. The attempt to recreate Caesar's victory at Alesia had seemed promising initially. More than fifteen miles of fortifications hemmed Pompey against the coast while dams were built to block the streams. A similar length of opposing defences prevented Caesar from advancing, but the combined constructions deprived the Republican army of water for its soldiers and fodder for its horses. By July, the bodies of hundreds of pack animals lay rotting in the sun, increasing the risk of disease among Pompey's troops. If something wasn't done, men would begin to die of cholera and dysentery. Meanwhile Caesar's legionaries, who were short of supplies, ground up charax vegetable roots and mixed them with milk. The resultant dough was baked into loaves, and in a measured taunt of Pompey's men, some of this bitter-tasting food was tossed into the enemy lines.

Fortunately for Pompey, it was then that two of Caesar's Gaulish cavalry commanders defected. Discovering from them that parts of his enemy's southern fortifications were incomplete, Pompey launched a daring attack at dawn the next day. Six legions took part in the massive assault. Uncharacteristically, Caesar refused to admit that his blockade was failing and launched a counter-attack, which failed miserably. Outnumbered and demoralised, his legionaries had fled the field en masse. Not even the presence of their legendary commander could stop the rout. One *signifer* was so panicked that when confronted by Caesar, he actually inverted his standard and menaced the general with its butt-end. Only the timely intervention of one of Caesar's Germanic bodyguards – who sliced off the man's arm – prevented him from coming to serious injury. The same could not be said of Caesar's army, which lost a thousand legionaries and more than thirty centurions. Strangely, Pompey had soon called off his pursuit, allowing his opponent's battered legions to escape the field. 'The fools could have won the war that day, if they but possessed a general who knew how to win,' Caesar had sneered. Brutus knew it was true.

A month passed. Again the two sides faced each other, but on an open plain this time. Caesar's army had been depleted by injuries and the garrisoning of towns to nine legions, while Pompey still had eleven.

Superstitiously, Brutus prayed that Dyrrachium would not be repeated here today, at Pharsalus. That he would survive, and be reunited later with Fabiola. With seven cohorts as protection, she, Docilosa and Sextus were safe in Caesar's camp, nearly three miles to the rear. If the battle was lost, the senior centurion in charge had orders to retreat to the south. It was best not to think of that eventuality, he reflected, hastily burying the thought. Then Brutus grinned, remembering Fabiola's demand to march out on to the plain and watch the struggle. She was a lioness, he thought proudly. Fabiola had accompanied him everywhere since Alesia and now felt like his good-luck talisman. Discovering that she was also a devotee of Mithras had reinforced this feeling. They had prayed together for victory at dawn, before his departure. In that department, Brutus reflected, everything was going well. Almost everything. He sighed, thinking of Fabiola's unexplained reticence towards Caesar. Still, it was rarely a problem. Plenty of other officers had used the excuse of the prolonged campaign to bring their mistresses along, diluting Fabiola into the mix.

'Sir!' shouted one of Brutus' centurions. 'It's begun. Listen.'

Brutus sat up in the saddle, cupping his right hand to his ear. The sound started as a low thunder, but quickly intensified until the ground shook. Without doubt, it was the noise of hooves. Pompey's cavalry was attacking, and in response Caesar's German and Gaulish horsemen trotted forward, to the north-west. There were a thousand of the experienced warriors, with a similar number of specially trained light infantry interspersed between. Yet their task was hopeless. Against more than three times their number all they could do was slow the speed of the enemy attack: a delaying tactic. Brutus' pulse increased, and he looked around, checking that his men were ready. They were, he saw proudly. Two thousand of Caesar's finest troops, who would follow him wherever he led.

The clarion sound of *bucinae* ripped through the air all along the host. *Vexilla*, red flags, were also raised and lowered, repeating Caesar's orders to ensure accuracy. Instantly the rhythmic tread of *caligae* upon the hard ground added to the noise. Two of the three lines in front of Brutus were advancing. Only one, the third, remained to hold their position. He grinned. Undeterred by the cavalry charge, Caesar was taking the battle to Pompey.

Brutus and his men waited, watching and listening to the battle commence. Impatient, nervous, none of them enjoyed holding back while their comrades began fighting and dying. Yet this was different. They had to stay put because their mission was all important.

The first to meet were the two forces of cavalry. Brutus could see the clash in the distance. Sunlight glittered off polished helmets and spear tips, clouds of dust rose and battle cries rang out. Brutus knew what it was like; he had done it before. Within moments of hitting the enemy, all semblance of formation would be lost. The struggle would immediately become a mass of confusing, individual fights, rider against rider, foot soldiers against horsemen. Hack, slash, bend in the saddle. Reassure the horse, wipe sweat from your eyes. Look around, check where one's comrades are. Dodge a spear thrust. Move forward.

He turned to look west, wondering why the infantry had not yet met. Roman soldiers advanced towards each other in total silence, but there would still be an enormous crash of weapons against shields when it happened.

A legionary messenger came from Caesar's position, to the rear of the third line. 'Pompey hasn't allowed his men to advance, sir,' he panted. 'They're just standing there, waiting.'

'What did you say?' Brutus demanded. No general ever held his troops back like that.

Grinning, the messenger repeated himself. 'When our lot realised, they stopped and re-formed.'

Brutus swelled with pride. With his first and second lines already committed, Caesar would not have been able to give such a command. With astonishing initiative, his soldiers had shown their top quality by regrouping before the combat began.

A whistling sound filled the air.

Pila, thought Brutus. A volley from each side at twenty or thirty paces and they'll hit.

Screams and cries began ringing out as the javelins landed. A few moments passed. And then, with a noise like thunder, fifty thousand men smashed into each other.

'Caesar orders you to prepare yourselves, sir,' said the messenger, darting off again. 'All his trust is in you. But do not advance until his flag signals.'

'Do you hear that, boys?' Brutus cried to his men. 'Caesar trusts us completely. And we will repay that confidence. Venus *Victrix*, Bringer of Victory!' He roared out the password given to them that morning.

A great sound of approval met his words, swelling as it moved along the cohorts.

Brutus smiled. His legionaries' morale was high. But that could not rid him of the anxious feeling in the pit of his stomach. Even if Caesar's hardened veterans in the front two lines won the day against Pompey's less experienced soldiers, it would all mean nothing when the enemy horse swarmed around their right flank. There were no men on earth who could withstand a cavalry charge from behind. Everything depended on him and his six cohorts. Great Mithras, Brutus thought fervently. Give me courage. Grant me success.

Dismounting, he had a legionary take his mount to the rear. This task was for foot soldiers only, and Brutus wanted to be in the middle of it. He was no officer to lead from the back. Handed a *pilum* and a spare *scutum*, he took his place in the front line, nodding encouragingly to his men.

They waited in silence, baking in the hot sun.

An ominous feeling soon took hold of Brutus and he peered into the distance.

Covered by the Gauls and Germans, Caesar's light infantry were beginning to retreat. Without this protection, they would be run down and killed to a man. But the cavalry's discipline was good, Brutus saw with relief. Wheeling and turning to confuse the enemy, the tribesmen hurled the last of their spears into the advancing mass of Republican cavalry. Aware that their mounted comrades could not do this for long, the infantry broke into a sprint, towards the side of Caesar's right flank. They were aiming to pass to the side of Brutus' position.

The Republican horsemen surged forward, pushing ever harder. Lightly armed with spears and swords, few bore shields or wore armour. They were Thracians, Cappadocians, Galatians and a dozen other nationalities, all vying for the honour of turning the tide in Pompey's favour. Behind them charged thousands of archers and slingers, the next attack wave.

Brutus chewed a fingernail. This was the most critical point of the battle.

Losing more and more men, still the Gauls and Germans did not break.

The light infantry tore around Brutus' cohorts, and headed east. If everything went to plan, they would re-form with their mounted comrades in a few moments.

The battered cavalry were perhaps three hundred paces away. Still much too far for an attacking foot soldier to run at a horseman, thought Brutus. Mithras, bring them nearer.

'Close order!' He shouted at the nearest centurion. 'Shields up. Ready *pila.*'

His order was obeyed at once. *Scuta* clattered off each other, forming an impenetrable wall. Angled up in the position to throw, his men's javelins poked forward over the shield wall. Ranks of determined faces peered into the dust cloud before them.

A hundred and fifty paces separated the remnants of the Gauls and Germans from Brutus' six cohorts. They could hear the excited shouts and cries of the pursuing Republicans. Faces began to grow nervous, and the officers looked to Brutus for orders.

In turn, Brutus glanced anxiously at Caesar's location. He could just see his general's red cloak amidst the mass of senior officers and bodyguards. But no damn flag. Come on, Brutus thought, his heart thumping in his chest. Give us the command.

Less than a hundred paces.

Their cavalry were close enough now for Brutus to see the sweat lathered on their tired mounts, the wounded men barely upright in the saddle, the numerous horses without riders. Respect filled him at the heavy sacrifice the tribesmen had made.

Protected by the horses' height, the six cohorts were still hidden from the enemy. This was precisely Caesar's purpose.

Seventy paces.

Fifty.

At the last moment, the Gauls and Germans turned their mounts' heads and rode across the front of the shield wall.

Now, thought Brutus. By Mithras, it has to be now.

Again he looked for the *vexillum*. This time it was there, a piece of scarlet cloth, urgently bobbing up and down. Typically, Caesar had waited until the last possible moment.

'At the double,' Brutus screamed, pointing his javelin. 'Charge!'

With an inarticulate roar, his men obeyed. Trained relentlessly as new recruits to keep their shields together when running, they presented a fearsome sight to any enemy. Particularly to horsemen, who were never charged by infantry. And for the previous few weeks, Brutus had taught the six cohorts to stab their *pila* at enemy riders' eyes and faces. The legionaries were delighted by this novel tactic. As everyone knew, cavalrymen were dandies who thought themselves better than any other soldier.

Shouting at the top of their lungs, they pelted forward, emerging from the dust like grey, avenging ghosts.

The Republican cavalry did not know what had hit them.

As expected, they had driven off Caesar's horse and light infantry, causing heavy losses. Now the entire enemy rear was exposed and they could break into smaller squadrons, free to ride along it at will. Pompey's inexperienced soldiers were holding up well, so Caesar's legions were trapped between a hammer and an anvil. Very soon they would be crushed. Whooping exultantly at the thought of victory, the Republicans trotted forward.

And were met by a shield wall over eleven hundred paces wide.

Stunned, they came to an abrupt halt.

Brutus' men slammed into them at full tilt. Hundreds of *pila* stabbed upwards in unison, biting deep into the Republicans' open mouths, eyes and unarmoured flesh. Plenty of horses were struck too, suffering painful wounds which made them rear up in terror. Keen to cause as much distress to the mounts as possible, the legionaries screamed fierce battle cries. Keeping their *scuta* locked together, they ripped out the barbed javelin heads and thrust at their enemies again. And again. The shocked cavalrymen quailed before the savage and totally unexpected attack. This was not what was supposed to happen!

The six cohorts managed to move forward a step. Then another.

Brutus was like a hound which has just found the scent. They had to keep the advantage that their surprise had granted them. Considerably outnumbered by the enemy horse, causing panic was their main weapon.

'Forward,' he screamed, the veins bulging in his neck. 'Push forward at will!'

The centurions and junior officers repeated his order.

Seizing the opportunity, groups of legionaries shoved into the gaps between enemy horsemen. Protecting themselves with their *scuta*, they used their *pila* to strike terror into the Republicans' hearts. Here and there, a slashing sword cut down a soldier, but the impetus was all with Brutus' cohorts. And a few moments later, he saw the most welcome of sights in a battle. Men's heads turning to the rear. Fearful expressions twisting faces. Cries of alarm. Turn and flee, you whoresons, Brutus thought fiercely. Now.

It was like watching a flock of birds change direction. Entirely consumed by terror, the leading Republican cavalry wheeled and urged their horses away from the merciless javelins, which offered nothing but death. Panicked, shouting incoherently, they collided with the squadrons behind, which were dividing up in preparation to assault Caesar's rear.

Sick with tension, Brutus held his breath. If there were solid, disciplined officers in the enemy's ranks, this was the moment to pull back, regroup and then charge them on the flanks and rear. If that happened, all his preparations and Caesar's hopes would be dashed, and the struggle lost.

But faced with a retreating wave of terrified and injured comrades, the astonished riders did what most men would do in the circumstances. They turned and fled. In an instant, the Republican cavalry attack had become a rout. Trailing a huge cloud of dust, the horsemen galloped away into the distance.

Raising his bloodied *pilum* in the air, Brutus cheered. His cry was echoed by two thousand exhilarated legionaries, but their task was not over, nor the battle won.

The enemy cavalry's panic and cowardice completely exposed thousands of advancing archers and slingers, who were there to support the mounted attack. Wails of fear rose up as they saw their protective screen vanish like so much morning mist. Ready for this exact moment, Caesar's regrouped cavalry and light infantry swept forward again, creating a bloody slaughter that scattered the terrified, lightly armed soldiers across the plain.

The way to Pompey's left flank was wide open now, thought Brutus delightedly. Looking around, he saw that his men had realised the same thing. It was time to deliver a hammer blow of their own.

'Come on,' Brutus shouted, trotting forward. 'Let's show those fuckers what real soldiers can do!'

It was half a mile at least to the Republican lines, but Brutus' men charged forward like hunting dogs let slip from the leash. As they ran, he was aware of the third line moving on his left side. Caesar was making his final play by committing all his troops to the fray. Its legionaries would provide a much-needed input of fresh energy to the two sections which had now been locked in battle for some time.

Brutus' main worry now was Pompey's response to his attack. Like Caesar, he had probably held back his third line, which meant that his own cohorts' advantage could be swiftly dispelled by Republican reinforcements. All the more reason for speed, Brutus thought, pushing himself into a sprint. Wearing a transverse crested bronze helmet and mail shirt and carrying a heavy *scutum*, it was an exhausting effort. The sun had been beating down on the dry plain since dawn and was near its zenith now. The air was hot and still, difficult to breathe. Most men had not drunk for hours and every throat was parched. Yet no one held back.

It was at moments like this that victory could be achieved.

And Caesar had placed his trust in them.

An hour later, and Brutus knew that the day was theirs. In a wonderful stroke of luck for Caesar, Pompey *had* committed all three lines of his army against his opponent's two. Presumably an effort to bolster his raw troops, the measured decision had left the Republican leader with no reserves to counter Brutus' wheeling attack. In addition, his cavalry were scattered to the four winds, and his missile troops butchered. Brutus and his six cohorts had fallen on Pompey's unsuspecting left flank like wolves on helpless sheep. Driving the soldiers in it sideways, they watched delightedly as the panic spread.

When Caesar's third line had crashed against the Republican front a few moments later, the end was nigh. Brutus had to give the enemy legionaries credit – holding their ranks, they fought on, refusing to run. It was a different story with Pompey's allies, however. When the fate of their cavalry was followed by these further setbacks, they turned tail and fled towards their camp. With renewed courage, Caesar's legions had pressed home their attack on the Republican legions. Step by step, they advanced, pushing their increasingly demoralised enemies backwards.

Brutus grinned mercilessly. It always started at the rear, when men who could see that their comrades in front were losing, looked back. Armed with long staffs, *optiones* and other junior officers were positioned here to prevent any retreat without orders. Thinly spread out though, they had no chance of stopping men from flight when the panic reached a critical mass. Inevitably that was what happened. Preceded by their commander, Pompey's shattered legions had deserted the field as a disorganised rabble. Reaching the supposed safety of their fortified camp a short while later, they had been horrified when Caesar's men followed and placed them under siege. After a short, vicious encounter, the gates had been forced, requiring Pompey and his soldiers to go on the run again.

Urged on now by Caesar himself, the exhausted legionaries were in hot pursuit of their defeated enemies, who were to be denied rest, water and food. The victory, thought Brutus, would be nothing less than total. Once again, Caesar had stolen victory from the jaws of defeat, this time using one of the most inventive tactics in the history of warfare.

Swallowing the warm dregs from his leather water carrier, Brutus grinned.

All they needed was to capture Pompey, and the civil war was virtually over.

In the event, that was not to happen. Although twenty-four thousand soldiers were taken prisoner, with numerous high-ranking officers and senators among them, Pompey and many others made good their escape that night. Included in this number were Petreius, Afrianus and Labienus, Caesar's former friend and ally on the Gaulish campaign.

Early the next day, Brutus stood on a nearby hill, studying the battlefield. Fabiola was by his side, silently aghast. While not as bloody as Alesia, the human cost of Pharsalus had been high: over six thousand Republican legionaries lay dead below them, while Caesar had lost more than twelve hundred. Uncounted numbers of Republican allied troops were strewn everywhere, worthless in death as they had been in life. Clouds of vultures, eagles and other birds of prey already filled the air overhead.

'Will they all just rot?' asked Fabiola, revolted at that thought.

'No. Look,' answered Brutus, pointing. Small groups of men could be seen stacking wood in rectangular piles all across the plain. 'Funeral pyres,' he said.

Fabiola closed her eyes, imagining the smell of burning flesh. 'Is it over then?'

Brutus sighed heavily. 'I'm afraid not, my love.'

'But this . . .' Fabiola pointed at the carnage below them. 'Have enough men not died?'

'The losses are terrible,' he agreed. 'Yet the Optimates will not give up this easily. Word has it that they will take ship for Africa, where the Republican cause is still strong.'

Fabiola nodded. About the only area where Caesar had suffered a setback so far was in the province of Africa. The year before, Curio, his former tribune, had made the foolish mistake of being lured away from the coast and into the barren hinterland. There he and his army were annihilated by the cavalry of the king of Numidia, a Republican ally. 'That will require another campaign,' she said, wishing the bloodshed were already over. When it was, she could reactivate her plans to take revenge upon Caesar. 'Won't it?'

'Yes,' Brutus replied simply. 'But you can go back to Rome at any stage. I'll make sure you have enough protection.'

Pleased by this, Fabiola kissed his cheek. 'I'll stay by you, my love,' she said, still wary of the potential danger from Scaevola. 'What of Pompey?'

Brutus frowned. 'The scouts say he headed east to the Aegean coast, unlike the others. From there, my guess is that he will sail for Parthia, or Egypt.' He saw her questioning look. 'The man won't just give up. He needs more support for his cause.'

'It will never end! Pompey still has two sons in Hispania. They've got to be untrustworthy too,' cried Fabiola despairingly. 'Africa, Egypt, Hispania. Can Caesar fight a war on three fronts?'

'Of course,' Brutus smiled. 'And he will win. I know it in my heart.'

Fabiola did not answer, but despair filled her. If Caesar truly was capable of defeating so many foes, he would prove to be the most formidable general ever seen. How could she ever take revenge on someone so powerful? Brutus loved her, she was sure of it, but it seemed doubtful he would ever betray Caesar the way she wanted him to. What chance, there-fore, had she of convincing anyone else? Disconsolate, Fabiola stared out over the plain, searching for a clue. For a long time there was nothing. At last she saw it, a single raven flying apart from the other birds, coasting on the warm currents of air which rose from the baking ground below. Rapt, Fabiola watched it for a long time. And then she knew. Thank you, Mithras, she thought triumphantly. The worst enemies were always the ones within. So Brutus and his compatriots were still the key.

'If he succeeds,' Fabiola said calculatingly, 'you cannot trust him ever again. Rome must beware of Caesar.'

'What do you mean?' asked Brutus, confused and a little angry.

'The arrogance of a man with such ability knows no bounds,' Fabiola answered. 'Caesar will make himself king.'

'King?' The mere concept was now anathema to every citizen. Almost five hundred years before, the people of Rome had committed their proudest act: overthrowing and then expelling the city's last monarch.

Fabiola knew one more vital detail.

An ancestor of Brutus had purportedly been the main instigator.

Exulting, she watched the blood drain from Brutus' face.

'That can never be,' he muttered.

Chapter XXVI: The Bestiarius

Off the coast of Ethiopia, summer/autumn 48 BC

Romulus crashed into the sea on his back. At the last moment, he remembered to hold his breath. Disorientated, he panicked as his heavy chain mail immediately began to pull him into the depths. Soon his lungs felt as if they were about to burst, and it took all Romulus' effort not to let his reflexes take over. Yet he had no desire to die with a chest full of seawater, and his desperate desire to help Tarquinius gave him extra strength. Righting himself, Romulus kicked his legs vigorously and pushed upwards. To his relief, the salinity aided his buoyancy. Romulus burst through the surface, exhaling as he did so. Air had never tasted so sweet. Wiping his stinging eyes, he frantically scanned the sides of the dhow for his friend.

All he could see was cursing pirates lining the rails. Some were shaking their fists, but others were stringing bows or aiming spears.

'Quickly!' screamed Ahmed. 'You fools! Loose!'

The danger was not over.

Romulus cursed. What hope had he of climbing aboard? Of rescuing Tarquinius before the trireme struck? Certain death from two directions awaited if he even tried. Yet he could not just swim away.

'I'm here,' said a voice from behind him.

Romulus nearly jumped out of his skin.

Tarquinius was bobbing a few paces away, a wide grin on his face.

'How . . . ?'

'There's no time for that,' the haruspex replied. 'Let's put some distance between us and the dhow.'

Right on cue, an arrow hit the water between them. It sank harmlessly, but another followed, and then a spear was launched.

Romulus had no desire to linger. Taking a quick look around to establish which way the shore was, he pushed himself through the warm sea with strong strokes.

'Fucking dogs!' Ahmed's voice echoed across the waves. 'Curse you both to hell and gone!'

More poorly aimed arrows splashed in nearby, but none of the crew had Romulus' skill with the bow. And the infuriated Nubian could not afford the time to pursue the pair. It had been a perfectly timed moment to flee.

Their armour was not enough to stop them reaching dry land. Soon afterwards, they pulled themselves up an abandoned beach, which was covered in stones and pebbles. As one, they turned to see what had become of the dhow.

They had a grandstand view of the unfolding drama, which was about to reach its climax.

The pirate vessel had managed at last to come about, and was picking up speed towards Arabia, the wind bellying her sails. But it was too late. The dhow's poor tacking had proved to be its undoing. Before the corsairs could gain any ground eastwards, the trireme had reached ramming speed. And it showed no sign of slowing down. The drum was pounding out a thudding rhythm faster than a man's heartbeat, forcing the oarsmen to row at an exhausting pace.

'There's been no signal to heave to,' said Romulus.

'They're going to ram them regardless.'

'Poor bastards.'

Raised slightly from the water by the speed of the trireme, the bronze head of the ram became visible as they watched. Both were riveted to the spot. Extending fifteen paces or more in front of the ship, it provided the Roman navy with one of its most devastating forms of attack. Yet Ahmed and his crew were unaware of this. All they could see was the trireme bearing down at an acute angle, aiming for a head-on collision.

Cries of alarm carried across the water, intermingled with the screams of the captive women.

With an incredible crash, the ram hit the dhow near its prow. Even though they were some distance away, it was possible to hear the cracking of timbers. The overwhelming impetus of the Roman vessel drove the smaller boat sharply to one side. Several pirates were thrown overboard from the sheer force of the impact. They flailed about in the water, help-lessly watching their comrades, most of whom had been knocked off their feet. Shouts of terror and confusion rang out.

The dhow had been dealt a mortal blow.

To finish it off, the *trierarch*, the Roman captain, roared out a single command. As one, archers on the trireme peppered the other vessel with arrows. Falling among the stunned corsairs like a deadly rain, the volley was devastating. Undisciplined, panicked, the surviving pirates died where they stood or crouched. The unfortunate women fared no better. Remarkably though, Ahmed was still uninjured. Courageous to the last, he shrieked orders in vain at his crew.

The *trierarch* barked out another command, and the catapults twanged in unison. Stone balls swept through the air to crush men's ribcages; a huge arrow pinned Zebulon to the mast. Only a handful of pirates were left unwounded. Now there would be no need to risk the lives of any marines. This was Roman military efficiency at its brutal best.

Romulus felt a pang of sorrow as he watched. The pirates were dying miserable deaths, unable to even close with the enemy and fight hand to hand. For all that they were bloodthirsty renegades, they had lived and fought together for nearly four years. Romulus felt some degree of kinship with them. And then there were the innocent women. He turned away from the sight, unwilling to watch any more. But a moment later, he was compelled to look back.

Using long poles, the marines pushed the trireme away from the dhow, revealing the gaping hole that had been punched in its hull. Yet the manoeuvre was not being done to admire their handiwork. With the space empty of the ram's bronze head, seawater was now free to rush in, destroying the *olibanum* and spices the pirates had stolen. And sinking the pirates' vessel.

Romulus had never seen how devastating the ramming of a ship could be.

The dhow sank in a matter of moments. Soon the only trace remaining was a few spars of wreckage floating on the sea, accompanied by the bobbing heads of four or five survivors. Among them, Romulus recognised Ahmed. But there was to be no mercy. In a final act of ruthlessness, archers on the trireme loosed another volley.

Still the Nubian's head was visible.

Above the noise and confusion, Romulus fancied that he could hear Ahmed's voice shouting curses. It was the way he would always remember the pirate captain.

Dozens more arrows hissed down, ending the show.

He was very glad now that Mustafa had been left behind in Cana. With luck, his fate would be different to the rest of the crew. As always, Romulus wondered if the haruspex had known what would happen.

'Let's go,' said Tarquinius.

With a start, Romulus came to his senses.

'Before the *trierarch* sees us and sends some men ashore.'

'Of course.' He had been so wrapped up watching the one-sided battle that he had forgotten about the hostile reception they too would get from the Romans. After what they had witnessed, it was unlikely that any time would be granted to explain their status. Opting for discretion, the two friends crouched down and beat a path away from the trireme's sleek shape. A gentle rocky slope led them up off the beach. Once over the crest, they were out of sight.

The warm sun beat down, drying them fast. But all they had with them was their clothes, chain mail and swords. Tarquinius also had his axe. There was one half-full water bag and no food. Neither had a bow, so hunting would be difficult.

We're alive, thought Romulus grimly. That's what counts. 'How did you get away?' he demanded.

'I managed to grab one of Ahmed's legs and knock him over.'

'Without him splitting you in two?'

Tarquinius shrugged eloquently.

'You could make it in the arena,' laughed Romulus, clapping him on the shoulder.

The haruspex grimaced. 'I'm getting too old for that,' he said.

Romulus ignored his answer. It was not something he wanted to consider. A confident and assured young man now, he still relied on the other for psychological support.

'Africa,' announced Tarquinius with a grand gesture.

It was an amazing sight.

Before them, rich grassland rolled off to the west and north. A range of smooth, undulating hills filled the southern horizon. Small trees and scrubby bushes were dotted here and there. Irregularly shaped termite mounds projected upwards, fat red fingers of packed earth. The birdlife was richer here than anywhere Romulus had ever seen: as well as seabirds, there were honeyguides, orioles, kingfishers and countless other varieties. The animal life was no less varied. Several types of antelope, large and small, paced along, grazing as they went. Nearby, a group of magnificent horse-like creatures covered in wide black and white stripes was doing likewise, their tails flicking away flies. A herd of elephants stood around a waterhole, using their trunks to drink noisily and spray themselves with water. Elegant white birds walked along their backs, searching for parasites. If hit by a stream of water, they would indignantly fly away to alight upon another individual.

The peaceful scene was a stark contrast to the last occasion that they had seen elephants. Romulus did not want to dwell on that thought. 'Look,' he said in amazement, pointing at the striped animals.

'Zebras,' came the reply.

Tarquinius' knowledge never failed to surprise Romulus. 'How in the name of Hades do you know that?'

'I saw one presented at a triumph for Pompey in Rome,' replied Tarquinius.

'And those?' Romulus pointed at three strange-looking animals, which were feeding off the branches on the upper reaches of the trees. Their short coats were sandy-coloured with dark brown patches of different shades, and they had immensely long necks and legs. A short, upright mane ran up their necks and odd, stubby horns protruded from the tops of their heads.

'Giraffes.'

'Are they dangerous?'

'Not really,' laughed the haruspex. 'They're plant-eaters.'

Romulus flushed, embarrassed. 'There must be lions, though.' He had seen close up what the large cats could do to a man. Meeting one in the wild was not something he particularly wished to do.

'Those we must look out for,' agreed the haruspex. 'As well as rhinos, buffaloes and leopards. It's a pity that we have no spears.'

'I've seen lions and leopards before, obviously,' said Romulus, his eyes wide at the density of wildlife. 'But not the others.'

This was an invitation for Tarquinius to begin one of his lessons. Naturally enough, he did not just mention the flora and fauna, but also the histories of Ethiopia and Egypt and the details of their civilizations and peoples.

When he had finished, Romulus felt more at home in this new and alien land, which had a much longer and richer past than his own. Like many others however, it was gradually falling under Rome's influence. 'How far is it to Alexandria?'

'Many hundreds of miles.'

The scale of what faced them began to sink in. 'Must we walk the whole way?' he asked.

'Possibly. It is unclear.'

'Best make a start, eh?' sighed Romulus.

They began to march north. Towards Egypt.

By the time they reached the waterhole, the elephants had gone. The shallow pool had been left muddied by the massive beasts, but there was nothing else on offer. Slaking their thirst and filling the leather water carrier, they moved on. Hunger was also gnawing at their bellies. In the circumstances though, that could wait. Putting a good distance between themselves and the trireme just off the coast was far more important than searching for food. While there was no sign of pursuit, both were careful to keep glancing in the direction from which they had come.

The morning passed without event, and Romulus began to relax. Keeping roughly parallel to the shore, they had covered perhaps eight or nine miles; they had escaped. Or so it seemed.

The young soldier felt little elation, however. Travelling on foot through Ethiopia and then Egypt, without proper weapons or enough companions, would be a Herculean task. While a similar distance, their journey down the Indus had been easier because it was by boat. This, on the other hand, felt akin to the odyssey that the Forgotten Legion had endured after Carrhae.

At least they had not been alone then.

By late afternoon, the pair had walked a further ten miles. Making their way to the sea again, they scanned the horizon for a long time. Nearly two decades younger, Romulus had the keener eyes. Happy that there was no sign of the trireme, he searched out a sheltered depression in the sand dunes which rolled back from the beach. Chopping the spiked lower branches from some nearby trees, the pair soon fashioned a high-sided, circular enclosure. It was large enough for them to lie down, and sleeping inside its protection would be safer than nothing at all.

They did not risk a fire. It was still quite warm and they had no food to cook. Any blaze would only attract unwanted attention anyway.

Tarquinius offered to take the first watch.

Gratefully accepting, Romulus fell asleep within moments. He dreamt of Rome.

When he awoke, thoroughly chilled, Romulus was unsurprised to find Tarquinius keeping vigil beside him. A faint light on the horizon hinted that daybreak was not far away. His friend had let him rest uninterrupted for the whole night. Feeling guilty, Romulus was about to say something, but held back. Facing east, the haruspex did not seem aware of his presence. Sitting perfectly still with his arms folded, Tarquinius resembled a well sculpted statue.

'Forgive me, mighty Tinia,' he whispered. 'For what I have done.'

Romulus' ears pricked up at the mention of the Etruscans' most powerful god. As a Roman, he called him Jupiter.

There was a long pause, during which Tarquinius sat watching the myriad stars above gradually fade away. His lips moved in silent prayer.

Fascinated, Romulus lay still, doing his best not to shiver.

'Great Mithras, accept my repentance,' Tarquinius muttered. 'I did what I thought was best. If mistakes have been made, then let me be punished as you see fit.'

Romulus was intrigued. What did his friend mean? Had it anything to do with their voyage? Although it had taken almost four years to reach Africa, the young soldier could not envisage how they could have got here more quickly. He held no grudge against the haruspex for this, for without his aid and the invaluable *Periplus*, Romulus would never have made it. For years now, his friend's wisdom, guidance and prophetic ability had been as solid a support to Romulus as steering oars were to a ship.

Or was it something else altogether?

A feather of memory tickled the edge of Romulus' mind, but frustratingly he could not recall it. At last the cold bettered him, and he shivered.

Instantly Tarquinius' demeanour changed, and he became his usual calm self. 'You're awake,' he said.

Romulus decided to be bold. 'What were you saying?'

'I was praying, that's all.' The haruspex' face was an unreadable mask.

'It was more than that.'

Tarquinius did not answer.

Sudden fear gripped Romulus' throat. 'Have you seen something about Fabiola?' he demanded.

'No,' Tarquinius denied.

'Are you sure?'

'I swear it.'

Full of suspicion, Romulus studied his friend's face.

Thin beams of orange sunlight crept over the edge of the nearest dunes. The temperature began to climb, which was a relief to both. Without blankets, their rest had not been the best quality. But before long it would be warm: uncomfortably so. And they needed to find food that day. Water alone could not sustain a man marching in this extreme environment.

Then it came. Romulus had no idea what made him think of it, the most passing of comments by Tarquinius nearly seven years earlier.

'There was a reason that you fled Italy,' he said softly. 'You would not tell me before. What was it?'

Surprise registered in Tarquinius' dark eyes and Romulus knew that he had hit the nail on the head.

'I cannot say,' replied the haruspex in a reluctant tone. 'Yet.'

'Why not? Because you still feel guilty?'

The acute observation sank deep.

'Partly,' Tarquinius admitted. 'And the time is not right.'

'Will it ever be?' Romulus demanded angrily.

'Soon.'

A braying sound broke in on their conversation, and the pair looked around in surprise. It was some distance away, but only horns could be responsible for that level of noise.

Horns blown by men.

And there was nowhere for them to run.

It would be best to stay hidden. Dragging Tarquinius with him, Romulus crawled to the edge of the depression. Nothing could be seen yet. They waited, an awkward silence between them. Long moments passed, until it was full daylight. Approaching from the south, the din grew louder and louder. Men's shouts mingled with the clamour from the drums and horns, but it was impossible to make out words.

Over the nearest hill came a pack of hunting dogs in full cry. They were followed by an immensely wide line of figures walking shoulder to shoulder, beating drums and playing all manner of musical instruments as loudly as possible.

'It's a hunt,' guessed Romulus.

Tarquinius' eyes narrowed.

Of course every animal within earshot immediately headed north or west. There was no escape in the east, where the sea lay. The two friends watched, engrossed. Antelope and giraffe, elephant and zebra stampeded alongside each other, uncaring. Bush pigs squealed in terror, raising their tails as they ran. A herd of buffalo thundered along, shaking the ground. Even predators such as lions and jackals were affected by the fear and fled for their lives. Romulus saw a solitary, terrified leopard leave the safety of its tree to join the throng.

A group of zebra to the north was already lifting their heads at the noise. Seeing the approaching men, they twitched their tails and moved away. Instinctively their companions began to do the same. A few moments later, all were on the hoof, galloping away with long graceful strides.

The friends' curiosity was up. Whether those they had seen were hunters, or *bestiarii* capturing animals for the arena in Rome, it was likely that they had come from the far north. Which was where they wanted to go. The excitement allowed their previous disagreement to subside, but Romulus had not forgotten it. There would be another time to talk, and he would not let the haruspex avoid answering his question then.

A sea change had just taken place in their relationship.

Tarquinius peered into the distance. 'They'll be heading for a narrow ravine.'

'We can follow the beaters once they've passed,' said Romulus. 'Should be easy enough.'

'If we're careful,' warned Tarquinius.

'Of course,' Romulus growled, irritated.

They squatted down on their haunches and waited. Romulus judged that the dogs and hunters would come within two hundred paces of their position, but no nearer. Fortunately the contour of the land angled away from them, towards the north. This meant that the wild beasts passed well clear of them, and in turn their pursuers did too. The pair remained hidden as the baying of hounds came closer and then died away. It was followed by the racket being made by the men, which also eventually faded into the distance. When there had been silence for a while, they stood up slowly. To the north, a large haze of dust was visible, driven up by the mass of fleeing animals.

The passage of hundreds of hooves left an unmistakable trail; Romulus and Tarquinius followed it for a good mile. The plain gradually narrowed as its sides rose to form low hills. On the tops of these slopes, primitive wooden fences had been built to stop any animals escaping.

'Very clever!' said Tarquinius, pointing. 'Whoever is in charge has organised this hunt well.'

Romulus understood. Although he had never seen a beast hunt, he had lived for tales of them as a child. 'It leaves more men to be used as beaters and hunters.'

'Or spearmen.'

'At the bottleneck?'

Tarquinius nodded.

Carefully they made their way down the valley, seeing an occasional injured antelope or zebra lying stricken on the ground. Panicked by the noise and the other animals, some beasts had fallen and been trampled. They would be easy prey later, thought Romulus hungrily. Food for the pot.

Neither had any real idea of whom or what they would find at the neck of the trap. The sight that greeted them moments later was most impressive. They reached a point where the ravine narrowed as it dropped down to a flat surface some hundred paces below. Instead of hunters' hides, the pair saw long nets strung in a line from one side of the valley floor to the other. Some distance in front of the thick mesh were rows of deep pits in the ground. Everywhere they looked, there were figures trapped in netting or the traps, struggling frantically to escape. It was a scene of pure chaos. Lone uncaught animals darted here and there in blind panic, uncertain where to run. Loud neighs and cries mixed with the hunters' shouts.

Groups of men were running to each successive animal in the nets, freeing them but immediately binding their limbs with ropes. Their task was urgent, and dangerous, and Romulus saw a number get badly injured. Kicked, stamped upon or gored, they dropped to the ground, bleeding and screaming. No one came to their aid, and their comrades were so plentiful that the operation continued without interruption. Directing the proceedings from the centre of the valley floor was a short figure in dark clothes, armed with a long staff.

'This is no hunt,' Romulus exclaimed. 'It must be for the circus in Rome!'

'A possible way home,' added the haruspex.

Elated, Romulus' attention was suddenly drawn by loud brays of anger. Just below them, a huge zebra stallion had been trapped. In the ensuing struggle to free itself, its hindquarters had come free of the net. Now a ring of men surrounded the magnificent beast, trying without success to rope it and bring it to the ground. The enraged zebra kicked and bucked around in circles, swinging its head violently from side to side. In an effort to ensnare one of its back legs, one of the braver hunters stepped in too close. The stallion sensed the man's presence and whirled around, driving both hind feet into his face. Like a puppet with its strings cut, the figure crumpled to the ground and lay still.

'Fool,' said Tarquinius quietly.

Romulus winced. No man could survive a blow like that. Unlike the one I delivered to Caelius that night, he thought bitterly. It wasn't me. So who else could it have been?

Terrified of suffering the same fate as their companion, none of the hunters would now approach the zebra. At length, it struggled free of the weighted mesh and galloped off through a gap in the traps.

Romulus wanted to cheer. The promise of freedom was a powerful drug.

'Let's go down,' said Tarquinius.

Romulus hesitated, but it made sense to make contact with the *bestiarii*. He didn't know what reception they might receive, but any risk was outweighed by the possibility of joining their party. That would greatly increase the two friends' chance of reaching Alexandria. There were few travellers in this empty land, and journeying on their own would be fraught with danger.

For some time, the men wrestling with the animals did not notice them approaching. They were engrossed in subduing as many as possible, before the beasts smothered in the netting, injured themselves or escaped, as the zebra had just done.

When they were quite near, Tarquinius called out in Latin. 'Have you need for more men?'

The nearest hunters turned round in surprise. Ill-fed, dressed in rough tunics and for the most part barefoot, they looked like slaves. In unison, their mouths opened in surprise.

'Where is your master?'

None answered.

Romulus was not surprised by their silence. With light brown skin, black hair and dark eyes, the cowed-looking men looked Egyptian. Slaves to a man.

Even when Tarquinius addressed them in Egyptian, they did not reply.

A bulky, long-haired figure came striding over from a bull buffalo that had just been restrained. He was dressed similarly to the hunters, but the whip and dagger hilt protruding from his wide leather belt told a different story. Noticing Tarquinius and Romulus, the *vilicus* came to an abrupt halt.

'Where the hell have you come from?' he demanded suspiciously in Egyptian.

'From there,' said Tarquinius, waving vaguely to the south.

A little wrong-footed by the blond newcomer's confidence, the *vilicus* scowled. 'Your names?'

'They call me Tarquinius. And this is Romulus, my friend,' replied the haruspex quietly. 'We were hoping for some work.'

'This isn't the marketplace in Alexandria. Or Jerusalem,' the *vilicus* sneered. 'We don't need any more labour.'

Romulus could not understand what was being said, but the *vilicus*' aggressive manner did not need translating. This fool is both stupid and bad-tempered, he thought. Yet they could not afford to antagonise him. There weren't many other options available. He kept his face impassive, while Tarquinius simply folded his arms. And waited.

'Gracchus!' There was no mistaking the tone of command. 'What's going on?'

The man fell silent. A moment later, a short figure in dark brown robes arrived, the same the friends had seen earlier. He moved to confer with his *vilicus*.

'These two just breezed in out of nowhere, sir,' Gracchus muttered. 'They're looking for work!'

The deeply tanned newcomer had a mane of grey hair, a wild beard and shrewd brown eyes. With its metal-shod tip, the well-worn staff in his hands looked more like a weapon than a crutch. A weighty purse dangled from his leather belt, while a number of thick gold rings adorned his fingers. This was a wealthy man.

Romulus and Tarquinius waited patiently.

At length the short man had heard enough. 'I am Hiero of Phoenicia. A *bestiarius*,' he said, speaking Egyptian in a sonorous tone. 'And you are?'

The haruspex repeated their names slowly and calmly.

Romulus racked his brains. He had heard of a man called Hiero before.

The *bestiarius* frowned at Tarquinius' accent. 'You're Roman?' he asked, switching without effort to Latin.

His men looked on uncomprehendingly.

'We are,' replied Tarquinius.

'What are you doing here in the wilderness?'

'We were guards on a merchant vessel,' announced Romulus in a confident voice. 'It was attacked by pirates south of here two days ago. When the ship was taken, the two of us managed to swim ashore. The others weren't so lucky.'

'Guards, eh?' Hiero's beady eyes lingered on Tarquinius' scarred face and Romulus' rusty mail shirt. 'Not pirates?'

'No,' Romulus protested. 'We're honest men.'

'Curious,' said the *bestiarius*. 'The local trireme only left its mooring near our camp yesterday. Before he left, the *trierarch* mentioned that he hadn't seen any pirates for a while.'

Romulus did not rise to the bait.

Tarquinius intervened. 'A trireme? On the Erythraean Sea?' he scoffed. 'No such thing.'

'There is now, my friend,' replied Hiero smugly. 'We merchants complained so much that the Roman authorities in Berenice saw fit to commission three ships. They now patrol the seas south of Adulis, and piracy in the area has dropped, thank the gods.'

'Excellent,' cried Romulus. 'With Jupiter's blessing, they will find and punish the whoresons who killed our friends.'

The haruspex murmured in agreement.

Clearly sceptical of their story, Hiero stroked his beard. There was an uneasy pause. 'Why have you approached my men?' asked the *bestiarius* at length. 'Do you need some water? Or food?'

It was patently obvious that the ragged-looking friends needed more than this. Hiero is playing with us, thought Romulus bitterly. He wants to know if we can benefit him in any way. But we have no ruby now, like the one Tarquinius had to buy the silk from Isaac. Nothing to buy our passage.

'My thanks for your kind offer,' murmured Tarquinius, bowing his head.

Romulus was quick to emulate him.

There was a small smile of recognition, but nothing more.

'We had actually hoped to join your party,' ventured Tarquinius. 'As you know, the journey to Alexandria is long and dangerous. Especially for two men travelling on their own.'

Hiero pursed his lips. 'I have little need of more mouths to feed every day.'

Tarquinius hung his head, waiting. It was time for Romulus to act on his own.

Romulus' heart sank. No doubt the *bestiarius* had plenty of labourers and guards on his well-planned and well-funded expedition. He stared upwards, and a flock of small, brightly coloured birds caught his eye. Darting this way and that, their feathers shimmered brilliantly in the sun.

Tarquinius watched him sidelong.

We are worth far more than the average man, Romulus thought angrily.

Hiero turned to go.

'My friend here has some medical knowledge,' Romulus volunteered. 'He can clean and stitch wounds as well as an army surgeon. I can also, although not to the same level of proficiency.'

The *bestiarius* spun around, suddenly beaming from ear to ear. 'Why didn't you say? Men with your abilities would be most welcome. There are many injured animals that will die without treatment.' He laughed. 'And some slaves.'

While exotic beasts were worth huge sums of money, Romulus found it chilling that their lives were more important than those of men.

'Come! Come!' Beckoning eagerly, Hiero led the pair away from the nets and pits, leaving Gracchus staring suspiciously after them. Recounting the trials and tribulations of his trip, the old *bestiarius* walked half a mile to the rear. Here, over a large area, sprawled a large collection of wooden pens and cages. The enclosures were all made of rough-hewn timber planks, fashioned from the trees that stood nearby. Many held antelope, from delicate ones with a white belly and black stripe along the flank to larger ones with graceful spiral horns. All of them clustered together, milling fearfully about their enclosures and sending clouds of dust into the air. Others contained buffalo or zebra. They paced to and fro, pawing the dirt and bellowing to register their distress. A single pen nearby had much taller sides than the others, and contained a pair of giraffes.

'Strange, aren't they?' said Hiero. 'The first two I've ever managed to catch alive and unharmed. They usually break their legs in the nets or pits.'

'How will you get them on a ship?' asked Romulus curiously.

'That is something I'm working on,' cackled Hiero. 'But the money they'll fetch in Rome will keep me thinking of ways!'

An old memory surfaced, and Romulus knew why the name Hiero was familiar. Shortly before he was sold into gladiator school, he had overheard Gemellus, his former master, having a conversation with his bookkeeper. They were talking about a venture to capture wild animals deep in the south of Egypt. Raising the necessary capital had been the only problem. And the expedition was to be led by a Phoenician *bestiarius* named Hiero! Romulus stole a glance at the old man. It seemed utterly amazing that he might have dealt with Gemellus. Old rage flared in his heart, and he resolved to find out what he could.

Angry roaring from a nearby cage drew Romulus' attention.

Hiero saw him glancing at the large crate, which was made of extra thick logs. 'That's where I need your help most,' confided the old *bestiarius*. 'It contains a big lion we caught a few days ago. He tore open one of his front legs on a wooden spike, and the wound has become infected. It's getting worse by the day.'

Reaching the cage, Romulus peered between the bars. The smell of pungent urine from within was overpowering. Inside he saw a male lion with a magnificent mane; it was pacing up and down, but with a heavy limp. When the beast turned to walk back, Romulus saw the injury Hiero had mentioned. Deep, ugly and infected, it extended in a ragged line all the way from the left elbow to the shoulder. Thick clusters of flies had been attracted by the smell and they buzzed around the confined space, trying to land on the wound at every opportunity. The lion lashed his tail from side to side in frustration, unable to disperse the annoying insects for more than a moment at a time. Romulus moved closer for a better look. The wound looked awful, and would certainly prove to be fatal if left untreated. Noticing him, the huge male snarled angrily and, despite the bars separating them, Romulus jumped back. Its canine teeth were as long as his fingers.

'Well? Can you cure the beast?' demanded Hiero. 'It's worth a damn fortune – alive.'

'I'm not sure,' Tarquinius replied. 'First we will have to restrain it.'

Romulus looked in at the lion once more and was mesmerised by its deep amber eyes. He wondered if it felt the same as he had in the cells below the arena before a fight. Trapped. Alone. Angry. How could it be right to capture the big cat for sport? As he had been forced to fight and kill other gladiators? Yet to satisfy the bloodthirsty Roman public, it and countless thousands of others were ensnared and then transported huge distances to be slaughtered in the amphitheatre. Hunting the lion in the wild was acceptable, but not this. Romulus was filled with revulsion, but there was nothing he could do. This was life.

'And if my slaves manage to tie it down?' Hiero's voice was insistent.

'We can assess how bad the wound actually is,' answered the haruspex. 'That's before cleaning and stitching it.'

'Will your treatment work?' queried the *bestiarius*. His face turned crafty. 'If it doesn't, I can offer you little more than a meal and a couple of full water bags.'

'I'm sure that my friend here will be up to the task,' Tarquinius announced.

Romulus' stomach turned over with shock. He had never operated on an injury this severe. *What is he thinking?* He threw an angry glance at Tarquinius.

'Excellent,' said Hiero, now looking expectant. 'I'll gather a dozen men.'

Chapter XXVII: Alexandria

Three months pass . . .
Lake Mareotis, near Alexandria, winter 48 BC

Hiero was ecstatic. The long, difficult journey from Ethiopia was drawing to an end. All that remained was a relatively short voyage to Italy, and then he would be able to sell every last damn animal in his caravan. Another year of hard work was almost over, and the *bestiarius* would be heartily relieved when it was and his purse was bulging. After being trapped, the beasts had been transported hundreds of miles, by ship and in cages on wagons drawn by mules. The process had not been without its problems. It was simply not possible to capture so many creatures and confine them without some losses.

One of the giraffes had broken a hind leg in the bars of its enclosure and had to be killed. A number of antelope died without any apparent cause. Hiero knew from long experience that stress was the probable reason. It was the loss of a valuable bull elephant which pained the *bestiarius* most though. Panicking when his men tried to herd it on to one of the open, flat-bottomed transports, it had jumped into the sea, attracting attention of the worst kind. Even close to shore, there were always plenty of sharks about – hammerheads and other large types. Hiero had grown used to their constant presence at certain times of the year. Everyone had watched in awe as one daring shark had swum in and attacked the elephant. Feeling the first bite, the trumpeting bull became even more terrified and swam out further. It was a fatal mistake. Attracted by the blood staining the sea, more sharks soon arrived. By the end there were more than twenty, but it still took an age to kill the enormous creature. The piteous noises it made tore even at Hiero's jaded heart. Eventually the elephant had succumbed though, a small grey island that bobbed back and forth in the reddened water.

But there were still reasons to be content, thought the *bestiarius*. Thanks to Romulus' ministrations, the lion with the terrible leg wound had completely recovered. Many other animals, as well as injured slaves, had benefited from his and Tarquinius' treatment. In truth, the expedition had been a resounding success. He had dozens of the more common animals like antelope and buffalo. As well as the big male, there were several other lions, four leopards, a giraffe and three elephants. But the greatest prize of all was a great armoured beast with a horn on its nose, something that Hiero had only ever heard of before. The rhinoceros had short legs for its size but could run faster than a man. Its immensely thick skin resembled metal plates, making it almost invulnerable. Possessed of poor eyesight but a keen sense of smell, the bad-tempered creature had gored two of his slaves to death when being captured. Others had been severely injured since.

That did not concern the *bestiarius* in the slightest. Such minor losses were all factored into his costs. If the gods continued to smile on him as they had up till now, his arrival at Alexandria would make him an even wealthier man. One or two more trips like this and he would be able to retire. Hiero stared surreptitiously at Romulus. Appearing out of the wilderness so unexpectedly, the young man and his quiet, scarred companion had been useful additions to his party. He had spent weeks trying to persuade them to stay on in his employ. While the pair had professed interest, the wily *bestiarius* had gathered that reaching Italy was their main aim. Still, he couldn't complain. The work they had done had more than paid for their food and transport costs.

'Well?' he asked, stepping on to the shore. 'What do you think of that?'

Romulus could scarcely believe his eyes. Beyond the far edge of the lake, the great walls stretched for miles. This, the capital founded almost three centuries earlier by Alexander of Macedon, was absolutely vast.

It had been so long since Romulus had seen a large city. The last had been Barbaricum, and before that, Seleucia. Yet the metropolis which sprawled from east to west dwarfed both. Even Rome, the heart of the mighty Republic, could not compare.

Tarquinius was lost for words. For him, reaching Alexandria was the culmination of a lifetime's expectations. All those years before, Olenus had been correct. It was overwhelming – and frightening. Tarquinius felt as if fate were rushing in on him.

'A magnificent sight, eh?' cried Hiero. 'Practically every street is wider than the biggest in Rome, and the buildings are made of white marble. And then there's the lighthouse. Ten times taller than any house you've ever seen, yet it was built over two hundred years ago.'

'Don't forget the library,' said the haruspex. 'It's the largest in the world.'

'And?' The *bestiarius* waved a dismissive hand. 'What do I need with all that ancient learning?'

Tarquinius laughed. 'You might not read it, but others do. Scholars come from far and wide to study here. There are books on mathematics, medicine and geography which cannot be found anywhere else.'

Hiero's eyebrows rose in surprise. The slight, blond-haired man was constantly revealing new qualities. He and Romulus were obviously well educated, which had made their company far more appealing than that of Gracchus or any of his other employees. It was part of the reason that the *bestiarius* found himself discussing what to do with two strangers. They had spent long hours together on the journey, during which a certain level of trust had developed between them. Hiero had also come to fear Tarquinius a little, although he could not explain why.

'Look,' said Romulus.

A fine stream of smoke was rising into the air above the centre of the city.

'That's no household fire,' breathed the *bestiarius*. 'A large funeral pyre, perhaps?'

'No,' answered Tarquinius. 'There's a battle going on.'

Romulus stared in shock. This was most unexpected.

'How could you know?' Hiero demanded. He had seen no need to mention the civil war between Ptolemy and his sister Cleopatra, and his slaves knew little of such affairs.

'It is written in the sky overhead,' said the haruspex.

Unusually bereft of words, the old man's mouth opened and closed.

Romulus hid a smile.

'You're a soothsayer?'

Tarquinius inclined his head.

Hiero looked aggrieved. 'You never mentioned it before.'

Tarquinius' dark eyes bored into the *bestiarius*. 'I saw no need.'

Hiero swallowed noisily. 'As you say.'

'Who's fighting?' asked Romulus.

'There's been trouble recently between the king and his sister,' interrupted Hiero, anxious to retain control. 'It's probably just some rioting. Nothing to worry about.'

Romulus studied the sky over the city. There *was* something there. A different air, was it? He wasn't sure, but a bad feeling entered his mind and he looked away.

'But foreign troops are involved,' said Tarquinius.

'Greek or Judaean mercenaries,' Hiero responded triumphantly. 'They're commonly used in Egypt.'

'No.'

Cowed by the haruspex' ominous tone, Hiero fell silent.

'I see legionaries, thousands of them.'

His countrymen, here? Romulus wanted to shout out loud with joy. 'Romans fighting Egyptians?' he cried.

Tarquinius nodded. 'They are hard pressed, too. Badly outnumbered.'

Romulus was amazed by the strong urge to help that overcame him. Before, he would not have particularly cared what happened to Rome's citizens, or its troops. After all, they cared little for slaves. But life had changed him. He was an adult now, bound to no one. Surviving constant and bloody combat as a gladiator, soldier and pirate had given Romulus an unshakeable belief in himself.

And helped me realise what I am, he thought proudly. I am a Roman. Not a slave. And my father is a nobleman.

Beside him, unnoticed, Tarquinius looked on in approval.

Romulus sighed. It was pointless thinking like that. Without proof of his status as a citizen, he would always be open to the charge of being a slave. The tattoo of Mithras on his upper right arm could not entirely conceal the scar where his brand had been. All it would take was an accusation from someone like Novius. No doubt there would be plenty of men like him among the beleaguered soldiers within the city. Romulus' new-found confidence soured. 'What are they doing here?' he asked.

'Could the Roman civil war have spread this far?' the *bestiarius* asked, stroking his beard.

'Possibly,' replied the haruspex. 'But there is no wind, so the smoke is rising in a straight line. I cannot tell much.'

There was a long silence as they pondered the significance of Tarquinius' words. Naturally, Hiero was very unhappy. It was he who stood to lose out if normal port business had been affected by any trouble in the city. Yet the presence of Roman soldiers in Alexandria affected them all. Romulus and Tarquinius needed a vessel that would carry them to Italy. They didn't want to attract any untoward attention.

His mind working overtime, the *bestiarius* spoke first. 'Are they Pompey's men, or Caesar's?'

Tarquinius frowned. 'Somehow I sense the presence of both men in the city. The struggle is not over yet.'

'Who cares?' remarked Romulus angrily. 'Let's wait here until it all calms down. We have supplies, and water. There's no need to rush in and get ourselves killed. Normal trading will resume as soon as the dust has settled.' With plenty of maritime experience, the friends would have little problem finding a ship home. The fact that they had been part of the *bestiarius'* expedition would make them even more valuable as crew to any captain with intentions of carrying wild animals. And by concealing their armour and weapons, it would be easy enough to avoid unwanted scrutiny.

At this, Hiero grew agitated. 'I can't sit here like a fool. Do you have any idea of how much food those beasts consume every day?' he demanded. 'If Tarquinius is correct, the best policy might be to move on. Journey to another port.'

'There is another option,' said Tarquinius.

They both turned to him.

'Wait until it gets dark and then check it out for ourselves.'

Romulus began to feel uneasy, but Hiero's face grew eager.

'We could reconnoitre the situation. Talk to the locals.'

'That sounds risky,' challenged Romulus. Relations between him and Tarquinius were still strained thanks to the haruspex' repeated refusals to explain why he had left Italy.

'For seven years we have lived and breathed constant danger,' Tarquinius answered calmly. 'And yet here we are.'

Romulus feared the faraway look in Tarquinius' eyes. 'Carrhae and Margiana just happened though,' he cried. 'We had to deal with those situations as they happened. This can be avoided!'

'My destiny is to enter Alexandria, Romulus,' said Tarquinius solemnly. 'I cannot turn away now.'

Hiero's gaze switched eagerly from one to the other, fascinated.

Romulus felt unhappy at the prospect of walking into an unfamiliar city that was at war. And the air currents he had seen over Alexandria were full of dark possibilities. He stared at Tarquinius, whose face was set. It was futile to argue with him. Unwilling to look again at the sky over the city himself, Romulus hung his head. Mithras, protect us, he prayed. Jupiter, do not forget your faithful servants.

Hiero was oblivious to the deep emotions flowing between them. 'Good,' he proclaimed. 'I can think of no better men for the job.'

Neither Tarquinius nor Romulus replied. The former had fallen deep into thought. The latter was struggling to control his fears.

Alexandria awaited.

The couple's rooms were large and airy, the floors covered with thick carpets, the furniture made of ebony and inlaid with silver. Long, column-filled and painted corridors led to a succession of similar chambers interspersed with courtyards and gardens. These last were filled with fountains and statues of the bizarre Egyptian gods. Everywhere the windows afforded stunning views of the Pharos, the lighthouse. Even these could not make Fabiola like Alexandria. Egypt was an alien place, full of strange people and customs. The pale-skinned servants who bowed and scraped obsequiously were driving her to distraction. And luxurious surroundings could only do so much to dispel her claustrophobia. After weeks of being cooped up indoors, she was struggling not to despair. Nor could she go on avoiding Caesar for ever.

Fabiola listened to the baying mob outside. Although the sound had grown familiar, it still chilled her blood.

Sextus gave a reassuring look, which helped a little.

Brutus also saw her glance at the shuttered window. 'Don't worry, my darling,' he said. 'There are four cohorts just outside. The rabble can't get anywhere near us.'

Something inside Fabiola snapped. 'No,' she cried, 'but we can't go out either! We're trapped like rats in a sewer because Caesar bit off more than he can damn well chew.'

'Fabiola—' Brutus began, his face strained.

'I'm right, and you know it. Once he knew Pompey was dead, Caesar sauntered in here as if the place were his,' she retorted hotly. 'Is it any surprise that the Egyptians didn't like it?'

Her lover fell silent. His general's habit of acting so fast that his enemies were caught off-guard almost always worked. This time, Brutus had to admit, it had not.

Fabiola grew even more indignant. 'And to let his *lictores* clear the path before him? Is Caesar the king of Egypt now?'

Docilosa looked worried. This was dangerous.

'Lower your voice,' Brutus ordered. 'And calm down.'

Fabiola did as he said. Other senior officers were billeted nearby and might overhear. It was pointless losing control, she thought. A waste of energy.

Rather than take his entire army to Egypt, Caesar had split it into three unequal parts, sending the larger portions back to Italy and into Asia Minor, where their missions were to enforce the peace. Meanwhile, he himself was to pursue Pompey. This decision had not augured well for their arrival in Alexandria. And so it had proved. Sailing in not long after Pharsalus with about three thousand men, Caesar had ordered his ships to anchor safely offshore until he knew what type of reception the Egyptians would offer him. When a pilot vessel emerged a short time later, its crew was instructed to carry the news of his arrival to Alexandria's ruling officials. Their reply was swift. As Caesar landed, he was greeted by a royal messenger who solemnly presented him with a package.

In it were Pompey's signet ring, and his head.

Full of sorrow, Caesar promised revenge on those who had killed his former friend and ally. Ultimately, it might have served his purpose for Pompey to die, but Caesar was not the cold-blooded killer some Republicans made him out to be. His clemency towards the senior officers who had surrendered at Pharsalus had been remarkable. And his very public grief for Pompey was genuine. Perhaps it was this pain which led to his use of his *lictores* upon their arrival, thought Fabiola. But Caesar's move went down badly with the locals, and things had grown worse from there. Although the quarrelling Ptolemy XIII and Cleopatra were both absent, the city was no walkover for an invading force. The local population did not take kindly to foreign soldiers invading their streets, or to their royalty's palaces being seized. When Caesar had two of the ministers responsible for Pompey's murder executed in public, the simmering resentment created by his arrogance flared into open anger. Aided by the Alexandrian mob, the Ptolemaic garrison began to launch daring attacks on the foreign troops. It started with barrages of rocks and broken pottery, but soon progressed to more deadly violence. Using their intimate knowledge of the city, the Egyptians cut off and annihilated a number of Roman patrols over the space of a few days. Almost overnight, the entire place turned into a no-go area. In a humiliating climb-down, Caesar was forced to withdraw his outnumbered legionaries into one of the royal palaces near the docks. There, with all the approaches blocked by barricades, they remained.

After two years of constant marching and fighting, their time in Alexandria was meant to be an opportunity to relax. Instead, confined by the unrest to their quarters, Fabiola had been brooding constantly about Caesar. In her mind, his sexual assault on her in Ravenna utterly proved his guilt. And her parentage. The latter discovery had not afforded her any of the joy that might be expected in such circumstances. In its place, Fabiola was filled with a dark, vicious satisfaction. After years of searching, she had been granted one of her most desired wishes. Now her revenge had to be plotted, but she wanted far more than to slip a sharp knife between Caesar's ribs one night. It was not that Fabiola cared whether she died in the attempt. She did not. With Romulus in all likelihood dead, what purpose was there in living? No, her restraint was because Caesar did not deserve a swift end. Like her mother's in the salt mines, his had to be a lingering death, full of suffering. Preferably at the hands of those he trusted most. Yet Fabiola had to be careful. Since Alesia, Caesar did not trust her and keeping Brutus happy in the face of his master's disapproval was a task in itself.

Currently, however, the most likely risk was that an Egyptian rabble would tear them all to pieces. For someone who wanted to engineer a man's death with precision, it was immensely frustrating. Here Fabiola could do nothing other than work on Brutus, and her resentment was reaching critical levels.

Fierce street battles were still raging daily. While a type of status quo had been reached, Caesar and his small force were cut off from his triremes, their only way out of the situation.

'Help is on its way from Pergamum and Judaea,' offered Brutus. 'It will arrive in a matter of weeks.'

'Really?' cried Fabiola. 'That can't be certain, or there'd be no need for this pointless attack on the harbour.'

'We have to regain access to our ships. And seizing Pharos Island will give us an advantage over the Egyptians,' he replied, the colour rising in his cheeks. 'You know that I cannot disobey a direct order.'

Tread carefully, thought Fabiola. Although he had been deeply affected by her words after Pharsalus, Brutus still loved Caesar. 'I'm worried about you.' She was not lying. Hand-to-hand combat at night was very dangerous, and the Roman casualties had been heavy. Brutus was dear to her, but he was also her sponsor and protector. Without him, Fabiola would lose all the security in her life. Prostitution would beckon again. It might only be for one client, but the reality would be no different. Fabiola did not allow herself even to contemplate this option.

Brutus' face softened. 'Mars will protect me,' he said. 'He always does.'

'And Mithras,' replied Fabiola. She was gratified by his pleased nod.

'Caesar plans to do more than just regain the harbour tonight. He's sending me back to Rome so I can take counsel with Marcus Antonius, and assemble more reinforcements,' Brutus revealed. A sudden scowl twisted his mouth. 'He also ordered me to leave you here. Apparently you'll distract me from my duties.'

Fabiola stared at him, aghast at that possibility. 'What did you say?'

'I stood up to him. Argued the point,' answered Brutus stoutly. 'Politely, of course.'

'And?'

'He wasn't too happy,' grinned Brutus. 'But I'm one of his best officers, so he gave in eventually. Happy now?'

Surprised and delighted, Fabiola hugged him fiercely. She had had enough of this hot, foreign place.

And if Caesar survived, she would be waiting for him. In Rome.

* * *

By late afternoon, the caravan was encamped in a secure location by Lake Mareotis, which flowed right to the city walls. Donning their armour and weapons, the two friends readied themselves as best they could. They had made use of badly made shields and shoddy iron helmets while serving with Ahmed, but these had been left behind on the dhow.

'I suppose we should be grateful,' said Romulus, throwing a light woollen cloak over his shoulders. He felt naked at the prospect of meeting hostile troops without proper equipment. 'No one will take a second look at us.'

'Exactly. That's the point,' replied Tarquinius, who was wearing one as well. He pulled out a silver chain which always hung round his neck. On it was a small gold ring, which was finely decorated with a scarab beetle. For the first time that Romulus could remember, the haruspex put it on.

'What's that for?'

Tarquinius smiled. 'It will bring us good luck.'

'We need plenty of that,' said Romulus, casting his eyes at the heavens. Now prepared to interpret what he saw, Romulus could read nothing, and his friend would answer no questions at all. Once again, he had to trust in the gods. It was a completely helpless feeling, but Romulus gritted his teeth and readied himself. There was no other way.

Calling down the blessings of his own deities, Hiero also provided them with a good description of the city layout. This would be invaluable. 'Don't do anything stupid,' the old *bestiarius* counselled. 'Find out what you can and come back here safely.'

'We will,' replied Tarquinius, his face impassive.

They all gripped forearms in the Roman manner.

It felt as if they would never see Hiero again, and Romulus could bear it no longer.

'Have you ever had dealings with Roman merchants?'

The *bestiarius* looked surprised. 'Of course,' he said. 'I've done business with them all. Noblemen, merchants, *lanistae*.'

'Anyone called Gemellus?'

Hiero scratched his head. 'My memory is not what it was.'

'It's important,' said Romulus, leaning closer.

Curious, Hiero decided not to ask why. There was a fierce, intimidating look in the other's eyes. He thought for a moment. 'Gemellus . . .'

Romulus waited.

'I remember,' the *bestiarius* said at last. 'From the Aventine?'

A pulse hammered in Romulus' throat. 'Yes,' he whispered. 'Like me.'

Tarquinius frowned.

'A friend of yours?' demanded Hiero.

'Not exactly,' Romulus replied, keeping his tone neutral. 'Merely an old acquaintance.'

The *bestiarius* did not react to the obvious lie. It was nothing to him. 'Gemellus, yes. He invested a third share in a venture of mine nearly ten years ago.'

'That's about right,' agreed Romulus, feeling a pang of deep sadness. Fabiola had been there too, eavesdropping on Gemellus while he planned his involvement.

'The whole affair was cursed from start to finish.' Hiero scowled at the memory. 'Many animals seemed to know where the traps were, and those we did catch were poor specimens. I lost dozens of men to strange fevers and afflictions. Then the Nile flooded on the way back, so it took twice the normal time to reach Alexandria.' He paused for effect.

Romulus nodded in apparent sympathy. Inside, though, he was fuming. Even a few wild beasts would make a man's fortune. No doubt Gemellus was still enjoying the proceeds.

'That's not all,' sighed the old man. 'Often I sell the animals on the dock at Alexandria, but Gemellus wrote demanding that we take them to Italy.'

Tarquinius sucked in a breath, feeling rather stupid. How could he have not realised before? A winter afternoon in Rome, eight years earlier. Gemellus, a merchant from the Aventine, desperately wanting a prophecy. The bad omens that resulted from it. Ships with their holds full of wild beasts, crossing the sea.

Romulus was so caught up in the *bestiarius*' tale that he did not notice. 'That makes perfect sense. You'd get a far better price there.'

Hiero nodded. 'For that reason, I foolishly agreed to his request. Thank the gods that I travelled on a lightly laden liburnian, not one of the cargo vessels.'

'What do you mean?'

'There were freak storms on the voyage across,' revealed the *bestiarius* gloomily. 'Every last transport sank and all the animals drowned. I lost an absolute fortune.'

Tarquinius brought back every possible detail of the merchant whom he had met outside Jupiter's temple on the Capitoline Hill. Ill-tempered, fat and depressed, Gemellus had been crushed by his revelations. The last of these had been the most powerful. *One day there will be a knock on your door.* At the time, there had been far more important things on the haruspex' mind, and he had not really pondered the significance of what he had seen. An unknown stranger's worries were of little concern to him. Now though, it made perfect sense. Gemellus had been Romulus' owner.

Oblivious to Tarquinius, Romulus could barely conceal his exultation. 'And Gemellus?'

Hiero shrugged. 'The same. His investment of one hundred and twenty thousand *sestertii* is still lying on the bottom of the Mediterranean.'

'Gemellus is ruined?' Laughing aloud, Romulus clapped the *bestiarius* on the shoulder. 'That's the best news I've had in years!'

'Why?' Hiero looked confused. 'What's it to you?'

Guilt suffused Tarquinius that he had not made the connection before, and told Romulus. It was a failing of his to focus entirely on grand issues when smaller ones, like this, could make such a difference. Yet he rarely told his protégé anything. I have become too secretive, he thought sadly. And I love him like a son. More remorse washed over Tarquinius. Deep down, the haruspex knew that his fear of revealing why he had fled Italy was the cause of his reticence. Wary of letting this information slip, he had deprived Romulus of a possible source of hope.

I have to tell him. Before it's too late.

Hiero's eyes narrowed. 'Did Gemellus owe you money?'

'Something like that,' said Romulus evasively.

The old man waited to see if any more information would be forthcoming.

It was not, and the two friends prepared to leave.

The last piece of news had altered Romulus' black mood for the better. Tarquinius was pleased by this. Whatever the night held in store would be better faced in good humour. Ill fortune and the gods' displeasure were sometimes directed at those who entered dangerous situations fearing the worst. Chance and destiny favoured the bold, thought the haruspex.

Given what he had seen in the sky, it was the only way to think. More than twenty years after Olenus had done so, Tarquinius had read his own fate. If he was correct, the next few hours would reveal all.

And somehow he would find the right time to tell Romulus.

Night had finally fallen, and the temperature was dropping. Overhead, a clear sky promised at least some visibility in the dark streets. Wall-mounted torches illuminated the large, colonnaded courtyard, which was packed with four strengthened cohorts of legionaries. Caesar was committing almost half of his forces in Alexandria to this manoeuvre. The general had lost none of his daring.

Wrapped in a warm, hooded cloak, Fabiola stared at the silver eagle. She had rarely been so close to one before, and was deeply stirred by it. Since her *homa*-induced vision, the metal bird had come to represent not just Rome, but the last of her hopes that Romulus was still alive. Tears pricked the corners of Fabiola's eyes, but she wiped them away. This was her private grief and she had no wish to share it again with Brutus. Thankfully, her lover was out of earshot, conferring with Caesar and another staff officer.

It was not long until they were ready. To light their way, every fourth man had been issued with a pitch-soaked torch. Marching in darkness might have attracted less attention, but soldiers needed to see enemies to kill them. Seeing each other's faces also helped to keep up morale. Caesar was well aware that the setbacks of the previous weeks had dented his legionaries' usual confidence. He gave a short but stirring speech, invoking Mars and Jupiter, and reminding his men how they had defeated far greater armies than faced them here.

A cheer rose into the air, but was instantly quelled by the centurions.

Without further ado, the gates were opened, and two cohorts marched out to clear the barricades on each side of the entrance. Following the blast from an officer's whistle to sound the all-clear, the third unit emerged, led by the *aquilifer* carrying the eagle. This was followed by Caesar, Brutus and Fabiola, the senior officers and a hand-picked century of veterans. Also in their midst were Docilosa and the faithful Sextus. The fourth cohort was last to exit. At once the doors slammed shut behind them.

Fabiola felt a tremor of fear. They were on their own.

Beside her, Brutus' eyes were glinting in the dim light. Seeing her apprehension, he kissed her cheek reassuringly. 'Courage, my darling,' he whispered. 'You'll be at sea within the hour.'

She nodded, keeping her gaze fixed on the silver eagle. Torchlight bounced and reflected off its polished wings, giving it a distinctly forbidding air. It was a powerful talisman, and Fabiola took strength from it. From the fervent looks being thrown in the eagle's direction, it was clear that many of the men did too. Even Docilosa was muttering a prayer to it.

In close formation, the legionaries headed towards the harbour. Thanks to Alexandria's wide avenues, they were able to move at double pace. Impressive buildings passed by on either side: temples and government offices. They were constructed on a massive scale, greater than most similar structures in Rome. Rows of thick stone columns formed their porticoes, each the height of many men. Even the doorways were enormous. The walls were inscribed with hieroglyphs from floor to ceiling: dramatic representations recounting the country's glorious past. Immense painted statues of the half-human, half-animal Egyptian gods stood before many buildings, their dark eyes blankly watching the passing soldiers. Fountains pattered to themselves and the palm trees moved in a gentle breeze.

Not a person was to be seen. All was silent.

It felt too good to be true.

It was.

Rounding a corner on to the quayside, they found their path had been blocked by waiting lines of heavily armed enemy soldiers.

Many were dressed similarly to Caesar's men, which felt disconcerting to Fabiola. Yet the reason was simple, according to Brutus, her adviser on all things military. After a series of humiliating defeats a century before, Egypt had stopped using its Macedonian-like hoplites in favour of troops trained like legionaries. In addition, a Roman force which had arrived in Alexandria seven years before had largely gone native. This meant that recent confrontations between the two sides were often evenly matched. If anything, it was the Egyptian soldiers who had had the advantage, fighting as they were to dislodge the Romans from their own city. And tonight, even more forces had been gathered. Behind the enemy legionaries stood rank upon rank of slingers, archers and Nubian light skirmishers, their weapons ready. This was to be a crushing defeat upon the invaders.

Caesar's lead cohort ground to a sudden halt, forcing the units behind to stop.

Fabiola's first view was across the water to the lighthouse. It was a dramatic sight, one which never failed to impress. Built on a projecting spur of Pharos Island, the immense white marble tower was awe-inspiring. A single-storey complex surrounded its great base, which was square. Statues of the Greek gods and mythical sea creatures decorated the whole outer surface of this building. Entrance to the lighthouse itself was gained by a wide ramp, which was visible above the outer complex. Even now, Fabiola could see laden mules toiling up it, carrying firewood for the huge fire which burned high above. Many floors up, the second section was octagonal, with the final part being circular. The room at the very apex was formed by supportive pillars, and contained vast polished bronze mirrors. These reflected sunlight during the day and flames at night. On the roof of this chamber was a large statue of Zeus, greatest of the Greek deities.

Fabiola eventually tore her eyes away. The blaze at the top of the Pharos illuminated the main harbour quite well. Grand buildings and warehouses lined the quayside. A dense forest of masts clustered together, belonging to the Egyptian fleet which had been ferrying soldiers into the city. The water was so deep that even the largest vessel could moor here. Groups of sailors filled the ships' decks, shouting and gesticulating at the confrontation about to be played out before them.

Craning his head from side to side, Brutus cursed loudly and vigorously.

The Egyptians had chosen the site for their ambush well. Thanks to a high curtain wall on the right-hand side, there was only room for two cohorts on the dock. The others were trapped in the wide thoroughfare which opened on to the harbour. The instant that these men came to a halt, loud battle cries filled the air. From the rear came the familiar hissing sound of arrows, followed immediately by the screams of those who had been hit.

'The bastards must have been hiding in the side streets, sir,' shouted Brutus.

'To prevent us withdrawing,' said Caesar calmly. 'The fools. As if I would run away!'

'What shall we do, sir?'

Before he could answer, guttural orders from the Egyptian officers rang out. A volley of stones flew into the night sky, causing heavy casualties among the unprepared legionaries. Following close behind came a shower of javelins, invisibly arcing up and then scything down in a second torrent of death. Scores of men were hit, many fatally. Others had an eye taken out, or were simply knocked to the ground, wounded or concussed.

Ten steps from Fabiola, a centurion collapsed. He kicked spasmodically and then lay still.

She stared at him in horror.

The officer had just taken off his horsehair-crested helmet to wipe the sweat from his brow. Now an egg-shaped depression visible through his short hair was leaking a mixture of blood and clear fluid. His skull had been smashed.

'Shields up!' roared Caesar.

Grabbing a discarded *scutum*, Brutus darted to Fabiola's side and drew her to him. With it over her head, she was able to witness the Roman legions in action at first hand. Although the volleys of missiles had caused many casualties, the other soldiers did not panic. The gaps in the ranks closed swiftly, and the next stream of stones and javelins clattered down harmlessly on their shields.

'We can't stay here like this,' said Fabiola. 'They'll slaughter us.'

'Wait.' Brutus smiled. 'Watch.'

'Those with torches, hand them to the men behind. To the second cohort,' ordered Caesar. 'Quickly!'

His command was obeyed at once.

'Front ranks,' Caesar shouted. 'Ready your *pila*! Aim long!'

Hundreds of men drew their right arms back.

'Loose!'

The Roman response rose up in a steep trajectory, flying high over the Egyptian legionaries. As Fabiola watched, the metal-tipped rain landed among the unarmoured slingers and skirmishers, striking them down in great swathes. Distracted by the screams of their comrades to the rear, the enemy troops' front ranks visibly wavered. They were given no chance to recover.

'First cohort, CHARGE!' Caesar's order rang out crisp and clear. 'Loose *pila* at will!'

His men had followed their general for years, through thick and thin. From Gaul to Germania, Britannia to Hispania and Greece, he had never failed them.

A swelling roar of anger left their throats and the front ranks swarmed forward at the Egyptians. Javelins were hurled as they ran, lodging in enemy *scuta* and injuring scores more soldiers.

Caesar was not finished. 'Those in the second cohort, ready your torches.'

Still Fabiola did not understand, but a huge smile was spreading across Brutus' face.

'Aim at the ships! I want their sails to catch fire!'

Caesar's men bellowed their approval.

'Loose!'

Turning end over end in graceful, golden cartwheels of flame, dozens of torches flew through the darkness. It was one of the most beautiful things Fabiola had ever seen. And the most destructive. Loud screams rose from the ships and gilded barges as sailors were struck by the burning pieces of wood. There were muffled thumps as some torches landed on the vessels' decks and hissing sounds as others fell into the water.

Just a few caught in the tightly furled sails. It was enough. Dried out by the sunshine and sea breezes, the heavy fabric was bone dry. Lit for some time, the pitch on the torches was red hot. It was a perfect mix.

Here and there, tell-tale yellow glowing patches appeared. They spread fast, reaching the masts within a matter of moments. Fabiola could not help but admire Caesar's ingenuity.

Wails of dismay rose from the watching Egyptian soldiers. Their fleet was going to burn.

And then the legionaries hit them.

Reaching Alexandria had not proved difficult. After a long march in late-afternoon sunshine, the two friends had arrived at the southern outer walls. Gaining entry was similarly easy. Plenty of guards were on duty, bored-looking Egyptians in Roman-style mail and helmets, but they showed little interest in a pair of dusty travellers. Closing the Gate of the Sun at sundown was of more concern. Although keen to find out what was going on, Romulus and Tarquinius had not asked any questions of the sentries. It was not worth the potential problems they might encounter if their own armour and weapons were discovered. They would have to find out what they could from ordinary citizens.

But there had been little activity within the city. In fact, it was almost deserted. Even the Argeus, the main street which ran north to south, was virtually empty. A few people scuttled here and there between the obelisks, fountains and palm trees on its central parade, but the usual stalls selling food, drink, pottery and metalwork were abandoned, their wooden surfaces bare. Even the huge temples were vacant of worshippers.

It looked as if Tarquinius' predictions were right: there had been fighting.

Their suspicions were raised further by the sight of Egyptian troops assembling outside what looked like a large barracks. Aware that they could be regarded as enemies, the pair ducked out of sight into an alleyway. More soldiers filled the next street as well. Using Hiero's directions and the position of the sunlight, they worked their way through the rectangular grid of thoroughfares towards the centre. Romulus' uneasiness grew steadily as the distance from the southern gate increased. But they could find no one to talk to. And Tarquinius was like a man driven: his expression eager, his pace fast.

By the time darkness fell, they had passed the tree-covered Paneium, a man-made hill dedicated to the god Pan, and the immense temple to Serapis, the god invented by the Ptolemies. Romulus was awestruck by Alexandria's architecture and layout. Unlike Rome, which had only two streets wider than an ordinary ox-cart, this city had been built on a grand scale to an imaginative master plan. Rather than single impressive buildings or shrines dotted here and there, whole avenues of them were laid out. Everywhere there were grand squares, splashing fountains and well-designed gardens. Amazed by the Argeus, Romulus was bowled over by the Canopic Way, the main avenue which ran east to west straight across the city. At its intersection with the Argeus, he was able to appreciate its extraordinary length thanks to Alexandria's flat terrain. The junction itself was dominated by a magnificent square filled with an obelisk and a huge fountain, which was decorated with marvellous statues of water creatures, real and mythical.

Romulus had been especially thrilled to see the outside of the Sema, the huge walled enclosure that contained the tombs of all the Ptolemy kings, as well as that of Alexander the Great. According to Tarquinius, his body was still on view inside, encased in an alabaster sarcophagus. He would have dearly loved to pay his respects to the greatest general who had ever lived, in whose footsteps he and Tarquinius had marched with the Forgotten Legion. But Romulus had to content himself with just seeing the site of Alexander's final resting place. It helped him to feel that, in some way, his life had come full circle. Italy was not far away. What a pity Brennus was not with them too, Romulus thought sadly. But that had not been his fate.

Like all the other public buildings though, the Sema was shut, its tall wooden doors barred. As the sun set, its dying light turned the structure's white marble an ominous blood-red colour.

At the same time, a bright yellow glow lit up the sky to the north.

Romulus stared in shock.

'The lighthouse,' said Tarquinius. 'It can be seen thirty miles out to sea.'

There was nothing like that in the whole Republic, thought Romulus in amazement. The Egyptians were obviously a people of great ability. Everything he had seen here today proved that. And now, as it had done with so many other civilisations, Rome had come to conquer. Except, as Romulus was shortly to discover, things were not going to plan.

'How far is the harbour?'

'A few blocks.' Tarquinius grinned boyishly. 'The library is near too. Tens of thousands of books all in one place. I have to see it!'

Romulus was momentarily infected by his friend's enthusiasm. But his fear soon returned as shouts and the clash of arms reached their ears. The noise was not far away, and it was coming from the direction that they were heading in. 'Let's go back,' he urged. 'We've seen enough.'

Unslinging his battleaxe, the haruspex kept walking.

'Tarquinius! It's too dangerous.'

There was no response.

Romulus cursed and ran after him. His friend had been right so many times before. What could he do but follow?

Each man's destiny was his own.

It did not take long to reach the western edge of the main harbour, which was still peaceful. Here it was separated from a smaller one by a raised, man-made causeway running out to Pharos Island. At each end was a bridge which allowed ships to pass on one side of the port to the other.

'The Heptastadion,' revealed Tarquinius. 'It's almost a mile long.'

Romulus could not take his eyes off the lighthouse, which was taller and more magnificent than anything he had ever seen. 'That's a marvel,' he muttered.

The haruspex watched him indulgently for a moment, but then his face grew serious. 'Look,' he said.

In the small anchorage to the left of the Heptastadion were nearly two score triremes. A cohort of soldiers was on guard nearby, protection for the vulnerable docked vessels.

Romulus gasped as the familiar sound of Latin carried through the cool air. There was no mistaking the troops' identity. They were Roman.

'Caesar's men.'

'Are you sure?' Romulus asked, excitement running through him.

Tarquinius nodded, sensing that something important was about to happen. Precisely what, he could not tell.

Not that it mattered whom the legionaries served, thought Romulus. It made little difference to them which Roman general had a presence in Alexandria.

Renewed sounds of combat came from their right and they turned their heads. A few hundred paces away, past some warehouses, stood a large group of Egyptian soldiers. There were archers, slingers and light infantry to the rear, with legionaries at the front. All of them were facing away from the two friends. As they watched, a volley of stones and javelins shot up into the air, disappearing beyond the front ranks. Loud screams erupted as they landed.

'They've ambushed our lot,' cried Romulus. His mind was telling him that they should escape, but his heart wanted to fight with his countrymen. What's the point? he thought. This is not my war.

'You will have a choice very soon,' said Tarquinius.

Startled, the young soldier looked around.

'I sense a link between you and Caesar. Will you embrace or reject it?'

Before he could respond, Romulus heard the words 'Ready *pila*!' above the din. His eyes were drawn back to the fighting.

Roman javelins thrown in response to the Egyptian volley came showering down on the unprotected slingers and skirmishers. There was a moment's confusion and then they heard the legionaries charge. At the same time, burning torches were tossed out into the harbour on to the ships tethered below. Within the space of thirty heartbeats, plenty of sails were aflame.

Romulus admired Caesar's tactics, which caused instant panic in the Egyptian ranks. So there was a connection between them? He watched the fire spread in a kind of daze.

'No,' hissed Tarquinius. 'Not like that.'

'What's wrong?'

'If it moves down here, those will burn.' The haruspex pointed at the large warehouses nearby.

Romulus did not understand.

'That's the library,' said Tarquinius, his face twisted in anguish. 'The ancient books in there are totally irreplaceable.'

Horrified, Romulus turned back. Already a quarter of the Egyptian ships were on fire, and the blaze was spreading fast. It was easy to see how the library might burn. Yet there was nothing they could do.

Tarquinius studied the conflagration for a few heartbeats and then his eyes opened wide with grief and awe. His faint hope that the Etruscan civilisation would see a new ascendancy was a false one. When the civil war was over, Rome would grow bigger and even more powerful, suffering nothing else to grow in its shadow. And Caesar would play a major role in beginning this process. He sighed, thinking that was all there was to see. But as ever, there was more. It was now he must tell Romulus, before it was too late.

Romulus was getting anxious. It was time to go. 'Come on,' he cried.

'You asked why I left Italy in a hurry,' the haruspex said suddenly.

'Gods above,' muttered Romulus. First the revelation about Caesar, then this. 'Don't tell me now. It can wait.'

'No, it can't,' Tarquinius replied with a real sense of urgency. 'I killed Rufus Caelius.'

'What?' Romulus spun around to look at the haruspex.

'The nobleman outside the Lupanar.'

All the background noise died away as Romulus struggled to take in the impossible. 'You? How . . . ?' His voice trailed away.

'It was me,' Tarquinius hissed. 'I was there, sitting near the doorway. Waiting for him.'

Romulus' eyes widened with shock. There *had* been a small hooded and cloaked figure by the brothel. At the time, he had presumed it was a leper or a beggar.

'But when Caelius came out,' Tarquinius went on, 'you picked a fight with him. I held back for a moment, but the breeze told me that I had to act fast. So I stabbed him.'

Romulus could not even speak. His hunch had been correct all along: the crack on the head he had delivered had not killed Caelius. Instead, Tarquinius had delivered the fatal blow. Confusion mixed with rage and Romulus' mind reeled with the enormity of it. He and Brennus need not have fled Italy at all. 'Why?' he shouted. 'Tell me why.'

'Caelius murdered the man who taught me haruspicy. Olenus, my mentor.'

Romulus wasn't listening. 'You ruined my life that night,' he retorted furiously. 'And what about Brennus? Have you thought about that?'

Tarquinius did not reply. His dark eyes were full of sorrow.

'Making prophecies is one thing,' Romulus went on, outraged now. 'Men can choose to believe or disbelieve what you say. But committing murder and letting an innocent man take the blame, that's directly interfering with someone's life. Mithras above! Did you have any idea of the effect you might have?'

'Of course,' replied Tarquinius quietly.

'Then why did you do it?' Romulus screamed. 'I might have earned the *rudis* by now, and found my family. And Brennus would be alive, damn you!'

'I'm sorry,' faltered Tarquinius. Real sadness filled his face.

'That's not nearly enough.'

'I should have told you long ago.'

'Why didn't you then?' Romulus shot back bitterly.

'How could I?' Tarquinius replied. 'Would you have kept as a friend the man responsible for all your troubles?'

There was no answer to that.

And then the gods turned their faces away.

The heavy tramp of men marching in unison came from behind them. It was very close. Sprinting to the corner, Romulus risked a look around it. The street down which they had come was entirely filled with approaching Egyptian troops. He spat a curse. They were marching to the aid of their comrades, or to attack the triremes. In the process, the soldiers had unknowingly blocked off their escape route.

They had two choices: to flee over the bridge and along the Heptastadion and risk being completely trapped, or to take their chances along the water-front. Find a small alleyway to hide in until the battle had passed.

Tarquinius materialised at his shoulder.

Romulus clenched his jaw until it hurt. He wanted to throttle the haruspex, but this was no time to continue the feud. 'What shall we do?'

'Head for the island,' Tarquinius replied. 'We'll be safe there until dawn.'

Shedding their cloaks, they turned and ran for the Heptastadion, some two hundred paces away.

Shouts rose from the triremes as they were spotted. Although they were illuminated against the light from the huge conflagration, Romulus was confident that they were beyond javelin range.

They sprinted on.

More cries rose from the Egyptian soldiers who had just reached the quayside.

Romulus glanced over his shoulder and could see some of them pointing in their direction.

'Don't stop,' yelled Tarquinius. 'They've got more to worry about than us.'

One hundred paces.

Romulus began to think that they would make it.

Then he saw the sentry picket: a squad of ten Roman legionaries standing on the edge of the Heptastadion, their attention focused on the heavy fighting. He glanced over himself. Caesar's cohorts had smashed through the Egyptian lines and were pounding along the dock towards their triremes. The sentries cheered at the sight.

Mithras and Jupiter, Romulus thought frantically, let us pass unseen.

Tarquinius' gaze rose to the heavens. His eyes widened at what he saw.

Fifty paces.

The gravel crunched beneath their *caligae*.

Thirty paces.

One of the legionaries half turned, muttering something in a comrade's ear.

He saw them.

Twenty paces.

Now they were well within range of the sentries' javelins; things happened very fast. A single *pilum* hummed through the air towards them, but landed harmlessly in the dirt. Another five followed, also falling short. The next four, thrown by men eager to bring down potential enemies, flew too long.

A pair per man, thought Romulus. Ten left. Still too many. He cringed inwardly, knowing that the best shots always held on to their *pila* until the last moment. At this range, the legionaries could hardly miss. And that was before drawing their *gladii* and charging them down. They could not make it.

Tarquinius realised the same thing. 'Stop, you fools,' he shouted in Latin. 'We're Romans.' He slowed to a stop and raised his hands in the air.

Quickly Romulus did the same.

Remarkably, no more *pila* were launched. Instead, the sentries ran over, shields and swords at the ready. In the lead was a middle-aged *optio*. Within a few heartbeats they were surrounded by a ring of *scuta*, the sharp points of *gladii* poking between them. Hard, unshaven faces suspiciously studied the two friends.

'Deserters?' snarled the *optio*, looking at Romulus' rusty chain mail and Tarquinius' leather-bordered skirt. 'Explain yourselves, fast.'

'We work for a *bestiarius*, sir,' Romulus explained smoothly. 'Just got to Alexandria today, after being in the far south for months.'

'Why are you creeping round like spies then?' he demanded.

'Our boss sent us in to check out the situation. We're the only ones who can handle ourselves, see,' replied Romulus with a knowing look. 'But we got trapped by the fighting.'

The *optio* rubbed his chin for a moment. Romulus' explanation wasn't unreasonable. 'And your weapons?' he barked. 'They're Roman style, except for that thing.' He pointed curiously at Tarquinius' double-headed axe. 'How come?'

Romulus panicked. He had no wish to call down the attention, or opprobrium, that admitting to being veterans of Crassus' campaign would bring on them. But what could he say? Keeping silent was not an option.

To his relief, Tarquinius broke in. 'Before the *bestiarius*, we served for a while in the Egyptian army, sir.'

'Mercenaries, eh?' growled the *optio*. 'For those bastards?'

'We knew nothing of any trouble with Caesar,' added Romulus quickly. 'As I said, we've been gone from the city for more than six months.'

'Fair enough.' His eyes flickered with satisfaction at their military appearance. 'Right now we need every damn sword we can get.'

'But . . .' said Romulus, not quite believing what he was hearing. 'We want to get back to Italy.'

'Don't we all?' asked the *optio*, to roars of laughter from his men.

'We're not in the army though,' protested Romulus, fighting a sinking feeling.

'You are now,' he snarled. 'Welcome to the Twenty-Eighth Legion.'

His soldiers cheered.

Romulus looked at Tarquinius, who gave a small, resigned shrug. Romulus scowled. The haruspex' actions had led to this, had led to everything. There was no forgiveness in his heart, just a searing anger.

'Don't try and run,' warned the *optio*. 'These lads are free to kill you if you do.'

Romulus studied the circle of smirking faces. There was no mercy in any.

'Remember the penalty for desertion is crucifixion. Understand?'

'Yes, sir,' they both replied quietly. Miserably.

'Cheer up,' the *optio* said with a cruel smile. 'Survive six years or so and you can leave.'

Bizarrely, Romulus took some heart at this. While the penalties for indiscipline in the military were savage, he was being treated like a Roman citizen, not a slave. Perhaps this way – in the legions – he could win acceptance. On his own, without Tarquinius.

Something drew Romulus' eyes back to the dock.

Gaining momentum, Caesar's legionaries had now pushed past the Egyptians whose arrival had caused the two friends to flee. While the first cohort pursued their demoralised enemies back into the city, the remainder were marching down to their triremes. Near the front marched an *aquilifer*, holding the legion's silver eagle aloft. Romulus swelled with pride at the sight of it. Hurrying behind was a party of senior officers and centurions, recognisable by their transverse horsehair-crested helmets and red cloaks.

One of them could be Caesar, Romulus thought.

'There's our general,' cried the *optio*, confirming his suspicion. 'Let him know we're here, boys.'

His men cheered.

Romulus frowned. There were two women in their midst too. Then a blinding flash of light seared his eyeballs and he looked around.

In the harbour, most of the Egyptian ships were burning. Long yellow tongues of flame were reaching across the narrow quay to lick hungrily at the library buildings. The immense conflagration lit up the whole scene.

Curious, Romulus turned back to stare at the newly arrived Romans, who were now no more than a hundred paces away. Along with some officers, the women had been helped on to the deck of the nearest ship. But other red-cloaked figures remained on the dock. Sailors were already loosening the trireme's moorings, preparing to cast off into the harbour. Caesar was sending for reinforcements, thought Romulus, and sending his mistress and her servant away to safety.

Then one of the women pushed back the hood of her cloak.

Romulus gasped. It had been nine years, but there was no mistaking the features. She had grown up, but it was his twin sister. 'Fabiola!' he shouted.

No reaction.

'FABIOLA!' Romulus bellowed at the top of his voice.

Her head turned, searching.

Lunging forward, Romulus managed to run a few steps before two legionaries blocked his way.

'You're going nowhere, scumbag,' snarled one. 'We're on sentry duty until dawn.'

'No, you don't understand,' cried Romulus. 'That's my sister over there. I have to speak to her.'

Derisive laughter filled his ears. 'Really? I suppose Cleopatra's your cousin, too?'

Helplessly, Romulus screamed the same words over and over. 'Fabiola! It's me, Romulus!'

Incredibly, amidst the press and the confusion she saw him. Long-haired, bearded and in rusty chain mail, he could have been mistaken for a lunatic, but Fabiola knew her brother at once. 'Romulus?' she yelled joyfully. 'Is it you?'

'Yes! I'm in the Twenty-Eighth Legion,' he shouted, giving Fabiola the only clue he could think of.

His last three words were swallowed in the pandemonium around Fabiola. 'What?' she cried. 'I can't hear you.'

It was pointless trying to speak. Officers' commands, sailors' cries, and the pounding drum filled the air in a cacophony of sound.

Fabiola ran to Brutus' side and muttered in his ear and an instant later, he was beckoning to the *trierarch*. And shouting at him.

Reluctantly the captain ordered his men to stop what they were doing. All activity on the deck ceased.

Romulus' heart thumped with joy.

But then waves of screaming Egyptians emerged from the nearby side streets, called by their defeated soldiers from every slum and dirt-bound hovel to help drive out the Roman invaders. The legionaries suddenly had a major battle on their hands.

On the ship, Brutus looked helplessly at Fabiola. Sorrowfully. 'We can't stay. Our mission is too important,' he said and turned to the *trierarch*. 'As you were.'

Fabiola felt her knees begin to shake. With a supreme effort, she held herself upright, forced down the faintness. Take courage, she thought. Romulus is alive, and in the legions. He *will* return to Rome one day. Mithras will protect him. She raised a quivering hand in farewell. For now.

'Cast off. Quickly!'

Hearing the shouted order, Romulus understood Fabiola's gesture. Utter wretchedness filled him. There was to be no joyful reunion.

Pushed out into the harbour by long poles, the trireme turned ponderously. Slow drumbeats directed the sailors, and the three banks of oars dug alternately into the water, positioning the ship to leave. The *trierarch* paced up and down, shouting rapid-fire commands. Other crewmembers unlashed and prepared the deck catapults while the ship's marines readied their weapons. Nothing lay between them and the open sea to the west, but they would be ready all the same.

The baying crowd of Egyptians was nearly at the dock. Moving fast, Caesar had marshalled his cohorts into a solid line across the Heptastadion. Just a few moments remained before the two sides clashed.

'Let's get over there. Every legionary will count against those whoresons,' shouted the *optio*. 'Draw swords!'

A dozen *gladii* hissed from their scabbards, including, instinctively, those of Romulus and Tarquinius.

'At the double!'

Struggling to contain his emotions, Romulus glanced at the haruspex as they ran with the others. 'Fabiola's gone.'

'Safely on her way back to Italy.' Tarquinius found time to smile. 'And your road there is clearer now.'

Italy, thought Romulus, readying himself for the fight.

My road to Rome.

Author's Note

M any readers may be familiar with the events which led to the downfall of the Roman Republic. Where possible, I have stuck to the historical record. Clodius' death, the rioting in Rome – including the use of gladiators – and the burning of the Senate all really happened, although my full-scale battle in the Forum Romanum is imaginary. To my knowledge, the targeting of Caesar's supporters by Pompey is also fiction. Pompey did restore order in Rome with his legions, but we do not know who commanded them. Marcus Petreius was a real military commander, whose actions after his fictional meeting with Fabiola and marching to Rome are accurate. The remarkable events at Alesia also took place, and interested readers may want to see a reconstruction of Caesar's bicircumvallation near modern-day Alise-Sainte-Reine, or the Musée des Antiquités Nationales in Saint-Germain-en-Laye, near Paris, where the finds from the nineteenth-century archaeological dig are displayed.

Gaius Cassius Longinus was a real person, although he was Crassus' quaestor (deputy), not a legate. Longinus was the only senior officer to survive with his honour intact after Carrhae. Was this coincidence? After all, he was about the only nobleman who could recount the battle! He became an enemy of Caesar's and fought against him at Pharsalus, after which he was pardoned. His brother (or cousin) Quintus Cassius Longinus was a tribune in January 49 BC, and was one of those who carried the news to Caesar at Ravenna, thus precipitating the civil war. To ease the plot, I have amalgamated the two characters. The battle of Dyrrachium is documented, including Caesar's men tossing charax loaves at their enemies, his near escape from the panicked *signifer*, and his comment about Pompey not knowing how to win. The manner of Caesar's victory at Pharsalus is also well known, and recorded as the first occasion when infantry were used to attack cavalry in such a daring way. In making Brutus the commander of the legionaries responsible, I have strayed into fiction.

Caesar's arrival in Egypt a few weeks later was typically rapid, and he very nearly came unstuck when the Egyptians reacted violently to his presence. He had with him the depleted Twenty-Seventh Legion, not the Twenty-Eighth, but the reader will find out in the next volume in the series why I made that change. During the civil war, we do not know how long soldiers had to serve in the legions before they could leave, with opinions varying between six and sixteen years. They carried two javelins on campaign, with some sources reporting that only one was carried in battle. I have stuck with two. The battle in Alexandria's harbour did take place, but I have slightly altered what we know of it. Contrary to popular opinion, only part of the library burned down – the worst damage to it took place centuries later, at the hands of a zealous Christian mob! I have also delayed the arrival of Cleopatra on the scene.

As readers of *The Forgotten Legion* will know, the Parthian recurved bows were made of layers of wood, horn and sinew, and were tremendously powerful. Punching through the Roman *scuta* like paper, their arrows annihilated Crassus' legions. My use of silk coverings on the shields is fiction. After consulting experts in the field, however, I am told that layers of cloth used in such a way – especially if cotton were included – would act like a bullet-proof vest, dispersing the force of the arrow and probably stopping it from penetrating. For simplicity, I chose to use only silk. An unfinished project of mine is to test the theory on a silk-covered Roman *scutum*, helped by re-enactors who use such recurved bows. The long spears used against the heavy cavalry did exist, and were used successfully against Parthian cataphracts by Roman armies in the third century AD.

Legionaries were possibly first introduced to Mithraicism in the first century BC, although its practice did not become more common until a few decades later. With its origins in modern-day Iran, it is highly likely that the Parthians knew of Mithras, or even worshipped him. And there are two surviving references to women being part of this supposedly men-only religion. See also the entry in the glossary.

Roman surgeons were very skilled, successfully performing operations that would not be repeated in the western world for over fifteen hundred years. Tarquinius' thoracotomy to remove an arrow, though, is pure fiction, as is his use of penicillin powder from Egypt! It is highly unlikely that even this antibiotic would have saved Pacorus from the effects of *scythicon* (see glossary). Morphine was commonly used by the Romans, however.

What happened to the survivors of Crassus' army after Carrhae nobody really knows, although it has been suggested they fought as mercenaries for the Huns (see the note at the beginning of *The Forgotten Legion*). But if those described in Chinese records were Roman legionaries, they would by then have been old men, for it is known that many of Crassus' soldiers were veterans of the campaign against Mithridates in the 60s BC, and the Chinese description dates from 36 BC. However, the Sogdians and the Scythians were definitely peoples that the Forgotten Legion could have encountered. The Scythians' practices of beheading, skinning and scalping their enemies are well recorded, as are their penchants for warfare, red (presumably chestnut) horses and poison arrows. I could not resist setting the final battle against the Indians on the banks of the River Hydaspes. This was the site for one of Alexander the Great's most famous victories, against a superior force which included over a hundred elephants. Although there is no evidence for the encounter described in *The Silver Eagle*, it could have happened. Invading tribes were sweeping through the area at roughly this time. The practice of coating pigs in grease and setting them alight to frighten elephants is recorded. So too is the use of elephants in 'musth' (when bulls are much more aggressive, and liquid streams down the sides of their faces), and of feeding them alcohol before battle.

Barbaricum was known to the Romans, and by the first century BC the trade to Egypt and thence Italy was already well established. Ships sailed in each direction once a year, following the relevant monsoon. Although the Romans had a presence in the towns on the Red Sea by then, I know of no record of triremes being used in these waters. To supply Rome's ever-growing demand, wild animals were being caught everywhere they existed, and Ethiopia was one of those places. While exceedingly dangerous, the occupation of a *bestiarius* was a lucrative one. We know that the animals were moved north by ship and by wagons, but not much more. I have used some of the information from Hannibal's crossing of the Rhône when referring to the transports used for elephants.

Thanks to the many holes in our knowledge, much has to be left open to interpretation when describing the ancient world. While I have changed some details, I have also tried to portray the time as accurately as possible. Hopefully this has been done in an entertaining and informative manner, without too many errors. For those that might be present, I apologise.

Lastly, my heartfelt thanks to the multitude of authors without whose works I would be lost. First among these is *A History of Rome* by M. Cary and H. H. Scullard; closely following are *The Complete Roman Army* and *Caesar*, both by Adrian Goldsworthy, as well as numerous fantastic volumes from Osprey Publishing. Thanks also to the members of www.romanarmy.com, whose rapid responses to my questions often helped so much. It is quite simply one of the best Roman reference resources there is. Sorry I couldn't make it to RAT Mainz 2008!

Glossary

acetum: sour wine, the universal beverage served to Roman soldiers. Also the word for vinegar, the most common disinfectant used by Roman doctors. Vinegar is excellent at killing bacteria, and its widespread use in western medicine continued until late in the nineteenth century.

Aesculapius: son of Apollo, the god of health and the protector of doctors.

amphora (pl. *amphorae*): a large, two-handled clay vessel with a narrow neck used to store wine, olive oil and other produce. It was also a unit of measurement, equivalent to 80 pounds of wine.

aquilifer (pl. *aquiliferi*): the standard-bearer for the *aquila*, or eagle, of a legion. To carry the symbol which meant everything to Roman soldiers was a position of immense importance. Casualty rates among *aquiliferi* were high, as they were often positioned near or in the front rank during a battle. The only images surviving today show the *aquilifer* bare-headed, leading some to suppose that this was always the case. In combat, however, this would have been incredibly dangerous and we can reasonably guess that the *aquilifer* did wear a helmet. We do not know either if he wore an animal skin, as the *signifer* did, so that is my interpretation. The armour was often scale, and the shield carried probably a small one, which could be carried easily without using the hands. During the late Republic, the *aquila* itself was silver and clutched a gold thunderbolt. The wooden staff it was mounted on had a spike at its base, allowing it to be shoved into the ground, and sometimes it had arms, which permitted it to be carried more easily. Even when damaged, the *aquila* was not destroyed, but lovingly repaired time and again. If lost in battle, the Romans would do virtually anything to get the standard back. The recovery of Crassus' eagles by Augustus in 20 BC was thus regarded as

BEN KANE

a major achievement. My placing of an *aquila* in Margiana is obviously conjecture.

as (pl. *asses*): a small copper coin, originally worth one-fifth of a *sestertius*.

atrium: the large chamber immediately beyond the entrance hall in a Roman house or *domus*. Frequently built on a grand scale, this was the social and devotional centre of the house. It had an opening in the roof and a pool, the *impluvium*, to catch the rainwater that entered.

aureus (pl. *aurei*): a small gold coin worth twenty-five *denarii*. Until the time of the early empire, it was minted infrequently.

Azes: the history of north-west India at this time is poorly described, but we know that in the second century BC different Scythian tribes and Asian nomads conquered much of the area, including parts of Margiana and Bactria, fighting the Parthians and the remnants of the Greeks descended from those left by Alexander. In the following century, they were variously defeated in turn by other Indo-Scythian tribes. The ruler of one such was Azes, of whom very little is known.

ballista (pl. *ballistae*): a two-armed Roman catapult that looked like a big crossbow on a stand. It operated via a different principle, however, utilising the force from the tightly coiled sinew rope holding the arms rather than the tension in the arms themselves. *Ballistae* varied in size, from those portable by soldiers to enormous engines that required wagons and mules to move them around. They fired either bolts or stones with great force and precision. Favourite types had nicknames like 'onager', the wild ass, named for its kick, and 'scorpion', called such because of its sting.

basilicae: huge covered markets in the Roman Forum; also where judicial, commercial and governmental activities took place. Public trials were conducted here, while lawyers, scribes and moneylenders worked side by side from little stalls. Many official announcements were made in the *basilicae*.

Belenus: the Gaulish god of light. He was also the god of cattle and sheep.

bestiarius (pl. *bestiarii*): men who hunted and captured animals for the arena in Rome. A highly dangerous occupation, it was also very lucrative. The more exotic the animals – for example elephants, hippopotami, giraffes and rhinoceroses – the higher the premium

408

commanded. The mind boggles at the labour required, and hazards involved, bringing such animals many hundreds of miles from their natural habitat to Rome.

bucina (pl. *bucinae*): a military trumpet. The Romans used a number of types of instruments, among them the *tuba*, the *cornu* and the *bucina*. These were used for many purposes, from waking the troops each morning to sounding the charge, the halt or the retreat. We are uncertain how the different instruments were used – whether in unison or one after another, for example. To simplify matters, I have used just one of them: the *bucina*.

caduceus: a Greek symbol of commerce, adopted also by the Romans. It was a short herald's staff covered by a pair of intertwined serpents, and occasionally topped by wings. It was often portrayed being carried by Mercury, messenger of the gods and protector of merchants.

caligae: heavy leather sandals worn by the Roman soldier. Sturdily constructed in three layers – a sole, insole and upper – *caligae* resembled an open-toed boot. The straps could be tightened to make them fit more closely. Dozens of metal studs on the sole gave the sandals good grip; these could also be replaced when necessary. In colder climes, such as Britain, socks were often worn as well.

cella (pl. *cellae*): the windowless, rectangular central room in a temple dedicated to a god. It usually had a statue of the relevant deity, and often had an altar for offerings as well.

Cerberus: the monstrous three-headed hound that guarded the entrance to Hades. It allowed the spirits of the dead to enter, but none to leave.

congiaria: free distributions of grain and money to the poor.

consul: one of two annually elected chief magistrates, appointed by the people and ratified by the Senate. Effective rulers of Rome for twelve months, they were in charge of civil and military matters and led the Republic's armies into war. Each could negate the other and both were supposed to heed the wishes of the Senate. No man was supposed to serve as consul more than once. But by the end of the second century BC, powerful nobles such as Marius, Cinna and Sulla were holding on to the position for years on end. This dangerously weakened Rome's democracy, a situation made worse by the triumvirate of Caesar, Pompey and Crassus.

contubernium (pl. *contubernia*): a group of eight legionaries who shared a tent or barracks room and who cooked and ate together.

corona muralis: a prestigious silver or gold award given to the first soldier to gain entry into a town under siege; other awards included the *corona vallaris* for similar success against an enemy encampment, and the *corona civica*, made of oak leaves, given for the saving of another citizen's life.

denarius (pl. *denarii*): the staple coin of the Roman Republic. Made from silver, it was worth four *sestertii*, or ten *asses* (later sixteen). The less common gold *aureus* was worth twenty-five *denarii*.

dolia (sing. *dolium*): giant earthenware jars that were buried in the ground and used for storage of liquids such as oil or wine, and solids like grain or fruit.

domus: a wealthy Roman's home. Typically it faced inwards, presenting a blank wall to the outside world. Built in a long, rectangular shape, the *domus* possessed two inner light sources, the *atrium* at the front and the colonnaded garden to the rear. These were separated by the large reception area of the *tablinum*. Around the *atrium* were bedrooms, offices, store-rooms and shrines to a family's ancestors, while the chambers around the garden were often banqueting halls and further reception areas.

equites: the 'knights' or equestrian class were originally the citizens who could afford to equip themselves as cavalrymen in the early Roman army. By late Republican times the title was defunct, but it had been adopted by those who occupied the class just below that of the senators.

Fortuna: the goddess of luck and good fortune. Like all deities, she was notoriously fickle.

fossae (sing. *fossa*): defensive ditches, which were dug out around all Roman camps, whether temporary or permanent. They varied in number, width and depth depending on the type of camp and the degree of danger to the legion.

fugitivarius (pl. *fugitivarii*): slave-catchers, men who made a living from tracking down and capturing runaways. The punishment described in *The Silver Eagle*, of branding the letter 'F' (for *fugitivus*) on the forehead, is documented; so is the wearing of permanent neck chains which had directions on how to return the slave to their owner.

garum: an extremely popular sauce in Roman times, it was made by fermenting a fatty fish in brine and adding other ingredients such as wine, herbs and spices. *Garum* factories have been found in Pompeii, and soldiers on Hadrian's Wall ordered and ate it as well. Some modern authors compare garum to Worcestershire sauce, which has anchovies in it.

gladius (pl. *gladii*): little information remains about the 'Spanish' sword of the Republican army, the *gladius hispaniensis*, with its waisted blade. I have therefore used the 'Pompeii' variation of the *gladius* as it is the shape most people are familiar with. This was a short – 420–500 mm (16.5–20 in) – straight-edged sword with a 'V'-shaped point. About 42–55 mm (1.6–2.2 in) wide, it was an extremely well-balanced weapon for both cutting and thrusting. The shaped hilt was made of bone and protected by a pommel and guard of wood. The *gladius* was worn on the right, except by centurions and other senior officers, who wore it on the left. It was actually quite easy to draw with the right hand, and was probably positioned like this to avoid entanglement with the *scutum* while being unsheathed.

haruspex (pl. haruspices): a soothsayer. A man trained to divine in many ways, from the inspection of animal entrails to the shapes of clouds and the way birds fly. As the perceived source of blood, and therefore life itself, the liver was particularly valued for its divinatory possibilities. In addition, many natural phenomena – thunder, lightning, wind – could be used to interpret the present, past and future. The bronze liver mentioned in the book really exists; it was found in a field at Piacenza, Italy in 1877.

homa: the sacred liquid drunk by members of various eastern religions such as Jainism. It was common practice for devotees in ancient times to take hallucinogenic substances when worshipping their gods. With secret rituals and rites of passage, it is not unreasonable to think that those who practised Mithraicism did the same.

intervallum: the wide, flat area inside the walls of a Roman camp or fort. As well as serving to protect the barrack buildings from enemy missiles, it could when necessary allow the massing of troops before battle.

Juno: sister and wife of Jupiter, she was the goddess of marriage and women.

Jupiter: often referred to as '*Optimus Maximus*' – 'Greatest and Best'. Most powerful of the Roman gods, he was responsible for weather, especially storms. Jupiter was the brother as well as the husband of Juno.

lacerna (pl. *lacernae*): originally a military cloak, it was usually a dark colour. Made of dyed wool, it was lightweight, open-sided and had a hood.

lanista (pl. *lanistae*): a gladiator trainer, often the owner of a *ludus*, a gladiator school.

latifundium (pl. *latifundia*): a large estate, usually owned by Roman nobility, and which utilised large numbers of slaves as labour. The origin of the *latifundium* was during the second century BC, when vast areas of land were confiscated from Italian peoples defeated by Rome, such as the Samnites.

legate: the officer in command of a legion, and a man of senatorial rank. In the late Roman Republic, legates were still appointed by generals such as Caesar from the ranks of their family, friends and political allies.

liburnian: a faster and smaller ship than the trireme, the liburnian was adapted by the Romans from its origins with the Liburnian people of Illyricum (modern-day Croatia). With two banks of oars, it was a bireme rather than a trireme. It was powered by sail, by oars or by a combination of both.

licium: linen loincloth worn by nobles. It is likely that all classes wore a variant of this: unlike the Greeks, the Romans did not believe in unnecessary public nudity.

lictor (pl. *lictores*): a magistrates' enforcer. Only strongly built citizens could apply for this job, essentially the bodyguards for the consuls, praetors and other senior Roman magistrates. Such officials were accompanied at all times in public by set numbers of *lictores* (the number depended on their rank). Each *lictor* carried a *fasces*, the symbol of justice: a bundle of rods enclosing an axe. Other duties included the arresting and punishment of wrongdoers.

ludus (pl. *ludi*): a gladiator school.

manica (pl. *manicae*): an arm guard used by gladiators. It was usually made of layered materials such as durable linen and leather, or metal.

mantar: a Turkish word meaning 'mould'. I have taken advantage of its exotic sound to use it as a word for the penicillin powder that Tarquinius uses on Pacorus.

manumission: during the Republic, the act of freeing a slave was actually quite complex. It was usually done in one of three ways: by claim to the praetor, during the sacrifices of the five yearly *lustrum*, or by a testamentary clause. A slave could not be freed until at least the age of thirty and continued to owe some formal service to their former master after manumission. During the empire, the process was made much simpler. It became possible to grant manumission verbally at a feast, using the guests as witnesses.

Mars: the god of war. All spoils of war were consecrated to him, and no Roman commander would go on campaign without having visited the temple of Mars to ask for the god's protection and blessing.

Minerva: the goddess of war and also of wisdom.

Mithraeum (pl. Mithraea): the underground temples built by devotees of Mithras. The internal layout described in the novel is accurate. Examples can be found from Rome (there is one in the basement of a church just five minutes' walk from the Coliseum) to Hadrian's Wall (Carrawburgh, among others).

Mithras: originally a Persian god, he was born on the winter solstice, in a cave. He wore a Phrygian blunt-peaked hat and was associated with the sun, hence the name *Sol Invictus*: 'Unconquered Sun'. With the help of various creatures, he sacrificed a bull, which gave rise to life on earth – a creation myth. The sharing of wine and bread, as well as the shaking of hands were all possibly initially Mithraic rituals. Unfortunately we know little about the religion, except that there were various levels of devotion, with rites of passage being required between them. A mosaic in a Mithraeum at Ostia reveals fascinating snippets about the seven levels of initiate. With its tenets of courage, strength and endurance, Mithraicism was very popular among the Roman military, especially during the Empire. Latterly the secretive religion came into conflict with Christianity, and it was being actively suppressed by the fourth century AD.

mulsum: a drink made by mixing four parts wine and one part honey. It was commonly drunk before meals and with the lighter courses during them.

murmillo (pl. *murmillones*): one of the most familiar types of gladiator. The bronze, crested helmet was very distinctive, with a broad brim, a bulging face-plate and grillwork eyeholes. The crest was often fitted with groups of feathers, and may also have been fashioned in a fish shape. The *murmillo* wore a *manica* on the right arm and a greave on the left leg; like the legionary, he carried a heavy rectangular shield and was armed with a *gladius*. His only garments were the *subligaria*, an intricately folded linen undercloth, and the *balteus*, a wide, protective belt. In Republican times, the most common opponent for the *murmillo* was the *secutor*, although later on this became the *retiarius*.

olibanum: frankincense, an aromatic resin used in incense as well as perfume. Highly valued in ancient times, the best *olibanum* was reportedly grown in modern-day Oman, Yemen and Somalia. For obvious reasons, I have not used today's name as it refers to the Franks who reintroduced it to Europe in the Middle Ages.

Optimates: an historical but informal faction in the Senate. Its members were dedicated to maintaining the honourable traditions and standards of the Roman Republic, while its main opponent, the Populares group, stood more for what the people wanted. At the time of *The Silver Eagle*, the most prominent member of the Optimates was Cato, who had been harbouring ill-feeling towards Caesar since 59 BC. Then a consul, Caesar had acted illegally by using physical force to further his cause. Damningly, he had also founded the triumvirate which took nearly all the power from the Senate and placed it in the hands of just three men. Then he had taken it upon himself to conquer Gaul, making himself incredibly wealthy. In the process, Caesar formed the largest and most battle-hardened army Rome had ever seen, one which was loyal only to him. Attempts by the Optimates to recall Caesar prematurely from Gaul were unsuccessful, but then a successful charge of corruption against Gabinius (see the final chapter, set in Alexandria), the acting governor of Syria, gave them heart. But without an army to back them up, the Optimates had little real power to force Caesar into a court. After making a deal with Pompey to restore the peace in 52 BC however, the faction saw a golden opportunity. Over the following months, they assiduously courted Pompey, the only man with the military might to help them. Ultimately, and against the initial wishes of the majority of the Senate, they were successful. Their actions, and Caesar's refusal to stand down, precipitated the civil war.

optio (pl. *optiones*): the officer who ranked immediately below a centurion; the second-in-command of a century.

Orcus: the god of the underworld. Also known as Pluto or Hades, he was believed to be Jupiter's brother, and was greatly feared.

papaverum: the drug morphine. Made from the flowers of the opium plant, its use has been documented from at least 1000 BC. Roman doctors used it to allow them to perform prolonged operations on patients. Its use as a painkiller is my extension of that.

Periplus (of the Erythraean Sea): a priceless historical document from approximately the first century AD. Clearly written by someone familiar with the area, the *Periplus* describes the navigation and trading opportunities along the entire coast of the Red Sea to eastern Africa and as far east as India. It details safe harbours, dangerous areas and the best places to buy valuable goods such as tortoiseshell, ivory and spices. I have changed its origins and contents slightly to fit in with the story.

phalera (pl. *phalerae*): a sculpted disc-like decoration for bravery which was worn on a chest harness, over a Roman soldier's armour. *Phalerae* were commonly made of bronze, but could be made of more precious metals as well. Torques, arm rings and bracelets were also awarded.

pilum (pl. *pila*): the Roman javelin. It consisted of a wooden shaft approximately 1.2 m (4 ft) long, joined to a thin iron shank approximately 0.6 m (2 ft) long, and was topped by a small pyramidal point. The javelin was heavy and, when launched, all of its weight was concentrated behind the head, giving it tremendous penetrative force. It could strike through a shield to injure the man carrying it, or lodge in the shield, making it impossible for the man to continue using it. The range of the *pilum* was about 30 m (100 ft), although the effective range was probably about half this distance.

Priapus: the god of gardens and fields, a symbol of fertility. Often pictured with a huge erect penis.

primus pilus: the senior centurion of the whole legion, and possibly – probably – the senior centurion of the first cohort. A position of immense importance, it would have been held by a veteran soldier, typically in his forties or fifties. On retiring, the *primus pilus* was entitled to admission to the equestrian class.

principia: the headquarters of a legion, to be found on the Via Praetoria. This was the beating heart of the legion in a marching camp or fort; it was where all the administration was carried out and where the unit's standards, in particular the *aquila* or eagle, were kept. Its massive entrance opened on to a colonnaded and paved courtyard which was bordered on each side by offices. Behind this was a huge forehall with a high roof, which contained statues, the shrine for the standards, a vault for the legion's pay and possibly more offices. It is likely that parades took place here, and that senior officers addressed their men in the hall.

proconsul: the governor of a Roman province, such as Spain or Cisalpine Gaul, of consular rank. Other provinces, e.g. Sicily and Sardinia, had slightly lower-ranking praetors to govern them. Such posts were held by those who had previously served as consuls or praetors in Rome.

pugio: a dagger. Some Roman soldiers carried this, an extra weapon. It was probably as useful in daily life (for eating and preparing food etc.) as when on campaign.

retiarius (pl. *retiarii*): the fisherman, or net and trident fighter, named after the *rete*, or net. Also an easily recognisable class of gladiator, the *retiarius* wore only a *subligaria*. His sole protection consisted of the *galerus*, a metal shoulder-guard, which was attached to the top edge of a *manica* on his left arm. His weapons were the weighted net, a trident and a dagger. With less equipment to weigh him down, the *retiarius* was far more mobile than many other gladiators and, lacking a helmet, was also instantly recognisable. This may have accounted for the low status of this class of fighter.

rudis: the wooden *gladius* which symbolised the freedom that could be granted to a gladiator who pleased a sponsor sufficiently, or who had earned enough victories in the arena to qualify for it. Not all gladiators were condemned to die in combat: prisoners of war and criminals usually were, but slaves who had committed a crime were granted the *rudis* if they survived for three years as a gladiator. After a further two years, they could be set free.

Samnite: a class of fighter based on the Samnite people who occupied the central Apennines, but were finally defeated by Rome in the third century BC. Some accounts describe them with triple-disc metal breast-plates, but other depictions have the Samnites bare-chested. Plumed helmets and greaves were common, as was the typical wide gladiatorial belt. Carrying round or rectangular shields, they usually fought with spears.

scutum (pl. scuta): an elongated oval Roman army shield, about 1.2 m (4 ft) tall and 0.75 m (2 ft 6 in) wide. It was made from two layers of wood, the pieces laid at right angles to each other; it was then covered with linen or canvas, and leather. The scutum was heavy, weighing between 6 and 10 kgs (13–22 lbs). A large metal boss decorated its centre, with the horizontal grip placed behind this. Decorative designs were often painted on the front, and a leather cover was used to protect the shield when not in use, e.g. while marching.

scythicon: the poison used by Scythians on their arrows, the purported recipe for which has survived in the historical record. Small snakes were killed and left to decompose, while vessels full of human blood were buried in dung until the contents putrefied. Then the liquid from the jars was mixed with the substances from the rotted snakes to make a poison that, according to Ovid, when applied to a hooked arrowhead 'promises a double death'.

secutor (pl secutores): the pursuer, or hunter class of gladiator. Also called the contraretiarius, the secutor fought the fisherman, the retiarius. Virtually the only difference between the secutor and the murmillo was the smooth-surfaced helmet, which was without a brim and had a small, plain crest, probably to make it more difficult for the retiarius' net to catch and hold. Unlike other types of gladiator, the secutor's helmet had small eyeholes, making it very difficult to see. This was possibly to reduce the chances of the heavily armoured fighter quickly overcoming the retiarius.

sestertius (pl. sestertii): a brass coin, it was worth four asses; or a quarter of a denarius; or one hundredth of an aureus. Its name, 'two units and a half third one', comes from its original value, two and a half asses. By the time of the late Roman Republic, its use was becoming more common.

signifer: a standard-bearer and junior officer. This was a position of high esteem, with one for every century in a legion. Often the *signifer* wore scale armour and an animal pelt over his helmet, which sometimes had a hinged decorative face piece, while he carried a small, round shield rather than a *scutum*. His *signum*, or standard, consisted of a wooden pole bearing a raised hand, or a spear tip surrounded by palm leaves. Below this was a crossbar from which hung metal decorations, or a piece of coloured cloth. The standard's shaft was decorated with discs, half-moons, ships' prows and crowns, records of the unit's achievements and which may have distinguished one century from another.

stola: a long, loose tunic, with or without sleeves, worn by married women. Those who were unmarried wore other types of tunic, but to simplify things, I have mentioned only one garment, worn by all.

strigil: a small, curved iron tool used to clean the skin after bathing. First perfumed oil was rubbed in, and then the *strigil* was used to scrape off the combination of sweat, dirt and oil.

tablinum: the office or reception area beyond the *atrium*. The *tablinum* usually opened on to an enclosed colonnaded garden.

tesserarius: one of the junior officers in a century, whose duties included commanding the guard. The name originates from the *tessera* tablet on which was written the password for the day.

testudo: the famous Roman square formation, formed by legionaries in the middle raising their *scuta* over their heads while those at the sides formed a shield wall. The *testudo*, or tortoise, was used to resist missile attack or to protect soldiers while they undermined the walls of towns under siege. The formation's strength was reputedly tested during military training by driving a cart pulled by mules over the top of it.

Thracian: like most gladiators, this class had its origins with one of Rome's enemies – Thrace (modern-day Bulgaria). Armed with a small square shield with a convex surface, this fighter wore greaves on both legs and, occasionally, *fasciae* – protectors on the thighs. The right arm was covered by a *manica*. A Hellenistic-type helmet was worn, with a broad curving brim and cheek guards.

tribune: senior staff officer within a legion; also one of ten political positions in Rome, where they served as 'tribunes of the people', defending the rights of the plebeians. The tribunes could also veto measures taken by the Senate or consuls, except in times of war. To assault a tribune was a crime of the highest order, making the Optimates' threat to Antonius and Longinus in January 49 BC an act of real political skulduggery.

trierarch: the captain of a trireme. Originally a Greek rank, the term persisted in the Roman navy.

triplex acies: the standard deployment of a legion for battle. Three lines were formed some distance apart, with four cohorts in the front line and three in both the middle and rear lines. The gaps between the cohorts and between the lines themselves are unclear, but the legionaries would have been used to different variations, and to changing these quickly when ordered.

trireme: the classic Roman warship, which was powered by a single sail and three banks of oars. Each oar was rowed by one man, who was freeborn, not a slave. Exceptionally manoeuvrable, and capable of up to 8 knots under sail or for short bursts when rowed, the trireme also had a bronze ram at the prow. This was used to damage or even sink enemy ships. Small catapults were also mounted on the deck. Each trireme was crewed by up to 30 men and had around 200 rowers; it also carried up to 60 marines (in a reduced century), giving it a very large crew in proportion to its size. This limited the triremes' range, so they were mainly used as troop transports and to protect coastlines. By the time of the late Republic, they were being replaced by even larger ships.

valetudinarium: the hospital in a legionary fort. These were usually rectangular buildings with a central courtyard. They contained up to 64 wards, each similar to the rooms in the legionary barracks which held a *contubernium* of soldiers.

Venus: the Roman goddess of motherhood and domesticity. At Pharsalus, Caesar used her name to inspire the thought of victory in his men, adding the 'Victrix', or 'bringer of victory' to her name.

vestiplicus: a specially trained slave whose job it was to take care of a wealthy man's toga. Togas had to be kept properly creased when not in use; when worn, each fold had to be carefully arranged to lie properly. The toga was the ultimate symbol of Roman manhood, and was donned when assuming citizenship, taking a new wife from her father's house, receiving clients and when discharging duties as a magistrate or the ruler of a province. It was worn in the Senate, during the celebration of a triumph, and of course in death.

vexillum (pl. *vexilla*): a distinctive, usually red, flag which was used to denote the commander's position in camp or in battle. *Vexilla* were also used by detachments serving away from their units.

vilicus: slave foreman or farm manager. Commonly a slave, the *vilicus* was sometimes a paid worker, whose job it was to make sure that the returns on a farm were as large as possible. This was most commonly done by treating the slaves brutally.